D1526026

NECTAR
OF THE
WICKED

USA TODAY BESTSELLING AUTHOR
ELLA FIELDS

For the hearts that once shined so bright

ONE

THEY ARRIVED AT THE SAME TIME EVERY YEAR.

Not a moment late and never a second early.

The clock in the town square struck seven with a screech. The moon sat full and high in the starless sky. Against it bobbed silhouettes—flapping wings and swaying caravans of the monsters descending toward the vast field of shivering wildflowers.

Businesses and homes locked up hours ago, but the streets were not empty.

In groups for presumed safety, townsfolk, farmers, the curious, and those from neighboring villages formed a crowd of more than one-hundred daring souls. All of us were headed toward the same destination.

Toward the most excitement we'd see until they returned.

It was my first time. Those under the age of twenty years were not permitted to conduct business with our yearly visitors. Many called them the traveling traders. Others, those who knew better, called them exactly what they were.

The Wild Hunt.

"Come *on*, Flea." My guardian dug her fingers into my wrist and tugged. "If we get stuck too far back, we might miss our chance."

I loathed the word. *Guardian.*

It implied the woman had raised me. Nurtured me. With the exception of indulging herself until she'd lost consciousness, Rolina nurtured nothing. One could argue that I'd spent a great portion of my life taking care of her.

I was never to call Rolina my mother, which she'd insisted as soon as I could begin to understand why. As soon as I could grasp that I wasn't like her and never would be.

Cracked cobblestone soon gave way to grass. The overwhelming scents and heat of clustering bodies enveloped as we joined the awaiting and gathering citizens of Crustle in the field.

Why the hunt even bothered with the soggy river-flanked prison commonly referred to as the middle lands, I didn't know. I was just grateful they did, or I might have remained trapped in this place of in-between forevermore.

Anticipation swelled. Together, we all slowly shuffled forward, careful to give our visitors room but unwilling to cease moving out of fear of losing our place in line.

My eyes glued to the night sky, my breath quickening as the advancing darkness of those silhouettes blocked out the moon. My attention returned to the ground when a boot squashed my slipper-encased foot.

My toe throbbed, making my whisper harsh. "Are you certain this will work?"

The question was redundant.

We weren't leaving this field until Rolina seized the only thing she wanted more than wine and narcotics and opulence. It was my own desperate eagerness that had me seeking reassurance.

"Of course, it will," Rolina snapped. "It has to."

She'd had this planned for years. We both had. For so long, I'd almost begun to think this night would never come. For so long, it would seem I'd forgotten to be fearful of what awaited us.

I'd spent those years researching what to expect when everything I wanted finally arrived. Endless nights wasted to wondering over the evening I would be taken home. For although the middle lands were home to faerie and human and more, I'd always felt within my bones that it wasn't where I was supposed to be.

Residents of Crustle consisted mostly of humans who'd been discarded from their homeland for unlawful and immoral conduct, and faeries. I'd never understood why any faerie would choose to leave Folkyn for this damp and miserable land that sat squashed between it and the human realm of Ordaylia.

Gane, the town librarian and my only friend, often reminded me that not all Fae chose to leave. Many had been forced to because they'd gone against one of the four ruling houses by breaking their archaic laws, or they'd done the unthinkable...

They'd fallen in love with a human.

Humans were not permitted in Folkyn. Somehow, many still slipped through the cracks in the warded veil that separated Faerie from the middle lands. That, or they'd been captured by faeries to be kept for various dark needs.

Then there were those who remained in Crustle because they'd been born here—their parents faerie, human, or even both.

I was none of the above.

I was a changeling.

Though I was certainly not the only creature who'd been dumped in the middle lands as a freshly born babe, I was still something of a rarity. For if there was one thing the Fae valued above nearly all else, it was family—especially their young.

A fact that only made my impatience to find answers all the more burning.

Rolina ceased rising onto her toes in an attempt to see past the group of burly men in front of us. My guardian tossed me a cold glance. "It's worked before. There is no reason it won't now."

Indeed. If that were not true, we would not be so willing to believe we'd get what we both desired.

"It was hundreds of years ago," I reminded her, and though I'd tried desperately to research it, we knew nothing of the circumstances of the changeling who'd returned to her home in Folkyn via a trading visit with the Wild Hunt.

An elbow jabbed into my ribs.

Not from the murmuring crowd awaiting the arrival of the growing mass of darkness above, but from Rolina. As with any touch from her, pain sparked, but I didn't wince. I bit my tongue until it nearly bled and drew in a deep breath through my nose.

Incessantly, I'd had to remind myself that my guardian's hatred of me was not my fault. That she'd spent twenty years in the type of pain that filled her heart with poisonous rot while longing for her true daughter. But her ire no longer burned as it used to. I'd long ceased desiring a scrap of affection from a woman who would only ever resent me.

"But it's what is right. What is *fair*," Rolina said with quiet venom. "Your ilk is many ghastly things, but they are always fair."

Fair.

Such a word did not exist in this world of eternal gray.

Rolina should know that better than anyone. Yet so many souls held tight to the false security of right and wrong. I'd ceased believing any such security existed before knowing what the words meant.

No matter what realm you stood in, the expansive and diverse continent of Mythayla was cruel and unjust—perhaps far more than even the guardian I'd been stuck with.

Regardless, after years of being trapped, I was ready to embrace every inch of what awaited on the other side of that invisible veil. A veil I'd seen shine in the distance from the puddled rooftop of our apartment building, the only sign of its presence unless you dared to breach the wetlands and woods to approach it.

Supposedly, the vibration and heat of the wards were enough to repel humans from nearing, while those with faerie blood could walk right up to it. Some had even sworn they'd glimpsed the gigantic wolves and scaled beasts of Folkyn that roamed the ever-stretching forests and rivers on the other side.

The shuffled movement of huddled bodies came to a stop.

A hush descended over the field as both steed and monster alighted one by one.

Grass and flowers lurched. The very soil beneath our feet rippled. No one moved. I wondered if many had ceased breathing, and if they too felt it. The way the air grew colder—thicker—as if the horde of wild faeries had brought the night sky closer to land.

"*Move,*" Rolina snarled, nails curling into my skin once more.

I did, and right as someone stepped on my dress. I heard it tear and cringed. I loathed sewing, and Rolina would insist I mend it right away. I hoped I wouldn't have to. Hoped I might never see our sewing kit again.

We stopped again, and over the many bobbing shoulders and heads before us, I tried to make out what awaited. I'd seen it before, but only from atop our apartment building. Never, ever so wonderfully close.

The horses were the first thing I glimpsed, jet black with wings and so tall their heads reached the top of the giant tent being erected. The dark material shimmered into place in slow rippling curls that could've been mistaken for a shudder in the night sky.

A place of feigned privacy for trade.

Just as the crowd moved forward again, a roar split through the growing chill. It seemed to crack open gaps between time to freeze us all. Awaiting Crustle citizens cried out and covered their ears, including Rolina. All those who weren't like me.

Rolina cursed and swung her eyes up at me, a glimmer of something that looked alarmingly like fear within.

Impossible.

The creature who'd ignored me at best, belittled and abused me at worst, cared nothing for me.

I'd lost count of all the times I'd imagined what life might look like if I'd been her human daughter rather than a faerie who'd been forced to take her place. Until I'd learned there were far better things to spend my time imagining. Things that might prove achievable.

I didn't know who I belonged to, but not a day nor night could pass without Rolina making sure I knew it wasn't her.

My heart dipped, then began to race. After all this time, I would receive the chance to find out exactly where and to whom I did belong.

As the growling and roaring of caged beasts settled, we again pushed forward. Two flames danced to life upon steel poles, signaling the entrance to the tent. No one would ever find it otherwise. Rumor stated there was no opening in the tent. No entering without a faerie guiding the way.

Rolina's impatience returned. Muttering to the backs of the men in front of us about the selfishness and slowness of those already paying their way into the tent to trade, she fidgeted. She scratched at her arms and attempted to look ahead, but she was too short to see much.

I pressed my lips together.

My unseemly height was one of Rolina's favorite things to insult. At six-foot, I didn't believe I was tall by faerie standards, but of course, I would forever be anything but seemly to her.

Closer and closer, the tent of faeries loomed.

I supposed I should have been scared, and I was. But mostly, I was just anxious. Worry of failure unfurled into worry over the outburst that awaited if we were turned away and I was left to clean up the aftermath of irate Rolina while also choking on my own crushing disappointment. A disappointment that would surely break my heart.

Three people now remained in front of us.

I felt Rolina's desperation. If this didn't work, then that was it. Just like every other citizen of Crustle, I was as good as stuck here. There was always talk of those risking their lives to escape, but I'd heard nothing of real use that might help me do the same.

It wasn't that I had a death wish. I knew people lived here both out of choice and necessity, and I knew of the horrors awaiting in the faerie lands of Folkyn.

But I also knew that I'd been dumped here in Crustle for a reason.

Whether that reason be wretched or plain stupid, all I wanted was to know what it was. Perhaps then, I would learn who I was.

Perhaps then, I could join my family or find a home within a community that allowed me to live a life of my own choosing.

A life that didn't involve saving myself from all the world had to offer to appear nurtured and protected and, therefore, easier swapped with the hunt. A life that did not involve serving a woman who made a mess of our apartment just to keep me away from my few enjoyments to clean it.

A life that *was* a life—not a waiting game within a pretty cell.

Sacks of coin encircled the large boots of a muscular faerie taking names and payment. Silver glinted from the weapons strapped to his woven belt, in his arched ears, and from a glimpse of his large nose.

Two men remained.

People leaving the tent pocketed the coin they'd exchanged their prized possessions for, and headed quickly toward the dim glow of town.

One lone man holding an armful of books stepped forward.

Before I could get a good look at the titles or the female who exited the tent to whisper something to the coin and name collector—a sword sheathed at her back between two dark braids— Rolina latched onto my wrist and burst forward.

The man before us had yet to enter the tent, but she didn't care.

She dragged me with her and tossed our entry fee into an open sack at the faerie's feet.

The *clink* created a silence that screamed.

The female who'd been in talk with the collector froze and eyed us with glowing moss-green eyes. Laughing silently, she shook her head and patted the male's arm. Then she rounded the tent and disappeared.

The male sighed. "Name."

She spoke as soon as he did. "Rolina."

"And the..." The male finally looked up from the handful of walnuts he'd retrieved from a pocket in his tight leather pants. A sharp brow rose as he chewed and stared at me. "Faerie?"

Rolina shifted her short brown hair behind her ear. "Her name is Flea."

I nearly snorted at the way she'd casually pronounced it, as though I hadn't been named after an insect because the woman hadn't cared to name me at all.

The male looked back and forth between us with gold-brown eyes and dark brows. One of them was also full of silver rings. "Flea?"

"It's short for Fleanna," Rolina said, exasperated.

I chomped down on my lips, tempted to say she was lying. The male's amused assessment of us told me he'd already guessed as much as he extended his hand for mine.

Certain creatures could detect age. In this case, full maturity could be confirmed by touching a faerie's pulse. My stomach tightened, though I wasn't sure why. I'd reached twenty years during the full moon just last month.

"Fresh," the male confirmed, a tilt to his lips as he gave me another—far slower—once-over.

Heat rose up my neck to fill my cheeks when his thumb brushed over the sensitive skin of my inner wrist. Never had anyone touched me in such a way before, and though it was but a touch and expected, it still startled me.

I ducked my head, both ashamed and terrified and...

And something else.

Rolina snarled. "Eyes and paws off. We've important business to tend to."

"I'll bet you do," the faerie muttered, but he released me and nodded to a bald female wearing an eye patch.

We walked toward her, and she eyed me curiously as she stepped aside to let us pass.

I felt it and almost gasped. A gap in the air right before the entry to the tent. The midnight material dissolved over our skin like water, cool and rushing.

Rolina shivered and made a low sound of disgust.

Another faerie with dark eyes stepped before us and gestured for us to wait. He then moved back to the shimmering wall of the tent.

Rolina huffed indignantly as we did as instructed.

Lining the large circular space were crates, sacks, and woven baskets, most already filled with wares. Numerous faeries sorted through them while others kept guard with weapons at their sides and backs.

It was then I began to understand why the Wild Hunt bothered with trade visits to Crustle.

At the tent's center stood a dark metal table loaded with treasure and trinkets that glittered and gleamed. They spilled over it like stars reflected across a cloud-covered lake. As someone stepped away from the table, I glimpsed the embossed and worn spines of piles of books.

Faeries ushered some of the treasure aside, presumably what they considered high value, as we awaited permission to step forward.

I'd been too preoccupied with attempting to read the titles of the books to notice Rolina's patience had run dry yet again.

I should have known it would. Regardless, shock seized me as she daringly crossed the grass floor of the tent to the creatures who sat at the trade table.

"Lady," snapped the same male who'd halted us upon our entry. "You will wait to be called forth."

My mouth opened and closed, fear and mortification keeping me frozen.

"I've waited long enough," Rolina said. "Twenty years, to be exact."

Unsure what to do, I gave the faerie what I hoped was an apologetic look and hesitantly trailed Rolina.

The male frowned. I feared he would throw us out when the creature who seemed to be in charge drawled in a cutting tone from his high-back chair behind the table, "Then, by all means, do show us what you've got that is of such importance."

All kinds of folk lived in the middle lands.

But I'd never seen a being quite like this one.

He had the body of a giant man and a head that resembled a serpent. Where most men would have facial hair, scales flanked his cheeks. An off-green hue darkened his forehead and brightened his reptilian eyes. A sheet of parchment hung between his fingers. Each scaled hand had only four, half the length of a typical faerie digit. Darkened nails sprouted and curled, resembling sharpened claws.

"... she is clearly not mine."

Busy studying the male's unique features, I almost missed the exchange between him and Rolina.

"Why wait this long to bring her to our attention?" the male said, seeming more interested in an old watch he lifted to inspect closely. "There is nothing to be done—"

"*Why* wait?" My eyes widened as Rolina hissed, "Because the hunt do not trade with anyone under the age of twenty years."

Those strange eyes flashed back to the flustered woman beside me, and I was certain the scaled faerie hadn't once even glanced at me. "If she is indeed a changeling and you've kept her for all these years, then I'm afraid there is nothing that I nor anyone else can do for you. Your lost offspring is likely dead." He looked at a male with similar scaled features who'd stepped forward. He gestured for us to be escorted out, then looked at the tent entrance. "Bring in the next."

That was it.

My ears filled with a screeching buzz. Something cracked within my chest.

It widened as Rolina refused to heed the dismissal.

"Wait, wait," she pleaded, her sharp tone now gentling with panic. "Please, I just know that if we tried—"

"Hush." I placed my hand upon her upper arm and clasped it firmly in warning. "Come, we need to go." It was far from wise to anger one of the Fae. Especially the hunt, who belonged to no royal house and therefore did not need to abide by their rules.

It happened too fast for my tense limbs to respond.

I was shoved with enough force to send me stumbling face-first into the trade table.

My hands grasped it, nearly tipping the heavy metal over as I righted myself. Fear hitched my instant apology, but no one was paying me any mind.

Everyone in the tent had risen to their feet. Every eye was pinned to my incensed guardian.

"I don't want her!" Rolina screamed. "Twenty fucking years I've waited for this night. *Twenty years* I've waited and hoped for the return of my *real* daughter, you filthy, cheating, vermin scum—"

Before she could utter another word, her eyes went wide.

Her thin frame went eerily still.

Then crumpled to the grass.

Fright and shock became a storm that emptied my mind and lungs as I beheld the corpse of the woman who'd given me both refuge and peril. The guardian who'd kept me alive but had smothered something fundamental inside me.

The monster who'd held me captive while never wanting me at all.

All of it—gone.

So many years of hoping and planning just...

Done.

My throat constricted. My eyes burned. "No," I rasped and fell to my knees. I crawled to her, pulled her close, but I needn't have bothered. I knew. I could already hear it.

Nothing.

Her heart was as good as stone. Unseeing eyes bulged, wide open beneath the orbs of firelight bobbing across the tent ceiling. Closing them with trembling fingers, I bowed my head, unsure how I was supposed to get her home. I could carry her, but then what?

My skin hummed in warning. I glanced up to find a silver mist descending.

"Get back," a sharp voice commanded. "Unless you wish to join her in the pits of Nowhere."

I dropped Rolina to the grass and shuffled back on my rear a second before the mist met her lifeless body. It seemed I wouldn't need to fret about burying her—as right before my very eyes, she began to decompose.

Living in this prison of eternal in-between with both creature and human, I'd heard and seen a great deal of odd things. Magic used for entertainment, miraculous healing, and plenty of stealing. I'd even seen someone shapeshift for coin on the street. But this...

I couldn't look away. The grass, soil, and even some weeds glowed brighter as if hit by a flare of sunlight.

As if they were absorbing Rolina's flesh and bones like one would a hearty meal.

Someone cursed and groaned. "Every fucking time you're here, I swear."

A female snorted. "Never can help yourself, Vin."

Laughter sounded. A roaring and unfitting orchestra that reminded me where I was and what could befall me.

"Your tyrant, I presume?" That voice again. The one that had told me to move. It was different. Not the same as the snake-skinned male who'd refused to trade with us.

I didn't ask if he'd ended Rolina's life. I supposed I didn't need to know. She was gone, and trying to swallow that was more than enough for right now. I couldn't have asked a thing if I'd tried, being that I couldn't seem to make words form to answer his simple question.

Hands snuck under my arms, lifting me from the ground.

Instinct returned. I whirled as we exited the tent, smacking the male's hard chest to be set down. The breeze gathered force, reviving me enough to realize I was making a grave error. But it was too late.

He dropped me to my feet and snatched my wrist, though not as violently as Rolina was prone to—*had been prone to.*

Sharp like the edge of a blade and as rough as a stone used to sharpen it, his low voice lured my eyes to his. "You might be lovely to look at, but that doesn't mean I won't kill you."

My eyes widened upon his, and my cheeks bloomed with both anger and terror.

Eyes of molten gold gazed down at me, then narrowed. His large hand was cool, the pads of his fingers roughened, as he lowered my own.

I blinked and pulled my hand to my chest, cradling it although he hadn't hurt me. Peering behind me to the tent, I stepped back from him before he did.

But looking was pointless when I'd seen it happen. There would be no trace of the woman I'd spent my entire life with. There was only a portable house of horrors veiled behind impenetrable canvas blending perfectly with the night.

"You..." I swallowed. "You killed her."

The faerie's thick brows crinkled. "That you care when the woman clearly cared nothing for you makes you awfully stupid." There was a pause as he eyed my hands, then carefully, my face. "Your name."

Most had left the field for town, leaving only a few stragglers awaiting entry into the tent. I turned in a circle, wondering what to do, where to go, what came next...

Home. I had to return to the apartment that had never been mine. Tomorrow, I would try to figure out what might happen next. Tomorrow, I would try to accept that nothing might ever change. That I'd still be stuck—

A throat cleared. I'd forgotten I had company.

The cloak-wearing murderer snapped, "*Name.*"

I startled, flinching as I spun back and had my first proper look at the male awaiting an answer from me. "Flea," I croaked.

The giant with golden eyes tilted his head, watching me shift on my feet as my cheeks flamed. Of course, there was no need to repeat myself and say it clearer. He'd heard me just fine.

Those catlike eyes crept down my body. Not in a lewd way, yet I still grew hotter—more uncomfortable—by the moment. "Flea?"

"Yes," I rasped.

"You're lying." He set loose an impatient breath and cursed quietly. "I'll give you one more chance to tell me your true name."

"I don't have one." My shaking hands grasped my brown skirts, clutching them tight. Perhaps I'd hit him again otherwise. Perhaps I'd seize the throat of his high collar and howl at him for changing and ruining everything within one measly second.

Perhaps I'd even thank him.

A death sentence, any and all of it, I was sure.

But as he lifted his hair-dusted chin, his gaze meeting mine down the bridge of his slightly crooked and slightly too long nose, I found myself asking this cruel stranger, "What am I to do now?"

He blinked, as if he were just as taken aback by the question as I was.

Then he scowled.

After a moment of unbending silence, he turned so swiftly for the tent, the breeze kicked up with the swish of his night-absorbing cloak.

And I was left more alone than ever before.

TWO

FREEDOM.

For so long, I'd imagined what that might look like.

Not once had I imagined merely a larger cage. Not once had I guessed that the freedom to live a life of my own would actually leave me with little choice at all.

I'd never worked. Not for coin. I'd cooked, cleaned, washed, shopped, and dreamed of a world beyond the warded borders of Crustle and the recesses of my imagination.

The rare escape I'd found hid amongst the pages of books. Whenever Rolina was out, I would study pictures and read or sneak downstairs to the library to exchange books for more.

In the stairwell of our apartment building was a wooden door barely big enough for a grown creature to squeeze through. I'd discovered it one night when I'd been too young and afraid to leave the building.

After sitting upon the landing for countless minutes, I'd failed to find the courage to venture down the last curl of steps and outside.

Hesitant to climb back upstairs to the woman with a temper I'd been desperate to escape, I'd wandered over to look closer at the door. The wood was worn, hinges rusted and flaking. Yet the padlock gleamed like that of true gold with intricate engravings of birds and leaves.

With one touch of my curious fingers, the metal hadn't just moved—it had unlatched.

The goblin who'd greeted me inside with such fright he'd nearly dropped his teacup had mercifully never had the padlock replaced.

And though I shouldn't have been permitted to borrow anything at such a young age, Gane had never sent me away.

My only companions, a lifeline and a bridge to adulthood, I'd handed myself over entirely to fiction and the tales and lore of other realms.

It was possibly the one and only thing I would eternally remain grateful to Rolina for—that she'd taught me my letters, the basics of reading, and numbers.

Of course, she had merely wished to make it seem as though she'd done whomever my faerie parents were a great service in caring for me so well. Not a year passed before she eventually grew tired of bothering with me at all. By the age of eight years, I could clean myself and parts of the apartment. I'd discovered the library during that year, and I'd learned enough to continue learning without her.

Books couldn't save me now.

And after days spent cleaning the already pristine apartment and staring at Rolina's extravagant belongings, I didn't know what to do. There was nowhere else to go, and only one creature who might have cared.

Gane grew paler by the second as I finished informing him of all that had happened.

"That vile and foolish woman." The goblin's furry and crinkled arched ears twitched with discomfort as he glanced to the street-facing doors I'd never once used. "You're lucky to be alive."

"I know," I said, sighing as I perched atop his tall desk, which sat giant and imposing in the middle of the narrow library. Due to his short stature, he had a set of wooden steps behind it, as well as a stool. I'd once asked him why he'd never sought a smaller desk for himself. He'd said that he'd rather people not look down upon him when requesting his assistance. "I don't know what else to do."

"You count yourself blessed by Mythayla to still draw breath, and that you can now do so without living under Rolina's tyrannical rule."

I snorted, though he was right. I was fortunate, I knew, but I was so many other conflicting things that I couldn't seem to feel any one feeling for too long. "Is it bad?" I asked, hesitant. "That I do not grieve her."

Gane scoffed. "You are too human for your own good. She was a monster of a woman."

"But she gave me shelter." I traced a fractal of light spearing through the aisles and over the worn desk from tall rectangular windows too grimy to see beyond. "Food, and some semblance of safety."

"And you were required to slave after her in return until she could send you away. If you ask me, that woman was far more faerie than you and those she despised. Hypocrites always meet their matches in the end."

Indeed, Rolina had.

Gane laid his quill down on his afternoon checklist and placed his gnarled hand over my fidgeting fingers. "You're feeling bereft because you did not get what you want after hoping for all these years, and now you're afraid you never will. But Flea..."

I studied his hairy fingers, and how my own far exceeded their stubby length, but I looked up at him when he said, "You have a chance to live a life of your own choosing now. You don't need to cower nor answer to anyone. Nothing is stopping you from doing exactly as you wish. You do not need Folkyn."

Nothing stopping me.

Those words rang through me, bittersweet. "I still need answers," I said, and I'd told him as much hundreds of times before.

The goblin did as expected. Taking his hand from mine to remove his spectacles from his almond eyes, he shook his head as he cleaned them with his plaid shirt. "You only think you do, but that you were dumped in Rolina's care says otherwise."

Rolina had always loathed to be reminded that her daughter was likely dead. All these years, she'd refused to believe it. Her few friends in town and at her place of work—the Lair of Lust—had supposedly ceased trying to convince her to grieve and move on long ago.

"But I can't just ignore it," I admitted. "I've spent too many years believing it will happen."

I could understand why Gane thought it was a waste of time to worry over creatures who did not worry over me, but... what if they did? What if they'd spent twenty years hoping I was okay, and that they might one day see me again?

What if I'd been stolen from them and left here in Crustle? As vengeance, or for my own safety? What if my parents were dead, and there had simply been no one to care for me? There were so many what-ifs, I could make a list as tall as the rafters in the library.

And I would never learn anything if I stayed here.

Gane set his spectacles back upon his wide face, then scratched at the white hair climbing his cheeks in tiny curling clouds. "You have to ignore it. There's no other option, so cease breaking your own heart. Crustle is your home, Flea."

But he knew that wasn't entirely true; otherwise, he wouldn't have left his podium with another exasperated shake of his head as soon as he'd finished speaking.

"Wouldn't you wish to at least know where you came from?" I called after him as he traversed the awaiting piles of books in the aisle closest to the desk. "I have to find a way, Gane."

"You don't *have* to do anything. Go home and enjoy Rolina's lavish life."

His unwillingness to talk of a land he had chosen to leave when his wife had perished some decades ago did not surprise me.

But his desire for me to leave him alone did.

I jumped down from the desk, hope rekindling and warming my blood. "Gane, if you know of a way, then you must tell me."

He'd never claimed to, but then, I'd never thought to ask. I'd believed, almost as strongly as Rolina had, that the Wild Hunt would swap me. At the very least, that they would find enough reason to take me home.

My fingers swept over the spines of books as I trailed the hobbling goblin from one aisle to the next. "Gane, *please.*"

He stopped and feigned rehoming a thick volume on the history of merfolk. One I'd read cover to cover five times. "There isn't a way. None that I would dare suggest."

"Then how did you come to Crustle?"

All he'd ever said was that he'd left Folkyn. Which I now suspected wasn't true.

His silence was telling.

He sighed and turned to squint up at me. "I went to the royal house of Hellebore with the intention of stealing a statue as old as the land itself."

I blinked, then I smiled broadly. "*Really?*"

His lips quirked before he made a sound of irritation and shuffled away. "Be gone, Flea. You are no criminal, and I won't see you endanger yourself."

I followed him to the back of the library. "But you did it."

"The king took pity on me because one of his warriors told him of my wife, and he could see I merely wished to have no part in the land that stole her from me."

"The frosty king of Hellebore took pity on you?" I almost laughed. "But he is a known tyrant."

"Tyrants have souls too, Flea. Besides..." He waved a hand, entering the swinging waist-length door to the small kitchenette and heading straight to the tea kettle. "Leaving Folkyn and leaving Crustle are two very different feats."

"Perhaps the governor will take pity on me now that I've lost my guardian."

"You are of age to no longer need a guardian, and the governor couldn't give two shooting stars about anyone but herself."

He was right. Ruthless in a way that was almost admirable, the half-fae female who'd fought dirty to earn her role as keeper of the middle lands cared nothing for exceptions unless it suited her own greedy desires.

And despite foolishly feeling like one, I was no exception.

I was far from the first faerie to be thrown out of Folkyn as a babe, and I certainly would not be the last.

Gane set the kettle on the stovetop, and I snatched a piece of cheese from the chopping board.

He glared at me.

"Rolina spent the last of her pay on wine, celebrating the arrival of the hunt for days prior to their visit." I shrugged and took another piece. "I'm almost out of food."

"Then I suggest you find yourself employment and quit worrying over finding a way into Folkyn."

"So there *is* a way." I grinned around the cheese, and he snatched the board from beneath my hand when I reached for more. Goblins did not like to share food with anyone but their families, no matter how much they tolerated someone else's company. "I know there is, and I know that you know what it is."

"Flea," he said, beyond exasperated now. "Even if I did know exactly how to get you in, I would take the answer with me to my grave."

Cheese and disbelief clogged my throat. I swallowed thickly with a wince. "You would do such a thing to me?"

"I would."

I scowled. "Why?"

"Because I care about you, and I will not see you die because I gave in to your fanciful dreams. Go home and get to thinking about where you might like to work." With that, he stole through the swinging door of the kitchenette with his cheese to his private quarters on the other side.

I waited to see if he'd return when the teakettle whistled. He didn't.

It was odd to feel both relieved and saddened by someone's absence.

Staring at the corner of the kitchen I'd cowered within as a youngling, I couldn't decide where the sadness even came from. I healed quickly, yet I'd received a thin scar upon my arm at the age of seven years from a plate Rolina had thrown at me while I'd huddled with my arms over my head.

I shook off the memory and finished the last of the raisins.

The sadness wasn't from missing her, I surmised as I changed into my finest gown of pleated emerald cotton with a cream satin bodice. Rather, it stemmed from knowing the woman who'd never wanted me had lived more than half of her life with nothing but grief and hatred.

And an unshakable belief that had failed her in the end.

I couldn't bring myself to do anything with her belongings. This entire apartment, even the scant furniture and belongings within my own room, was all hers.

Never mine.

She'd always made it abundantly clear that I was a guest—an unwanted one—so the only comfort I found was when I could forget that fact by escaping into books.

I looked at Rolina's room one last time.

The bed I'd made that she hadn't slept in the night before she'd died. The clothing and wineglasses she'd left scattered over the large space for she knew I would clean up after her. The white and brown toadstool dust speckling the small mirrors upon her dressing table.

Then I closed the door.

It was time to search for employment, lest I head back downstairs to the library in a few days to beg Gane to help me when I ran out of food.

I was tucking my feet within my scuffed slippers when a tapping sounded upon the door.

We rarely had visitors. Rolina loathed for those she drank her time away with to pay any attention to me, and no one had come knocking since she'd died.

I wondered if word would spread, or if I'd need to inform all of whom she'd known.

Madam Morin stood upon the other side of the door, her high cheeks adorned in a bright-pink rouge and the tight rust-colored ringlets sweeping down from her updo. "Flea, darling." Her shrewd apple-green gaze danced over me from head to toe. "My, how you've grown."

I'd hardly dealt with the madam who was our landlord. There was no need when Rolina saw her every other evening at the pleasure house. The half faerie was also a friend of Rolina's, which was how she'd gained employment after her husband disappeared.

Yet a slow blink of her kohl-painted lashes was the only reaction when I informed her of my guardian's fate.

"Rolina's gone."

Morin's ivory-gloved hand touched her ample chest. "I heard. Ghastly, isn't it? What those wild ones can get away with." Tutting, she said, "Such risky business, trading with the lawless folk. Why, you're lucky to have escaped unscathed, dear darling."

I nodded. I fell asleep each night to the memory of that flesh-and-bone-eating mist, knowing I had indeed been fortunate.

Sensing she was not here to offer condolences, I did my best to keep from growing stiff as I clenched the door and awaited the reason for this visit.

Morin's smile waned, her hand sliding from her chest. "I do wish we could put off such a conversation, but it's already been some days, and I'm afraid the matter cannot wait any longer." Her gaze flicked over my shoulder. "Not if you wish to keep such a fine roof over your head."

"The rent," I said, my stomach sinking slightly. I'd begun to assume that was why she was here.

I opened my mouth to tell her I was looking for employment, then closed it when she spoke between pursed lips. "And there's also the matter of Rolina's other debt."

"Other debt?"

Morin sighed and folded her hands before her. "As we both know, Rolina was fond of beautiful things, and beautiful things cost a lot of coin, my darling."

I shook my head. "I'm afraid I still don't quite know what you're saying."

"I'll put it plainly, then." The madam lifted her pointed chin. "Rolina was my friend, so I gave her exceptions I cannot grant to others. She spent her coin boldly and recklessly, and ahead of her scheduled payments from the Lair of Lust."

"Oh." My stomach churned. "But I have no coin to offer you. She spent it all. She—"

"I know." Morin and her husband managed one of the most profitable businesses in Crustle. I understood exactly what it was, and I understood what was coming when her eyes gleamed a second before she said, "But as sweet as you are, your problems are not my own. The gold must be repaid."

Gold.

I was nearly too afraid to ask, "How much?"

She arched a brow at my audacity, but then relented with a sigh that failed to stir one tight ringlet. "Ten gold coins, plus the remainder of this month's rent."

Shit.

The remaining rent was almost an entire gold coin by itself.

Color drained from my face in a rush that chilled my blood. I had no way of finding such a large sum of coin, and this greedy female knew it.

"I can give you two days to come up with the funds, or"—a slight smile was given with her suggestion—"you can work for me until the debt is repaid and you are a month ahead in your rent."

I failed to keep from scowling. "But Rolina was never a month ahead."

"Again," she said, the sugar slipping from her tone, "Rolina was my friend. You are a faerie I barely know."

I shouldn't have been shocked. I'd known where this was headed. I could scent it in the air between us—the thirst for coin beneath her cloying apricot perfume as the madam stepped forward.

I still tensed when she grasped my chin and gently tapped her long nail beneath it. "You're of mature age now, dear Flea." She tipped it up with a smile that revealed her sharp canines. Her green eyes roamed my face. "A very fine replacement you shall make."

The words escaped me before I could trap them. "I cannot work in a pleasure house."

"No?" Morin stepped back with high brows and a fluttery laugh. "It would seem you've been left with no choice, my darling." Turning away, she said, "I'll send for you when it's time."

Misunderstanding what I'd meant by that statement, she sauntered down the hall to the stairs. All the while I grappled to find a way to inform her that she didn't want me, and that I would certainly fail in such employment.

I'd never even been kissed.

THREE

I SHOULD HAVE BEEN HEARTBROKEN.

The woman who'd ensured my survival, no matter how grim it had been, was gone. Forever washed from this world. Some tiny part of me should have felt guilty for not doing more to save her. For not adequately warning her of the danger that would befall us if her temper were to flare.

And I had been heartbroken. I'd lost my chance.

Now, I felt nothing but annoyance and an expanding anxiety for whatever loomed ahead.

Pacing the two-bedroom apartment while the bath filled, I stared at the gilded paintings of gowns and lamp-lit streets upon the walls and I thought of the coin. I thought of what it might cost to even so much as attempt to find another way to get what I wanted. To gain what might be my only chance at true freedom.

To finally find all the answers.

The Wild Hunt wouldn't return for another year. Regardless, I understood now that it had been more than foolish to assume what I needed would be found with the likes of those who would end a life so swiftly because they'd been offended and lacking in patience.

No, there had to be another way. And whatever it was, it was sure to be expensive.

The sky had barely darkened when a gentleman wearing a mustard bow-tie and a monocle over one of his murky blue eyes arrived with a heart-stalling thud on the door. "Madam Morin awaits your escort to the Lair of Lust."

"Of course she does," I muttered, knowing better than to refuse although I didn't need an escort to the building just down the street from the one I resided in.

I still hadn't decided what to do. I hadn't determined whether Morin had spoken true regarding Rolina's debts, nor if it mattered. If she hadn't, there was no way to prove such a thing. Especially when the evidence filled our apartment in the form of beautiful art, furnishings, wine stains upon the linen and carpets, and fine clothing.

In the end, there was nothing left to do but follow the gent and hope that I could make this meeting short by being honest with Morin about my lack of... uh, romantic experience. Then I would ask for more time to repay the debt, and find employment doing something I could actually do tomorrow.

With the exception of blaming me for her husband's departure and therefore her fate, Rolina had never spoken of her work at the Lair of Lust. At a young age, I'd eventually pieced together what working for Madam Morin required due to the scents she'd bring home.

The idea of exchanging pleasure for coin had never concerned me, but I wasn't what they were looking for. Though I'd too often wished differently, I hadn't any experience with bedding someone. Rolina had wanted me untouched out of fear that my Fae family might not accept me if I'd been sullied by anyone in the middle lands of Crustle.

I found it hard to believe that would be true, given the hungry sexual appetites of faeries. Then again, I'd heard and read multiple contradictory tales regarding my own kin.

The Lair of Lust was a narrow three-story structure jammed between another apartment building and the long-abandoned florist on the corner. The ornate front doors opened to a high-end bar and lounges. Glass chandeliers were visible through the heart-shaped window.

Light glowed within, illuminating finely dressed patrons seated at the bar and around candle-topped tables. The walls were supposedly spelled to keep the noise from leaking out onto the street and into the neighboring buildings along it.

My escort walked past the front entrance.

Fear was soon replaced with curiosity as I was led down the tight alleyway beside the dark florist and around the corner to a metal flight of stairs. If anything, after another night spent tossing and turning with inescapable images of flesh-eating mist falling from a rippling sky, I could do with the distraction.

We climbed all the way to the third floor, the door opening with a quiet creak. "After you," the gent murmured, his bushy mustache hiding his lips.

I nodded my gratitude out of habit and waded into a dimly lit hall. Brass lamps lined the bowing walls between a long row of closed plum-colored doors.

"Down the end and to your left. She's waiting for you."

I turned back, but found no sign of the monocle wearing fellow, whom I assumed might have been Morin's husband. The wood floor groaned beneath my slipper-encased feet. The sound of laughter and clinking glasses drifted up the stairwell from the bar below. But other sounds could not be heard. At the end of the hall, I stopped, each breath growing slimmer.

The rooms must have been spelled for privacy, too.

Perhaps a distraction wasn't what I needed after all. A night of unbroken sleep and a week to make more plans and better sense of all this sounded much better.

"Have you any idea of the time?" came a shrill voice and a cloud of that apricot perfume. "I was beginning to think you might have escaped Darold's escort."

"I, uh..." Before I could form proper words, Madam Morin's hand curled around my wrist and tugged me into a large room. "Wait, I think we should talk about something," I said, and swallowed as I studied the piles and rows of garments and lace and wigs choking nearly half of the room. "First, I mean."

Waving my request away, Morin released me. "In case you haven't noticed, the third floor is predominantly staff quarters. This is where you will arrive and leave. Quickly now"—a wary look was given to the door I'd been dragged through—"there's no more time for dawdling."

She then hurried me behind a privacy curtain in the corner of the room and thrust the heavy velvet closed. "Your client arrives any moment, and he does not like to be kept waiting."

A dress flew over the curtain and landed upon my head.

After enduring Rolina for so many years, I was more than skilled at handling those with no patience. Yet alarm speared through me at the mention of *he*.

Struggling into the filmy mixture of elastane, lace, and organza, I snapped the peach concoction into place over my arms and hips with a wince. "Skies squash me," I whispered, turning to the side to inspect the skintight bodice in the scratched mirror. "I look like a peacock."

A volcano of organza and ribbon rose at my waist to then spill beneath my hips. It fell to the floor to barely cover my toes.

The curtain was ripped open.

Morin's crimson lips pursed as she eyed me. "Hair up," she said, a finger in the air as she circled me. "Leave a few curls out. He is sure to love the kiss of winter-touched hair over a slim neck such as yours." Lowering to the floor, she clucked with disapproval as she attempted to pull the skirts down. "No shoes. Too tall as it is."

Straightening, her shrewd gaze dragged slowly over my physique. Unaccustomed to being so overtly scrutinized, I lifted my chin and curled my fingers into my palms to keep from covering my breasts. Which were at risk of bursting from their lace and satin enclosure, no matter how tightly wrapped. "Just how faerie did you say you are again?"

"I..." I frowned because I hadn't, while wondering why it would matter. "I don't know." I tried not to laugh as I said, "A lot?"

A brow raised, Morin licked her teeth. "Show me those ears." Lifting my hair, I did as requested, and a smile that appeared more hungry than pleased lit her green eyes. "Whatever you are, dear darling, you'll certainly pass as full."

Said ears heated and filled with my racing heartbeat as I attempted to ignore unwanted thoughts of what awaited.

"Come." Turning, she beckoned for me to follow her back down the hall to a room at the very end near the exit. "Finish preparing in here. Hair, rouge, you know what to do. Hurry."

The door slammed. Powders plumed from pots upon the once white and now stained furniture surrounding me.

There was only one other creature present. A male who sat at a stretch of mirror-lined tables edging the far wall. He'd paused in applying kohl to his eyes, and met my gaze in the mirror. "Fresh meat?"

I looked at the trays of glitters and powders scattered before him, unsure what to do. "I'm..." I swallowed thickly. "I think I might be sick."

"Sit down," he said with a scowl, then returned to lining his bright-emerald eyes. "You'll ruin our tips with the scent of vomit clinging to us." He was a faerie, or at least half, judging by the near-point of his ruby-studded ears.

I did as he said, but my hand shook as I reached for the jar of rouge brushes. Instead, I shoved it in my lap and stared at my reflection. My cheeks, high and sharply curved, were drawn, making my soil-dark eyes appear black.

I bit my lips to bring back their color. I could certainly do with the rouge. A ghost. My client was about to meet with a wraith. I was about to meet with a stranger, and I...

I couldn't move.

Silence permeated like another flesh-eating mist. I twisted my fingers while silently reciting my letters in an effort to quell the unease noosing around my throat.

The male's rich voice was gentler when he eventually spoke once more. "The first night is always the most daunting, but you never know..." He set the tiny brush back into a vial. "You might enjoy it."

"Do you?" I asked, unsure why but needing his answer all the same.

He laughed, a buttery sound that both jarred and soothed. "Darling, do I look like I hate it? It's the best job I've ever had, and believe me," he huffed, "I've had many in my hundred years of existence."

At that, I turned on the cushioned stool to better look at him. He appeared not a drop older than twenty-five years. Though that was no surprise. Even half-fae could live a few hundred years before signs of aging slowly took hold.

The male twisted on his stool, too. His thigh-high leather boots creaked when he reached down to his feet.

His focus sharpened on my face as he paused in tying the maze of laces. "Who in the skies are you, innocent one?" He sniffed. His neck rolled as he straightened, gaze brightening. "Such dark eyes for such a seemingly pure soul."

I refrained from saying I wasn't pure. I couldn't be when I was more grateful than distraught over Rolina's demise.

The door burst open.

Morin cursed viciously. "You haven't done your hair." I watched her scowl in the mirror. "Or so much as touched your face." She looked over her shoulder into the hall, her complexion paling when she stared back at me and chewed her red-painted lip. She sighed. "Never mind. We've no time. Come."

I offered a slight smile to the male who was now smirking at me and rose on weak legs.

As I entered the hall, the fear I could scent dampening the air grew stronger. Strong enough to realize it was not merely emanating from me but from the stiff-backed madam I trailed.

"Room twelve." Halfway down the hall, she stopped and turned to me. Her apple-green eyes were glossy. "Whatever you do, *do not* displease him." With that, she gestured to the slim stairwell beside her.

"But..." I frowned, thinking she would surely tell me more. "I don't know anything. I don't know what I'm expected to do or if—"

"You do whatever he tells you to. Now go."

She waited as I hesitated. It was now clear there was no escaping this, and that informing her of my inexperience would be pointless.

So I gripped the railing tight and waded down to the second floor.

Adrenaline fled. Terror froze my feet to the floor before the closed purple door of room twelve. The room sat at the end of the hall. Firelight in the lone lamp upon the wall caused the aged brass of the numbers one and two to darken and then glow.

Could I truly do this? Not only was I ill-prepared, but apparently, I was also a coward.

The silence of the entire floor was too telling. Too stifling. Indeed, the rooms had been masked by spell-work to keep all sound trapped within.

Claws, sharp and sinking, dug deep into my stomach.

I shifted over the cool wood floor beneath my bare feet, unsure how I should proceed.

Was I supposed to knock or simply enter the room and introduce myself? Would he decide to just get straight to... business? What would such *business* entail when it was a transaction? I had some idea of what to expect when I one day gave myself to another, and I'd imagined passion, heat, and a magic that could not be explained. Would this gent want any such thing?

Perhaps he was expecting me to merely offer myself and forget about any enjoyment of my own. Was I permitted to enjoy it? What if I loathed it? How should one even offer themselves? Naked? Half clothed? Sprawled upon the bed and hopefully not shaking with fear of the unknown?

Behind me, the stairs halfway down the hall tempted like an alluring siren I wasn't sure I could muster the courage to become.

If I fled, then I would face yet another gigantic setback and certain danger. Like so many with business in the middle lands, Morin would have people to punish those who dared to disrespect her. If I stayed, then I would face the stranger awaiting the use of my body on the other side of the door that seemed to pulse with the uneven thud of my heart.

As if plucking a piece of broken glass from my foot, I seized the handle with gritted teeth and opened the door.

Of course, the first thing I noticed was the bed. Deep purple gauze was secured with black ribbon to the four posts surrounding it. It waited dressed in similar colored bedding in the center of the far wall.

I saw nothing else.

My teeth unglued, my attention stolen by the commanding presence of my first client.

He stood at an oak liquor cabinet mere feet from where I was frozen in the doorway, his hair only a shade lighter than the rippling black silk of his loose shirt. I drew in his staggering height, then the long fingers leaving the crystal decanter of whiskey he set down.

The most beautiful man I'd ever seen turned, his thick hair whispering over a broad shoulder. "You're late."

I was unable to keep my eyes from widening as my heartbeat stalled.

Man was the wrong word.

Every inch of him was pure and cold-blooded *faerie*.

My heart restarted with a violent patter. Unsure how to respond—how to talk at all—I uttered dumbly, "I am?"

He stilled, and I knew I'd displeased him. The air changed, growing chilled with talons and teeth as he turned in full.

I almost wished he hadn't.

His eyes were a blue so deep, they resembled the sky before an evening storm. Fringed in dark lashes, their uncompromising weight caused my heart to cease racing in my chest.

It stopped beating entirely as the male's thick brows furrowed and he gave the glass of whiskey to his parting mouth. His nose was strong and straight without a trace of past injury, and his lips so full I couldn't help but wonder how soft they'd feel against my own when he lowered the glass.

He licked them, and my stomach tightened. The odd sensation worsened when he swallowed the liquor.

Hypnotized by the dipping of his throat, my gaze traversed the olive skin as though I could follow the whiskey's journey into his body. A body that, even covered in clothing, overwhelmed. Burning with shame and something I failed to recognize, I couldn't remove my eyes from the small smattering of dark hair revealed where he'd left his shirt unbuttoned at his throat.

His voice was bark wrapped in silk. His order one I didn't even consider disobeying as he said with quiet authority, "Do close the door."

I tore my eyes from his chest and turned to do as he said, using the opportunity to take a moment. I took a few more as I locked the wooden barrier with the golden chain, unable to believe what I'd just done.

I'd blatantly ogled my client.

A client of whom I'd need to bed.

A male of whom was both breathtakingly beautiful and extremely terrifying.

As though he could read my mind, and likely scent what I was undoubtedly flooding the room with, humor thickened his tone. "Do you not wish to look at me some more?"

My cheeks caught fire. "I apologize. You just..." I turned back, but found I couldn't meet his eyes. I fastened my own upon the large velvet divan beside me. "Well, I suppose you shocked me."

Shocked was putting it mildly.

It was not for me to discern why anyone visited this establishment, but curiosity had me wondering what beneath the stars would possess such a creature to pay for pleasure? He had no need, surely, regardless of whatever his tastes may be.

"Were you expecting someone else?"

I shook my head and clasped my hands before me to keep them from trembling. "I wasn't told anything about whom I would uh..." I winced, deciding on, "I would meet."

The faerie said nothing for a moment, but his attention was a frost pressing upon every part of me. I heard him swallow as he drained the whiskey. The glass hit the wood behind him with a thud that nearly made me jump.

"Frightened, little butterfly?"

At that, I looked at his brown leather boots. They were giant and pointed at the toes. "No."

"If you're going to be so bold as to lie, you will at least do me the courtesy of looking me in the eye while you do."

His crisp words washed the heat from my cheeks. My spine locked, every instinct screaming to flee.

I could already hear Madam Morin's threatening disapproval, so I did as he wished. I met his gaze, expecting to find a glower—more displeasure within the endless dark blue.

Instead, I found a calm stillness to his features, rendering them sharp like stone, and a studious glow that brightened his eyes. "Much better," he murmured, and his head tilted slightly. "Now try again."

"Try again?" I asked, confused.

"Answering the question."

Oh. I squeezed my fingers together.

It was growing abundantly clear that I was doomed.

Whoever this male was, he was not from Crustle. His demeanor, the power roiling from him like a second shadow carried as an ever-fluttering invisible cloak, was too much.

It was as lethal and true to every word I'd heard and read of those with enhanced magical abilities. Of those native to Folkyn.

He was going to punish me by speaking of my incompetence and disrespect to Madam Morin. I could feel it. Or worse, he might even hurt and humiliate me until he'd felt I'd sufficiently learned my lesson.

At a loss for what to do, I bit the inside of my cheek and felt the sting of tears grow stronger.

All the while the creature radiating a power that shortened each breath did not blink. He waited for my answer, lashes curled toward his dark brows.

My chest tightened and tightened. I'd never felt more trapped, more like prey, as this faerie refused to set me free of his gaze. "I'm nervous," I finally confessed, my words rasped. "And scared, yes."

His blank expression did not change. "Was that very difficult to admit?"

"No," I said, but when his head cocked, I corrected myself. "Y-yes."

"Why?" he asked, his eyes never leaving mine as he crossed from the liquor cabinet to the divan. The nearing of such energy, of all that he was, raised the hair on my arms. "Because I frighten you?"

"I do not know you..." I stopped, for I was digging a deeper grave with every passing minute.

He huffed and lowered to the divan with eye-drawing grace, his form far too large although the seat was designed for two. "Try again."

"Yes, you frighten me," I admitted, turning to fully face him.

He placed his leg over the other, black trousers snug over muscular thighs. "What is your name, butterfly?"

I attempted to choose from the many names I'd always dreamed of having. In the end, I knew he'd see any of them for the lie they were. "I do not have one."

That earned a surprised lift of his brow. He repeated in a slow drawl, "You do not have one."

I shook my head.

He hummed. The arm spreading atop the divan caused his shirt to open more at his chest. "Come closer."

Unsure how close he wanted me, I stopped mere inches from where he sat.

His leg dropped. "Closer." My heart kicked at my sternum as his scent, an earthy caramel, deepened and lured. His knees opened, revealing the hard bulge at his groin that threatened to burst the seam of his pants.

My eyes stayed fastened upon it a moment too long, but thankfully, he did not comment.

"Closer," he almost rasped. When I stood right between his knees, he said, "Yes, stop."

The heat of him was overwhelming. A warmth so crystal sharp, it burned like the touch of iced water.

My lips parted, and my stomach clenched, as he stared at my mouth while saying, "Much better."

I didn't know what to say to that. He spoke before I could feel forced to say anything at all. "Surely, the people of this bustling town must call you something." The word bustling was said as though he'd meant rotten.

"Flea," I said. "My guardian called me Flea."

His bark of laughter was unexpected, the throaty melody trans-forming his features from mouthwatering perfection carved from marble to ethereal. The sound died far too quickly for my liking as he said, "I do hope you're trying to evade giving me an honest answer. If so"—he dragged his teeth over his bottom lip—"you are rapidly im-proving in the art of deception."

"I wish I were," I said quietly, attempting to smile.

His features flattened, eyes flaring so fast and bright, they turned an iced blue. The temperature in the room dropped. Before I could understand why, the faerie licked his teeth behind closed lips. "This guardian must have truly loathed you."

"She did." And I couldn't avoid recalling the one time I'd asked Rolina if she would call me something else—couldn't help but lose the nervous excitement that had thickened my blood as I remembered what my request had been met with.

Laughter followed by a slap across the face.

"Where is she now?" the male asked softly, daringly—as if he had already guessed.

"Dead."

Another hum. "This pleases you."

I shouldn't have said anything, but he was crossing a line I did not think needed to be crossed. "I don't wish to speak of it."

I awaited reprimand. A demand to divulge whatever he sought. It never came.

"Very well." I stared at him in surprise and felt the tension slowly leave my shoulders. "But I will not call you such a thing."

I nodded once, my lips unwilling to open.

His chest rose and fell with a deep inhale as his eyes briefly left mine to traverse my body. "Do you like that gown?"

"Not really."

"Why not?"

Confused by all his questions when I thought he'd only wish to get to know my body, I couldn't help but gently ask, "Why do you care to know?"

He laid his other arm over the headrest of the seat, fingers strok-ing lazily along the steep angle of his hair-peppered jaw. It firmed under his touch as he studied me. "You are brave." Noting the furrowing of my brow, he explained, "To ask anything of me unless it pertains to how you can please me."

I knew I had to, though it still irked me to say, "I'm sorry."

"Are you?" he said, his teeth flashing bright as they caught his pointer finger. "I do not think you are."

I flushed, loathing it.

"Answer the question, and perhaps I shall forgive your carelessness."

My eyes met his, and in them, I found a darkness gathering. His thumb rubbed his upper lip. "It itches," I said, tracking that movement intently. "The dress."

"Then take it off." It was not a request and also not an order. It was not a suggestion, either. Rather, the words grazed the skin like the daring tickle of a blade's point.

A taunting test.

Whatever it was, it didn't matter. I was here to do more than un-dress for him, and it seemed it was time for the reason he'd visited this pleasure house.

Yet fear did not seize me as I'd guessed it would. As I clutched the mass of material at my hips and pulled upward until the entire mon-strosity was falling from my hands to the floor, a rush of unexpected liquid heat swept through me.

The heady taste of anticipation shocked as I looked from the pile of peach organza to the male whose eyes hadn't left me.

My cream satin slip reached my thighs and showed almost half of my heavy breasts, the material sitting just shy of my nipples. I re-sisted the urge to fold my arms over my chest, and the urge to cover the wide flare of my hips.

My client's hand had fallen slack, hanging beneath his hewn chin. But his expression remained impassive save for that glow of amusement in his gaze. I'd have worried that I wasn't what he desired to indulge in until he said thickly, "Take a seat."

I made to move from between his knees to the other side of the divan when his hand caught mine.

The touch singed and stilled.

Smooth and slightly roughened fingers curled around my own. "On my lap."

I blinked, but he merely stroked his long fingers over mine and waited. I shivered, though I wasn't the least bit cold. Then I awkwardly moved forward.

"May I touch you?"

My answer was whispered. "You already are."

He smirked, all the warning he gave before he grasped my hips and lifted me as if I were nothing but feathers. My thighs fell astride his, my core close to his groin, and my hands splayed over his hard chest.

I withdrew one to tug at my slip before I could remember that it didn't matter if he glimpsed between my thighs. Not when he was here to see and have all of me.

And as he snatched my hand to set it back on his chest, I was growing more excited than fearful of that by the second. "Much better," he said.

I wasn't sure if that were true. My heart pounded, and my stomach flipped.

Seeming to sense that, and I supposed he could, the male's gaze momentarily dipped to my breasts. Slowly, it returned to mine as his hand slid up my back, tangling in my long curls. "Hair of pure snow and eyes of damp soil."

My shoulders loosened, as did my fingers over his chest, when he gently traced the strands of hair at my back. "You are full faerie," he said, almost a whisper, "yet so dreadfully innocent and full of heart."

It hovered upon the edge of my tongue, the desire to refute his correct assessment. I didn't. I watched his long lashes curl up and down as his eyes fell to my stomach, then to my thighs. "How is that possible, especially in a place such as this?"

I didn't know he was referring to the middle lands in general until I said, "This is my first evening here," and he smirked.

Apparently, he was well aware of that.

My eyes narrowed. "That is why you wished to meet with me?"

His lips lowered, eyes roaming back up my chest to meet with mine. "I prefer not to waste time with those who don't know how to please, but I will admit to being too curious for my own good."

I wasn't sure why a knot of disappointment formed at hearing him say that. Perhaps it was because I'd long-wished to experience many things, pleasure at the hands of another included, and maybe this was indeed a test.

One I was failing miserably.

Fingers clasped my chin. I hadn't realized my gaze had fastened to the peeling ivory paint upon the wall behind the divan until it was forced to collide with the male's once more. "I am not deterred."

"You're not?" I surprised myself by saying aloud.

His thumb brushed beneath my lower lip, his eyes following. "Something tells me you will be eager to please me."

Irritation spiked, causing me to open my mouth when it would have been wise to remember who held the power in this room. "Presumptuous and awfully arrogant of you."

His brows jumped, and I braced.

He chuckled again, and a relieved exhale left me. "Is it, though?" he asked, and the way his mouth curved distracted. So much so, that when he leaned forward, I grew tense again. "I can smell you, sweet creature. You're aroused."

Heat drenched my cheeks, and he skimmed the side of his finger over one. This close, I could make out a small scar at his hairline, and notice the way his pupils swelled while I studied his soft-looking mouth.

"Indeed." He groaned, and the hand at my lower back pushed my body into his until his length sat flush against my core. "I cannot help but think you will please me more than what is good for me."

My head swam from the contact and his throaty words. Dizzied and feeling drugged, I leaned back with my hands braced upon his chest, needing to breathe.

He didn't seem to mind, his touch at my face remaining and tickling as he traced my cheekbone.

Fear slipped away as I watched him—his rapt focus as he absorbed my every feature. The arch of my brows and the crest of my lashes were gently brushed.

His curious touch and hungry gaze emboldened me to study him in kind.

He was giant yet lean. Beneath the loose silk that gaped at his defined chest were rock-hard muscles. My fingers hesitantly crawled down to his abdominals. His hardness twitched against my core. It shocked me still, and he clasped my cheek.

My eyes lifted to find his were upon my mouth, his thumb pressed at the corner. "Such lovely lips. A perfect, silken bow. Tell me," he said, nearly absently, "has anyone ever kissed them?"

Heat threatened to engulf my neck and face again, but I sensed what he wanted and shook my head.

"Kiss me, butterfly."

I couldn't deny that I wanted it, too, so I leaned forward. Doing so made his erection press harder against me, and a startled breath with low sound slipped free.

His hand clutched my cheek tighter. "Does that feel good?"

I swallowed, not needing to answer when my body leaned instinctively into his in response, seeking more of that sparking warmth.

"I'm still waiting," he murmured, lashes dipping and his words heating my mouth.

"Yes," I said and closed the small gap between our mouths, nerves long forgotten when my eyes closed upon the first touch of his lips meeting mine. I sat them against his carefully, savoring that I was truly doing such a thing.

That I was doing something I'd only ever dreamed about doing.

Then I slowly moved them. His lips parted at my urging, and a soft sound rumbled from deep within his chest. I skimmed and pressed, and after a minute, I licked just under his upper lip.

He was whiskey and winter. A poison so intoxicating, I greedily sought more.

I lost myself and grasped his cheeks. He tensed beneath me at my boldness, but when I made to withdraw, he clasped my rear. Firmly.

And then he kissed me back.

His silken lips claimed with hungry prying and pressing. He groaned and tilted his head, his tongue entering my mouth to meet mine.

I forgot why I was here. I forgot this male was a stranger willing to pay for my company. I forgot I'd ever been afraid and uncertain.

All I could feel was fire.

A moan stunned me, falling between us when his hips jerked and his length dug hard against me. He tore away, his eyelids heavy and his pinkened mouth tempting me to reclaim it. He swallowed, and I had the sudden and extreme urge to lick his throat.

The hand upon my rear squeezed then left, my skin chilled in its absence. My slip had risen, I realized.

He'd touched my bare skin.

Though it shocked, I didn't mind. Especially when that same hand rose to my chest. A lone finger dragged along the edging of my slip over the swells of my breasts. I waited, almost asking him to tug it down to expose more of me.

As though at war with himself, the male's jaw hardened, and he straightened until our noses were close to touching.

His hold upon my face gentled, his thumb caressing the curve of my cheek and luring my eyes to his. "You are the most exquisite treasure I've ever laid eyes on," he whispered against my mouth. He bit my lip—hard enough that I flinched. I gasped when he sucked it clean of blood and dragged his mouth over my cheek to vow to my ear, "And I'm going to do such filthy, dishonorable things to you."

I should have been afraid.

Many Fae, especially those with immense magical abilities,

hungered for blood. They relied on it for strength and to appease addiction if they were prone to feeding too much.

I had no time to decide what either of us might be.

I was lifted, then dumped upon the divan beside a fat pouch of coin I hadn't seen sitting next to him. That magnetic heat from his body had left the velvet of the chair toasty warm. I stared up at him while he rolled his shirtsleeves, my lips and flesh tingling.

Goddess damn me. Even his forearms, thick and sprinkled with dark hair, were tantalizing.

This unexpected client of mine dragged a hand through waves of darkest brown. The strands fell back over his shoulders to brush his granite jaw. "Do not speak of this meeting or meet with anyone else."

"You're leaving?" I blinked and blurted, "But we..."

The glare he gave me was glacial. "Understood?"

Alarmed and speechless, I blinked some more. Then I nodded my acceptance and pulled my slip over my thighs as though he hadn't just researched my body like he was learning a map.

"Moving your head about is not an adequate answer, butterfly."

I frowned but acquiesced. "Understood."

"Good. Await my sparrow."

The door opened, but before he could step through, my confusion and the mess he'd made of me demanded *something.* "You've not even given me your name."

He stilled. I expected him to be irritated by my audacity or that he might just leave.

But as he stepped out into the hall and the door slowly creaked closed behind him, he said far too simply, "Florian."

My heart clattered to a violent stop in my chest.

Then fell with a sickening splash into my stomach.

I'd never seen the royals of Folkyn. Given how little they wanted to do with Crustle, and of how little they thought of the citizens, any paintings and depictions of them had been forbidden in these lands eons ago.

But due to my research of the place in which I'd been born, I knew of all their names. And no one would dare name their offspring after a royal unless they too were part of that royal family.

My eyes remained stuck to the door. As the swift return of fear threatened to expel the meager contents of my stomach, I forced them to the coin next to me.

Not only had I kissed a royal faerie of Folkyn.

I'd made a deal with the winter king.

FOUR

H IS NAME HAUNTED ME FOR THE NEXT TWO DAYS.
Florian.
My first and only client was king of one of the four rul-
ing houses of Folkyn.

The winter-wielding king of Hellebore.

King Florian.

The succinct way he'd given his name befuddled, as if he'd known
it would leave me thinking of nothing but him until we met again. As if
it were not an unusual thing for a faerie king to visit a pleasure house.

It was.

Kings and queens had their own personal harems, lovers, and
even spouses. Whatever and whomever they chose. They had no need
to seek indulgences elsewhere. Even more unusual was that a king
would seek such a thing here in Crustle—in the middle lands the folk
of Folkyn thought far beneath them.

And all of that coin...

It sat upon the tea table before Rolina's favored armchair, catching starlight and sunshine as the hours passed, barely touched.

I'd been burning with the need to talk about it, yet I couldn't decide whether to tell Gane of the meeting. Besides a quick visit to the
grocer yesterday to buy more food, I hadn't left the apartment. I was
behaving as though Rolina were still here, though I'd seldom had room
to think of her since my first evening at the Lair of Lust.

I'd seldom thought of anything but the bone-chilling memory
of kissing a faerie king.

I'd lost hours to sitting upon the cushioned window seat and staring at the busy town street, pondering why such a powerful creature

would want something like me. Not because I thought there was anything particularly wrong with me, but because of the overabundant perfection of him.

King Florian could bed anyone of his choosing without paying for it.

Sleep came in bursts of midnight-sky eyes and flesh-eating mists.

Dawn delivered quiet but busy streets.

With what I hoped was enough coin in tow—I didn't dare bring it all—I hurried across the street from the apartment building and cut through the alleyway to Main Street. Freshly baked bread and steamed fish coated the brisk morning air.

I squeezed between the bakery and the vendor cart parked outside of it, ignoring the leering gazes of some of the miners and tradesmen who waited in line for beverages and breakfast. Farther down the street, beyond the myriad of shops and apartment buildings yet to open their drapes and shutters, awaited the market.

Amid the permanent display of mismatched carts, tents, and rickety tables and stands, row after row of vendors were setting up or already at work. A maze, I'd thought upon my first trip to the market crowding the broken and weed-infested cobblestone of an abandoned street. I was greeted now as I had been then, by the misty reek rising from the canal behind it.

Rolina had never liked to be seen with me, nor had she trusted me to venture out too often on my own.

But after contracting a violent stomach flu when I was fourteen years, she was bedridden for nearly a week. Reluctantly, I'd then been granted my first taste of independence. Though the cackling and shouting and incessantly stalking eyes had frightened me so much that I'd returned to the apartment with only half of what I'd been sent for, and I was never permitted to return again.

I was only permitted to shop for what we needed at the grocer on Main Street and ordered to return straight away. Failing to do as I was told was always met with repercussions too painful to warrant appeasing any desire I had to explore.

That was then, I thought soberly as I began the walk through the numerous stalls.

Discomfort curled into my chest and scoured through my limbs like slithering barbed wire when it came knocking again.

Relief.

Only a monster would be glad for the passing of another soul. Yet I still felt only an odd sense of confusion at the sight of her belongings, and a curious sadness for that of her missing mortal daughter.

All my life, Rolina had lived with nothing but crumbs of hope.

It was the one thing that had bound us—the only thing we'd had in common—our desperate hope for answers. I couldn't decide if it were best she'd left this world without knowing of her true daughter's fate. All I knew was that I couldn't rest until I found the answers to my own.

Some traders muttered greetings as I passed. Others watched on while I scanned their wares. Healing implements, tonics, sweets, clothing, rare pelts, and...

Up ahead, the smallest of the stalls remained empty. But the beadwork upon the jewelry pulled my feet and fingers close. Sapphires of milky blues and crystal skies had been entwined into bracelets, necklaces, and even diadems.

A large hand slammed over mine.

My heart stopped at the sight of three long fingers. Two were nothing but gnarled stubs.

"Hello," I said and cleared my throat as I attempted to snatch my hand back. "They're beautiful."

Slowly, the hand slid from mine. When I looked up, my eyes met with an orange set.

"So are those fingers of yours." The faerie's voice was gruff. "If you wish to keep them, don't fucking touch unless you're buying."

Right. I'd forgotten that the rule as old as the Fae themselves extended to many business dealings here in Crustle, too. "Is that how you lost yours?"

The bald faerie raised a white brow. "Did you wake up this morning and decide to look for trouble, or are you always so reckless?"

At that, I couldn't help but smile. "Merely curious."

"Curiosity kills far more than cats, pretty thing." My heartbeat slowed, then grew heavy as he sank onto the tree stump behind the table and reached for a copper mug of coffee. "A forlok got them, if you must know."

Forlok.

My astonishment was mistaken for cluelessness, for he said proudly, "'Bout as tall as you. Skeletal but deadly." His eyes glinted. "Their bones sell for a real handsome price to certain witches. Anyway, I got what my young and foolish self deserved instead."

It seemed I was indeed in the right place.

I tried to keep my tone mild and casual. "You've visited the faerie realm."

He paused with his coffee halfway to his mouth and eyed me as if I were born yesterday. If I only knew that I might as well have been with my lack of worldly experience. "No one visits Folkyn. I was born and raised there, and I left." His clipped words implied there was far more to the story. That he likely fled before he was forcibly removed or worse.

Looking back at the jewels, I said, "These aren't from here."

He thumped his mug onto the table and loomed over it, startling me. "All right, who the fuck are you?" he sneered. "*Huh?* One of those good for nothing royal spies? I haven't done a damned thing wrong, you hear? It's all legal enough." He flicked his hand. "So be gone."

I stepped away and raised my hands. "I swear I'm nothing of the sort. I just..." I sighed, then confessed, "I just need a little information."

Taken aback, the male's face scrunched as he surveyed me once more. "I've nothing worth knowing. Go back to bed."

"But I think you might." Gathering two gold coins from the pocket of my dress, I opened my hand and gave him a glimpse of them. "And I'm willing to pay."

His fire-colored eyes narrowed on the coins, then my thread-bare cotton dress. "What's the likes of you doing with coin like that?"

"It's not stolen, if that's what you're inferring," I clipped, then reminded myself to keep my emotions at bay. Now was not the time to be offended. For all I knew, he could be one of the few with the ability to help me in some way. "All I need to know is how to get in."

He snorted. "Get in?" A bark of laughter. "To Folkyn?"

I nodded.

His smile waned. "You're as insane as you are stupid."

I gritted my teeth and made to tuck the coins away.

"All right, all right," he said quickly. "Fine. I'll tell you one thing and one thing only."

I placed one coin away, and the male cursed. "You're meaner than you look." I waited, and he grumbled, "You need to know someone."

"Someone?"

"Exactly," he said, glancing at the quiet stalls on either side of us. "You know what I mean."

"Someone from there, you mean," I said, my hope deflating even as I recalled the heat of Florian's mouth upon mine, his branding touch.

Other than the payment his visits provided, the king would be of no help. Merely alluding to my lifelong desire for answers could prove an irreversible and disastrous mistake. The royals of Folkyn did nothing that did not serve them, and if King Florian knew of my plan...

He could kill me for so much as dreaming of entering a land forbidden to me.

Snatching a cloth tucked within his belt, the jewel trader polished a large sapphire as an elderly woman walked past. "Good morning, Hal."

Hal huffed indignantly. "When is morning ever good, Issle?"

She chuckled as if accustomed to such a greeting from this Hal, and after eyeing me up and down, she continued to a wagon of old produce parked by the curve of the canal.

Hal waited, then went on a good minute later. "Two options,

really. If you wish to survive. You need someone from there or high up in the ranks here."

I withheld the urge to groan and curse. "Of course." I couldn't keep my eyes from rolling. "I'll just go pay the governor a nice little visit, shall I?"

I made to return my coin to my pocket when he said, "Or you could find yourself one of her corrupt henchmen."

I blinked. "Her guards?"

He shrugged. "Whatever you wish to call them. With eighty of those..." A nod of his head to the coin in my hand. "You might be able to hire one to get you through the wards."

"*Eighty?*" I nearly shouted.

That was far more than the king had left me with. More than another four meetings with him would accrue, providing he even gave me as much coin again.

"I don't make the rules, pretty thing, and very few have the means to break them."

My chest tightened at the thought of never leaving this place of in-between. Never knowing. All the many nevers I would fail to erase.

"What's Folkyn got that you want so badly?"

"Answers," I said, my tone flat as I placed the single coin on the table.

"Answers to what?" He immediately pocketed the gold. "Don't know who your shit-stain father is?" His laughter was rough and scornful. "You and hundreds of others, pretty thing. Trust me, some truths aren't worth finding."

My smile was weak, as was my desire to correct him. So I didn't. I turned to leave. "Thank you, Hal."

"Wait a second." Folding the cloth, he released a heavy breath and beckoned me closer.

Too curious and with little else to do, I turned back.

"Listen." He peered at the stalls astride his before lowering his voice. "Whatever it is you're seeking..." His eerie eyes met mine. "Goddess knows it won't be worth getting."

I almost rolled my eyes again, as he'd already said as much.

But then he added, "You'll have more luck sneaking into those warded woods"—he jabbed his thumb behind him to the south—"and making a home for yourself in the mortal lands than you will any kingdom of Folkyn. Ain't no such thing as sneaking about in any court, no matter who gets you in nor how. If they don't want you there, then mark my words..." His voice dropped to a rasped whisper. "Eventually, they will find you, and if they don't kill you, you'll spend what remains of your days wishing they fucking had."

The sparrow arrived with the waking moon.

Content to stay in bed, I ignored it. I hadn't moved since arriving home from the market, my mood flat enough to neglect the growling pleas of my stomach.

Hal's parting words were a constant spinning wheel through my mind, erasing all I'd clung to for years.

Insistent, the sparrow hopped along the ledge at the window and chirped.

"I'm not interested," I said, though the creature wasn't able to hear nor understand.

Perhaps it did.

The bird paused and watched me from across the apartment. Then it plucked the piece of parchment that'd been tied to its leg. It fluttered to the chipped row of low shelving beneath the window to land on a lace doily next to the small wooden clock.

The bird chirped again, wings spreading.

"Oh, fine." I threw off the bedding and rose from the same single-sized mattress I'd slept on since I could remember.

Though I'd often wondered what it might be like to sleep in such comfort, I couldn't bring myself to enter Rolina's room again, let alone use her bed. Which was large enough for two grown men and overflowing with frills and feathered pillows.

The bird finally took flight, but not until I'd unrolled the small note that read, *Midnight, same room,* in a heavy and almost illegible cursive.

The note slowly crunched in my closing fist. I tossed it onto the kitchen countertop before opening the bag of cherry tomatoes and the cheese I'd purchased upon leaving the market. While eating, I contemplated what might happen at this next meeting.

I drained a glass of water and set it down with a trembling hand. He was a king.

And it was therefore outrageous of me to lose myself to thoughts of his mouth devouring my own, and the way he'd felt so perfectly larger than life beneath me.

It would be equally as outrageous yet also wise to take his gold and never return—to continue seeking a way to sneak into Folkyn now that I had some means to do so. After all, there was a good chance Hal might have been lying about the sum of coin needed to persuade the right people.

His warning flattened that plan before it could grow wings. He hadn't been lying, and even if he had, it would still cost more than I could afford.

And if I did not return to the Lair of Lust when sent for, what might Madam Morin do? She would undoubtedly be furious at my snubbing of any client, but a client such as he?

Whether I liked it or not, Crustle was where I must remain for the foreseeable future. So I popped another tomato into my mouth and drew a bath.

The squeak of the faucet and the water crashing against the porcelain tub echoed throughout the hauntingly empty apartment.

I'd spent my entire life feeling lonely. Now, I was truly alone.

Alone and unsure how to remain afloat while already sinking in these punishing and cage-resembling middle lands. To make an enemy out of anyone, especially a king, could cost me my life. Gane was the only one who might notice if I disappeared, and by the time he did, it could very well be too late.

I sank into the warming water and gazed at the coral tiles through a film of honeysuckle-scented bubbles, knowing none of this was new. I'd just made sure to never acknowledge it too closely before, my heart and mind always glued to a future I could not see.

For although I refused to admit it, I knew a future outside of Crustle was as good as nonexistent. If I wished to ensure my survival, it was best I make peace with that—and with my loneliness.

If this was it, then maybe there was no need to seek different employment. Maybe, with clients like the blue-eyed king, I could work for Madam Morin long enough to buy a small farm beyond the marshes surrounding the mayhem of town.

Dark-blue eyes blazed behind my closed eyelids, and I gasped as I rose from the water.

Excitement unfurled and exploded in my chest, shaming me.

I wanted to see my unexpected client again.

The king wanted me. For reasons I had yet to understand, being that he'd even said he preferred his lovers more experienced. If anyone could grant me all I'd dreamed of, everything that now seemed so irrevocably out of reach, it was a king of one of the ruling houses of Folkyn.

Impossible. He would certainly punish me.

But perhaps he wouldn't.

Perhaps with enough patience and careful prodding, he could be convinced to help me, I thought, as the memory of his warm mouth and his warmer warning returned with frosted fire.

I'm going to do such filthy, dishonorable things to you.

I stopped my hand from sliding down my body and closed my thighs. Only because he might scent what I'd done, regardless of bathing. I groaned with a myriad of frustrations as I sank into the water again before washing and preparing to leave.

I wasn't willing to wait and see if I would have an escort this time.

Arriving at the Lair of Lust a half hour before midnight, I made good use of my earliness by searching for a gown.

After trying on three that were either too tight or too large, I settled on a lemon number that fell to the floor in a single sheet of satin-backed lace. It resembled a night gown for someone with the coin to spare on the indulgence, but I couldn't deny how much I liked the way it molded to my curves.

Gentle but fitting, it cupped my breasts, hips, and upper thighs before falling to touch my toes.

In the dressing room, I attempted to do as Madam Morin had said last time and wear my hair up. But the pins wouldn't hold the wild and thick waves. Instead, I braided and pinned a few pieces behind my ears.

A woman entered as I contemplated doing something with my face, her own and her upper body flushed. Adjusting her tasseled dress, she froze at the sight of me and flicked strands of bronze hair from her cheek. "You must be Rolina's replacement."

I nodded and set the powder puff down. I had no idea how much to use anyway. "Hello."

"Pretty," she said, a little curl to her lip as she inspected me. "Rolina always dealt with the rogues. Dennis is a biter, so be sure to watch those lovely tits."

I coughed to hide my shock. I had no intention of meeting other clients. At least, I hoped I would not have to. I didn't bother saying so, though. "I'm afraid I've yet to meet him."

"Count yourself lucky, then," she muttered, closing the stall door to the tiny bathing room in the far corner.

I stared at my reflection in the mirror, the subtle paling of my cheeks, and decided to forgo putting anything on my face. Being that the woman hadn't so much as offered her name, I didn't doubt she wanted privacy. And I had no business hoping for something as elusive as a comrade, let alone a friend.

The door to the dressing room had barely closed behind me when Madam Morin appeared atop the stairs to the third floor. "Oh, merciful Mother. You're actually half decent this eve." She strode briskly down the hall. "Though I must say, a little color on those lips wouldn't hurt."

"I'm not well-acquainted with the art of such things."

Knocking a ringlet from her cheek, Morin slowed and raised a brow. I was quickly studied from head to toe. "Get friendly with it,

Flea. This one seems content, to be sure, but future clients might want a little more..." She pursed her crimson lips. "Flavor."

I frowned, but before I could find anything to say to that, she snapped her fingers. "Well, what are you waiting for?" She gestured to the stairs. "Move, darling. He's already here."

"Already?" It couldn't have been midnight yet, surely.

"You speak as though it's a bad thing." Laughing low, Morin scooted behind me to enter the dressing room. "Keep him eager, and you'll keep his coin. But do hurry on now."

The door closed, and I was left wondering if perhaps it was not such a bad thing indeed—to have a male as powerful as he so keen to see me.

Yet on the second floor, my confidence began to melt. I paused with my hand over the door handle.

His scent permeated. His presence a silent hum upon the air.

Belatedly realizing that if I could sense him through the wood, then he could sense me, I opened the door. As I quickly locked it behind me, I said without thinking, "You could have told me you were a king before we..." Remembering myself, I shut my mouth.

I winced, then turned and curtsied.

King Florian raised a brow. He was already lounging upon the divan, an ankle over his knee. "Before we what?"

Unable to conjure the right words, especially with those eyes traveling from my heating cheeks to my chest to my covered legs, I blurted as I straightened, "Before we fornicated."

He coughed, and I could have sworn it was to cover a shocked bark of laughter. "Fornicated?"

My nose twitched. It was the wrong word, I knew, but it was too late now. I clenched my skirts. "You know what I mean."

"I don't know that I do," he drawled dryly. "Would you care to explain?"

"I would not." I was more red than a ripe tomato, made worse when I failed yet again to respect him properly. "Majesty."

Another laugh. This one a melodic rumble that accompanied a

flash of straight teeth and extremely sharp-looking canines. "You look like a lemon pie, butterfly."

More embarrassment threatened to bloom. Doubting I had room for more, I curled my bare toes over the cool wood and forced a response. "Not fond of pie, Majesty?"

His lips twitched. "Sit."

Laying a large hand next to him upon the divan, he waited for me to settle beside him.

"It would have been helpful to know you were a king." I smoothed my fingers over the satin hugging my thighs and felt him track my every movement, perhaps even my slow-to-calm breath.

"How so?"

I glanced at the untouched liquor cabinet. "I could have been far more respectful." I quickly added, "Majesty."

"Florian."

"King Florian."

His nose crinkled ever so slightly. "Florian."

"Oh," I breathed, officially mortified. "Understood."

He hummed as if amused. "You've been busy." When I finally met his glowing dark gaze with a frown, he elaborated. "The market."

"What of it?" I asked, feigning confusion—for visiting the market was nothing but normal.

The king of Hellebore dragged his teeth across his lower lip. Apathy and that strange cold heat pulsed, then leaked from him. After a moment, he huffed lightly. "You were hunting for something. I wish to know what it is."

"Why?"

"I wish to know everything about you," he stated, and so matter of fact, it took a moment for those words to sink beneath my skin.

It trembled in response, my fingers curling into the thin fabric of my gown. "There is really nothing much to know."

"Humor me." He turned to fully face me. "For now."

I did the same, leaning into the lowering back of the divan. "For now?"

"I loathe repeating myself."

Indeed, a tiny crease formed between his brows.

A huge risk, yet I supposed there was no better time than now to take it. I supposed there wasn't going to be a good time for something so audacious as attempting to ask assistance from a king.

I chewed my lip, then released it when I decided on saying, "I would like to ask something of you first."

His expression didn't change. His eyes didn't leave my face, roaming every feature with slow study. "Ask," Florian clipped.

Fear drummed in my chest.

I silently prayed to the goddess that it did not quake my voice and cleared my throat. "If I am to meet with you," I started, then corrected, "if I am to meet *only* with you, then I wish for something in return."

Surprise cracked his facade, but only slightly. "Gold is not enough for you, daring creature?"

Heat infused my cheeks once more. "Some things cannot be purchased, no matter how much I wish and hope and try."

"That is why you were poaching known criminals at the market."

The word criminal alarmed me. At the same time, I hoped Hal was okay. "I was sent away."

"And that is why he still breathes."

My eyes bulged, and I forgot who I was seated with. "You followed me?"

An impatient and slow blink was all the response he gave.

Of course, such a thing was beneath him. Florian likely had loyal people everywhere—including the market.

His silk shirt, buttoned only to mid-chest as his other had been, gaped when he lifted a knee to the chair and leaned closer. He slid an arm along the back, his thumb and forefinger rubbing together right beside my shoulder. "Tell me of these things that cannot be purchased."

His scent and pheromones crawled over and into my body, making my words meeker than I intended. "Will you consider my request if I do?"

Mouth quirking, the king said, "You are not exactly in a position to barter for much of anything, sweet butterfly."

"Why do you call me that?"

"Your aroma and your delicate..." He paused, then said flippantly, "Beauty, shall we say."

My cheeks and neck caught fire, and I ducked my head as I scrambled for lost words. He was referring to my lack of experience with, well... *anything*. I knew that, but for some reason, I still liked it—liked whatever he called me far more than I should. Perhaps because it was not done out of hatred.

Perhaps because it was not Flea.

Emboldened, I lifted my head. "Why come to the middle lands for pleasure?"

"Why not?"

I scowled. "That is not an answer."

He raised a brow, and I tensed.

He noticed, and perhaps decided to keep what was sure to be a scolding behind his closing lips. A moment later, he said irrefutably, "You are quick to grow highly anxious."

"You are a king." And it would be wise for me to remember that.

"Let us not pretend it is merely because of me." My eyes narrowed, but he spoke again, his tone milder. "We shall get to the matter of my visits with you in good time, but right now, I wish to know what it is you seek so that I might take your request under advisement."

I wasn't certain I breathed as I studied his unmoving features. *Mother maim me*, he'd meant it. He wouldn't punish me, then, surely. Not when he wanted to know.

My heart shook, hope bursting the confession from my chest and past my lips. "I want to go home."

King Florian didn't blink for the longest time.

After enduring that intense midnight stare for an agonizing half minute, I feared I might vomit my heart into my lap. I had to look away. I gazed down at my trembling and twisting hands.

A finger curled under my chin, lifting it.

Those depthless eyes searched mine, and I hadn't realized I was on the cusp of tears until he studied the damp awaiting to fall with his head tilted. "When making a request that means so much to you, leave your heart out of it." His thumb glossed the edge of my lower lip. "For there are many who will find endless pleasure in robbing you of such rare innocence and wonder."

I wasn't sure what compelled me to dare ask aloud, but the words escaped before I could hope to stop them. "Like you?"

"Sweetest creature..." His lips curved, and he closed the space between us to whisper against my mouth. "No one's intentions for you are more wicked than my own."

I believed him. I had much to learn about the royals of Folkyn, but I knew enough to know there had to be some truth to the rumors and tales of their mischievous and often cruel natures.

His mouth hovered. Our eyes locked, and our breath mingled.

Despite knowing I was wading into water too deep to navigate, I didn't want to retreat.

I wanted to place my lips upon his. I wanted to touch his face. His throat. His arms. All of him. I wanted to see if the rest of his skin and bones were as sharp and smooth as the goddess-carved stone of his features.

"You're aroused," he said, a thin note of shock in his voice.

I swallowed and tried to ignore it, but with his lips so close to mine, his powerful energy encaging me, and something wild and unknown awakening within my body... I failed. My exhale shook with my words. "I think I would like to kiss you again."

His eyes flared as I finished speaking and did just that. My own closed.

A relief that both burned and made me itch for more swept through me as soon as my mouth settled over his. I breathed him in, not knowing what to do—not confident that I was doing anything normal or correct but uncaring.

Hands seized my face.

Stunned, I stared up into the vibrant darkness of his gaze. "You are daring indeed."

Fear returned, a flush entering my skin that nearly overpowered the madness that'd stolen my brain just moments ago.

I blamed him, and I said as much. "Did you do something to me?" Maybe he was one of the few faeries who could manipulate desires.

The king's hold gentled. His thumbs rubbed over the warmth in my cheeks with something akin to fascination in his tight features. "No more than you've done me."

Then he released me and stood.

A swift chill arrived and left me swaying.

I didn't dare stand. I stayed seated and on the verge of shaking as he crossed the room to the liquor cabinet.

His tone was calm, everything about him seemingly unaffected as he poured himself a drink. "I assume you do not know where this home of yours is."

"No," I said, glad for the return of conversation after a stretched and tense silence. "That is what I long to find out. I want answers, and I need help to get them."

"Because you are a changeling."

Not a question. He already knew.

He tossed the whiskey down his throat. I admired the broad expanse of his back and the way his shirt molded to his large shoulders but floated over his torso like rippling night. The glass was set down sharply upon the oak. "Answer me."

"You do not need me to," I said but then surrendered what he wanted. "Yes, I'm a changeling."

He turned and tucked his hands into his trouser pockets. Leaning back against the cabinet, he eyed me over the strong bridge of his nose. "You've lived in Crustle your whole life, and you now wish for that to change?"

"Desperately," I admitted, knowing it was far too late and futile to hide it.

His lashes lowered with his eyes, their journey down my body one that changed their color when they returned to mine a shade brighter. "That is why you attempted to trade yourself with the hunt."

My stomach sank. "How did you...?"

Fool, I inwardly scolded.

He was a king. Whatever he desired to know, the information would be found.

As if reading my thoughts, King Florian's mouth curved. He untucked a hand to scratch at the bristle dusting his jawline. "I've heard all about your encounter with the hunt."

"Is that why you wished to meet with me?"

"Partly." The confession was toneless. "I'm also informed when someone new is hired here at the Lair, especially when they're young and full faerie."

"Why?"

His teeth flashed, blinding. "Because I own it."

I didn't get the chance to recover from my surprise and the shock of such cruel beauty, nor ask him more questions.

The temperature in the room dropped, the air rapidly frosting.

"Until next time, butterfly."

Right before my eyes, the king disappeared, leaving me staring at the melting wisps of flurries he'd left in his wake.

FIVE

G ANE'S FEATURES CREASED AND BULGED CONTINUOUSLY with shock and horror.

I'd have found it comical if it weren't for the fact I hadn't told him everything. The goblin would have likely fallen from his perch behind the desk if so.

If I'd told him that not only was I indebted to Madam Morin but I was also meeting and playing dangerous games with a king.

"The Lair of..." The goblin shook his head and growled, "You are but an *infant* in such matters."

"I've reached full maturity."

"*Just*," he spat. "And you've barely scraped the surface of what that truly means, Flea. You know what awaits you. It could begin at any moment—"

I raised a hand, stopping him.

Indeed, I knew what would befall me during the months following my twentieth year of existence. The heat. I wouldn't have him speak of it to me. This conversation was mortifying enough.

"Gane, I'll be okay." I lifted a shoulder. "My client isn't too bad, and he's the only one I'm seeing." I refrained from making a face after saying those words.

"Too bad?" Gane sputtered.

The king was as cold as the frigid room he'd left me in the evening prior.

I hadn't heard from Madam Morin since, nor had I received a sparrow from Florian. After what I'd admitted to him, I half feared I wouldn't, and that maybe he'd decided, despite whatever he'd wanted from me, I wasn't worth the trouble.

The other half was terrified of the impossible—that the winter king might actually consider helping me.

It was all I wanted. All I'd dreamed of for endless nights.

And perhaps, I thought as I recalled Florian's drugging curiosity of me, it would be my doom.

I shivered.

Gane frowned. "Flea, I urge you to speak with the madam and come to another arrangement."

"What other arrangement could we possibly conjure?" I nearly laughed as I said, "Should I offer to clean the pleasure house instead?"

Actually, that was not such a bad idea.

Gane agreed, his cheeks red with outrage. "Yes. Something exactly like that. The creatures who visit that Lair are not looking to court and befriend you." He sighed and lowered his voice. "Some might even hurt you."

Florian's warning returned.

No one's intentions for you are more wicked than my own.

"It's too late. I'm making good coin," I said, uneasy and desperate to keep it from showing. "Good enough to be free of Madam Morin in no time." I straightened from where I'd been leaning against his desk. "I know what I'm doing."

The anger in Gane's dark eyes was soon replaced with sadness. "Flea, you have no idea what you're doing. You've lived your entire life inside of books and this rotting building, and your naivety will land you in disaster."

He was likely right, but I had nothing else. All I had was this slowly opening doorway to everything I'd ever wanted.

Even if it might cost me more than I could have ever imagined.

The sparrow came mere hours after I left the library.

In nothing but a towel, I padded across the apartment to where the bird ceaselessly tapped against the kitchen window. It chirped when I pushed open the glass, and as I reached for the note, rubbed its blue-feathered cheek against my finger.

I smiled in wonder as the sparrow took flight, but then quickly collected the tiny roll of parchment before it was lost to the soapy water in the kitchen sink.

The note was the same as the first.

With little else to do besides try and fail to read, I arrived at room twelve an hour before the scheduled meet time of midnight.

I'd dressed simply in a gown of my own. A sky-blue cotton tunic that cinched at the waist and dropped to my ankles. The flowing sleeves gathered at the wrists, and the neckline dipped right above my breasts. It was worn but lovely, and it would do.

Even so, I fidgeted and paced, worrying if I had time to change into something better. Something more seductive. Then I took a seat upon the end of the bed and finger-combed my hair. I hadn't touched it after washing it.

I wasn't sure what had possessed me to present myself in such a bland way. Impatience, maybe. Perhaps it was because I'd barely been touched at all during our last meeting after I'd gone to some effort to seduce.

I knew too little of such things, so if I were to be embarrassed again, it would not be because I'd tried to be someone I wasn't.

Someone I perhaps wanted to one day be.

The air stilled then changed as the king materialized.

Warmth spread throughout the room, followed by blistering cold. More of those small flurries danced and melted upon touching the floor as the king appeared wreathed in fading midnight tendrils of shadow. He wore a tight, long-sleeved black tunic with similar armor-lined pants and matching knee-high boots.

He looked as though he'd just left a battlefield, though not a trace or scent of blood could be detected.

Every impressive inch of his enormous physique was outlined. Every inch of him dangerous in a way I'd already known but had perhaps failed to wholly realize.

Amusement sparked within his eyes as he surveyed my expression.

I closed my mouth and averted my gaze to my bare feet. I'd kicked my slippers off before perching upon the end of the bed.

"No curtsy this time?" Panic had me ready to spring to my feet until the king said, "Don't bother. I like you where you are." Three long strides brought him within touching distance, and touch he did. He tipped up my chin until I met his eyes with mine. "Ready and waiting for me."

I blinked, without words.

His lips parted as he stared. "I dreamed of you," he murmured as if unwillingly. "It has been a long time since I've dreamed of anything."

"Truly?" I heard myself ask. I couldn't imagine merely sleeping when dreams were all that had kept me floating from one day to the next.

"Well..." His luscious mouth tilted. "Not of anything sweet, at least."

His admission created a strange twinge within my chest. "I've thought of you," I said, thinking it only fair to give him something in return.

"I expect you have." His touch fell away, leaving a crisp burn. "Been wondering over my answer to your request?"

I frowned. "That's not what I—"

"Trust I will not leave without giving you one, but first..." He yanked at the sleeve of my gown. "What is this?"

"A gown."

"It is a tent to hide within."

He wasn't entirely wrong, but annoyance still flared. "No one is telling you to wear it." My eyes widened at my foolish audacity.

Florian stilled, as did my heart.

It pounded hard when he unleashed a devious grin. "My, you're something else when a little riled, sweetling." His humor died as rapidly as it came. "Take it off."

Though I would have loved nothing more than to see what he

had planned for me, my annoyance refused to budge. "And if I don't want to?"

"Then you do not have to." He turned for the divan. "We will conduct this meeting as you wish."

The question left me without thought. "What will you do if I remove the gown?"

He stopped, and with his back to me, said with a softness that grazed, "What would you like me to do?"

I shouldn't have said anything.

I should have just told him I would like him to kiss me again. To touch me again, wherever his hands desired to roam. Instead, I blurted, "You did not even wish to kiss me during our last meeting."

He stalked back to me with slow grace, a brow raised. "Did I leave you disappointed?"

I couldn't deny that I had been. He saw as much when I again averted my attention to my feet.

"Cease trying to hide. Look at me." My eyes rose, and his knee knocked open my own as he loomed above me. "You shocked me. You continue to shock me in ways I find myself ill-equipped to handle, but I've decided something."

"You have?"

"I've decided that I like it." He cupped my face, brought it close to his, and ordered to my lips, "Now, I want this tent gone and your back upon the bed."

He helped me pull the gown over my head. Slowly, I eased down on the bed. He stepped away, and I rose to my elbows in nothing but my slip. "What are you doing?"

"Admiring the treasure I've found." But his expression remained unmoved. He stood with his hands clasped before him, his feet braced apart. "Open your legs."

My heart stopped galloping and climbed into my throat.

King Florian cocked his head. "Are you uncomfortable, butterfly?" He knew I was, but still he said, "Answer me."

"Yes."

"Good. Make your choice."

"And if I choose not to?"

"Then you choose not to," he said as though not having me however he wished would not bother him when we both knew it would.

It thrilled me that it would.

My skin burned beneath the weight of his attention. But as each second ticked by, my breathing evened, and the itch to see what he would do to me became a need impossible to ignore.

He knew I was nervous. He knew I wanted to play regardless.

My knees rose. Then slowly, they opened.

My slip slid over my thighs as they did, and though he made not a sound, I could feel it. The flood of tension emanating from him crackled, an iced breeze before a blizzard.

"Sweet indeed," he murmured, as if to himself. "Tell me something." His voice was closer, and I tore my eyes from the filigree etched into the mildew-dotted ceiling to find him standing at the end of the bed.

And staring between my thighs.

"Do you touch yourself?"

I hesitated only a moment before whispering, "Yes."

He hummed. "But no one has touched you, correct?"

"Correct."

I waited, my stomach tightening. As if knowing he was tormenting me, he seemed pleased as he said, "Would you like me to be the first to touch your lovely cunt, sweet creature?"

My next breath caught. Skies stab me, he was unmerciful.

And it would seem I wanted nothing less, a heady anticipation and impatience rushing through my body in the form of venomous heat.

"Yes," I croaked.

"Then open nice and wide for me."

I did as I was told, which earned me a soft hum of approval that swept over my skin like a whisper in the dark.

I tried to watch him, every part of me strung tight as the warmth of his touch hovered over my core. But as the first drag of his finger stroked through me, parted me, my eyes closed.

Bright light flashed behind my eyelids. My hips bucked.

"Do you wish for me to stop?" Humor thickened his question. He already knew what my answer would be.

"No," I said instantly.

His finger returned, trailing from my clit and opening me slowly as it moved to my entrance. He paused there. "Your thighs shake already, butterfly." A gentle dip inside me with the tip of his finger. "And you're so fucking excited."

His touch left me again.

I opened my eyes to find him sucking my arousal from his finger. His eyes closed as if he was savoring the taste of me. My stomach fluttered when I heard the low and almost imperceptible rumble in his throat. When I noticed the slight tremor of his broad shoulders.

His eyes opened. A blue so bright they matched a sunlit sky.

Our gazes locked. The tension in the room bubbled.

Then, with his eyes still on mine, he returned his hand to my core. Featherlight, he stroked his fingers over the sensitive skin of my inner thighs and tickled them over my mound. "Tell me, sweet creature." His voice was different, hoarse and sharp. "What would you do in order to get everything you desire?"

I couldn't concentrate. Not with his expert touch blinding me to all else.

He pressed the pad of his finger right above my clit and applied the slightest pressure. A rasped moan flew through my lips, and then he paused. "I'll resume when you answer me."

"Anything," I breathed, desperate for the pleasure to return and for all I'd ever wanted.

My answer apparently pleased him.

Enough that he dropped to his knees before the bed. His hands gripped my thighs, bruising as they dragged my body forward and straight to his hot mouth.

"Skies," I almost shouted, my back curling off the bed as the king dug his nose into my core and rubbed it up and down.

He inhaled deeply, his exhale a ragged groan against my slick flesh. "Fucking divine." Then warm, velvet heat dragged from my entrance to my clit. There, he circled and lapped as though I were a treat he would take his time to devour.

The sounds that left me would have been mortifying, had I any ability to care.

I had none.

But I clenched the bedding to keep from reaching for his hair as one thing repeated with sparkling loops in my starlit brain—he was a king.

A king of Faerie had his face buried between my thighs.

The room twirled. A cool sweat broke out over my skin. His hold on my thighs grew more painful. Burning—I was igniting from within and seconds away from feeling the flames dance all over my skin when he stopped.

Breath panted from me. Before I could protest, a fingertip gently pressed into my body.

I tensed, and Florian felt as much. He withdrew and pushed the tip of his digit back in. He would go no farther, only allowing my body to swallow his fingernail. I whimpered for more, my hips rolling.

His wicked words were steeped in unbending promise. "When I break you, it will be with my cock, and certainly not in a rotting pleasure house."

Then his mouth latched onto my clit, and everything within me seized.

And exploded.

He held me firmly as a storm of pleasure assaulted in waves. From my scalp to my toes, it roared through me. I writhed, moaning and breathless and attempting to make him stop.

He didn't.

He seemed intent on torturing me. His eyes, still a brighter blue, glowed with satisfaction beneath low lids.

Uncaring who he was, I reached down to make him end such exquisite punishment. Yet as soon as my fingers encountered his thick and shockingly soft hair, I surrendered.

As though he'd been waiting for just that, he ceased torturing me and crawled over my body on the bed. The size and darkness of him was a threat I couldn't find the energy to be wary of. He'd ensured I was nothing but rapture-wrung limbs and uncatchable breath.

"I will give you everything," he said, low and coarse directly above me. "And I will take everything in return. That includes every drop of pleasure I draw from your body."

Unable to speak, I could only stare up at him in a daze.

His words ricocheted through my mind like a warning. A warning I would ignore, even if it had been more blatant. For the way he looked at me, large hands braced on either side of my head as he studied my flushed face, my heaving breasts straining against my filmy slip...

It made me want him all over again.

It made me desperate for everything and anything he was willing to give.

His nostrils flared, and his eyes darkened. He lowered his mouth to mine and rasped, "You are the sweetest fucking nectar I've ever tasted." Our lips grazed with each word. "Kiss me."

I did so gently. Once, twice, and on the third press of my lips against his, my confidence blossomed. I licked my own essence from his upper lip and ran my fingers over the thick material encasing his torso. My hips rose for my bare body to meet his clothed erection.

He hissed between clenched teeth and tore away with a light growl.

It didn't escape me that he'd visited a pleasure house, yet I was the only one who seemed to be receiving pleasure.

I was about to ask if he did not wish to be touched in return when his earlier words about breaking me came back. Fighting off a shiver, I pulled my slip down over my thighs and sat up.

The king of Hellebore poured himself a drink, his fingers steady but his jaw ticking. "I think it's time for me to admit to being somewhat..." He set the stopper in the decanter. "Deceptive."

Not alarming, considering who I was dealing with. Still, a nervous patter in my chest began to overpower the lusty fog he'd left me in.

"I require a bride."

Those words cut through the fog and the room like an iced wind.

He turned and leaned against the liquor cabinet to assess my reaction.

There was no hiding my shock, nor my confusion. I blinked ceaselessly and stammered out, "Do you mean me?" He couldn't, surely.

I was a nameless nobody from a land he and his fellow royals despised.

He sipped the whiskey. "There is no one else in this room, butterfly."

My cheeks threatened to stain with heat. The outrageousness of what he was saying kept it from happening. "But..." My voice dried. I shook my head and cleared my throat. "I'm a changeling. I have no noble family. I have no family or name at all," I said, almost wincing at hearing myself spill the sad truths aloud. "I don't even have friends."

That last one wasn't exactly true.

I loved Gane, but admitting that the goblin who ran the town library was my only friend would not help. A goblin King Florian had exiled from his kingdom at Gane's desperate request, no less.

"Which makes you perfect," Florian said, the words soft but with a coating of steel that sent a spike of alarm trailing down my spine.

I wondered if he might even remember Gane, but I quickly pushed the thought away when I realized what this king was asking.

He was asking for a queen.

"Why?" I gripped the crinkled satin bedding, needing a tether to know this was real and not one of my dazzling dreams.

Florian lifted a shoulder and took another sip of whiskey. "I intend to go to war, and although I intend to win, it would be irresponsible of me to attempt as much without someone to rule in my stead should death find me."

War.

My mind spun and spun so fast, I feared I'd snatch the whiskey from his hand to drain the lot. There had always been rumors of cruelty and tension between the ruling courts of Folkyn, though never anything that would make one think they would go to war.

There had only ever been one war on this continent.

A war that had created the middle lands.

Crustle was formed eons ago when the Fae of Folkyn grew tired of humans leaking into their lands. All the while, the human royals of Ordaylia had never cared who stole into Fae territory and what they did while there, as they had supposedly gained many riches from the daring folk who lived to steal from faeries.

But when the stealing and treachery bloomed into murder—of both Fae and their wildlife—the four courts of Folkyn moved against Ordaylia.

From the recounts I'd read, it was not so much a war but a journey with few battles to the doorstep of the mortal royal home. By the time the Fae armies had reached the castle, the king and queen of Ordaylia had pledged to surrender and find terms for peace.

The king was killed and the queen forced to provide a solution that, while not well thought out, had indeed provided a tremulous peace across the continent of Mythayla for thousands and thousands of years.

Florian downed the last of his drink. "Afraid of a little bloodshed, butterfly?" He smirked. "Fear not. You would not accompany me. Risking your life would defeat the purpose of what I'm hoping to achieve, of course."

"I'm just..." I trailed off, at a loss for words. "I'm so confused."

"What confuses you?"

So many things. All of it.

I didn't say that, but rather, "You could have anyone you desire. Anyone."

He stroked the perfect curve of his lower lip, staring into his empty glass as though pondering whether to speak more on the baffling matter. "You are beautiful and of pure blood, yet you have nothing." When I frowned, he added simply, "Therefore, you will expect nothing."

He didn't need to fill in the gaps between those words. The females he'd perhaps considered in his court, or even in all the realms of Folkyn, were Fae.

They would expect everything.

And I could not blame them. A small fire burned low in my gut at his expectations and assumptions. "What makes you think I would make such an easy wife?" Realizing what I'd said and the way it could be received, I blushed.

Noticing, Florian smirked as he set his glass down. "I don't expect you to be..." He crossed to the bed with steps that kicked at my slowing heart. "Easy." Standing before me, he went to open my knees.

They opened for him on instinct—further cementing his beliefs.

His smile was devastating. His fingers gentle at my chin. He lifted and stroked it. "I already know you wish only to please me."

I swallowed, loathing that he was right. Denying it was pointless. Still, I challenged, "And what has you so convinced?"

His brow arched. "You are malleable." His eyes crawled down my body to halt between my thighs. "You do as I tell you."

"One could argue that's because you've paid me to."

His lips twitched, eyes slamming into mine. "We know that's not why you came on my tongue within a minute."

Want fired through my blood and gathered low in my body.

He inhaled, deep and grinning, as he murmured, "Smells like confirmation."

It was then I knew with a certainty that should have made me turn his outrageous request down but instead, only made me curl closer, that this male would indeed be my doom.

"Answers," I said, my voice strangled and wrong as I grappled for some semblance of control. "I require answers as to who I am and where I belong. Is that what I shall receive?"

A flash of darkness swept over his eyes. His touch firmed before he released me and turned away. "Of course."

I closed my knees and chewed my lip.

This was insanely stupid. So much so, I shouldn't even be tempted. Marriage was a contract few rarely escaped. Surely, I was not so desperate that I would marry a king.

But I *was* that desperate.

Though maybe it wasn't stupid at all. I'd be there. I'd be in Folkyn. I would not have to work for Madam Morin. I would not have to watch through our apartment windows as birds flew wherever they wished and I remained trapped.

Florian now stood close to the door, staring at me.

Perceptive or merely guessing wildly, he said, "You will wish for nothing, butterfly. You will have every comfort you need, including the protection of my court in your precious search for this home you desire. Just be mindful that should you find whatever that might be..." Flurries emerged, his words a cold and overt warning. "You will belong only to me."

Before I could ask if I would have him, he was gone.

The answer to my unasked question became clear in his absence. He wouldn't have sought a creature as desperate and foolish as me if he wished to belong to someone in kind.

SIX

AS THE FOLLOWING DAWN LOST ITS JEWELED LIGHT, ANOTHER sparrow arrived with a request to meet the king.

Having slept for only a handful of hours, I was already awake and surprised I'd slept that much given the never-ending spiral of thoughts and fears plaguing me.

Marriage. War. Queen.

Answers.

I stared at the small piece of parchment, at what I was sure was the king's handwriting, and I knew. He would want my acceptance of his proposal tonight.

I should refuse. I shouldn't have even been considering it.

Yet for some reason, the idea of turning down his offer filled me with more dread than the absurdly ridiculous idea of marrying him.

Trusting King Florian was not an option.

But neither was trusting that I could find a way to Folkyn on my own and survive. He was a risk with countless hidden and dangerous facets but also a guarantee. By agreeing to this, I would make it into Faerie.

I would finally be free of Crustle.

I donned a lime-green cotton dress that covered my arms, legs, and most of my chest. I brushed my hair but left it free and wild. Tonight, I would need to have my wits about me. Florian would not distract me by having me almost naked and at his mercy again, languid and pliant from pleasure.

The wind howled in greeting as soon as I stepped outside.

Fire within the street lamps flickered and swayed with the incoming storm. Smoke danced through the fogged dark as some extinguished.

The light tap of my slippers upon the moss-dusted cobblestone matched the erratic beat of my anxious heart.

Though the hour was late and the weather had turned, the Lair of Lust was aglow. The grimy street-facing window gave view to patrons dancing and drinking at the bar. Briefly, I wondered what that might be like—to lose all inhibitions in such a way.

Then I pondered if I'd already experienced it beneath the touch and taste of a devious king.

More than a little distracted while entering the alleyway that led to the back of the pleasure house, I nearly jumped when a rat skittered out from behind a pile of waste and ran from the darkness toward the street.

Heart pounding, I choked on a laugh as I watched it go. My smile fell when boots appeared and stopped.

A male in a hooded cloak blocked the end of the alley.

I could see nothing of his shadowed features from where I stood, but I remembered those eyes. Eyes of bright and pure gold.

Fear fell into every sluggish heartbeat, a dragging gong in my ears.

About to ask him what he was doing here when he'd been with the Wild Hunt, I struggled to form words. He didn't blink. His gaze held mine, and he didn't move.

Move. The word was a punch to the gut. The stairs to the rear entrance were just a few short feet away, yet both of us stood so very still, seemingly trapped.

Laughter spilled onto the street from a group leaving the Lair of Lust via the main entrance. It broke my terror-frozen trance. I jerked backward.

The golden-eyed faerie took a step forward.

An owl flying overhead gave an ear-piercing screech, and I finally ran for the stairs.

I flew up them, not breathing and half expecting to be yanked back down by the cloaked male.

A male of whom I swore was the same one who'd been traveling with the hunt. The same male who'd sent me away after I'd watched that strange mist dissolve Rolina into nothing but the soil and grass she'd died upon.

I opened the door to the third floor and threw myself inside, then closed it and peered through the sliver of streaked glass in the wood to the stairs.

No one was there. At least, not that I could see.

The Wild Hunt did not return between their yearly visits.

Unease curdled within my stomach, weighing my steps down to the second floor. I didn't linger on the third. Not only because I was in a hurry to escape the feeling of being hunted but also because I had no reason to use the dressing rooms.

I stopped beneath the stairs and leaned back against the wall, attempting to organize my scrambled thoughts.

Perhaps it hadn't been the same male, and he was merely waiting for one of the employees of the Lair to leave.

Whoever he was, it didn't matter. I had bigger things to tend to.

I smoothed my clammy hands over the bodice of my gown and continued down the hall to the room harboring a king.

With so many questions vying for answers, there was no controlling what left my mouth first. "Did you do all of that to me so I would be dazed and therefore more likely to agree to your needs?"

"Hello to you too, butterfly." Florian gave me an amused glance over his shoulder. His eyes narrowed on my gown, and his lip lifted in disapproval. He turned back to the liquor cabinet. "You'll be glad to know a dressing chamber filled with proper clothing awaits you."

Stunned, I almost asked how he knew what sizes I would need, and why he seemed so certain I would agree to this asinine bargain. But I refused to let him deter me. "I would appreciate an answer to my question." I swallowed. "Majesty."

"Florian." He continued reading a document I couldn't see.

My teeth gnashed.

"I am curious." The scratch of a quill sounded, and then he finally deigned to give me his full attention. "What exactly did I do to you?"

My ire dripped away as he leaned against the cabinet with his elbows upon the wood and crossed his booted ankles. The fabric of his silken black shirt tightened over his muscular arms.

No one had any right to look like him. As though the night sky and all of its stars lived within his eyes and the dark hair that fell in soft waves over his shoulders. As though Mythayla, goddess of the skies that watched over all, had crafted his bone structure from the marble statues created to replicate and honor her.

My tongue felt thick as I said, "You know what you did."

He waited, a maddening curl to his plush lips.

I nearly growled, so flustered and nervous and terrified and...

And unbearably excited.

"Say it, sweet creature." Florian straightened and strode toward me. "I'm starving to hear all about how I devoured your beautiful cunt to make you more amenable to my wicked plans."

I wouldn't, and he knew that.

As he reached me and collected a curl nestled over the curve of my cheek, my heart faltered. It dropped into my stomach when his amusement vanished.

Frosted anger hardened his features.

His eyes darkened to a blue so deep, they were nearly black. He sniffed, releasing my hair to circle me slowly. "Where have you been?"

"What do you mean?"

"I couldn't have asked the question any clearer," he said through teeth I knew were gritted before he stopped in front of me once again.

"I haven't been anywhere today," I said, confused. "Only here."

"You were followed, then," Florian surmised. "By a male."

Gold eyes. Dark hooded cloak.

My chin was taken, the king's grip firm but not enough to hurt. "You were aware?"

I saw no reason to keep the bizarre encounter with the golden-eyed faerie to myself. "The alley downstairs. Someone was standing at the end, watching me from the street. I ran to the rear entrance before he could approach me."

He searched my eyes, as if ensuring I spoke the truth. Still startled by his reaction yet having nothing to hide, I let him. "He scared you."

I nodded once.

"And he should," Florian said coldly. His touch fell, and he stalked back to the liquor cabinet. "There are some who seek to stop me."

"Those you are waging war against?" I pressed boldly.

He tensed.

Then, to my surprise, he answered me. "Yes. Should something like that happen again, you are to tell me right away."

I tried to keep the spark of fear those words gave from entering my voice. "You expect it to happen again?" The idea of seeing that male again frightened me more than marrying this frosty king.

"No, but it's wise to be cautious regardless." Florian looked me over, something moving behind that deep-sea gaze. "Did you happen to see what he looks like?"

"Gold eyes," I said instantly. "Nothing more."

Florian stared at me for a minute that seared each breath, his jaw ticking. He was agitated, and though I knew it was not my fault, an impulse to soothe gripped me. But then he looked at the cabinet, and I followed his gaze to what he'd been busy with when I arrived.

A contract.

He placed his finger between his teeth—between his canines.

Blood crawled from the tip of his forefinger when he lewdly removed it from his mouth. I watched it bead, then race down to his hand.

"Introducing you to the life force of our people will be a joy indeed."

Horror trickled down my spine. All the while, something stirred awake within me. Something unfamiliar yet hungry that slumbered deep within my bones.

I didn't dare meet his gaze while I failed to blink at the sight of his blood and warred with that strange entity, but I felt it. His own hunger and curiosity pushed upon my skin like the bruising touch of his hands.

His bloodied finger was then pressed to the contract without hesitation.

Then again, there was no need for him to hesitate. This was his plan. This was why he wanted to meet with me in his pleasure house.

His hand rose, and as it fell to his side, I stepped forward and stared at the large fingerprint inked in blood above the black looping scrawl of his name.

The magnitude of what was happening settled like sharp rocks within my chest and stomach. I blinked heavily, my terrified heart all I could hear and the parchment all I could see.

A blood contract. Escapable only in death.

I'd already known as much. All marriages and contracts concerning the Fae were the same—eternally inescapable. Yet I stared down at the parchment spread atop the cabinet over rings of long-dried liquor, unmoving. Scarcely breathing.

There was no name beneath the awaiting space where I would leave my own fingerprint.

Knowing what had snagged and stolen my focus, Florian murmured, "You need not have a name. Your blood is all that is required." His heat enveloped as he moved in behind me. He shifted my heavy hair to one shoulder to graze his lips against my ear. "Your blood is all that matters."

A shiver rolled through me, and I felt him smile against my neck when he lowered his lips to it. My eyes nearly drifted closed, my shoulders loosening with a shaken breath. "Bite your finger, sweet creature, or"—another press of his lips, this time to my fluttering pulse—"I will gladly do it for you."

Temptation couldn't outweigh the song of trepidation screaming throughout my body.

"But..." This was real. This faerie king was truly asking me to promise myself to him in marriage. "When will we marry?"

"When I decide it's time, of course."

Of course.

Really, it wasn't as if it mattered. This contract would bind me to him in the same way a marriage contract would.

I closed my eyes and attempted to call forth all the questions I'd planned to ask, but they were jumbled and useless, and I knew he'd have an answer to all. "Where will I live?"

"At Hellebore Manor with me. Your rooms have already been prepared."

The instantaneous answer shocked. It also reeked of startling honesty. But it was to be expected—that I would not share rooms with Florian. He was a king, and I was but a tool to secure his kingdom.

A tool he liked to play with.

Though it was for the best, a smudge of disappointment still spread. Stupid, considering I wasn't ready for such a thing. Certainly not with a male who drew breath from my lungs with one word, one look, and one barely-there touch.

The contract blurred crimson and black as I recalled the images I'd glimpsed of Hellebore Manor within books. Its dazzling dark expanse was covered entirely in crawling blood-red ivy, the picturesque grounds in glowing snow.

I tried to resist losing myself to the awe of getting to see it all, and I promptly failed when I thought of living there.

Butterflies flooded my stomach. I cleared my throat and shook my head a little. Now was not the time for daydreams. I had to keep my feet and heart planted firmly on the ground. "How will you help me find my family?"

Florian was silent for a long moment, but his heat still warmed my back. "Should you have any, then I will have my people begin the search for the answers you seek immediately."

"And if I wish to seek those answers myself?"

He hummed. "I suppose you may, though you will be confined to my kingdom."

Something told me he was already aware that if I had any family, they did not reside in Hellebore. That perhaps he'd already done some searching of his own. Though that didn't mean I couldn't at least discover where they might be and do what I could to reach them.

My eyes drifted over the ink upon the parchment. Unease and

excitement tangled, making it hard to think. His drugging presence made it nearly impossible. "This is only escapable via death, Majesty."

"Florian."

I smirked. "Florian."

He made a sound close to a purr, as though he enjoyed hearing his name cross my lips. "These things are often dramatic. You can break such a commitment if both parties agree to it."

"And if I do wish to one day leave the marriage?"

His mouth skimmed my throat, silken and hypnotic. "You believe I will give you reason to want to leave me?"

"I do not know you very well." A ginormous understatement.

"Do you need to?" he challenged to my ear. "Know that I will keep you content, and you will want for nothing, including those answers you seek."

He stepped back, just far enough for me to stare at him over my shoulder. I couldn't help but believe him. Or perhaps I was merely so desperate it wouldn't matter if I didn't.

He had me, and he knew it. All I was doing was wasting his time, and my own, with my struggle to surrender completely.

Florian didn't gloat. He watched in warming silence as I read the contract three times over and slowly lifted my finger to my sharp canines. It took a moment to find the courage to bite hard enough to draw blood.

Still standing at my back, Florian's soft chuckle was a welcome and sensual distraction.

My heart shook, but my hand was steady as I lowered my finger to the thick parchment. Though the puncture I'd made was small, it was enough.

I pressed my blood to the awaiting space next to his own.

Florian snatched my hand when it rose from the contract and brought it to his mouth. The gentle heat of his tongue, the sucking pull as his lips enclosed the digit, created a string of fire that unraveled straight to my core.

Eyes glinting knowingly, he released me. "Sweet indeed."

I ducked my head and inspected my clean fingertip. "When will I accompany you to Folkyn?"

The king rolled the parchment, and it disappeared inside a flurry of snowflakes. I watched them fall to the wood floor in wonder, as he said, "Tonight."

Florian gestured for me to enter the apartment first.

It seemed surreal that he was here. A king in this place in which I'd spent most of my life trapped. But when I'd insisted on needing to visit the apartment before we left, he'd refused to let me do so alone.

We'd walked in brisk silence down the street, and though his hands had been tucked within his pant pockets and he'd been looking straight ahead, I'd sensed he was alert. I suspected it had nothing to do with the grumbling sky. Rather, it had something to do with the gold-eyed male from the alleyway.

I hadn't commented. I wasn't sure I was capable of saying anything coherent during those minutes I'd spent stunned by what was unfolding.

I was leaving. I was finally going to Faerie.

Truthfully, there was nothing I wished to take from the apartment. But that wasn't why I was here.

"I'll be right back," I muttered while Florian stood stone-still beside the kitchen and eyed it as though he were both equally fascinated and repulsed.

In my room, I retrieved and pocketed the gold coins. Then I reached for the pad of parchment beneath the bed and almost knocked over the inkpot on the windowsill in my haste. I snatched the quill from my nightstand drawer and sat on the floor as I wrote with a tremble in my hand.

Once done, I folded the parchment and looked up to find Florian filling the entire doorway.

His gaze roamed the shelves at the end of the bed, the nightstand,

and then the single bed. As if wading through mud and not into a small room, he carefully navigated his way to the books upon the shelves.

"Your bed is the size of a peanut compared to the monstrosity in the deceased's chamber."

"This is her apartment," I said, not in Rolina's defense but because it was true. "I was merely a guest."

Florian's long fingers skimmed the worn spines until he encountered one of my favorites. A book that had been read more than any other favorite. "For twenty years," he said.

Saying nothing, I rose to my feet and set the parchment and ink in my nightstand drawer. I no longer had to hide anything for fear of Rolina's temper striking my few possessions. The habit was hard to shake all the same.

"Magical Monsters of Folkyn," Florian murmured. "I'm surprised such a thing is allowed here."

I refrained from telling him that many books from Folkyn resided here in our library and for purchase at market stalls. I'd hate for anyone as curious and lonely as I had been to go without the ability to learn whatever they desired should he decide to make sure they were properly outlawed.

I stood beside him. His woodsy caramel scent forced me back a small step when it lured me closer—as it tempted me to dare find where the scent was strongest. His neck, I imagined, or maybe that thick hair...

Finished with inspecting the food and time-stained pages, the king swept his eyes to me. "Are you not going to collect your belongings?"

"No," I said.

He eyed the letter within my hand. "Can't say I blame you. The only thing of interest here is your scent and the books." With that alarming comment, he set the book back where he'd found it and turned for the door.

I followed, of course, but then quickly returned to grab the book he'd been looking at.

After tucking the letter beneath the cover, I found the king waiting at the door. "Have you ever materialized?"

"Not willingly."

His slight frown was nearly imperceptible. "Interesting." He stepped out into the hall. "Lock the door."

I did and pulled it closed. "Before we go, I would like to return this to the library downstairs."

"Your beloved book with the letter inside?" he asked what he already knew.

I held it to my chest protectively. "It will only take a moment."

He noted the action with a twitch to his lips, then nodded and stepped aside. "Very well."

I hurried down the stairwell to the tiny secret entrance to the library. I didn't enter. Carefully, I reached in to set the book on the floor inside.

Florian stood upon the landing, watching me latch the padlock. "I assume there is someone who means something to you in the library."

"My friend works there. He might wonder where I've gone, and I don't want him to worry."

"I thought you had no friends."

"Just the one." I rose to my feet and brushed my hands over my skirts. "Ready."

Florian was still looking at the small door behind me. I took a step closer, and his eyes met mine, a dark and twinkling blue. "Are you truly, butterfly?"

"I've waited so long," I confessed. "What I am is impatient."

Amusement momentarily curled his mouth. Then he extended his hands, and I placed mine within his. "Then let us not keep you waiting a moment longer."

He tugged me close. So close, my chest touched his and his fingers linked with mine. At my hairline, he inhaled deeply, then whispered, "Close your eyes, sweet creature."

Not a breath later, everything grew dark.

SEVEN

I WAS TWISTING, TWIRLING, AND SCREAMING WITH NO SOUND.
A vortex of nothing and everything pushed and shoved as though I were going against the laws of nature by traveling along the rifting tides of energy.

I was. We were. The few times I'd done it before, I'd been sick afterward.

It seemed this time would be no different.

Not even the king's steadying hold could keep me from stumbling to my knees in the snow. I clutched my stomach and retched. Mercifully, nothing came up.

Florian clasped me under the arms and pulled me to my feet. "Breathe through your nose, butterfly."

I did, but it didn't seem to be enough.

His large hands were a much-needed warmth at my cheeks, turning my focus from the swirling white at my feet to dark-blue eyes. I drew in a longer inhale and released it slowly. Again when he nodded.

It was then I finally felt the cold burn enveloping my feet.

I tore free from his searching gaze and took in our surroundings. We stood in a small clearing within the woods. Trees towered above us, branches bare and any foliage that remained drizzled with snow. "Where are we?"

"Hellebore, of course."

"It's so cold."

"Didn't your books tell you so?" he drawled, sarcasm soaking each word. "It's the coldest part of the continent."

"Books can only tell you so much," I said, my breath pluming before me. "Some things need to be felt to be truly known."

"I could not agree more." He then trudged through the snow toward a waiting carriage.

Horses, as tall as cottages and as dark as night, shifted and huffed from the disturbance our arrival had created. Beside them stood a driver dressed in a blue and black uniform with a matching scarf. His chestnut eyes looked me over once, dismissively, before he looked at his king.

Behind the carriage were more horses, white and just as giant. The five males with them stared at me as though I were a weed in a garden of flowers. A mixture of curiosity and disdain.

Florian took an awaiting black coat from a male with deep-red hair.

I forgot to care about their opinions of me when the king draped the beautiful fur over my shoulders, the sleeves lined with a luxurious wool.

Then he picked me up.

My heart tumbled, my hands unsure where to land and flailing. "I am capable of climbing into a carriage, Majesty."

"You wear miserable excuses for shoes. They're already sodden." He set me inside the large leather and earthy caramel-scented space. A pair of white boots awaited on the floor. On the leather seat, a thick pair of woolen socks.

I blinked at them. "For me?"

"Put them on," he said. He disappeared, presumably to talk with the males I'd assumed were some of his royal warriors.

I didn't argue, the shock wearing off and the cold seeping beneath my flimsy cotton dress and ruined slippers.

Florian returned when I'd finished and took a seat beside me.

The leather bench seat spanned the length of the ginormous carriage. His presence, the heat emanating from him, still made me far too aware of every breath I drew.

The carriage lurched forward, taking my stomach with it in a violent dip. Withholding an excited laugh, I pulled the velvet drapes covering the window aside.

Miles of snow and trees stretched beyond. Though peacefully picturesque, the darkness between the trees and the mountains warned
of the dangers within. Yet a feeling that alarmed as much as it com-
forted told me I had nothing to fear with a male more dangerous than
a horde of beasts seated beside me.

"I've never been in a carriage," I said to snap free of my thoughts
and the growing tension, and to try to slow the pace of my heartbeat
at his closeness. I'd have thought the king would materialize us straight
to his manor, but I wasn't about to complain. "Do you usually visit
Crustle this way?"

"Your body would not handle materializing over such a vast distance. It takes time to build resistance to the laws of energy that wish
to keep things as they are."

I kept my focus on the wilderness beyond the glass window, all
the while knowing he had every inch of it. "Is that why I've never ended
up far from home?" Each time I'd materialized, I'd found myself in the
library at the bottom of our apartment building.

The king didn't answer.

I could feel his gaze upon me. A weight that called for my full
attention. I gave it to him, turning and letting the drapes fall closed.

He watched me for a moment that warmed. "I assume wherever
you ended up, you felt safest there." A statement, but I still nodded.
He blinked, then looked behind me to the window. "Yes. Though
I'm sure if another place gave you refuge, you'd manage to materialize there just fine, too."

"No matter the distance?"

His eyes returned to mine, cold and dark. "Distance and energy
are no match for desperation."

Those words hung between us like thawing frosted webs.

I blinked first, my eyes dropping to his chest. He still only wore a
light, long-sleeved shirt. Another that revealed a glimpse of his chest.
His hands were folded in his lap, his thumb gliding idly across the
other.

His soft question brought my eyes back to his. "What happened before you unintentionally materialized somewhere?"

The desire to look away and brush off his question took hold. The knowing darkness to his blue gaze told me lying would be futile.

I adjusted my damp skirts and studied the smooth leather of the boots he'd given me. "I was feeling..." I chewed my lip before settling on, "Overwhelmed, I suppose."

Florian made a sound of contemplation. "In the young and untrained, the gift of materializing will present itself when one is severely injured, fears for their life, or..." He said with gentle lethality, "Both."

I swallowed thickly.

"Butterfly," he urged, low. "Which one was it?"

Rolina's wailing screams and silent violence threatened to take me back. I wouldn't go back. I refused to when I was finally going forward. So I said, "Both," in a tone that conveyed I would say nothing more.

The king didn't press further. Shifting the drapes aside, I gave my eyes to the landscape once more as we moved through the dense darkness of the woods.

A stroking touch of the strands of hair down my back startled me.

I looked over at Florian as he curled a lock of my hair around his finger. He rubbed it with his thumb. "Satin soft."

That light touch was felt everywhere. The rapt focus he gave to something I'd never paid much attention to evoked a strange curiosity to know what he saw when he looked upon me.

A wide-eyed, soft-hearted, and woefully naive female whose ignorance of this cruel world fascinated him? A creature ripe for manipulation due to a disturbing lack of experience with much of anything?

As he took his hand away and studied his fingers as if their encounter with my hair had somehow changed them, I wasn't sure I wanted to know.

The shadowed woods sweeping past us eventually brightened into dawn-washed towns.

I soaked every small and towering home in with my forehead glued to the cold glass of the window. Every shop and snow-flooded dirt road. Every fleeting glimpse of vibrant life that did not exist within written words or pictures.

I was here.

"What is this town called?"

Florian didn't respond. I wondered if he'd fallen asleep and looked behind me.

He was wide awake and watching me. His elbow perched upon the covered window next to him, and his thumb rubbed over his lower lip. "Glennaya."

"Glennaya," I repeated, and stared back out the window as we neared a farming region. "How long will it take to reach your manor?"

"We should arrive in time for dinner."

I settled back into the seat, but I was still unwilling to part with the views beyond the window.

I kept the drapes open, watching night bleed into morning. The colors of sunrise were the same in Folkyn—just as stunning and sparking with hope. I didn't know why I'd expected the sky to be different when Mythayla watched over us all.

Florian told me the name of the next town we encountered before I could ask, and I gave him a grateful smile. But before I could gaze back at the stone dwellings in the distance, he said roughly, "Come to me."

We were no longer in the Lair of Lust, so I wasn't sure what to expect from him now. Nor had I had the time to ponder it. Then I remembered.

I was to be his wife.

I didn't think that meant I had to do whatever he wished, but ignoring his request when I didn't want to was asinine.

I moved closer to him, and he said, "Take a seat."

Knowing what that meant, I climbed onto his lap, carefully and awkwardly in my coat and boots. He pushed the coat off my shoulders and draped it over the seat beside us. I supposed it was warm enough in the carriage that I could do without it.

It didn't matter.

Ice could hang from the wooden ceiling. For when his hands cupped my hips, my entire body flooded with heat.

He leaned close to rumble against my mouth, "Never thought I'd envy a town." The whisper of his lips expelled a fractured breath from me. "Nor the fucking snow."

"And why would you?" I asked, lost to his harsh grip on my hips and how it contrasted with the barely-there gentleness of his kiss.

"The wonder in your eyes."

Splaying my hands over his hard chest, I leaned back to better look at him. I laughed when I realized he was indeed envious.

The eruption of sound parted his lips. His eyes darted all over my face. My smile fell at the storm gathering within. "I need to touch you."

"You already are."

His ticking jaw warned not to toy with him.

I leaned forward to press my lips to his. "Then touch me, Majesty."

A throaty growl left him, and as though I'd handed him the blade, the hold on his restraint snapped. My dress was pulled from my body with an aggression that tore the skirts and made the coins tucked within the pocket clink.

If Florian noticed I'd brought them when he'd made it clear I would want for nothing, then he didn't let it show.

Left in only my slip, I shivered, but not from the cold.

The king's impatience had faded, his gaze upon my breasts. He traced the hardened peaks of my nipples through my slip in a lazy and stomach-snatching circle. "I want to see them."

The idea of being naked in a carriage did not exactly fill me with excitement. But the driver's window was closed and covered, and the look in Florian's eyes gave me the confidence to pull my arms from my slip.

I pushed the worn satin to my waist, suddenly self-conscious.

Florian was a king.

He'd likely seen more breasts in his existence than the number of times I'd left Rolina's apartment. Yet the way he stared at mine, with his lips slack and his hands molding to my ribs beneath them, erased the insecurity.

As my anxiety fell, my curiosity climbed. "How old are you, Majesty?"

"Florian," he grunted.

I smiled. "Florian."

"One hundred and thirty-seven years," he said absently.

I'd have thought him older, which did not bother me. Age was not something faeries worried about in the way mortals often did.

His hands squeezed my waist. "And in all those years, I've never seen..." His thumbs brushed the curving swells of my breasts. "Never touched anything so divine."

I trembled. "And have you ever entertained someone in a carriage?" A foolish question, for he certainly had.

"Never had a female in my lap," he said, watching gooseflesh rise over my skin. "Nor have I placed my mouth on their cunts."

My stomach shrank and then bloomed, flushing a thorny warmth through my bloodstream. It gathered in my core and my chest.

He was dangerous indeed.

Knowing so did not stop me from smiling.

His eyes roamed up my neck to meet mine, amusement glinting within. They were clouded with a lighter blue I'd come to learn was desire. "Does that please you?"

"It does, but it also makes me wonder why I'm here," I said carefully. "In your lap."

"It's where I want you." His thumbs glossed over my nipples as he kissed my chin. "And I always get what I want."

I believed him.

Such arrogance should have deterred me from wanting him. But when his mouth dragged to mine, his lips softer than silk as they parted my own for our tongues to lightly touch, I knew there was likely little he could say or do that would make me not want him.

I wanted Florian in a way I hadn't expected to want any

male—with a desperation and longing to peel back his every layer to claim and study what lurked beneath.

He groaned when I sucked his tongue, his teeth catching my lip and tugging. "I want to make you come." It was his only warning before he clasped my face with one hand and slipped the other between my thighs.

He tipped my chin back and cursed against my throat. "When you need me, you must tell me."

"I need you."

He chuckled, his finger sliding through my wet center. "I meant before you're dripping between my fucking fingers onto my pants."

I stilled, embarrassed, and made to scoot back off him.

"Don't move," he growled, teeth latching onto the delicate skin under my jaw. "Not until you've thoroughly soaked my hand."

His finger slid back and forth languidly, a teasing brush over my clit each time. I needed more, and rocked into the touch. His teeth sank into my skin in warning. "You take what I give you, how I want to give it to you."

Frustrated and ridiculously close to release just from the timbre of his roughened words, I moaned.

"Good." A kiss was pressed underneath my chin. "So very good."

I clutched his shoulders. My fingers curled into his shirt. I wanted his mouth on mine, but his hand left my face to seize my hair.

The sharp sting on my scalp shocked me.

He wrapped the long strands around his fist and tugged until my back arched and my breasts were caught by his hot mouth. He sucked and kissed and gently nipped, and I knew without asking that he'd left marks.

Back and forth, he stroked me softly while my fingers scrunched the hair at his nape, and his mouth bruised my breasts. His hungry and throaty rumbles joined my noisy breaths. I shuddered, the sensations too much. "Florian..."

He released my breast to watch as I trembled and unraveled with a slowness that tortured. "Look at me," he ordered, and I tore my heavy eyes open, his grip on my hair and his touch on my core unrelenting. "Perfect creature."

Then his hold gentled, and I broke free of it to fall over him.

He was all hard heat beneath me, but when I dared to kiss his neck and reach between us to unbuckle his pants, to finally see and properly feel him, he grabbed my arms. "When you first greet my cock, it will be upon my bed and nowhere else. Sleep."

I tried, but his gravel-coated promise and the hardness that failed to soften beneath me made it difficult. My eyes closed, my body languid and content, but my mind swirled with questions and anticipation over what lay ahead.

"This war you spoke of," I said through a yawn. "Why would you want such a horrid thing to happen?"

Florian remained quiet for so long that I gave up on waiting for an answer.

When he gave one, it was a low question that accompanied the skimming of his fingers through my hair over my back. "What makes anyone wish for bloodshed?"

"Anger," I said, unable to keep from thinking of Rolina. Unable to wipe one of many memories of hiding in my room when she drank so much that her fury made me an outlet for her grief. "Retribution."

The king of Hellebore hummed, the deep and delicious sound a vibration against my nose. "Sleep."

"Butterfly." The thickened voice and the name I'd grown fond of stirred me awake. "Get dressed. We'll arrive soon."

My face was still in Florian's neck. The soft wool of my coat draped over my back.

I groaned and lifted my head, blinking heavily.

Slowly, blue eyes, dark brows, and those devastating features became clearer.

The king smirked, swiping a tendril of hair from my cheek. "You slept through a parade of folk greeting us in the last town. Did I exhaust you too thoroughly?"

I was disappointed to have missed it, but I was also too tired to care. I blinked again in response, then felt the cool fingers of this winter-laden realm touch my bare skin. No wonder he'd covered me with the coat. My slip was still folded at my waist.

I rolled off the king to the seat beside him as he chuckled, frantically righting it.

"I do not share treasure, sweet creature. No one is going to see you."

Though those words were a relief, they didn't deter me from putting my gown back on. I finger-combed my hair and took greedy sips of water from the canteen the king offered.

He took it back while ordering, "Coat on."

I pushed my arms into the sleeves and then immediately opened the drapes.

"Butterfly."

I turned to find him holding my pouch of gold coins. Flushing, I ignored his amused gaze and snatched them from his hand with a mumbled, "Thank you."

I tucked them into my coat pocket and looked out the window.

Snow-covered cobblestone streets filled with wagons of produce and lined with tall wood and stone buildings greeted me.

Among them were civilians dressed in heavy coats, furs, long-sleeved gowns, and thick tunics. The kaleidoscope of color and fabrics—ranging from moth-eaten cotton to expensive silks—I was accustomed to glimpsing on the dreary streets of Crustle seemed an entire world away.

And it now was, I thought with a sprinkle of alarm, absorbing this faerie kingdom's dark blues, blacks, and varying shades of crimson.

Windows of colored glass dragged the eye to many homes. Some were two story, some three, and others tiny bungalows squashed between with adorable gardens.

Well-kept wooden signs with curling script hung from shop

fronts. Displays in long, oblong, and arched windows were cast aglow by strings of fireflies within crystal orbs. Smoke puffed from almost every chimney within sight, rising toward the early evening sky.

Many civilians continued to wave and bow and curtsy. Others merely continued with their end-of-day routines as if a royal carriage was nothing they hadn't seen a dozen times or more.

It might have been blanketed in snow, but it didn't matter. This place was so far removed from the mud and debris-flooded streets of the middle lands that I fell more and more in love with each new slice of winter-kissed perfection.

"Lurina," Florian said. "The royal city of Hellebore."

Turning to him, I said with an awe that made his head tilt toward the window behind me, "It's magical." I turned back, waving at a bouncing youngling held by a giant male. "You must visit as often as possible."

"I mostly just pass through," he said, apathetic.

I frowned at that. Then again, this was his world, and he'd been alive for a long time. It was only new to me. The reminder had my forehead sticking to the glass as I waited with my breath fogging the view to see what would come next.

"Your nose will turn blue if you don't straighten up."

"I'm fine," I said, but I rubbed it and my forehead regardless.

The king huffed, seeming to withhold a laugh.

Not a minute later, the city street we traveled became a slow and winding road uphill into the mountains of woods that overlooked the city of Lurina.

And then I saw it.

Hellebore Manor appeared in gaps and glimpses between the trees.

It would have been disguised by the deep-red ivy coating the entirety of the three-story fortress if it weren't for the windows. Arched glass glinted in the glow of dusk and stood in tall rows along each floor.

As we finally neared, I had to wipe the carriage window clear of the fog from my breath, unwilling to move an inch.

Willow and oak trees surrounded the manor's circular drive.

In the center stood a large statue of the goddess, her robe marked with mildew and her star-spun hair and features cracked from the elements.

"They say Mythayla was forged from the flames of colliding stars," Florian murmured, knowing what had caught my attention. "Forced to kill beasts until she could feed from those she loved to rejuvenate and survive during her reign of procreation with falling stars."

I'd heard similar, as well as many different beliefs, as to how the Fae and the continent of Mythayla had come to exist. Including that it had taken countless centuries for her offspring, faeries, to grow strong enough to survive without her aid. So strong that a jealous and vindictive harem of lovers supposedly killed her when they learned they were no longer needed.

"Do you believe that?"

I expected no response. Then, as we came to a rocking stop, he said, "It is a test." He leaped out of the carriage with distracting grace. "To trust in what you cannot see."

I frowned. "You think it unwise?"

"I didn't say that."

As he assisted with my ungraceful exit from the carriage, I silently questioned whether he needed to when he'd already suggested as much.

A smirk attempted to curl his stubborn and glorious lips when my hastily-donned gown snagged on the carriage door handle.

Glancing away to rid the heat entering my cheeks, I looked back to the statue of the goddess. Beneath Mythayla's feet spread a small garden of frosted roses, almost black in color. Upon closer inspection, I noticed they were a dark and glimmering blue—much the same as the king's eyes.

My fingers fell slack, leaving Florian's as I then looked at the manor.

"It's beautiful," I breathed, dragging my eyes from the circular row of stone steps. Above them were arched doors in a towering stained

NECTAR OF THE WICKED | 97

wood, and beneath the walls of crimson ivy hid a sparkling onyx stone. "And huge."

I hadn't realized I'd garnered an audience until Florian's boots crunched over the brown pebbled drive toward the doors. "This is Olin, our family steward."

I blinked and approached the tall and thin male who assessed me with sharp lavender eyes. "Hello, Olin."

The faerie's silver mustache shifted with the thinning of his lips. An incline of his head was apparently all the greeting I would receive.

I was too distracted by the majestic extravagance as we moved into the giant foyer to mind. Ahead, the ceiling rose through the second floor. A dark crystal chandelier housing dozens of candles glinted above me.

"Come, butterfly."

But I wasn't finished admiring the portraits of the Hellebore family.

A gilded frame contained a young Florian. Another a brunette female with eyes so much like his, she could only be his mother. A male with black hair stood beside her with dark eyes and a similar severe bone structure to his son.

He stood with the regal and proud look of a male who knew he'd been gifted a great fortune. Not merely because he wore a crown of onyx and diamond and sapphire jewels, but because of the female he held at the waist and the hand affectionately clasped over his son's shoulder.

Such a stark contrast to the portrait of the same late king of Hellebore on the opposite wall.

In this one, there was no queen, and Florian's father had lost that glow in his eyes. He still stood proud before his son and the young female of whom I guessed had been born some years after Florian had grown.

Here, Florian was taller than his father—broader. The arrogance he carried glinted in those ever-changing eyes. But the firmness of his jaw, the protective hand he'd placed on the very young female's shoulder, spoke volumes.

He had adored his sister. A sister I knew nothing about, and therefore I assumed she'd passed on quite some time ago.

My throat tightened as I wondered how old she'd been when that'd happened—as I reached out to touch the rosy cheeks covered in gentle obsidian curls. Her eyes were a brighter blue than her brother's, but there was a different mischief to them.

A darkness that no amount of color could hide.

"Her name was Lilitha."

Florian's toneless voice stunned me, and my hand dropped to my side.

It was wrong of me to ask. I'd barely stepped a few feet into his home. Regardless, I failed to trap the curiosity when he clipped, "Ask, butterfly."

"How young was she when she died?"

Expressionless, he said while staring at his sister, "Twenty-one years."

So dreadfully young, especially in Fae years. I was tempted to ask why, but I'd already pried too much.

Florian glanced at me, as if sensing and awaiting the question.

I said in jest, "She looks as though she would have caused you a great deal of trouble."

"You have no idea," he said with a huff, though he did not smile. He turned and marched from the foyer into the adjoining hall.

Beyond the staircase, a spray of moonlight washed over the smooth stone floors through a row of what seemed to be glass panes.

A courtyard sat in the very center of the manor.

Atop the landing, I leaned against the stone railing to glimpse it through the glass that rose from the first floor all the way to the ceiling.

Though it was now fully dark, the courtyard was aglow with lanterns of firelight in each corner. Hedges of those blue roses sat on either side of wooden bench seats, and behind them, ivy fell in curtains from the rooftop.

"There will be time to explore as much as you wish," the king said. "Right now, you should wash up and rest. I have some matters I must see to."

The tone of his voice, or rather the lack thereof, left no room for argument.

I followed him up the stairs, my eyes flitting over various artworks of ancestors long passed and earlier depictions of the manor we walked within. I was so engrossed with taking everything in, I nearly ran into Florian's back when he stopped before two large doors.

"My rooms," he said, then walked on to the right. The hall curved into another, and it contained only one door at the end. He opened it and gestured for me to enter ahead of him. "Yours."

The thought of sleeping so close to him both unnerved and thrilled me. Remembering I'd taken a long nap upon his lap in the carriage after what he'd done to me, I almost laughed at the absurdity of having any apprehension at all.

I stepped inside.

And I promptly lost all the air within my lungs.

The bedchamber was easily triple the size of the apartment I'd once thought I might never escape. Filigreed molding adorned the corners of the ceiling, which had been painted in a mural of stars and clouds and rays of sunlight in homage to the faerie mother, Mythayla.

White shelving rose toward the ceiling and stretched along one entire side of the room, books lining every available space. Upon the other side, farthest from Florian's chambers—to my foolish relief— was the bathing room and what looked to be a dressing chamber.

The bed in the center of the room was dressed in creams and crimsons and drowning in frilled and velvet pillows. Ivory netting was tied to the white posts with blood-red ribbon. Two wooden nightstands in matching white stood on either side, the brass-held candles atop them already aflame.

I'd almost forgotten the king stood behind me until he murmured with a slight touch of amusement, "I'll send for you at dinner, butterfly."

As soon as the door clicked closed, a loud breath whooshed from my lungs, followed by a disbelieving and uncontrollable laugh.

The sound echoed as I twirled into the room.

I fell to the gigantic bed on my back and stared up through the netting to the fascinating artwork on the ceiling.

My very own rooms.

Rooms inside of a royal house that would soon call me their queen. *Me.* A nameless changeling who'd spent her entire life cowering from a woman behind the pages of books.

Giddy exhilaration had me smothering another bubbling laugh.

It was then I realized that I'd almost believed all of this to be a lavish and vastly imaginative dream I'd concocted from desperation and hope. That at any given moment, I would be shaken awake by Rolina's rage.

As I stared at the slim door snug between rows of bookshelves, a door I knew connected to my future husband's rooms, it began to cement heavily in my bones.

This was wonderfully real.

EIGHT

NOT AN HOUR LATER, OLIN, THE STEWARD, INDEED delivered me to dinner.

But I hadn't expected to dine alone.

The grand room upon the first floor sat next to a library I longed to visit. And it was too large, too much oak and golden candlelit darkness, for one creature.

I'd bathed and cleaned my hair with vanilla and honeysuckle soaps in a tub large enough to swim in, and I'd wondered if Florian had known we'd used similar soaps, though far less lovely, in the apartment. I hadn't the heart to inform him that I'd rather never use scents Rolina had once adored again.

She could no longer rob me of luxuries or anything else, including manners.

I'd then perused the dressing chamber with my eyes bulging and my exploring fingers trembling as they'd swept along all the many stunning fabrics. Velvet, silks, the softest cottons and chiffon...

All of the gowns were hard for me to absorb, let alone decide on what to wear.

I'd settled on a long-sleeved navy-blue number that was most likely a nightgown due to the looser bodice and the figure-hugging silk. I'd paired it with my coat, although it probably did not suit, when Olin had knocked upon the door to escort me downstairs.

Stiffly, I picked at the delicious serving of lamb soaked in mint gravy. Even the beans here were different—larger and juicier.

The steward stood outside the dining room, utterly silent. When I'd greeted him upon opening the door to my rooms to find him with his hands clasped behind his back, he hadn't returned it.

He wore a similar uniform to the warriors who'd escorted us to the manor, sans the armored and bulky coat. His dark-blue waistcoat was lined in black and without a single crease nor a speck of lint, his matching trousers the same.

His silver hair was cropped close to his scalp. His mustache was impeccably trimmed. That, and his stubborn silence and posture, said this was a male who took his responsibility and loyalty to the Hellebore family seriously.

Perhaps too seriously, I thought, when he entered the dining room upon realizing I'd lost interest in finishing my meal.

"Is it not to your liking?" he said in a crisp tone that conveyed someone like me ought to be grateful and finish every morsel.

"It was incredible, thank you." I offered a weak smile. "My stomach might need time to adjust to such a large serving, for I'm already indecently full."

"The king will be displeased," he said tightly.

I feigned looking around the large and narrow room. My eyes settled at the head of the table where I knew Florian would sit if he'd deigned to join me. "He is not here," I needlessly said with a stronger smile.

Then I sipped my water and stood, collecting my plate and crystal glass.

The steward's disapproving look fell into a scowl when I walked the long length of the oak slabbed table to the doors. "Which way to the kitchen?"

Olin sputtered. "You may leave that for the staff to collect."

"I don't mind. I would like to see it, and seeing as the king is busy, I've nothing else to do but explore." I lifted my shoulders. "Would you care to show me?"

He glared at me for sweltering seconds that should have made me reconsider irritating him more than my mere presence evidently already did. Then the steward sighed and marched out into the hall. "This way."

He walked at such a brisk pace that I struggled to keep up, the cutlery threatening to slide from my plate.

At the opposite end of the first floor, we descended a steep and rocky flight of stairs. The kitchen was located a level below ground. Starlight still crept in through the slicing of windows squashed right below the ceiling.

Along the far wall, steam rose from sinks filled with soapy water and pots bubbling on stovetops. An island bench stood large and center in the humid room, fires burning beneath for yet another stovetop above.

Scraps overflowed from two pails by the door directly opposite the one we stood before. The other was open, giving way to stone stairs that presumably twirled up to the gardens astride the manor.

Regret kept me rooted in the doorway.

A ginormous male flitted from the sinks to the stoves with the grace of a trained dancer and barked orders in a melodious voice at two youths attempting to keep up with his needs.

Olin gave me a smug look.

I refrained from bristling and cautiously stepped forward. I had to see this through now. "Uh, hello."

A young male dropped something on his foot, muttering a curse that sounded like, "*Tullia.*"

All activity came to a crashing standstill. Three sets of similar eyes fell on me at once.

Olin cleared his throat pointedly. "Our guest would like to return her meal."

I frowned at the steward, as I was not a guest, and that was not true. At least, not entirely. Stepping forward again, I smiled and said, "It was delicious, thank you."

The intimidating male who'd been throwing commands blinked at me with large brown eyes. His matching hair was secured in a low ponytail by a black ribbon at his thick nape. Slowly, he looked from me to the steward, then he came to retrieve the plate from me. "You did not finish it."

"I'm not used to such large servings," I said softly, hoping my voice did not quake from his nearness.

But he gently took the plate and glass in his long fingers and nodded once. His golden features seemed a little drawn as he stared at me for a long moment before saying, "Then I will ensure your next meals are smaller to give you time to adjust."

The steward made a noise that sounded suspiciously like a scoff.

The male with my plate glanced at him with narrowed eyes. Then he nodded to me once more and disposed of my dinner's remains.

I was unsure what else to do, so I smiled at the other males and realized they were twins. One of them grinned brightly; the other glared and assessed me as if I were an insect who'd snuck inside his home.

"I am Kreed, and these are my sons, Thistle and Arryn."

Without a name to give them, all I could say was, "I'm pleased to meet you."

Kreed smiled, though it didn't touch his eyes. Something akin to concern pulled at his mouth when his sons snickered to one another, and I turned from the room.

Upon reaching the first floor, I couldn't help but remark aloud, "That was..." I gazed down into the humid gloom of the stairs. "Odd."

Olin laughed, short and barked.

I frowned but hurried after him down the hall.

"It is you who is odd, changeling," he said as he left me at the grand staircase that would deliver me to my rooms.

I watched him go, unease quickening my heart and keeping my feet still.

I was accustomed to being disliked, to being loathed, even, and I hadn't expected to be treated as though I was a much-needed addition to this royal house.

That wasn't what unsettled me.

It was the tension that stalked the halls. A reek of secrets and ghosts. It was the inescapable feeling that no matter who I was—a soon-to-be queen or a changeling—I would not be welcome here.

The war-hungry king had his secrets, this I knew. I'd thought I could get by without learning them. That I could find comfort in his realm without learning all of who he was.

Now, I couldn't help but worry that I'd been wrong.

The following morning, a walk of the grounds revealed a frozen lake far beyond the stables, but it failed to clear the uncertainty.

An uncertainty that haunted my dreams and sprouted thorns with the king's absence.

Florian had already indulged so many of my curiosities. Though each time he had, I was left with more questions and concerns that wouldn't be revealed until his presence no longer clouded my judgment.

Marriage wasn't something I'd ever thought too much about. While I was not opposed to the idea, I had harbored grand ideals of falling in love numerous times first. I never thought I'd one day agree to wed someone before I had experienced many lovers.

I was attracted to Florian. That much had been made abundantly and embarrassingly clear during the first moments I'd laid eyes upon him.

But one needed a heart in order to fall in love, and Florian...

If he had a heart, he'd hidden it too deep beneath his ice-crafted armor.

The longer his absence from this place he called home, the more I realized there was no care behind his actions. No empathy. Certainly no concern. There was only a ruthless and incredibly Fae-like interest to amuse himself while ensuring he received everything he desired.

And I was unassuming and insignificant enough to fit those desires.

There was no going back now, and though this attraction had grown claws and teeth that seemed to sharpen with every encounter the king deigned to give me, I didn't want to.

I reminded myself that I was right where I needed to be to see to my own desires. So any befuddlement and useless wonderings would need to be cast aside and ignored.

The stable hand was in the paddocks with two giant horses, similar or perhaps the same as the beasts who'd hauled our carriage through Hellebore to this estate. More of them shifted and nickered as I crept through the rear door of the stables and into the dark.

The building appeared to be constructed from thick layers of wood to keep the freezing gusts from entering. Eight horses eyed me. All of them monstrously tall and seemingly taken aback by my presence.

"Hello," I whispered, unsure why. Perhaps not to startle them.

Crossing the hay-dusted stone between the rows of large watching eyes, I marveled at how big the beasts truly were.

Intimidating, certainly, though not enough to stop me from offering my hand to a dark gray mare. She sniffed my chilled fingers, then nudged them away with a grunt.

"Bluebell won't humor anyone without a treat first."

My stomach flipped.

I spun to find Florian behind me, who'd entered soundlessly through the rear door I'd left open.

Dipping my head, I smiled. "Majesty."

He straightened from the stall of a stallion and unfolded his arms. "Florian."

I sucked my lips to keep from grinning and turned back to Bluebell. She was now watching Florian's approach with a spark of hope in her eyes. I knew the feeling.

"You shouldn't wander off without telling anyone," Florian said. "It's freezing out."

"I was bored." It wasn't entirely a lie. I couldn't be idle when a brand-new world awaited exploration. "And there's so much to see." I moved to the next, who eagerly tossed his large head over his stall door.

"Yet you chose to visit the horses."

The horse sniffed my cheek when I stepped too close, and I

laughed as I retreated and gave him my hand. "I've never ridden one, let alone seen creatures so huge this close."

Florian said nothing for a short while.

Curious, I asked, "What of the winged beasts?"

"The hunt are the only ones daring enough to tame and breed them for their needs." He watched the friendly horse attempt to chew my hair, then sighed and headed back to the door.

I'd thought he'd left, and I was still attempting to quell the disappointment when his booted steps sounded again.

His arm brushed mine as he reached for the stall door. "Step back."

"You're letting him out?" I asked, stumbling back with my eyes widening.

The reins in his hand swayed as he unlatched and opened the door. "You wish to ride a horse, and Bennington is the most tolerant of strangers."

"I don't have to," I said quickly. "This was not what I intended when I said that. I was just speaking—"

Florian turned and pressed a finger to my mouth, blue eyes dancing between mine. "Sweet creature, would you like me to take you for a ride or not?"

The double meaning in his words did not escape me, and my cheeks flushed. I still nodded.

His eyes brightened. His finger dragged my lower lip down, his gaze following as he brought it over my chin and then to his mouth.

He could have just kissed me. He could kiss me whenever he liked, and he knew it.

But he ran that finger over his lips as if tasting something so delicious it was forbidden, then turned back to Bennington.

I watched, my heart thundering with anticipation, as Florian readied the horse who had to duck his head to fit through the large entrance to the stables. Then I followed them out into the cold.

He mounted first, swift and with an elegance that shocked for a male of his size and a beast so large. The sun peeking through the gloom overhead blinded when I gazed up at him from the ground. His hair curtained his cheeks in dark waves, the breeze rustling it against his shoulders and lips.

Lips that curled when I failed to acknowledge the hand he'd offered.

I dropped my head momentarily—eternally feeling the fascinated fool around this king—then placed my hand within his cool grasp.

He tugged, pulling me forward a step. A shocked squeak left me as he reached beneath my arms to haul me up onto the horse to sit before him.

The saddle was bigger than average, of course, but not built for two. I failed to care about the rubbing of the leather pommel snug against my core while pressed so tightly to Florian's chest.

His rough exhale stirred my hair. His arm a tight band of muscle around my waist.

He adjusted my plum skirts, instructing, "Lift your legs for me." Taking his time, he gently tucked the wind-catching gauze and silk under my thighs.

Every stroke of his fingers singed. Every breath in my ear became more ragged. Until he cursed and snatched the reins, hard at my lower back as he commanded Bennington to leave the drive of the stables.

I gripped the saddle, my chest filled with a riot of fluttering butterflies as we passed by the paddocks.

The stable hand cupped a hand over his forehead, watching us. He bowed before we left his line of sight and disappeared behind a dilapidated greenhouse. Rows upon rows of dead fruit trees surrounded it.

"Lemon trees," I said, studying the bare branches. "Oranges, too."

"It's been a long while since they've produced any fruit," Florian said to my ear. "They need to be ripped from the ground." His tone hinted at a reluctance to do so, and I sensed something stopped him from getting rid of the greenhouse, too.

"Autumn will come," I said, as that was likely why he waited. Hellebore was the coldest kingdom in Folkyn and all of Mythayla, but its deathly winter would make way for enough respite to give birth to more life.

Florian didn't respond, and I soon forgot about the seasons as we approached the lake I'd seen from a distance earlier. The surface resembled a grimy mirror, shadows swaying from the snow-dusted trees we trotted within.

"Can we walk upon it?"

"Yes, but not with Bennington," he said. "It's thick, but not so thick that it will tolerate all of our weight combined."

As we moved on, I looked back to the lake with longing—with a wonder for what lurked in the water beneath its frozen ceiling. "Have you ever seen a pixiefish?"

"Many," he grunted, his fingers rubbing ever so slightly over my stomach.

"They were my favorite creature of Folkyn to read about when I was young," I said. "Are they truly unable to leave the water?"

"Worried their tiny teeth and claws will find you?" Florian teased dryly.

I didn't care if he wasn't interested. I still said, "No, I just cannot imagine only ever staying in one place. Never seeing anything else."

He sensed why that troubled me, but he took a minute to respond. "In Oleander, you'll often see them baking upon the rocks by the rivers and sea. So yes," he said, as though I'd forced him to, "they can leave their homes, but not for long."

Not for long.

Those words hung like icicles within my chest as we wended deeper into the woods.

Bennington seemed all too happy to explore despite the cold. His breaths steamed the air, but he trotted through the brush with what could only be described as merriment. I leaned forward and patted his neck.

"You shouldn't distract him."

"He's not distracted," I said. "He's happy."

Florian's hold tightened, almost as if he wanted to squeeze me for talking back to him.

I wouldn't have minded, and I was past the point of caring what my acceptance of his frosty treatment said about me. *Attraction*, I reminded myself. I was discovering what I liked, and there was nothing wrong with that. I wasn't worried that I liked to be told what to do.

The only thing that alarmed me was that I liked a lot of him.

Bennington leaped over a log, and I let loose a breathless and near-silent scream. Florian's chuckle warmed my skin. The sound one of rough and rare beauty.

As if knowing it pleased me, he sobered and cleared his throat. "You wear the same coat."

"I like it," was all I could think to say. Rolina had never given me anything that wasn't once her own, or unclaimed clothing she'd brought home from work.

"And do you like the rest?" he asked some moments later. "The clothing."

My eyes caught on the crimson ivy of the manor through the trees ahead. We'd almost circled back. "I do," I said. "Thank you."

"Ask."

I refrained from sending him a scowl over my shoulder. "How do you know I wish to ask anything?"

"You tense, and your tongue pokes at your teeth."

I frowned as we left the trees and crossed the dirt road to the pebbled drive. "You can't see that."

"I can see the change in your jaw when you do it."

Distant voices and wheels trundling over rock and dirt invaded our bubble.

"Perceptive," I said, admittedly kind of impressed. Also far too pleased that he'd studied me so thoroughly.

My smile waned at what I glimpsed behind us.

Wagons were being hauled uphill toward the manor. Many wagons and many warriors on horseback. I stared over my shoulder as we continued ahead of them all, attempting to see what they were doing.

Florian placed his lips on my cheek and whispered roughly, "Ask, butterfly."

So focused on whatever the king was having delivered—and in such large quantity—it took a moment to recall what we'd been discussing.

Another kiss to my cheek and I remembered, although his scent and the hand pressing against my stomach made it difficult to form the question. I hoped my insecurity came across as mere curiosity. "Who did all the fine clothing belong to?"

"You," he responded simply, and rather than continue toward the stables, the king urged Bennington into a canter that stole my breath and every thought from my head.

The breeze whipped and burned my cheeks. My heart seemed to soar through the crisp air in our wake. Florian slowed the horse as we again entered the woods beyond the stables, allowing him to cool down before he brought us to a complete stop deep within the icy foliage.

I turned to look at him, about to ask what he intended by stopping here.

His mouth immediately stole mine, and he swallowed my shocked gasp with a quiet groan.

The hand around my waist crawled higher to skim my breast through my gown. My stomach tightened, and I squirmed forward without thought, my core rubbing against the pommel of the saddle and causing sparks to ignite.

Florian noticed. Nothing seemed to escape him. He dipped his tongue into my mouth, then whispered, "Rock your hips."

He bit my lip as I did. A low rumble climbed his throat. It left him in a small growl when I clasped his hand and brought it to the low neckline of my gown. He needed no more permission. His hand slipped beneath the material, as well as that of my slip.

I moaned, rocking harder against the saddle when he squeezed my breast.

"So obedient," he crooned, kissing the corner of my mouth softly as pleasure seeped through every limb to coil and spread throughout my core. "You must really want to come." Another kiss to my lips, his eyes bright and wild on mine. "You make me so fucking hard, I could come just from watching you."

His thumb grazed my nipple, his other hand climbing beneath my skirts and slip. I stopped rocking against the saddle. He encountered my slick flesh and groaned again. "You're awfully wet, sweet creature." Then he circled my clit. "And so perilously swollen."

Indeed. I came apart at the second press of his finger against my clit.

Wicked delight shined in his eyes as he watched me shake and pant while gently rubbing me into pieces. My thighs squeezed, and Bennington huffed, shifting slightly.

Florian removed his hand. Gaze firm on mine, he brought his fingers to his mouth and sucked each of them clean with relish. Dazed, I stared, limp against him as he fixed my gown, and we slowly left the privacy of the woods.

We'd reached the drive to the stables before I'd wholly caught my breath and regained the use of my brain. "When will you let me tend to you?"

Florian climbed down from Bennington, then helped me do the same. "You already do," he said, a touch hoarse.

I stared up at him, confused by his meaning.

He grinned and stroked a curled finger beneath my chin, his head lowering and his lips molding tight to mine. He seemed to breathe me in, his mouth bruising and unmoving, the hand at my hip squeezing.

Then he broke away with sudden and swift force. He gave Bennington to the approaching stable hand and stalked toward the manor.

Memories of the day kept me restless and far from sleep.

Surrendering to failure, I decided to return my tea tray to the kitchen for something to do.

The stone walls might have kept the winter chill at bay, but they emanated a strange ice all the same. As though they watched, silent and all-knowing after providing refuge for generations of Hellebore royals.

The eerie yet somewhat comforting feeling stalked my quiet journey downstairs.

At the bottom of the staircase, I paused when I heard male voices floating between the cracked open door of a room to the left of the foyer.

"Hiding in the town of Jenmin, supposedly awaiting orders."

"How many?" Florian asked.

"Amber reported hearing of twelve, which means likely double that."

Florian scoffed. "Ignore them and press forward for more noise."

"The more we make, the more he seems to retreat." A pause before the other male said, "To continue with these direct and open attacks when he's bitten his tongue for so long is concerning, Flor."

The familiarity between the two struck me with surprise. Whoever this male was, he was not merely a warrior or general, but perhaps a friend, being that Florian did not protest the improper addressing.

There was no response from Florian.

His friend added, "Especially now that he has more reason to..." The male stopped abruptly.

As did my heart when the door creaked with the touch of a crisp breeze that opened it farther.

"Come here, butterfly."

Shit.

I looked down at the tea tray gleaming with firelight from the sconces and inwardly berated myself with a sigh.

The ticking of the clock above the foyer echoed in the silence.

There was a slight shake to my hands, probably from being caught eavesdropping. It caused a rattle as I set the tray upon the hall table next to a vase of pure gold awaiting fresh wildflowers that would come with morning.

Not much bigger than Rolina's room in the apartment, the king's study was surprisingly plain.

And intimidatingly dark.

The sconces were unlit, as if this meeting had not been planned or it was not meant to drag on given the hour. The only light to guide my hesitant steps was provided by the moon aglow in the two windows with drawn drapes beyond an oversized desk made of steel and oak.

Maps lined the expanse of one wall. It was too dark to see what locations had been marked with red wax.

Florian reclined in a high-back and winged leather chair, his coat open and his hair mussed.

He looked up from what appeared to be a miniature ice sculpture he'd been carving with a small dagger. He twirled the weapon between his fingers as he smirked, then set it down next to a stack of neatly piled documents. "It is unwise to listen in on conversations you were not invited to join, sweet creature."

I nodded, feeling his friend's gaze press upon me like an itch.

Florian carefully placed the sculpture next to the dagger. "And even more so to roam the halls at such a late hour."

Though those words should've further intimidated, they didn't. The gentle threat caressed my skin as though he'd brushed his fingers over it.

I half wondered if he'd introduce me to his friend, of whom I assumed was in fact his general, or if one of us would be dismissed.

Florian merely ordered, "Come to me."

I stepped forward onto a woolen rug and stopped between the two chairs facing his desk—one of which was occupied by the male. All I saw was a flash of bright eyes and white-blond hair and bulky boots crossed at the ankles. He said nothing, but his presence made it hard to shake the tension from my bones that had lingered since being caught loitering and listening.

Florian's gaze narrowed as if sensing as much, though it did not leave me. "Closer." I crossed to the desk, and the king reclined more in his chair with a twitch to his lips. "Closer, butterfly."

Heat began to bloom in my neck and cheeks. I was thankful for the darkness as I rounded the desk to stand directly next to Florian.

He patted the wood. "Closer."

Swallowing, I made to look at the silent male seated across from us.

Florian tutted.

I did as requested, my silk nightgown protesting when I pushed up onto the desk.

"Closer," he said again, and this time, he did not wait.

I was pulled to sit right in front of him, his hands remaining on my thighs. His thumbs rubbed, shifting the silk over my skin. A softness that grazed.

Florian crooked his finger. "Closer."

I leaned forward, gripping the edge of the desk as if it would help my heart cease racing.

The king stroked his knuckles over my cheek, his searching eyes a luminous light in the dark. "Kiss me."

Too aware of the warrior behind me, I hesitated.

Displeasure thinned Florian's lips. His eyes dropped to my mouth, the hand still upon my thigh squeezing gently. "Do you not wish to?"

"I do," I breathed.

Deadly in its deceptive beauty, his smile lifted his long lashes. "I don't know if I believe you."

My discomfort curled into a tight rope around my chest. Ignoring it, I leaned forward to place my lips upon the king's.

The tension rapidly left my bones.

Everything slowed and softened with the first silken touch of his mouth on mine. His taste awakened and soothed. I parted his lips, a breath carrying sound escaping me when he groaned and clasped my cheek and jaw.

Our tongues touched, and I shivered as he broke away and laid his forehead aside mine.

It took his next order for me to remember we were not alone.

Low, but not so low that our company would not hear, the king said, "Do close the door on your way out."

A little mortified, I scooted from between his legs and pushed off the desk to the floor. I kept my gaze on the ground as I passed the blond male I hadn't once dared to get a decent look at, and forced my weakened legs to the door.

As it closed, a boisterous laugh, unfamiliar and therefore not Florian's, failed to keep from sneaking through the spelled stone and wood.

NINE

I WOULDN'T SEE MY BETROTHED AGAIN FOR TWO DAYS.
After searching the three floors and discovering only parlors, a
ballroom, and locked chambers, I'd sifted through the grand library
downstairs. I had plenty of books to choose from in my rooms, but I
wasn't in search of something to read. Everything was still so new, so
glamorously different, I couldn't have read if I'd tried.

I didn't want to admit it. I couldn't help it, and I couldn't deny it.

I was itching to see Florian, hungry for more of his confusingly
cold yet heat-inducing company. Though the doors to his quarters
were locked, including the one adjoining our rooms, I could sense
he wasn't there.

When Olin escorted me to the dining room for another lonely
dinner, I'd asked of his whereabouts, only to be met with a rising of
his brows that conveyed his displeasure at my audacity.

I'd sighed and watched the fire burn low in the ornate hearth
while eating as much as I could. Kreed was the only one who'd been
half pleasant to me, and he'd indeed given me smaller servings for
every mouthwatering meal.

Today, I was tired of wandering the beautiful yet empty halls and
enduring Olin's stern disapproval of my lowly presence. After lunch,
I marched straight outside into the winter chill.

A guard who'd been loitering by the manor's entrance trailed me
to the edge of the drive. As I trudged in my boots toward the forest,
he mercifully made no effort to join me.

Twigs snapped underfoot. Frosted spiderwebs hanging from bare
branches glinted like jewels beneath the sun. I traced them with wonder and meandered deeper into the trees before I heard the faint growl.

I stilled, instinct warning me to retreat, when I caught a flash of white fur.

Then there was a whine, and that instinct changed with a jarring pulse I couldn't ignore.

I followed the sound as though it were a song on the wind rather than a keening I'd heard only once.

Behind a large oak, blood speckled the snow surrounding her.

A female. Confirmed with the first glimpse of her dark eyes.

I crouched beside the cub, allowing her to sniff me before I gently prodded her injured leg. She growled, attempting to move. I placed a hand on her flank, and she settled. Peering through the foliage, curious as to where her mother was, I sensed nothing nearby.

I inspected the bite on her leg. Another wolf had done it.

Indecision warred, but something stronger suffocated it. Something I'd not felt before arose and outweighed any uncertainty. Not only did I want to help her, I had to.

Carefully, I pulled the cub no bigger than a fat alley cat into my arms.

The wolf wriggled but stilled when my eyes met hers and I ran my fingers over her head. The admission left me on a whisper, though something told me that even if she didn't understand my words, she understood the emotion in my eyes. "I know how it feels to be discarded, young one."

We trekked back through the woods toward the manor. It winked at us, dark yet glowing red through the trees.

I crossed the dirt road and stopped at the entry to the circular drive.

It was flooded with wagons and carriages. Trunks were being unloaded and carried into the manor, with Olin leading the way.

At least thirty warriors milled about. Some talked, some watched their surroundings as if a threat might emerge at any moment, and others unpacked more trunks and sacks and tended to the horses. All of the warriors wore the black-edged blue uniform.

All of them wore weapons at their waists and across their backs.

"Skies," I breathed, knowing I could not move another step without all of them looking at me. Which would have been perfectly fine.

If I'd not been carrying a bloodstained cub I'd plucked from the forest.

I wondered where I might locate a side entrance. Then some warriors headed to the grandest carriage, and I caught sight of my betrothed for the first time in days.

My feet were moving before my brain could bleat at me to stop, the wolf almost forgotten until every pair of eyes felt like they were trying to burn a hole into my body. But it was too late to turn back nor care now.

Florian was not impressed.

Talking with one of his grumpy-looking warriors, he looked at me with a heat in his eyes that darkened to outrage when he spied the cub.

"His majesty returns." I smiled brightly. "Look what I found."

The fire-haired male Florian had been speaking with looked me over with a smirk, then took his leave with a bow to his king.

The king scowled at the tiny mound of white fur in my arms. His eyes narrowed on the blood covering the cub's leg. The wolf whimpered and seemed to recoil from his gaze.

I held her tighter and hushed her. "He won't hurt you."

When I looked back at the king, his features had flattened. But I didn't miss the way his lips twitched. "What makes you so sure?" His brow arched. "That is a wolf. A beast that has no place bleeding anywhere near my home."

"I know what she is, and she's just a babe who needs help."

"Put it back," Florian clipped in a tone that warned not to disobey him. "Messing with nature's way never serves well."

"And what if nature intended for me to happen upon her for this very reason?" I readjusted her weight in my arms. "I can help her, Florian." I nodded insistently. "I'll keep her in the stables. You won't even know she's here."

He glared, speaking through tight teeth. "You cannot keep a wolf with horses."

"I'm sure they won't mind, being that she's just a cub."

His clenched jaw shifted.

Sheepish, I grinned and spun to leave. "I'll see you later."

"Butterfly," he growled.

I hurried across the drive. The heavy stares of guards and warriors tracked my careful steps down the iced garden path surrounding the manor.

As tall as trees in the woods, the stables sat only half an acre behind Florian's giant fortress. It felt like a short eternity as I feared being followed and stopped.

Of course, the king was right. The horses were not happy.

Snickering and shifting echoed throughout the stalls when I entered the dark.

The stable hand jumped up from where he'd been taking a nap on bales of hay. A piece fell from his slack lips at the sight of me. "What in the skies—"

"Excuse me," I said and continued to the vacant stalls at the very end. They were not tended to, old hay and some excrement left to rot. I set the cub down and grabbed a rake.

The stable hand appeared. "I really cannot—"

"I'm in need of some horse blankets, please."

The tall and thin male blinked, scowling at me. Gripping his suspenders, he eyed me up and down with a sneer. "You're not leaving, are you?"

I smiled and offered my hand. "What is your name?"

He made a face at my hand, then stomped away in his knee-high boots to get me what I needed.

Florian was waiting on the side of my bed when I exited the bathing room after washing away the blood and muck.

Hands clasped between his knees, he rubbed his thumbs together. The darker bristle upon his face made me even more curious about what he'd been doing in his time away from the manor, if he'd been too busy to groom himself.

Admittedly, I rather liked it.

The cub, of whom I'd decided to call Snow for now, was tucked within a stall. Henron, the stable hand, had thankfully found a salve and a bandage for her wounds.

"Does it give you satisfaction?" I frowned, and he said, "To defy me?"

Wearing only a towel, I went to stand before the fire at the end of the bed to assist in drying my hair. Defying him had not been for the enjoyment of it, though I could not deny that it did please me to leave *him* wanting for once.

Before I could pass him, my hand was snatched. A shocked laugh escaped as he pulled me between his knees.

It died when his searing midnight eyes climbed my body to meet mine.

"Hello, Majesty."

His jaw ticked. "Florian."

"I'm afraid you've been gone too long for me to feel that familiar with you," I teased.

"I've had my tongue in your cunt and your drool on my neck," he said with far too much ease. He smirked when my eyes widened. "If that's not familiar, then please..." He clasped the back of my legs, hands slowly rising up my thighs, the towel taken with them. "Do tell me what is."

"You're awfully crude."

"Do not pretend to mind."

I raised a brow, but he was right. I didn't mind at all. "And I do not drool in my sleep."

His teeth flashed with a heart-thawing smile. "You do, and I've yet to wash my neck."

"That's..." My nose crinkled. "Rather unpleasant."

"What is unpleasant, butterfly, is your defiance." The towel was tugged to the floor, and I gasped as his hands roamed over my thighs and hips.

He stood, and in his absence, I'd almost forgotten his towering height and breath-robbing presence. His hands skimmed the curves of my breasts, one sliding my wet hair over my shoulder.

As the other hand wrapped around my throat.

Looming over me, he gently squeezed my neck and lowered his mouth to mine. "I should punish you for disobeying me."

I swallowed, unsure if I should be frightened or aroused. For I was an even mixture of both.

His finger pressed upon my screaming pulse. "Especially in front of my people."

I was tempted to ask what that punishment might entail, but when his lashes lifted with his eyes from my heaving breasts, the darkness within warned against it. Pheromones and his iced energy radiated in a vaporous heat, alluring and deadly.

It was on the tip of my tongue—an apology and a request for him to place that soft mouth on mine—when he dropped to his knees.

And pushed his mouth against my stomach with a low groan.

His heavier scruff tickled, coaxing a panted breath from me when he crouched lower. My thighs were gripped from behind. His fingertips bruised as he dug his nose and mouth into my core.

The sound that left him was animalistic.

I set my hands upon his shoulders, swaying slightly. "Florian..."

"Miss me, sweet creature?"

The desire to ask him where he'd been and why he'd left without warning—especially on what to do with his quiet home and ill-tempered staff—became a burn. But he'd chosen me to wed for a reason. He'd chosen me because I would be grateful enough for what he gave to let him be.

His teeth nipped my mound, and I yelped. He ordered, "Answer me."

"Yes," I confessed, then moaned when he kissed where he'd bitten.

His mouth dipped even lower, and after one lazy swipe through my core, he rose and licked his lips. His fingers brushed his mouth, but they failed to hide the pleased tilt when I reached for him and he evaded me.

It seemed this king I'd tied myself to enjoyed a little revenge.

He threw my earlier words back at me. "I'll see you later, butter-fly." Then he closed the door on his way out.

Once again, Florian did not attend dinner.

I was more relieved than disappointed. For the teasing he'd given me had left a tight coil of painful need, and I wasn't certain I was above apologizing for my defiance in order to have him remedy it.

I ate quickly, Olin glaring at me as I carried my plate from the dining room and down the hall. But I wasn't going to the kitchen.

I headed outside, passing the stunned guards patrolling the grounds, and toward the stables.

Henron was still packing up for the evening, his face smudged with dirt and a piece of hay in his mouth. It bobbed with his question. "You're going to feed the beast quail eggs?"

"And liver," I said, skirting around him and marching to the rear stalls.

He trailed me with a light laugh. "Do you truly intend to keep the wolf?"

"I intend to let her heal before releasing her back into the woods."

Henron returned to stacking hay bales as I greeted the cub who'd been sitting with her ears pricked, seemingly waiting for me.

Her rear wiggled as she approached the plate of food I set on the ground. She looked up at me, and at my nod, didn't hesitate a moment longer before mopping the porcelain clean.

Henron leaned over the stall door, tapping his knuckles on the wood. "She won't go, you know. Not now that you've altered her scent and given her a reason to stay." He eyed the wolf and scratched his long nose. "And you cannot domesticate a wolf." His apricot eyes conveyed what he knew I did not wish to hear.

She would need to be given a merciful death.

Florian's warning about messing with the way of things came back to me. I sighed, knowing he'd been right. I knew then, and I'd done it anyway. Regardless, I protested weakly, "She would have died."

Henron hummed. "Perhaps because she was supposed to, Princess."

My nose scrunched at the endearment. Before I could tell him not to call me such a thing, he disappeared, presumably to retire for the night.

Snow looked at me with eager eyes, wanting more to eat.

"In the morning," I promised and petted her soft head before checking her healing wounds.

Florian was in his rooms when I returned.

Like the rising of the sun minutes before the sky lightened, I could sense it—feel the energy reaching through the cracks in the stone of the manor.

I sat on the bed and stared down at the bedding, wondering if he would come to me while knowing he would not. Knowing that meant I should leave him alone.

It was hard to sleep when he was so close, rendering me lost to all the many reasons as to why he might not be interested in seeing me. Lost to wonderings of what he was doing, if he ever slept or merely lazed around in an arrogant kingly fashion, I kicked off the bedding as an unexpected sweat broke out across my flushing skin.

After breakfast, I was leaving the dining room when I felt the first ripple in my new and perhaps not-so-magical world.

A bellowed curse was followed by a crash.

Florian had a warrior pinned to the wall with his forearm at his throat. The golden vase from the hall table was now in endless pieces on the floor. "You know better than to have heart for those who had none for us. You will go back and fucking take it, understand me? There is no room for a pretty little conscience within this court."

The male started to protest, then shouted in pain as his cheeks changed from a ruddy red to blue. Ice crawled and crusted over his skin, cracking as Florian spoke. Cracking and peeling and tinkling to the floor with skin and blood.

I didn't hear what he said. All I heard was the ice hitting the ground with clinks that echoed.

My leftover breakfast—breakfast I'd intended to take to Snow—fell from my clammy and numb fingers to the floor.

I was staring at the remains of the vase, but all I could see was porcelain plates.

All I could hear was Rolina's voice. *If you didn't exist, then she would be here.*

Hands gripped my cheeks.

I flinched and stumbled free of Florian's hold.

He scowled, long fingers curling into his palms before falling slack at his sides.

The male he'd been furious with was gone. Not even Olin lurked in the hall. I looked at the ground, at the melting blood-tinged ice and broken vase, then to the oats and fruit.

My racing heart sank. "Snow's food."

"Snow?" Florian questioned.

"M-my wolf."

He stared at me for the longest time, as if unsure how to proceed. My chest was too tight. Air came and left me in short bursts.

My heartbeat was a drum I tried to ignore as I lowered to the ground and began to gather the broken porcelain and food.

Softly, Florian ordered, "Leave it be."

"She'll only get mad again."

"Snow?"

Realizing what I'd mumbled, I shook my head and drew in a deep breath. Perhaps the lack of sleep was to blame. My exhale hitched, the ringing in my ears decreasing.

Seemingly done with treading carefully, porcelain cracked beneath Florian's giant and polished boots as he crouched to the ground before me. He gently captured my hands and plucked and brushed the broken plate and food from them. "Look at me."

I lifted my eyes to his, and he swiped a tear I hadn't known had fallen to my cheek. His features lost their severity as he brought his damp thumb to his mouth and sucked. "She did this to you." It wasn't a question.

I frowned, about to ask who he spoke of.

He gave me a reproachful look that said not to bother lying. "The woman you were left with as a babe."

I swallowed and made to stand.

He stopped me with a hand at my chin. His eyes searched mine, and I said, "I'm fine."

His jaw rocked. "You flinched at my touch."

I tried to smile. It trembled as I said, "You are quite terrifying, Majesty."

He scowled again, though I didn't miss the spark of amusement, or perhaps something else, in his vivid gaze. "Go clean your hands." Taking my arm, he made me rise with him. "I'll arrange some proper food for this wolf you've stolen from fate."

"I didn't steal her," I protested. "Fate led me to her."

He brought my hand to his mouth with a lowering of his lashes and an inhale that loosened the stiff set of his shoulders.

Then he strode down the hall and left me forgetting why I'd ever been fearful at all.

TEN

I SAT IN THE ARMCHAIR WITHIN MY DRESSING CHAMBER FOR FAR longer than intended.

Perhaps it was the size of the room, which was more in line with what I was accustomed to, but I found comfort in the space. In the deep-blue, maroon, ivory, and crimson clothing that glinted and hung from wooden hangers.

I was no longer trapped within the middle lands.

No longer would I need to squeeze into a corner in the hope of going unnoticed to avoid someone's wrath. But lifelong insecurities and survival instincts were hard to escape, and I'd foolishly believed that crossing a warded veil with this king who wished to make me his wife would magically change everything.

Florian could clothe and shelter me and change my surroundings to suit his plans, but he couldn't change who I was.

Only I could.

Before I could be called for lunch, I decided to leave my preferred nightwear behind. I donned a dark-blue gown that fell to my feet in shimmering pleats, my coat, and a slim pair of black leather ankle boots.

Then I reached under the bed to the dusty corner that hid the gold coins I'd brought with me. I stared at them and tucked two within my coat pocket.

It was time to continue the hunt for what I needed.

Maybe then the life I'd left behind would not succeed at haunting me.

Florian's study was one of the first rooms in the hall adjoined to the entry foyer, and it would seem my quiet steps from the stairs weren't soft enough. He left whomever he'd been in discussion with. "Going somewhere, sweet creature?"

Though I'd been caught, I couldn't keep from smiling as I turned to him. "To the city."

He muttered something that sounded like, "Of course you fucking are," behind his hand. I frowned, but before I could ask why that was a problem, he said, "You cannot leave without a guard."

"What in the skies would I need a guard for?"

"Because I said so," he said, looking tempted to strangle something. Hopefully not me. He pinched the bridge of his nose. "And to keep you from finding trouble."

I scoffed and headed for the doors, although I longed to stay and study every inch of his powerful form wrapped in the fitted uniform of a warrior. "I'm an expert at avoiding that, don't you worry, Majesty."

"You've mothered a wolf." His hand seized mine. I squeaked in shock as he tugged me into his chest. He curled some of my untamable hair behind my ear. "You are my betrothed."

A fluttering erupted in my stomach at the reminder, at the sweltering wonderings of what that might eventually entail. "I am indeed." I clutched at the rough blue material of his royally decorated jacket.

His fingers traced the curve of my cheek. My eyes closed at the gentle touch. When he reached my chin, he tipped it high, and my eyes opened to deep blue. "You do not go anywhere without me or those I have assigned to escort you."

I blinked several times. I'd known he would not be impressed by my plan, but I hadn't realized it would be such an issue. "Surely that is un—"

"Hush." My brows rose, but I lost my annoyance when his lips squashed mine in an unyielding embrace. He was spearmint and whiskey, a spiced heat that forced my submission. I gladly surrendered, but then he tore away. "You're a thorn in my ass, butterfly."

I scowled. *He thought I was the thorn?*

As though I were wearing my thoughts, he smirked and walked to the stairs. "Just wait until tonight. I'll take you myself."

I had half a mind to say no and go without him.

"Leave, and I'll tie you to my bed to torture you for every minute you made me spend hunting you down." He paused before reaching the stairs, a look thrown over his shoulder that made my blood dance in my veins. "And sweet, I would love nothing more than to blemish your silken skin with my hands and teeth."

I stood there in shock, uncertain if I was worried or aroused.

Aroused, I determined as I looked at the doors with an almost unbearable desire to see just how long it would take him to find me.

We didn't materialize, and I was grateful.

I didn't want to miss the journey downhill into the city, no matter how dark and cold it had grown. Though it seemed I was not permitted to roam far either.

The king pulled me back with a look that said to wait as he rounded the carriage to talk with the driver.

I looked up at the night sky, the breeze a chilled kiss upon my cheeks. Smoke rose from chimneys toward the stars. The building beside me was slumbering, as were most others in the street.

I was led down an alleyway so narrow, my arms almost brushed the damp stone as I trailed the king to a door in the deep dark. He opened it, and I bumped against his coat-covered bulk in the tight space. "After you."

I looked through the door to the sconces glowing on either side of a steep set of stairs. "Where are we going?"

"Dinner." Noting my confusion, perhaps even my dismay, he asked dryly, "Problem?"

The right answer would be no.

The smart thing to do would be to smile sweetly and descend those stairs. But as I glanced down the alleyway to the awaiting carriage on the street, I couldn't ignore the twinge of disappointment.

I couldn't keep from answering honestly, "Actually, yes."

"You're not hungry?" Florian asked with puckered brows. "I know you didn't eat lunch."

Olin was a rotten tattletale.

Truth be told, my appetite was waning more and more each day. Likely due to a different hunger that was building with a near-painful impatience that stole my sleep each night.

But I didn't dare inform him of that. "I could eat," I said carefully, then, "but I wanted to visit the city for a reason, Florian."

I had hoped the use of his name would help lessen how much I was offending him by making him aware his efforts were not what I desired.

The king stared at me for a worrying moment. The frosted air around us began to bite. Finally, he blinked. "This is about your family."

I nodded.

He licked his lips, then sighed. "I do have news. We'll discuss it over dinner." Again, he gestured for me to enter the stairwell.

Gazing up at him, the light misting of dark hair that fell over one of his eyes, I struggled to keep from demanding that he tell me such news right this instant, for he should have certainly already told me. It was part of our agreement, and he was well aware of my desperation to discover all I could.

I reminded myself that it didn't matter how reverently he touched me—and how he made me wish he would touch me more—the male I was becoming grossly attracted to was still a king.

And I was to be nothing but grateful for what he deigned to provide me.

We climbed down to a surprisingly warm restaurant.

A female stood behind the bar made of glass, bottles of liquor aglow on the shelves behind her. Rounding the bar, she curtsied and brushed her hands upon her apron. "Florian," she said brightly.

I frowned at her casual address of him.

Florian smiled in a way I'd only seen a small number of times, real and warm. "Jessilba, thank you for accommodating us on such short notice."

"No need to thank us. It's always a pleasure." She gave me a curious once-over while tucking her golden hair behind her pointed ear, then said, "We've readied your table. This way."

We were escorted to a round metal table surrounded by circular booth seats. An entrée of some type of fish and a decanter of wine already awaited.

Florian made sure I was seated comfortably upon the rich brown velvet before settling opposite me. Jessilba waited, then reached for the wine. He stopped her. "I'll do it, thank you."

A dismissal, for the faerie smiled and dipped her head. "Your meals will be ready shortly."

I studied the rock-hewn walls adorned with brass sconces and gilded paintings of the sea. "What is this place?"

Florian sniffed the wine twice. "One of the best seafood restaurants in the city. A hidden gem, if you will. It was my father's favorite place to take us for many years." He poured a small glass, then lifted it to his nose to sniff again.

"Yet you believe they might poison you?"

"I believe nothing until it is proven," he said so flippantly, it made the slight ache in my head worsen. "And eons of history have proven it's wise to always be cautious, no matter how much any creature or place provides comfort."

Staring at the glass of golden wine he gently set before my empty plate, I wondered what had made him so rigidly cautious. He was a male of great power who ruled a kingdom of Folkyn. Perhaps it was because of his position that he felt he had to be.

I understood little regarding politics, nor had it ever interested me, but I did know that those in positions such as he did not keep them by being anything other than unapologetically ruthless.

"Comfort," I said, mulling over the word as I lifted the wine to my mouth. The king watched me take a small sip, his eyes upon my lips when I licked them. "I don't know if such a thing truly exists."

"It does," he said, his eyes rising to mine. "And it kills."

I held his gaze as those words blistered, questions turning through my mind. I was about to ask the most important one, regarding this news of my family, when he unbuttoned his coat collar and asked, "Is this your first time drinking wine?"

"No," I said, thinking back to the time I'd indulged my curiosity over Rolina's preferred method of escapism. "My guardian drank a lot. Sometimes, she'd fall asleep and leave some left over." My limbs tightened at the memory. "There wasn't enough left to fill half a glass, but she still noticed." I took another sip to give myself something to focus on—something to keep me from falling prey to another memory. "She was furious."

"She hurt you." The low words were not a question.

I still nodded, for he'd already guessed as much. I set the wine down and tucked my clammy hands within my skirts beneath the table. "Rolina preferred to escape me and her grief via toxins, but most of the time, it only made it worse."

"A rather gentle way of putting it," he remarked snidely.

"I suppose," I said, casting my eyes from his probing gaze to the tabletop.

He watched me for some time, a long finger circling the base of his glass. "And how did you escape?" he finally asked, so softly, it felt like a brush of his fingers over my bare flesh. "Books?"

I smiled, giving my eyes back to his. "Guilty."

His mouth curved, those endless dark blues unrelenting upon my every feature. So much so, I felt cold when they fell away and he served me a slice of the herbed fish. "Lemon?"

"Please," I said, slightly croaked.

I was tempted to remove my coat when he squeezed the fruit. Liquid poured from his iron grip, matching the flood of heat pooling low in my stomach.

I didn't need to meet his eyes to know he'd handed me a knowing look. The murdered slice of lemon was dropped cruelly to the side of the entrée dish.

"You are too pure of heart," Florian commented. "Considering."

I blinked. "Considering?"

"The woman abused you." Then, as if mystified, he asked, "How?"

Though he waited, I could find no answer for him. I picked up my cutlery and kept my eyes fastened to my plate as we ate in a silence that was anything but comfortable.

Mercifully, the tension was tamed by the arrival of a bushy-haired male.

He introduced himself to me with a wide smile and a ruddiness to his cheeks that met his brown eyes and made me instantly wish to trust him. "Don," he declared with a dramatic flourish of his hand as he bowed to both of us. "Welcome to a piece of my soul, beautiful lady."

The king looked at Don with his elbow on the table. His talented fingers skimmed his jaw, a smirk at his lips while the jovial male regaled me with tales of his beloved restaurant.

"... And my father was also a great fisher, but me?" He laughed, hearty and thick. "Oh no. The goddess cursed me with terrible seasickness." His eyes twinkled when I laughed. "Or did she bless me? For I have always been a master cook, my dear, never you doubt it."

"Father." Jessilba appeared behind him, wide-eyed and seeming almost concerned. She clasped his elbow, tugging. "Come along before you paint yourself a liar. The squid is done."

Don sputtered a myriad of colorful curses. Bowing with two jerks of his rotund form, he hurried back to his kitchen through a door beyond the bar.

I watched him go, feeling lighter from his presence.

That lightness bubbled when I found the king studying me, that smirk now matching the contemplative look in his eyes. "You have a musical laugh."

Unsure if that was a good thing, I only stared while my cheeks grew warm.

"Like birdsong beneath the rain," he murmured, almost as if to himself while lifting his glass of wine to his lips.

His throat dipped as he swallowed, and I imagined what it might feel like to run my tongue over his Adam's apple.

I hadn't realized I was still staring at his throat until a plate of squid was set before me. A glowing salad, drizzled with a sauce that smelled like nutmeg and ginger, was piled alongside it.

Florian sniffed and prodded at each dish until he was satisfied it was safe, uncaring if Don or his daughter watched from the kitchen.

While we ate, I thought of Snow and failed to hide the bite of panic in my voice when I asked, "Did someone feed the cub?"

Ever the refined king, Florian finished chewing while giving me an amused look.

He swallowed and dropped his gaze to his food. "I told you it would be taken care of." He cut into the squid, his eyes darker when they lifted to mine. "You do not trust me to keep my word?"

His question should have been answered with a confident and instant *yes*.

Instead, I said around a mouthful of food, "I trust you do not like that I disobeyed you and brought her to your stables."

I felt his stare like the burn of the sun while I focused on my meal. After a moment, he said, "You surprise me."

"I don't mean to offend."

"That's not what I mean."

Oh. I swallowed and gulped some wine, pondering what he did mean.

As we came close to finishing our meals, I then pondered how to broach the subject of the news he had yet to tell me.

As though feeling my itch to ask, the king's eyes rose from my plate to meet mine.

I was thankful my voice sounded more confident than I felt. "You said you have news regarding my family."

Again, Florian took his time chewing. He then set his cutlery down and dabbed at his mouth with a silver napkin. "They are not in my kingdom," is all he said.

My stomach sank with my heart.

I'd known there was a good chance anyone who shared my blood-line would not reside here in Hellebore. For if they did, then surely, the king would have sought them out upon first learning what I desired most from Faerie.

"Finish your meal, butterfly."

I'd eaten most of it, and I was now far more interested in the wine than anything else. "I've had enough to eat, Majesty," I murmured, and brought the glass to my mouth to drain it.

He watched me place it on the table, that familiar tic to his jaw. "Florian."

I should have smiled and said his name, as per what was growing usual, but I couldn't find it within me to care at that moment.

If my family wasn't here, then I would need to find a way to discover where they were. That, or I would need to travel to the other kingdoms of Folkyn—Oleander, Baneberry, and Aconite. Doing so would be no easy task, being that this king I'd agreed to marry said I was confined to his kingdom because he was in conflict with one of them.

We were settling into the carriage when I dared to finally ask him, "Which realm are you feuding with?"

Florian's gaze was bright with incredulity as it swept to me.

But I held it and said, "If I am to search for answers, then it would be helpful to know which kingdom I should avoid looking at first."

His shoulders sat tight and high, the name almost gritted. "Baneberry."

We lurched forward, and I stared at the clean and sharp lines of his profile as he stared at the closed driver window. He knew I watched him, yet he looked straight ahead and said nothing more.

He did not reach for me once during the short journey through the streets and up the mountain to the manor.

Something about his silence felt venomous, as though it were both a punishment and for my own good. I felt neither grateful nor remorseful. If anything, I grew more irritated and confused the longer this game of affection and rejection continued.

There was plenty Florian wasn't telling me. I knew that. I'd known it since I'd first pressed my mouth to his in that pleasure house. I just hadn't expected it to bother me this much—to eventually crawl under my skin and prod like a parasite that might kill.

I was merely insurance for his kingdom. I was to be his dutiful wife. I would likely be expected to provide him with an heir or two at some point, too.

But I was not permitted to truly know him.

Therefore, I was not supposed to ask him what this feud was about, nor why he seemed annoyed that I'd asked of it at all.

Left with no other options, unless I wished to return to Crustle and start anew with my quest to find the home I'd never had, I remained silent.

A familiar male with white-blond hair that stood in puffs reminiscent of the snow beneath the carriage's crunching wheels rushed to greet us. It was the same male who'd laughed in Florian's study after his king had kissed and dismissed me.

He wore a uniform that confirmed he was indeed a warrior, but the crest on his coat was different from the others I'd glimpsed. It was red, which I assumed signified his high rank.

A rank that allowed him to glare at the king impatiently as soon as he opened the door. As if he might pluck Florian from his seat to deliver him evidently urgent news.

The male looked at me with narrowed pale-blue eyes, his light-brown skin creasing as his lips curled a fraction.

I hadn't the time to decide whether it was a sneer or a smirk. Florian left the carriage and landed upon the pebbled drive in one shockingly graceful leap.

I climbed out with the help of the driver, who held my hand with a stiffness that conveyed he'd rather not touch me. Perhaps because I was betrothed to the king. I didn't care to analyze it when Florian barked at the blond male, "Fume."

The warrior, Fume, who'd been walking toward a wagon parked on the other side of the drive, backtracked.

Florian said something in his ear, the two of them similar in height. Then Fume crossed the drive to a small group of his awaiting brethren while I slowly made my way to the doors Florian and his ire had blocked.

A stupid question, yet I asked it anyway. "Is everything okay?"

Florian ripped his gaze from the wagon trundling from the drive. I peered over my shoulder, the frosted breeze lashing at my cheek.

Hands, bloodied and large, gripped the bars of the small oval window in the wagon's side, attempting to shake the grate free. A muffled bellow echoed in their wake.

"Go upstairs and get warm." An order, iced and final. The king disappeared with flurries that left a vapor where he'd stood.

I stared through the darkness for moments that numbed my fingers and cheeks until the sound of nearing steps broke my trance. A patrolling guard approached, and I retreated indoors before being told to.

Though I tried, I failed to forget the sight of those bloodied hands while I warmed up in the bathing pool. My mind in tangles and my gut twisting, I sat in a fluffy navy-blue robe before the fire until I heard Florian enter his rooms.

I was walking down the hall before I could talk myself out of it.

One of the doors had been left cracked open. I knocked and waited, tempted to peer inside my soon-to-be husband's private chambers.

"I've little time, butterfly," he warned from within. "I'll send for you tomorrow."

Dismissed without even opening the doors.

Annoyed and undeniably offended, I spun on my heel to return to my rooms. But that twisting in my stomach intensified.

I turned back and pushed the cracked door all the way open, letting myself in.

Then stopped at the sight of Florian's bare back.

Muscle twitched and shifted as he dropped a bloodstained shirt to the floor and then unbuckled his belt. "I told you—"

"What exactly does this feud with Baneberry mean?" I asked, done with being left to dwell in confusion. "I thought you were not yet at war."

"There are many facets to war besides battle, sweet creature." He dropped his belt, the leather hitting the stone with a resounding clank, and turned to face me. "And none are things I wish to speak of tonight."

"Or ever," I whispered, my eyes plastered to his chest—the scars and muscle and taut golden skin.

But it was the tattoo that stole my focus.

Such a thing was common within the middle lands, especially among humans, witches, and half breeds. It was rare to see them on a full-blooded faerie. Given the way we healed at a far faster rate than those with mortal blood, it would have taken countless sessions to become a permanent etching upon his body.

"You would do well to remember our agreement."

My eyes dropped, then reluctantly rose from his tapered torso with my resolve. "If I am to be your wife, I should at least know what issues this kingdom faces." I lifted my chin higher when his eyes darkened. "And why."

"Should you now?" Eyes clasped on mine, he reached down to unfasten his pants.

I would not let him deter me or shift my focus. I kept my gaze locked with his even as my blood burned with hungering interest while he kicked his trousers aside.

"Come to me."

I took a step forward, then stopped and scowled. "Florian, please."

His lips quirked. "Two words I've never loved hearing more." His expression hardened with his tone. "Come here, butterfly."

Knowing it was perhaps the only way I might get what I wanted, and that I wanted to surrender, I did. I crossed the long strip of plush night-blue carpet to stand mere inches from him.

An arm shot out to wrap around my waist. My breath fled when he pulled me to his body, and I was forced to place my hands on his bare and incredibly warm chest.

He tipped my chin, removing my eyes from the name written in the old language the Fae did not share with others upon his chest. It was forbidden to speak or teach it in Crustle. I knew little about it, but I knew just enough from my tireless research to understand what the ink said.

Lilitha.

"All I loved was taken from me." His thumb brushed my cheek, his eyes a never-ending darkness that stalked my flushed skin and parted lips. "My life irrevocably and unforgivably changed, and I've spent many years devising ways to rebalance the scales."

"Vengeance," I breathed.

Florian hummed. "I prefer to call it fair play."

That nearly made me smile. The scent of the bloodied clothing behind him on the floor stopped it. My lashes lowered to his chest. "Your sister?"

His silence was confirmation.

I wanted him to tell me what had happened to her, all the while accepting that the princess was no longer here was all I needed to know. "You've been punishing Baneberry," I guessed.

"I have been warning them of what's to come, yes."

Such few words, deliberately chosen for me to wonder over their every meaning. "You play games with me," I said, the tension between us growing taut. "But I am not one of your chess pieces."

His response drew my eyes to his. "I do not recall asking you to enter my chambers. In fact, I believe I advised against it."

"That is not what I meant." I swallowed the urge to apologize for my impatient tone. "Florian—"

His head lowered, the only warning I had before his mouth stole my own and erased what I'd been about to say.

He marched me backward to a bed twice the size of the giant one in my rooms. My legs hit the wooden frame, and I fell back onto the feather-filled bedding.

Florian loomed above me, dark hair and fever-bright eyes.

My heart swooped when he knocked my knees open with one of his, and his naked body dropped to press against mine. He groaned when his cock encountered bare skin beneath my robe, the flare of his eyes telling me he hadn't expected it. "Fuck."

He kissed me before I could find the strength to protest about what was surely going to happen.

Hot, wet, and toe-curling—his tongue and lips devoured mine with a hunger I'd yet to receive from him. Then he opened my robe and cursed at the sight of my breasts. My hands curled, lost in the thick gray bedding, as he gifted each breast the adoring heat of his mouth.

His hips rose, taking the heavy warmth of his cock that had nestled perfectly over my core and leaving me cold.

Until his finger slid through me and his mouth trailed a path over my stomach.

He stilled at what he found. "I see I have not been tending to your needs very well."

I could have certainly agreed, but he was not talking about my emotional turmoil.

"So fucking wet, sweet creature." He pushed my thighs wider, his mouth roaming lower to where I needed him.

Breaths growing panted, my back arched at the first slow swipe of his tongue over my swollen center. A groan vibrated against my slick and desperate flesh.

I knew what he was doing. I knew, yet all I could do was let him and admit, even if only to myself, I was weak and incapable of resisting him. Especially right now.

In my defense, he made it extremely difficult when the want that had indeed been awaiting his attention was finally given it. My body climbed higher with every lapping stroke of his tongue.

It seemed he was in a hurry this evening, as he didn't feast until I was clawing and mindless. Which only further proved he was attempting to placate me so he could return to whatever business I'd interrupted.

He flattened his tongue against my clit, and I ruptured so completely, I was still twisting on the bed with my thighs clamped together while he pulled on a clean pair of pants.

Beneath heavy eyelids, I watched him snatch a long-sleeved shirt from the leather chaise lounge in the corner and slip it on. He buttoned it as he leaned over me to pull the bedding atop my useless body.

He was still hard. The imprint of him pressed angrily to his pants.

What awaited him must have been important. That, or perhaps he found pleasure in depriving himself.

A kiss that warmed the cold he'd wrapped around my heart was given to my head. "Sleep, butterfly."

And after the doors to his rooms clicked shut, I almost did.

I blinked at the long oak dresser that sat nearest the doors. Then the matching slabs of shelving beside it that spanned the length of the wall to the chaise he seemed fond of tossing clothes upon.

There were no windows. Heavy drapes covered doors to a balcony stretching from the nightstand on the opposite side of the bed toward the open door of his bathing room, interrupted only by a fireplace.

He'd left me alone in his rooms.

So, of course, I decided it was only fair that I do some investigating.

Fair play, I believed he'd called it.

His bedchamber was the size of a small home. If a kitchenette had been tucked away behind the doors I opened and closed along the wall adjacent to my own rooms, then it very well could pass as one.

Florian's dressing room was riddled with those soft gaping shirts he preferred, and just as many pairs of tight-fitting black and charcoal trousers. Coats, some dark and spun with wool, others padded with built-in armor, lined the end of the chamber. In the center was an open unit of more oak shelving containing belts and boots—military and formal.

After checking his bathing room, my mouth falling open at the onyx tile-lined tub twice the size of my own, I checked the drawers and found...

Nothing.

Not a thing save for light clothing suited for spring or summer. Seasons that would not visit this kingdom.

A touch defeated, I sat on the side of his outrageously large bed and stared at the vines and thorns carved into the oak headboard.

An inkpot sat beside a golden candelabra on the nightstand. I leaned forward to clasp the brass knob of the top drawer. An empty pad of parchment was inside.

Next to a crown.

I almost laughed with shock, blinking down at the onyx vines and glinting diamond and sapphire leaves. Surely, I was not staring at the true Hellebore crown. But after seeing it in so many portraits within this manor, I knew I was.

Florian kept his crown in his nightstand drawer.

I shook the disbelief away and looked through the pad of parchment. I watched each bare page fall free of my fingers, then made to pull my hand from inside the drawer when a flash of silver behind the crown caught my eye.

A necklace.

Gently, I stroked the time-worn chain, the bright red stone that warmed under my touch, but I didn't dare pick it up.

With the odd exception of the crown, it was clear Florian wasn't so unwise as to keep anything of political importance in his personal chambers. In fact, aside from the necklace that appeared to be an heirloom, it seemed he kept hardly anything at all.

Nothing but clothing, books, ink, and empty pads of parchment.

I had little to no experience with socializing. Therefore, I didn't know what most might keep in their private quarters. Yet I knew there was nothing personal about my betrothed's rooms.

Perhaps he had hidden chambers elsewhere, filled with his secrets and desires and plans for vengeance. I nearly snorted because although there was so much I still didn't know, I knew right down to my bones that just wasn't so.

Either Florian Hellebore was as cold as the winter magic running through his veins, or he'd gone to great lengths to make sure no one would find anything that could ever be used against him.

There was no weakness when one held no heart.

"An engraved hairbrush still wouldn't hurt," I muttered to the necklace and carefully closed the drawer. "Skies, even a bookmark." *Something* to let me know this male contained a sliver of soul.

I looked down at his rumpled gray bedding, tempted to fall asleep in his scent and await his unpredictable return.

Annoyance danced with my growing doubt. Both feelings over-powered the temptation in his absence, and I returned to my rooms for another night of restless sleep.

ELEVEN

FLORIAN WASN'T AT BREAKFAST THE FOLLOWING MORNING. Considering the only meal he'd eaten with me had been in a hidden restaurant underground, I wasn't surprised, and I hadn't expected him.

Snow stood in thick piles, shoveled from the pebbled path encircling the manor by the groundskeepers. I smiled at the few who looked my way.

None smiled in return. They merely stared or glared. A burly male with cold-bitten cheeks even sneered.

I held the plate of raw beef that'd been delivered to the dining room with my breakfast tighter, unsure what I'd done to arouse such a lack of respect from almost everyone on this estate. It wasn't because they were Fae, who were known to be unwelcoming to outsiders, but perhaps because they knew I was from Crustle.

A place of which both lands of human and faerie despised.

Henron was in the paddocks with the horses. But I would have liked to think he would have waved in greeting had he seen me do the same to him.

Snow stirred awake from her nest of blankets in the corner of her stall, tail swishing. "Hello, my beautiful," I crooned, crouching to pet her chin.

She allowed it for a moment, then grew impatient for the meat to be set upon the ground. I watched her eat, marveling at how well her leg had already healed and how much she'd grown in just a handful of days.

Snow's ears pricked, her head rising. A low snarl peeled her lips back over tiny yet sharp teeth. "What is it?" I asked, and rose to look over the stall door.

She growled in earnest when I heard it—a faint hollering from outside.

I slipped out of the stall, the little wolf attempting to join me before I gently pushed her back inside and latched the door.

I followed the sound when I heard it again, taking the seldom used and rotting rear door of the stables into a small and abandoned field. I stood there a moment, looking at the greenhouse and the woods in the distance.

There was nothing but silence and branches, most bare and others laden with snow. It piled around tree trunks and drowned every dirt-worn pathway. So much so, I almost missed it.

A faded white hut, no bigger than an outhouse, stood just inside the tree line beyond the paddocks.

I peered around. But there was only Henron, whose back was to me as he worked with a giant and seemingly defiant black stallion.

Another shout echoed across the wintry landscape.

Henron didn't seem to hear. That, or he didn't care to know who was making such a noise.

Lifting my skirts high, I crossed the field. Snow neared the tops of my boots and threatened to pull them from my feet. The shouting increased in volume, and I pushed forward to discover the hut was not an outhouse.

It was an entry point. The door opened to crumbling dirt steps that led to some type of cellar hidden deep below ground.

"Back already, huh?" a voice called.

This close, the harsh echo startled. I raced back up the few stairs I'd descended and paused outside, my heart racing.

No one followed. Feeling my heart slow beneath my palm, my eyes fell to the lantern upon the ground by the door I'd left open.

I grabbed it and flicked the glass. Glowbeetles awoke, casting the soil stairwell in a golden gloom when I walked back inside.

"Who's there?" The voice came again. A male's voice, hoarse from yelling. "I'll peel your skin from your flesh, I will. Just try to fucking touch me again."

My nose wrinkled, and I knew I should simply leave.

But whoever was down there couldn't hurt me, or he would have already. He was stuck. Perhaps bound. Remembering the bloodstained hands in the wagon window, my curiosity and desire to find out what Florian was up to got the better of me.

Halfway down the stairs, I slipped on the flowing skirts of my crimson gown. Dirt crumbled beneath my feet. I smacked a hand against the wall to steady myself. When the male muttered something that sounded like, "Mother, save me," I seized my skirts and finished descending into the dark.

It was not an outhouse or a cellar.

It was a dungeon.

Iron cells, three on each side, lined the metal and soil constructed space.

"Skies," the prisoner whispered. "It can't be."

He stood in the first cage to my left. One of his eyes was so badly beaten, it was black and swollen shut. He lurched forward to grip the bars with those same hands I'd glimpsed yesterday, hissing as the iron burned his skin.

He released the bars and blinked. "It's you, isn't it? He found you after all."

"Who?" I asked, only to be met with a heavy furrow of his soiled brows. "I'm not sure what you mean."

His frown intensified. "Tullia." Then he cursed and stepped back to bow deeply. "Forgive me, Princess. The manners were obviously beaten out of me upon being found in this damned kingdom."

Princess?

I laughed nervously while retreating a step. "I fear you are mistaken. I am to be queen, yes, but I am not a princess."

"No." The male straightened and tilted his head, studying me a moment. "No," he said again, squinting with his other bruised yet functioning green eye. "It *is* you. You have her hair and his majesty's eyes." He shrugged. "A little soulless, if you don't mind me saying so, but the same nonetheless."

Fear and unease slithered through my chest, hitching my breath and my voice. "Who?" I said, dizzied, then sharper, "Tell me who you are."

"I am Frensroth, Princess. One of many who've been sent to retrieve you."

I stumbled back into the iron bars of the cell behind me.

Frensroth's bruised eye tracked me, a look of contemplation pulling at his split lips.

I barely felt the burn of the iron, numb to my toes, but I straightened when Frensroth said, "Smoldering skies, you do not even know who you are, do you?" A shocked laugh made him cough. He spat a glob of blood to the dirt while I grappled for my next breath. "Not your fault. That king is a cold and crafty beast indeed."

I squeezed the rusted handle of the lantern. "I am a changeling." It was all I could seem to mutter, and so low I was surprised he heard me. "A changeling from the middle lands."

Another choked laugh before his features settled grimly. "Not anymore. Listen..." He looked at the sunlight sprinkling down the stairs into the darkness, then back to me. "You are a princess of Baneberry, and you are being used—" His eye flared wide.

Then dropped to the dagger embedded in his chest.

I didn't need to look to know who stood at the bottom of the stairs. His presence cloaked like the energy before a storm.

I stared at the blood spreading over Frensroth's stained tunic, my heart still and each heaved breath shorter than the last.

The lantern fell from my slack hand to the dirt.

Frensroth stumbled and gripped the blade as though he'd pull it from his heart. Between gritted teeth, he rasped, "You are a plague upon this land, Florian, just as your sister was—" A dagger to his eye ended his frantic words.

And his life.

I screamed, but no sound was made as the prisoner crumpled to the ground. My knees quaked with my stomach.

Florian didn't move.

The damp dungeon became suffocating as the walls closed in. I couldn't draw enough breath as blood pooled beneath Frensroth's body and seeped into the next cell.

You are a princess of Baneberry.

It couldn't be true, yet...

Like a well-crafted poison that was now spreading to kill, everything locked into place.

The king's interest in me. The order not to meet with anyone but him during his visits to the Lair of Lust. The contract I could never hope to escape. The careful silence of this estate and the unkind looks cast my way.

Florian's maddeningly inconsistent fascination with me. The restraint when he would finally surrender and touch me.

I tore my eyes from the blood and looked at the male watching me with unreadable features. "Why?" I croaked, though asking such a thing was futile when I already knew. When he'd already told me.

You've been punishing Baneberry.

I have been warning them of what's to come, yes.

Florian merely stepped back and gestured for me to walk ahead of him up the stairs.

I didn't move. "I asked you a question."

"Without enough context for me to answer," he said coldly, then took two slow steps closer. "Why did I want you? Well," his tone softened, "I think you've discovered the answer to that already."

I tripped back, almost meeting the iron bars of the cell behind me again.

"Why did I kill him?" A smirk brightened his eyes. "That is obvious." His gaze dropped to my heaving chest, his brows lowering. "Regardless, he surrendered his life the moment he found the audacity to step foot in my kingdom with the intention of taking you from me."

"He was trying to save me." Sweat gathered across my nape, the narrow dungeon closing in further. I swallowed and whispered, "From you."

Florian smiled at that, beautiful and cruel. His eyes darkened upon my own. "Do you believe you are in need of saving, butterfly?"

"Don't call me that."

"The name Tullia derives from a species of butterfly." He closed the space between us, his scent venomous and his giant form blocking all light. Taking a lock of my hair, he studied it thoughtfully within his palm. "Did you know that, sweet creature?"

My stomach churned. His words confirmed.

His thumb stroked the curled strands.

While I'd been recklessly desperate for mere scraps of information, he'd known exactly who I was all along.

A princess.

"My parents." It was all I could manage to say, to think.

"Who rules Baneberry, Tullia?" He dropped my hair and tilted his head, awaiting a response I didn't want to give. "Surely, you know that much from your beloved books."

One didn't need books to know the names of Folkyn monarchs, but the barb stung all the same.

Baneberry was ruled by a king. And only a king.

The name was barely a sound. "King Molkan."

Whoever my mother was, perhaps she was not a part of Baneberry's court. I asked anyway, ignoring all he'd done in yet another moment of desperation. "My mother?"

"Queen Corina is long dead, butterfly." The words were flat, emotionless.

My eyes closed. "How long?"

Iced fingers caressed my cheek. "Shortly after your birth."

I flinched. Not only from his touch and what he'd said, but because I was trapped. I couldn't move. The iron bars warned in warmth behind me, and he was too close to escape unscathed.

Trepidation made the words a whisper. "Why am I here, Florian?"

"You know why, Tullia."

A name. *My* name.

After all these years of wondering if I would never have one, I now knew what it was. I knew, yet part of me wished I didn't. It was another weapon in this calculated king's arsenal. Hatred bubbled, erasing the sickness tightening my innards into knots and squeezing my heart in a vise.

Though I couldn't decide who I hated more—the king or myself.

I'd walked right into this spiderweb, willingly and so perilously desperate. I'd handed him my every desire without once digging deep enough to discover why he would want to know them. Without pushing harder for answers as to why he wanted me.

For it had sat there since my arrival in this ice-cold realm, a bone-deep knowing that something wasn't right. That things were not as they seemed.

His fingertip reached my lips.

I pushed it away and opened my eyes to glare up at him. They were damp, but I refused to let a single tear fall. "Why am I here, Florian?" I didn't need to know. I needed him to say it.

He feigned a pout. "No more majesty?"

"Why am I here, Florian?" I nearly growled.

He sighed as though answering the redundant question was beneath him. "You are here because your father owes me and my kingdom a debt he can never repay."

"He killed your sister," I guessed, and accurately, judging by the way his jaw hardened and he stepped back. "He killed Lilitha, so you plan to kill me."

"And yet..." His mouth curved. "You breathe, butterfly."

If he didn't intend to kill me, then Frensroth was right. He was using me.

"You're using me as a weapon in this game of fair play." I swallowed thickly, loathing the hurt I couldn't keep from my voice. "I wished only to know who my family was, and now you are using me against them?"

His brow arched. "Your father stole everything from us, Tullia.

Everything. He did so without hesitation and without remorse. Then he had the gall to hide you when your mother died, believing I would harm a babe."

Absorbing that, I said nothing. Couldn't have if I'd tried.

He licked his teeth behind closed lips. "I will destroy him by any means possible, but I would never do that. That he thought I would..." He let those words hang there. "Well, that tells you all you need to know about this precious father you've always wished for."

With that, Florian turned for the stairs. His dark coat kicked up wisps of snow behind him.

I didn't follow. I looked back at the cell containing a dead faerie. Questions and unease kept my feet stuck.

Frensroth had come for me. He'd said others had as well.

Which meant despite whatever my murderous betrothed had said, the Baneberry king cared. Enough to want me away from the male intent on ruining him.

Florian waited at the tree line, in quiet conversation with two of his warriors.

I didn't know what to do. All I knew was that I couldn't stay here. I couldn't stay, but I also couldn't leave. I'd made a blood vow, and I was bound to it unless we both agreed to break it.

Florian would not release me. I was the blade that would make his enemy bleed even more. I wasn't going anywhere.

That didn't mean I couldn't try.

I ignored him when he called for me. Seconds later, I felt him advancing at my back. I broke into a run, tripping through the snow in my haste to get away—from him and the image of Frensroth's battered face as the winter king's dagger had sunk so easily into his chest.

Florian's calm threat stalked me. "Run, Princess. Waste your time and harden my cock some more."

Florian didn't knock.

He entered my rooms as soon as the sun had set. He eyed the

coins I'd been fishing out from beneath the bed. "You won't get far with those, butterfly."

I'd spent hours trying to devise a plan of escape. I would rather live in the middle lands than be used as a pawn in his sickening game of vengeance. Of course, he would easily find me. The only way I would evade his plans for me was to reach Baneberry.

I couldn't materialize over such a great distance without risk of the energy rifts tearing me apart. But that didn't matter. I'd foolishly found my way to Folkyn. Somehow, I would find a way to the realm of Baneberry.

I left the coins and rose from the floor. "What do you want?"

"So many things." He closed the door and leaned back against it with his hands in his pockets, and that quiet snick was a bolt of thunder that caused my heart to jump. "Right now, I'll settle for hearing what you're concocting in that whimsical mind of yours."

"If you believe I'd dare share any part of me with you again, you're as delusional as you are cold."

He blinked but otherwise remained aloof with a dash of curiosity as he watched me wring my hands in my robe. "You're afraid of me."

I hated that he could scent as much, and the slight tremble within my voice. "You've just murdered someone, and you..." It felt bizarre to think, let alone say. "You've been attacking my kingdom."

"*Your* kingdom?" He tilted his head. "How sweet."

I ignored that, and how ridiculous it was to call Baneberry as such. Though it was indeed the stunning truth. "You intend to kill him," I said, and he knew I spoke of the male who'd sired me. "Before I even lay eyes on him."

He smirked. "Only after I'm done picking at every piece of his flesh, so you never know." He lifted his shoulder. "You just might catch a glimpse."

My heart sank.

The attacks he'd been ordering. The red wax upon the maps in his study. The wagons he kept receiving...

Me. He would destroy me.

"And that involves marrying the heir he went to great lengths to hide from you?" His silence was answer enough. He fully intended to humiliate us both, and it was working. "You're repulsive."

"Interesting," he said, grinning in a way I'd never seen before. It reached his eyes and brightened them to a dawn-touched sky. "For I'll wager I can still make you come undone within seconds, Princess."

"Do *not* call me that."

"But that is what you are, and now, what you are is mine to do with as I see fit." He closed the space between us until he'd backed me against the wall and clasped my cheek. "You are mine, Tullia. In time, you will learn to accept that as I have."

"I won't," I seethed, my eyes making the mistake of crashing into his. Endless blue threatened to hold me underwater until all breath left my lungs. My rage and fear dulled, but the ache it left me with would not. "You lied to me, Florian."

"Don't take it so personally," he whispered, brushing his nose over my cheek. "I will do whatever it takes to get what I want."

"I hate you," I rasped.

He tensed, then his hand slid down to my throat.

My heart kicked when he gently squeezed. I still said it again, hoping it wounded him—even if it was just a scratch compared to what he'd done and would likely continue to do to me. "I loathe you."

His mouth hovered over mine, our lips grazing with every low word that left his lying, manipulative mouth. "Hate me all you like, butterfly." His grip on my throat loosened, his thumb stroking my thumping pulse. "It changes nothing."

"It changes everything."

His eyes sparked. "You still hunger for me, and that is all I need from you."

"And to parade me at your side like a pet you keep only to punish those you despise."

His lips spread into a smile against my cheek. "You do not suffer, Princess."

Then his mouth stole mine.

I sank my teeth into his lip, and he snarled softly. This male was pure poison. Yet I licked his blood from my lips like it was an elixir.

His eyes were on my mouth. His teeth flashed as he rubbed my throat before releasing me. "Climb into bed like a good little pet. I'll return to tend to you when I finish carving Frensroth into bite-sized pieces for his return to your father."

Bile rose up my throat at the image he'd gruesomely painted.

He was stalking through the door when I said in an unintentional whisper, "Find another body to defile. I want no more of you."

His fingers gripped the doorframe, the wood creaking. "Ordering me to humiliate you further, my daring creature?" His eyes gleamed a depthless blue over his shoulder. "I highly advise against such foolishness."

The door slammed.

I sank down the wall with my hands in my hair, terrified, ashamed, and longing for the home I'd been so skies-damned determined to escape.

TWELVE

A GUARD WAS STANDING OUTSIDE OF MY ROOMS.
I didn't need to ask to know she'd been standing there
all night. She eyed me up and down with a smirk, her perfect features freckle-dusted and her dark hair trapped in a thick braid.

I was still in my robe, and I had no intention of remedying that
as I stalked down the hall. The sun was almost due to rise when I'd finally found sleep. After dreaming of flying blades and pools of blood
and unfeeling kings, it hadn't lasted long. I'd woken with a pounding
head and heart with the birds, and in a cold sweat.

The guard followed me, of course.

Olin waited beneath the stairs with that perfect posture and his
pointed chin in the air. Rather than bid him good morning as I'd done
every day prior, a greeting he'd never deigned to return, I said, "I know
why you detest me now."

The steward blinked and arched a brow. "Oh?"

I narrowed my eyes. "And I'll have you know that I find your un-
fair judgment almost as disgusting as your king."

I left him gaping after me and entered the dining room.

The guard stood by the doors in silence while I ate with my fingers, my teeth ripping into a strip of pork. "Olin detests most things
with a heartbeat, Princess, and I must advise against slandering the
king."

Shocked she'd spoken to me, I looked from the crackling fire to
her light-brown eyes. "Are you to follow me everywhere I go?"

The guard gave me a bland look. "Yes."

I dropped the pork to my plate. "What is your name?"

"Zayla."

"Pretty," I said absently. Then I knocked the plate of food toward her and rose to collect Snow's breakfast from the hutch. "You'd better eat, then."

"I've already eaten."

Of course, she had.

Zayla followed me outside into the gray morning. The wind tangled my untouched hair and whipped it over my cheeks. "Where are you going, Princess?"

"To feed my wolf."

"A blizzard nears."

I cared nothing for blizzards when I'd been swept into a storm I might never survive. "Then we'd better hurry."

In nothing but knee-high boots and my robe, I stomped through the ever-growing snow upon the grass to the stables. All the horses were in their stalls, Henron busy catering to their annoyance at being cooped up.

He laughed lightly as I passed. "Didn't feel like dressing in one of your evening gowns today, Princess?"

That word again—from him. I'd ignored it the first time. There was no ignoring it now.

Most would be delighted to discover they were a long-lost princess, including my stupid past self. Now, I couldn't think of anything worse.

"Shut your trap, Henron."

The stable hand whistled. "Never thought I'd live to see the day you were grumpy."

Zayla muttered something that sounded like, "Lucky me."

The two of them talked quietly while I tended to Snow and tried to calm down. But not even her soft fur or dark and inquisitive eyes could help settle me. My anger and self-loathing worsened with the weather that lashed at the wooden walls around us.

Snow shivered, and I withdrew my hand from her velvet ear as an idea came.

Once she was done eating, I picked her up and carried her back through the stables.

Henron's eyes bulged, a piece of hay falling from his mouth. "Where are you taking the wolf?"

"Out of the cold."

He cursed colorfully at my back, while Zayla raced after me. "I urge you to reconsider, Princess."

My hair flew in front of my face, making it hard to see. "Would you like to sleep in the stables in this weather?"

"If I were a wolf, yes," she said, almost pleadingly. "Much better than the woods."

I ignored her and tucked Snow's head to my chest when a giant branch fell in our path. Zayla grabbed my arm, but I didn't want her assistance. I pulled free and stepped around it.

She apologized, then tried to reason with me again. "Please, this isn't wise. The king will be furious."

I only smiled and thought, *exactly*.

I left Snow in my rooms and headed to the kitchen.

My nape prickled with awareness as I hurried past the king's study. He was in there. Hopefully wondering what I was up to.

I'd keep him wondering for the rest of his days if he insisted on keeping me. I had no doubt he'd already been informed of the cub in my chambers. I hoped his skin itched with irritation.

Zayla followed, but she stood atop the stairs, apparently confident I wouldn't flee from Florian via the underground rooms.

Approaching the island bench, I eyed the door shielding the set of stairs leading outside. Using it to escape would be impossible, especially with three males nearby and guards patrolling the grounds. I knew my chances of escaping at all were slim, and I was growing more and more certain that I would never see Baneberry.

Knowing didn't help—that surrender was my only option. I'd been backed into a corner and my hackles were raised.

I might have been a pet, but that didn't mean I would behave.

Kreed and his sons finally noticed my entrance over their laughter and chatter and the clang of pots and utensils when I cleared my throat.

They all turned at once. One of the twins blinked furiously.

Kreed wiped his hands on a towel and inclined his head in greeting. "Is there something you need?"

"A tunnel to Baneberry," I quipped before I could help myself.

Kreed's gaze darkened, his mouth tightening.

I leaned against the island. "You all knew, didn't you? You knew exactly what he intended for me."

The gurgling stew on the stove was the only sound.

I bit the inside of my cheek, then said, "I need a bowl of water, please."

One of the twins asked, "What in the skies for?"

His brother elbowed him.

"To lap at like a good little pet," I said coldly, shocking them and myself. I licked my teeth and sighed. "For the wolf in my rooms."

Kreed watched me while one of his sons resumed chopping an onion. The other dug inside the cupboard in the corner of the kitchen for what I needed. The cook's gaze burned, almost as if he wished to say something.

I refrained from telling him to spit it out already and averted my gaze to the tea tray at the end of the bench, ready and waiting to be taken upstairs.

Finally, Kreed said, "A wolf cannot be domesticated, Princess."

"Neither can females who've been tricked into marriage, yet here I am..." I forced a smile. "Stuck here doing whatever the king wishes."

Kreed leaned back against the sink. "You've only just discovered where you were born."

I nodded, staring down at the toes of my damp boots.

"Let the shock wear off before you make hasty decisions," he suggested quietly, then he stalked toward the door that would take him outside.

I looked back at the silver tray, Kreed's words unable to settle rationally. Especially when I realized the twins had curiously disappeared, too—leaving me alone with a tea tray headed for the king.

The sea salt sat by the stove beside me, the lid open and tempting. I scooped three spoonfuls into the teapot. Then I wiped the teaspoon on my robe and set it back beside the saucer.

The twins returned from a small room I couldn't see from where I stood, laughing. One grabbed the tea tray and took the stairs to the first floor of the manor.

The other handed me a bowl large enough to wash a babe in. "I'm Thistle." He pointed at a small cluster of freckles beside his right eye. "These tend to help people remember." I nodded and took the bowl. He glanced at it with a crooked smirk. "Thought you might need a big one, being that wolves don't stay small for long."

Apprehension threatened to make me reconsider allowing Snow indoors. I ignored his growing smile when I thanked him curtly, and returned to the first floor.

Zayla straightened from the wall that faced the stairwell. Her eyes narrowed on the slight smile that touched my lips as we heard the king curse viciously from down the hall.

"Olin, what in the rotten fucking skies is wrong with this tea?"

I chomped down on my lips.

Zayla asked with a rough whisper once we'd climbed the grand staircase, "You did that, didn't you?"

"Did what?" I asked, and in a dull tone that told her yes, I did—and no, I didn't care if she tattled on me.

"Tullia," she warned. "You mustn't toy with him. He might be fair, but he's also..." Looking at the doors of the king's rooms, she said softly, "Without heart."

"Oh, I'm well aware." I smiled, and felt it was at least a little bit earnest, as I met her eyes outside of my rooms. "Thank you for trying to warn me, though."

I closed the door on her worried expression, Snow rising from where she'd made herself comfortable on my bed. She entered the bathing room when I filled the bowl and set it down upon the stone.

I watched her drink, tempted to smack myself upon belatedly realizing I would need to take her outside numerous times a day until
she learned not to pee in my rooms.

A small price to pay for the only company I could trust.

Yet again, the king entered without knocking.

The slamming of the door should have warned me to be cautious.

It would seem the shock, and every other nasty feeling that
came with it, hadn't calmed enough for me to even consider mind-
ing my words. "It's rude to enter someone's private quarters without
permission."

Florian eyed where Snow was sleeping on the crimson carpet
before the fire, his jaw firm with displeasure. "So is putting salt in
someone's tea."

Snow only stirred in her sleep. Apparently not at all concerned
about the intruder who had entered our domain.

"Oh?" I hid behind the book in my hand. His boots, these ones
sharp-toed and crafted from what appeared to be reptile skin, were
only half blocked by it. "Whoever did that is rude indeed."

He hummed. "You are playing a dangerous game, *pet*."

The word pet singed like iron against my ears. But I turned the
page, saying airily, "I have no idea what you're talking about."

The book was snatched from my fingers.

Florian inspected the title, muttering, "*Romancing the Tyrant*,"
and tossed the rather fitting and steamy novel I'd just begun to enjoy
to the floor.

I straightened and gasped in outrage, but it was cut short when
the king stood over me and wrapped my loose braid around his fist.
He yanked my head back, his words a flame to kindling at my exposed
neck. "Do you think enraging me will benefit you?"

"Yes," I said, my heart beating hard. "For it makes me feel..." I
turned my head slightly, the words light and breathless at his bristled
jaw. "*So* much better."

He snarled. The sound rippled from his throat and coated my skin in gooseflesh. "Give me one good reason why I shouldn't fuck the insolence out of you."

I couldn't have stopped myself even if I'd imagined a million Frensroth's dead in a dungeon within the woods. I licked the bristle over his jawline, and whispered, "Because I'd enjoy it."

I was forced to my feet by the hand in my hair, pain smarting at my scalp when I was too stubborn to comply.

It mixed with a pleasure so complete when the king reached under my robe and between my thighs. They parted in permission— enough for his fingers to discover just how thoroughly my body liked to betray my mind.

"You speak true," he said, thick and perhaps even a touch shocked.

My head was then tilted for his mouth to brand the skin at the curve of my neck with a hard suck from his lips and a kiss of teeth. "You loathe me, yet your body melts from my presence."

I had nothing to say to that. Nothing wise, anyway. "The book I was reading before you so rudely interrupted was getting very..." I swallowed when he brought my arousal to my clit and circled. "Interesting."

My stomach tightened, and my thighs shook. I gripped his arms, my nails digging into the muscle beneath his thin shirt.

"If I find you've made yourself come without my assistance, I'll remove them all from the manor."

Surely, he couldn't be serious.

He pressed hard upon my clit, and I both flinched and moaned. Breathing heavier than I'd have liked, I asked, incredulous, "You're jealous of a *book?*"

His teeth sank into my neck, breaking the skin. The sharp bite of pain made me weakly attempt to push him away. "No one makes you squirm but me." He licked at the punctures he'd made.

The mere thought of him feeding from me, no matter how small an amount, both thrilled and enraged. "Don't you dare feed from me."

"Sweetest fucking creature..." His tongue flattened to my thudding pulse, then trailed up my throat. His hold on my hair loosened. His mouth fell over mine. The copper taste of my blood turned my heart over in my chest. "There will come a time when you'll plead for me to."

I wouldn't let him do that to me. Ever. "You've taken enough from me, wouldn't you agree?"

Florian reared back to meet my eyes and searched them. "I've not taken nearly half as much as I wish to, butterfly." Then his finger slid inside my body, and scalding pain lanced through me as it met resistance.

As it met the barrier he'd referred to.

He withdrew and spread my arousal again. Sparks of pleasure ignited—making me forget the pain, the lies, and every reason I shouldn't want more. My thighs shook harder, and I knew it wouldn't take much more for him to make me fall apart over nothing but his touch once again.

Then he stepped back, his eyes on mine as he placed his finger in his mouth and sucked. Unbalanced, I fell to the edge of the bed.

He groaned and stalked to the door. "Good night, *pet.*"

THIRTEEN

ANOTHER ENTOURAGE ARRIVED AT DAWN.

These wagons appeared to be filled with rice and grain and various other treasures I now knew were from Baneberry.

"Will he have the stolen goods disposed of?" I asked Kreed when I went to fetch my breakfast. "Or will he at least make sure they're not wasted?"

I was no longer interested in eating in the dining room—in pretending that this nightmare was the magical world I'd naively thought it to be.

Kreed did not protest when I grabbed the sugar-and-banana-dusted oats from my breakfast tray and sat on a rickety stool by the door to eat. But he did pause in slicing vegetables as he said carefully, "We live in endless winter, Princess. We waste nothing unless it has been contaminated."

"Poisoned, you mean?" I questioned. "How can you tell?"

"It's thoroughly inspected by those the king trusts with the sense for such things before we use any of it."

The sense for such things.

Briefly, I wondered what other types of magic the Fae of Hellebore possessed that I hadn't known, and if detecting poisons was something all of us could learn how to do. "And if it is poisoned?"

"Then it's dumped over the border into Baneberry with the severed heads of whom were involved."

The oats became glue in my throat. I coughed and forced them down. "They can sense that too?"

Kreed's voice held a notch of unmistakable pride when he smiled at me over his shoulder and said, "All of us have the ability to hunt, Princess. Some just more so than others."

He resumed chopping, and I stared at his broad back. "So Florian has been doing this for a long time." He didn't need to confirm as much. The weight that now sat in my heart ached. "Years of stealing from a land that is not his."

Kreed's tone hardened with his next words. "I do not meddle in the king's business, and he doesn't meddle in mine. Some things are better left alone."

"But you are his cook."

"Exactly. He trusts me as much as he can trust anyone."

Interesting. I knocked a piece of banana around in my bowl with my spoon. "How long have you served the Hellebore family?"

"A few decades now," he said.

Which meant he might've also served Florian's father. Perhaps his sister.

That weight became heavier.

Kreed added, "Though they were too little to be of much use, the king allowed my sons to stay and work here when their mother passed on five years ago."

This cook had the king's favor indeed.

"I'm sorry for your loss," I said, although it seemed as if he'd been estranged from their mother.

He nodded once but said nothing else.

I ate some more, mulling over all he'd said for a minute. "Why take Baneberry's food and valuables?"

Kreed swiped carrots out of the way and snatched a potato with a sigh. "Their king has committed egregious wrongs."

"My father," I said, the words so mystically foreign they evoked a slight flutter in my chest. Regardless of what he'd supposedly done.

Kreed huffed, but said, "He seldom tries to stop us, and he'll continue to lose the respect of his people by failing to engage with Florian besides that of defense."

I frowned. "But why wouldn't he engage?"

"Because he knows he won't win, and no king nor queen of faerie wishes to be humiliated in such a way. Pride, of course."

So Florian intended to force my father's hand. For if picking at every thread to King Molkan's pride, including wedding me, failed to encourage his surrender or retaliation, then Florian planned to do as he'd told me.

He would march upon Baneberry. He would take everything.

This soon-to-be husband of mine was growing more and more monstrous by the hour.

I kept those thoughts to myself, knowing to voice them would be futile.

Apparently, my stewing silence spoke volumes. Kreed turned and crossed his giant arms over his chest. Abundantly blessed with handsome features and muscle that pushed at the blue stitching of his tunic sleeves, he was not what I would expect to find hiding underground and cooking for a royal household.

"You hate him," he stated.

I almost laughed. "Whatever do you mean?"

His lips twitched. "Just..." He scratched at his clean-shaven cheek. "Be mindful of where you stomp." A look cast to the stairs beside me had me setting the spoon in my bowl. Kreed gave his brown gaze back to me. "A creature who has lost everything fears nothing, Princess."

I refrained from wincing—at what he'd said about Florian and the ill-fitting title.

"Please don't call me that." Not only did it not sit right, but it reminded me of what I was to Florian. Another toy in this game he played with my father.

Kreed frowned. "You truly knew nothing about yourself?"

"Nothing." I hopped down from the stool and scraped my leftovers into the compost. "And after wasting all these years wanting answers, I should have just left it that way."

The twins barreled down the stairs as I set my bowl by the sink. Olin followed, muttering words I didn't catch at their backs.

The steward glared at Kreed with a flaring of his nostrils. "Your spawn were annoying the newest and youngest member of our staff."

Kreed hid a smirk behind his hand as he rubbed his mouth. He crossed the room and waved Thistle and Arryn on. "Get washed up and start on lunch." He then looked at Olin and asked, "Annoying?"

"The poor thing was red in the face and hiding behind the mountain of bedding she was attempting to take to the washrooms."

Kreed snorted. "I see."

Olin shifted his weight to his other foot, his attention unmoving from the cook.

Tension warmed the already stuffy kitchen, and though Olin hadn't so much as glanced my way, I had a growing feeling that I should quietly excuse myself.

I smiled my thanks at Kreed, then climbed the steps right as Olin hissed, "You're conversing with the swine's daughter?"

"She's hardly his daughter when she's never even met the asshole, Ol."

"That doesn't make what she is any less real."

Kreed cursed. "She's young, harmless, and just trying to understand all of this. Sharing a few words with her won't hurt anyone."

The softer and lower tone of Kreed's voice, as well as the way he'd addressed the steward, had me pinching my lips together as I leaned back against the wall atop the stairs.

Olin's response was snide. "Providing you don't keep it a secret from Florian, of course."

"Must you make everything I do a fucking crime?"

"It's not my fault you're as trustworthy as a fox in a henhouse." Olin's steps sounded below, and I ducked into the hall.

Zayla frowned and straightened from the wall. "What have you done now?"

"Nothing," I said, smiling. Then shrugged. "Just a little eavesdropping."

Olin grumbled something behind us as he exited the stairwell. When he passed, he said sharply, "Your beast has soiled the carpet.

Take it outside before I have its head removed and hung above a mantel and her pelt made into a cushion for my feet."

Zayla watched Olin head into the foyer and out the doors, murmuring, "Well, he's certainly more surly than usual."

"He found me talking with Kreed."

She nodded, as if that made perfect sense, then whistled slightly.

I was tempted to ask her about it, but I had enough plaguing my mind. Not to mention a lovely mess to clean up.

Dinner was eaten in the kitchen while Kreed cleaned in a tense silence I assumed had nothing to do with me.

I wasn't hungry. Food wouldn't help to alleviate the tension in my head and muscles. The aches unsettling my flesh and bones. I ate what I could anyway, knowing I needed to and not wishing to offend Kreed.

Upon returning to my quarters, I found them empty of my wolf.

"Snow?" I called, inspecting the bathing and dressing chambers.

About to charge out into the hall and back downstairs in search of ghastly Olin, I stopped dead in my tracks.

The door connecting my rooms to the king's was wide open.

Beyond it was a dark and narrow hall squashed between his bathing and dressing room.

He'd taken her as bait. Yet I still walked toward the dim light of his bedchamber. To get her back, I had to, and I'd grown fond of having her comforting weight at my feet while I lost sleep in this manor filled with serpents.

Florian sat shirtless on his bed with a glass of whiskey in hand. My wolf dozed at his side, the novel he'd evidently stolen from my nightstand in his lap.

"I see what you mean," he said by way of greeting. "Though the descriptions do leave a lot to be desired."

Snow's ears pricked when I told her to come with me, but otherwise, she didn't move at all.

Traitor.

Florian smirked and ran a long finger over Snow's head. "She would make a lovely—"

"Do *not* finish that sentence."

His eyes flashed. "*Pet.*"

I gritted my teeth, growling as I spun to leave.

His chuckle quickened my heartbeat. "I do not intend to harm your wolf, butterfly, or she would already be dead." There was a pause, then threateningly soft, "Come to me."

The command lashed at my skin with caressing fingers. My own curled into my palms, temptation mixing with hatred and a myriad of other warm and cold feelings. It should not be a hard thing, ignoring this king after learning his true motives.

Yet it was.

Even without the needy changes occurring within my body, it was nearly painful to ignore a being so overflowing with wretched power. A being with a presence so commanding, it had rendered me submissive from the moment I'd first laid eyes on him.

It went beyond mere attraction.

The sound of his voice stirred more than the acute and growing want inside me. Florian Hellebore evoked a violent blend of hunger and curiosity. An unquenchable need to get as close as possible and burrow deep beneath his skin.

But surrendering would only give him what he wanted.

And I was now all too aware that his wants were not the same as my own, and that he'd tricked me with honest lies.

Kreed's earlier warning lingered. But it couldn't stop me from saying, "I'd rather not."

Though the words had been more gentle than I'd intended, they still created a silence that felt like a heartbeat thudding closer to my back.

The heat of his gaze was a winter breeze, and I swore some of my hair shifted over my shoulder before he made a sound of amusement. "Your little games of disobedience," Florian said, and my skin grew taut over my flesh, "are good for nothing more than exciting me."

I shouldn't have, but I'd already done so many things I shouldn't have, so I turned and said, "You only say that so I will stop disrespecting you."

A thick brow arched, his eyes darkening as I stepped closer to the bed he lounged upon as though it were a divan.

As if the growing tension in the room rankled, or she could sense what was about to happen before we could, Snow stalked back into my chambers via the door I'd left open.

Florian placed the book upon the bed, carefully and with his gaze moving from mine to the erection pressing into his loose cotton pants.

My stomach swirled, my eyes unfastening from the truth he'd shown me and roaming up his stomach. They took their time, counting his abdominals as I imagined what it might feel like to touch every muscled and defined inch of his bare torso.

He noticed. He noticed everything.

Rather than allow the embarrassment to creep up my neck to my cheeks, I forced a small smile and swayed closer to the edge of the bed.

He might affect me. That much I could never deny.

But that didn't mean I would do as he expected—flee from him with my cheeks heated and my heart thrashing through my limbs.

The only tell that he was surprised as I climbed onto his bed at his feet was the slight narrowing of those moonlit eyes.

Crawling between his knees, I prayed to the goddess he wouldn't hear the fear in my thundering heart, and said, "I'm afraid I do not understand what you're talking about."

"To be expected." He sipped his drink, then set it on the nightstand without taking his eyes off me. "As you are very much a hands-on learner, aren't you, sweet pet?"

My teeth met, even as thorny heat dropped to my core.

The challenge in his eyes said that no matter what I decided—if I stayed or if I stormed back into my rooms—he would win.

Regardless, I wouldn't back down now. I couldn't.

And not one part of me wanted to when I kept my eyes on his and dragged a fingertip over the waistband of his night pants. His breath hitched, his giant body instantly tensing.

My head spun with the knowledge that just one touch could elicit such a response in this arrogant and cruel creature. "Are you going to teach me, then?" I whispered with a smile and pushed that fingertip under the elastic of his waistband. "Majesty."

His skin was shockingly hot for a male with winter running through his veins.

"Of course," he said, voice thick. "Nothing has ever given me more satisfaction."

The air in the room became stifling. The flames in the sconces and fireplace guttered as the king regarded me with cool amusement that failed to hide the twitch to his jaw and the erection just a breath away from my hand.

Dipping lower, I encountered coarse hairs.

My stomach shook, and I sat back on my knees to tuck both hands into his waistband. Distracted by his warm and toned hips, I traced them, and gooseflesh arose.

Interesting, I thought. That a male as unstoppable as he would allow himself to produce such reactions.

"I half expected you to be an unresponsive statue," I admitted.

Low and humor-loaded, he asked, "Disappointed?"

He knew I wasn't. In response, I drew in a breath and tugged his pants to his thighs.

And almost flew backward off the bed when his cock bounced free right before my nose.

His laughter was a volcanic eruption that sent fire straight to my cheeks.

The heat melted quickly and settled into my chest as I gazed upon him in helpless wonder.

It was akin to cracking marble, the way that uninhibited sound transformed his cruel beauty into a hypnotic work of art. His cheeks rose high and tinged with color, his eyes ever so slightly creased and ashine.

He calmed, noting my fixation, and I found myself already miss-ing the deep and throaty song I knew I'd never forget. "You are far more beautiful than you deserve to be," I said with both awe and irritation.

Sobered completely, the king chewed the tip of his thumb as he surveyed me with some of that foreign light still lingering in his eyes. "One could say the same about you, *Princess.*"

The reminder of who we both were, of what I truly was to him, fell between us and chased all warmth from the room.

I ignored the bite of hatred that had me thinking of leaving and kept my eyes on his as I wrapped a hand around his cock. He jerked, almost imperceptibly.

His very thick cock, I realized, the heft and smoothness of him widening my eyes.

Florian bit into his thumb, smirking. My blood whooshed in my ears.

Needing to, I dropped my gaze before I did something more lu-dicrous than I already was, such as crawling over his body to kiss that smirk from his undeservingly handsome face.

Of course, lowering my eyes brought my attention to the heat pulsing in my hand.

He was long and large, which I'd already guessed from having him pressed against me, but nothing I imagined could have prepared me for the thick stone wrapped in soft skin.

Fascination warred with intimidation as I stroked my thumb over the vein beneath his shaft, from the engorged head right down to the base.

He groaned, the rumble spurring me to explore more with my fingers. Holding him at the base, I used my other hand to brush at the wetness leaking from the tip.

He shuddered, rising onto his elbows.

I paused, knowing I was doing this all wrong, and met his eyes. They were half-mast, his chest rising and falling heavily. His order rasped. "Keep going."

Emboldened that he seemed to like my curious fingers, I

did—until a sharp curse left him and he tucked the hair that curtained my face behind my ear. "Do you want to put my cock in your pretty mouth, butterfly?"

I blinked up at him, hating how the action likely conveyed my vulnerability and uncertainty. "I don't know what to do."

His fingers swept across my cheek to my jaw, pausing at my mouth. His thumb pulled at my lower lip, then caressed it. "Believe me when I say you cannot disappoint me." He eased back down, but kept his eyes on me, shockingly earnest as he said, "I will not force you. Only do it if you truly want to."

I looked at his cock, still snug in my hand, and moved back a little.

Again, I rubbed that vein with my thumb. I wanted to. He knew I wanted to. And as the fear of not knowing how to please him faded from his reassurance, I gave in and lowered to the reddened head.

My lips parted and skimmed the salty bead of desire. I licked his taste from my mouth.

Florian groaned, "Fuck." His hips bucked beneath me.

I licked him, then ran my tongue down the long length. As I traced that vein I was growing obsessed with, my body continued to warm rapidly with hunger.

I wanted more. Everything.

But when I slid my tongue back up his length to see how much of him I could fit into my mouth, I released him halfway down his shaft with a moan and wet pop.

Then I climbed off his bed while wiping at my lower lip.

"Butterfly," Florian warned between gritted teeth.

"Fair play," I sang on my way to the adjoining door, adding before I closed it behind me with a mocking curtsy, "*Majesty.*"

The sound of crashing glass made me jump, then smile with more satisfaction than any fool should feel after enraging a faerie king.

FOURTEEN

M Y SMUG SATISFACTION WAS FLEETING.
Not only because I spent the night twisting and turning in the bedding—so much so that Snow decided to sleep upon the carpet—wondering if Florian would barge through the adjoining door to finish what I'd started, but because of the visitor in the king's study.

The door was closed, and though it was spelled for privacy, I still heard it when I paused in the hall to wipe yet another bizarre gathering of perspiration from my brow.

Faint feminine laughter, followed by a rare and brief bout of Florian's own.

Zayla said nothing, but she gave Snow a tight look. The wolf had insisted on accompanying us to the kitchen once we returned from a quick visit outside, and her hackles rose when the guard got too close.

I hushed the tiny beast when she snarled at Zayla's continued assessment, and whispered, "You'll give away our attempt at eavesdropping."

Zayla snorted and stayed in the hall as I trekked downstairs to the kitchen for breakfast, Snow trailing.

Kreed did not comment on the wolf, but the twins were delighted. "It's true, then." Arryn laughed and crouched before the cub to offer his hand.

Her lips peeled back, but he waited. Slowly, she crept forward to sniff his hand, then allowed the young male to pet her.

I set her awaiting meaty breakfast on the floor. "I call her Snow."

"Creative," Thistle teased, arms folded and a smirk curling his lips, while I took my usual perch.

The stool now sat at the end of the island bench, my berried oats and a glass of water waiting. My eyes stung at the sight—at the knowledge I was welcome somewhere.

I swallowed the unexpected emotion and tried to ignore the other one I couldn't seem to kick aside. After a few mouthfuls, I failed miserably.

My spoon fell with an unintentional clatter into the bowl as I blurted, "Who is that female?"

"You'll need to be more specific." Kreed finished drying a saucepan and hung it upon one of the hooks dotting the ceiling above me.

I half rolled my eyes. "You know who I mean."

He grinned and tossed his worn towel over his shoulder. "You mean the female visiting with our king?"

I glared, lifting the glass of water to my lips and slurping.

The twins chuckled.

Kreed dismissed them, and they both cursed with relief and left via the door that would take them outside. That I'd seen them leave the same way before told me their private quarters were on the grounds somewhere and not within the manor itself.

"You seem..." The cook didn't even try to hide his amusement as he narrowed his eyes on my face and then my barely touched breakfast. "Bothered."

"I'm not."

He huffed and carried a pot to the sink, draining the water from it.

"I'm not," I said again, and ate another mouthful for good measure. "I wish whoever she is the best of luck in dealing with his insufferable attitude and overbearing presence."

"Overbearing?" Kreed questioned, sounding on the cusp of laughter.

I decided to shut my mouth, knowing I'd already said and implied far too much.

The king was under my skin. He'd made sure of that before I discovered his true intentions. Now, I could only hope it wouldn't hurt too much to peel it back and tear him out.

I didn't *want* to be attracted to him. I certainly didn't want to marry him.

And I didn't want the mere idea of him enjoying another's company to bother me as much as it did.

Gaining Florian's trust in the hope of finding enough freedom to escape was impossible when he didn't trust anyone. I was stuck, and I had to wonder if I loathed him more for that than for tricking me in the first place.

For trapping me in a larger prison.

I'd been so desperate for freedom that I'd stupidly signed over my life to Florian, believing he was fate sent to give me just that and more. All I could do now was rot within this cage of lust and loathing until an opportunity to get to Baneberry presented itself.

Then I would have the protection of the kingdom in which I'd been born.

Until Florian came for us with his armies, of course.

And I knew that such a betrayal would never be forgiven—regardless of him being wholly aware of my longing for answers and a place to truly belong.

Aggravated beyond measure, I shoved my breakfast away and ignored the urge to thump my head against the smooth stone countertop until my hopeless and desolate musings were knocked from my skull.

Kreed shot me a curious look over his shoulder, but I could handle no more talk of the king. "How long have you and Olin been dancing around one another?"

The cook's eyes flared slightly. The only tell he gave that perhaps I'd struck a nerve.

Giving his attention back to the soapy water, he sighed as if suddenly exhausted. "We haven't been involved for some years."

I didn't want to pry. However, I did want to distract myself and maybe learn why this steward was such a damned grouch. I pulled my breakfast close when my stomach growled for more sustenance. "Is that why he's always so miserable?"

Kreed chuckled. It quickly ended with a rough exhale. "He wasn't aware I had sons nor that I'd spent a few decades with a female before I met him. Can't say I blame him for how he feels." He shook suds from a large wooden spoon. "It's quite the secret."

"And why did you keep it?" I gently pressed.

Kreed didn't respond.

I resumed eating, believing he wouldn't.

Then, quietly, as though he did not wish for anyone to overhear, he explained, "I didn't know I had sons, either. By the time I did, and by the time I realized what we were doing was perhaps serious"—he shrugged—"well..."

It had been too late.

The door screeched open atop the stairwell, steps descending.

Her scent preceded her—sunlight and citrus with a faint hint of salt.

Her hair was the color of wet sand, falling straight and long over an ample chest and a torso with enviable curves. Dark-green eyes, reminiscent of seaweed, sparked with her slow-spreading smile as she stopped before me. "You must be the spawn of the enemy."

I coughed, almost splattering her beautiful ensemble with oats.

She smoothed her hands over the loose and gauzy tunic, the crimson material falling over tight-fitted slacks, and looked at Kreed.

Kreed was bowing.

She smiled wider and waved an elegant hand. "Oh, stop and come here."

The cook straightened and met the female in the center of the room to embrace her. "Glorious as always."

She tore away, gripping his large upper arms. "Where are the younglings?"

"Likely chasing some of the female staff into the woods until they need to return to prepare lunch."

My shock faded, but the awe remained as they talked about Kreed's sons and Mercury, Aura's wife. This was no ordinary female. She was a queen.

Queen Aura of Oleander, the southern kingdom of Folkyn.

A queen stood mere feet from me, and I hadn't even realized—hadn't shown any respect upon her arrival. To make matters worse, Snow snarled when the queen stepped too close to her breakfast bowl.

I hushed her, about to apologize when Aura's gaze lit, and she crouched before my beastly cub to offer her hand. "Darling," she said to Kreed. "Why is there a wolf babe in your kitchen?"

"Ask the spawn of the enemy."

I scowled at Kreed, but he merely began decluttering the island countertop with a smirk.

Snow sniffed Aura's hand and decided she was no threat, but refused to eat until Aura rose and stepped back.

The queen observed the cub, who'd already nearly doubled in size since I'd found her wounded in the woods, then looked at me as she placed a hand at her hip. "I can see why Florian's mood is more foul than usual."

Kreed chuckled. "Tullia has indeed kept him on his toes."

I would've glared at the cook again, but the queen tapped a short nail against her plump and rouge-painted lips. "They say you were a changeling." Interest had brightened her eyes to an emerald green. "Raised in the grotesque middle."

I nodded. "I did not know who you were until—"

My attempt at apologizing for not giving the respect owed to a queen was dismissed with a flick of her fingers. "And you've no idea what you've been dragged into."

"I'm starting to learn," I muttered, unable to hide my displeasure at being reminded of my own failings, and unable to keep from adding bitterly, "I was deceived."

Kreed coughed.

Aura looked at him, an eye narrowed, then back to me. "Indeed. Your anger and self-loathing are delicious."

Discomfort bit at my words. "Is it that obvious?"

"Darling, you wear it as a perfume." After a moment of inspecting me thoughtfully, her words softened. "You are so dreadfully young.

The art of careful trickery and deception has yet to touch your soul enough to teach you better."

Those words straightened my spine, a rebuttal forming and failing. I closed my mouth because she was right.

The glint in her eyes still irked.

My stomach then soured, and I clutched a hand over it.

Queen Aura noticed and hummed. She studied Snow when the cub sat at my feet and licked her breakfast from her lips, warning when I made to leave, "I wouldn't go up there for a while if I were you."

I frowned and lowered back to the stool.

Kreed groaned. "You refused him again?" His question would have concerned if it weren't for the fact that Queen Aura was mated and married.

Noting my confusion, Aura laughed. "War, darling. Florian seeks some of our military to sufficiently squash your father." The queen snatched a strawberry from the bowl Kreed set upon the countertop. Holding it to her crimson mouth, she said flippantly, "But he doesn't need us, of course."

"Then why does he seek your assistance?" I couldn't resist asking.

Aura chewed, licking the fruit from her teeth as she watched me. "Because he is obsessive in his pursuits. There will be no gaps in his armor and not a crumb of opportunity for defeat." Her green eyes roamed over my fluffy robe before she snatched another strawberry. "Though perhaps that is changing."

Kreed cleared his throat and shot Aura a look I couldn't decipher.

She sighed in a way that said he was spoiling her fun. Her gaze twinkled at me. "Another time."

I watched her leave the same way she'd arrived.

Kreed waited until she was well and truly gone before whispering, "Aura enjoys knowing everyone's business, Princess." He shook his head. "But that is all. She never gets involved in anything."

So that was why she was here when she had no intention of aiding Florian.

I pulled my breakfast back to me, hungry again. "You say that like it's a bad thing."

The look he gave me in return before he left the kitchen was some type of warning. But as my head began to pound, I lost the ability to care about the games of the Fae.

Apparently, Aura had meant it when she'd said we would talk another time.

My wolf cub bounded through the sludge and snow while I tried to shake the foggy residue my midmorning nap had left behind.

I hadn't intended to fall asleep, but after returning to my rooms to bathe and dress, I'd lain upon the bed to pet Snow, then woke to a gentle tapping upon the door.

Zayla had followed us outside, but after a look from Aura, she remained on the drive with an unmistakable grimace of displeasure. Guilt niggled at me, for she was surely going to earn a scolding from her king for not following my every move.

Sensing what was on my mind as I glanced back down the path behind us, Aura mused, "Does he think you'll fall through his fingers if he doesn't have someone watch you breathe?"

I laughed, shocked by it, and said thickly, "He doesn't trust that I won't try to get what I want."

"And what is that?"

The sun broke through the clouds overhead.

Ice clung to the snow-swept stones beneath our feet. Frost shimmered among the ivy crawling over the fortress we walked alongside, thorns glinting like diamonds. The chill of this kingdom was almost unbearable, but its beauty and magic were undeniable.

My captor's cold realm was everything I'd dreamed of one day experiencing, and I couldn't say that I wasn't excited to glimpse this estate once it was touched by autumn—the only other season to visit Hellebore.

All the while, I hoped I was long gone before it arrived, memories of wandering these grounds swept away with the melting snow.

"A way home," I finally said.

Aura slowed as we rounded the rear of the manor, dark crimson and blue roses within white-glazed hedges all that remained in the gardens. "You made a bargain with a king," she assumed correctly. "Believing that it would take you there?"

I didn't need to answer that, but she was a queen, so I nodded. "I should have known it was too good to be true."

"Desperation," she murmured as if to herself. "And fate." Before I could ask her what she'd meant by that, she surprised me by saying, "Florian wasn't always this way, you know. Calculated and cold to his core."

"Is that why you entertain him?"

She smiled, the touch of her fingers upon a thorny branch in the hedge causing the frost to instantly melt. "Yes and no. After hearing the rumors of what he's been up to, I simply wanted to see it and meet you for myself."

It should have shamed me to think of anyone in Folkyn learning what a fool I'd been.

Instead, I couldn't ignore the curiosity—the overwhelming desire to know more about this king who'd touched me like I was rare treasure while making plans to trap me. "Dare I ask what he was like?"

"Insatiable." She noted my immediate scowl and laughed. "In every way a faerie prince should be, darling." Exuberance filled her velvet voice. "He was reckless and wild, both unbearably cruel and sweet, and rarely without a substance to abuse."

"Substance?"

"Oh, he partook in every delight available, of course. Bodies, liquor, mushroom melts, toadstool dust..." The queen waved a hand. "My wife and I used to adore hosting him, even if we'd need to send him to the stables by the end of his stay. We cannot indulge the way we once did." Nostalgia tinted every word. "He was beloved and feared then, too, but in a way that was so very different to the stern loyalty and terror bestowed upon him now."

"Then his sister died," I said quietly.

"His father, too," Aura said, then nothing more for a minute as we walked on.

Snow roamed toward the trees beyond the paddocks. We passed an archway dusted with icy darkness that led to the courtyard in the middle of the manor, and I watched my breath plume before me, lost in thought.

Lost to imagining all Florian had once been.

"He raised that female," she whispered, throaty as though she might cry. "Florian might have been a typical ghastly and mischievous prince, but there was a wildness to Lilitha from the moment she was born. Florian lost his mother to the difficult birth, and Mercury and I have always wondered if perhaps his way of grieving her was to be the parent Lilitha never had."

I frowned. "But their father was still here?"

"He was here but also not," Aura said. "Hammond lost his mate, half of his soul, and he could seldom look at his daughter without being reminded of her."

"But she was his daughter."

A sharp look was cast my way. "And we are not human, my darling."

I swallowed and nodded. "So Lilitha rebelled because she lacked the nurturing love of parents?"

Aura laughed, the liquid velvet calming some of the tension that hadn't left my body in days. "Again, we are not human. Princess Lilitha would have been such a way, even if her mother had lived," she claimed. "I know it, and so does Florian." A light scoff. "Despite what excuses he would constantly make for the wildling."

Ahead, a curved row of small buildings came into view.

Arryn or Thistle—I couldn't be sure who, due to the distance—exited one and hurried through the snow toward the manor. As we drew closer, I noted the buildings were cottages for the staff. Smoke climbed from the stone chimneys toward the treetops beyond them, the other twin following moments later.

We watched them disappear down the side of the manor, Aura releasing a humorous breath.

I returned to our conversation. "Florian raised Lilitha, then."

"As best he could while tending to his own whims, yes," Aura said. "Though if you ask me, and I told him this hundreds of times, she was born for the Wild Hunt, not a royal house of Folkyn."

"The hunt do not belong to any house of Folkyn."

She raised a finger. "Exactly. Those who wish to disregard the laws and traditions we've upheld since the dawn of our existence have their options—the middle lands or the hunt. And she ignored as many as she could."

"Yet she didn't want to go anywhere else?"

Aura snorted. "Not to either of those places, no, and Florian would have refused." She sighed, stopping beneath an overflowing arch of roses as we rounded the corner. "No, Lilitha wished to go anywhere and do anything she desired, despite everyone's insistent warnings, and in the end, it was her end."

She shivered, though I sensed it was not from her lack of proper clothing in the cold. "Great goddess, I cannot wait to leave this cursed place."

I knew then that the conversation I greedily wanted more of was over.

Queen Aura might not wish to unite with Florian against my father, but she would not betray my betrothed by dishing out all the many secrets sitting behind her pursed lips.

We talked of Oleander, of the sea that hugged her palace and the sandy city district beyond, and of my futile desire to see it all for myself.

At that, she paused before we came full circle and met the drive at the front of the manor. "Your inexperience with the world you wish to know indeed assisted Florian, but you still breathe for a reason, darling." She patted my cheek and whispered, "Lean into that reason, and you'll find more freedom than you know what to do with."

Trying to comprehend what she'd meant, I watched her gaze darken and then brighten as she surveyed me. Her fingers clasped my chin, and she turned my head side to side. "Skies, you're nearing the heat."

My heart dropped, then pounded. For the mere brush of her fingers over my skin caused my flesh to come alive. "I know," I rasped. I refrained from saying that it wasn't near, and that I feared I was now deep within its punishing grasp.

I'd had my suspicions for the past week. My appetite for food and touch had changed from one minute to the next, and with such ferocity, the effects were now becoming debilitating.

Gane's warning of what it meant to reach the mature age of twenty years returned with an ice-layered burn to every part of me. It mercifully dulled the arousal I hadn't been able to shake—the increased change in my body I'd been warring with since Florian had left me desperate for release in my rooms some nights ago.

I missed the surly goblin. I'd known I would before leaving Crustle, but that was before I'd known I was walking into the lair of an inescapable viper.

The queen released me, and we walked on at a slower pace.

I even missed Crustle. I never thought I'd long for the crowded and polluted streets of the damp city-like town I'd always longed to leave. But I did. Now, I would rather be trapped outside of Faerie than inside it with those who had only ill intentions for me.

The thought of not seeing Florian again shouldn't have nicked at my chest nor burned my eyes. He was a blood-hungry asshole who'd used me so completely, so unapologetically, that I should wish him dead. Yet I didn't—knew I likely never could.

Perhaps the heat was to blame.

"How long will it last?" I eventually asked.

Aura slowed to flick ice and mud from an empty bird nest upon the ground, then inspected it. "However long it needs to."

That didn't help, and she laughed as she rose.

"Skies, this place is nothing but murderous ice nowadays."

Brushing her hands off, she returned to talk of the heat. "Once you start tending to it, maybe a few days, but for most, it's about a week. Depends on the individual and the creature in charge of satisfying your awakening."

That was yet another thing that worried me.

I chewed my lip for a moment, but I had to know. "Is there any way to go through it without..." I made a face when she looked at me. "You *know*."

Another laugh, her high cheeks and tiny pointed nose dusted pink from the chill.

She sobered when Florian left the manor and stalked down the steps with Fume at his side.

The two talked quietly. As we neared, Fume made to leave. When he realized who walked with me, he turned back to exchange greetings with Aura.

He clasped her hand and bowed, kissing it before he rose. "I hear you've broken our hearts by denying us yet again."

"You have no one to blame but yourselves..." Aura withdrew her hand and smiled tightly at the warrior as she gestured to me. "For believing I would visit for any other reason than to meet this divine creature."

Fume finally acknowledged me, his smirk becoming a forced smile that resembled a grimace.

Wishing he hadn't bothered, I returned it with only a nod.

His brown lashes dipped as he stared at me for a moment that made me grow more tense. Then he nodded to Queen Aura and headed to the middle of the drive to greet the band of warriors climbing uphill, more wagons in tow.

Florian stood stiffly, his hands clasped before him, and covered head to toe in black. His leather coat matched his boots, the breeze barely moving his near-black hair. His eyes stayed fixed on me, his expression unreadable, as Aura walked to him.

She rose to her toes to whisper something in his ear. The king bristled, casting a dark glance down at her before looking back at me.

The Queen of Oleander grinned, fingers wriggling my way before she vanished within a light cloud of sand-stained wind.

Nearing the king, I reached for some of it and rubbed the granules between my fingers.

Snow barreled across the drive, shaking wet from her coat. Thankfully, before she reached my side. I was given a look that told me she wasn't pleased to have been left behind.

I crouched down to swipe some dirt from her cheeks and murmured an apology.

Florian's question was low. "How much did Aura tell you?"

"More than you ever will." Taking in his unmoved expression as I straightened, I relented. "It was nothing you need to be grumpy about."

As I walked around him to take the stairs inside, Snow running ahead as if fearing I would leave her again, I couldn't keep from thinking about the small yet precious doses of information Aura had given me.

Hellebore's king hadn't always been this way—seemingly without a soul, or perhaps just a heart.

Florian snatched my wrist. "Grumpy?"

I stopped and eyed his large hand, then I made the mistake of meeting those fatal blues. "You're exceptionally talented at being in a bad mood."

His mouth twitched. "One could say I have every reason to be after being thoroughly teased, then left to milk my own cock."

Just the thought of the act ignited my blood and flared my eyes. At a loss for words, I appeased the need inside me by staring as his features slowly lost their fierce edge, and the smirk in his eyes tempted his lips to curl.

His fingers crawled up my arm. I shivered, hoping he didn't notice when he tugged me close and skimmed a knuckle over my too-warm cheek. "This fucking maddens me."

"What does?"

"The feelings you wear all over your face," he said, and tightly. "The arousal that colors your cheeks and glosses such dark eyes."

I wasn't sure how to do this anymore. Not now that I couldn't fall into his touch and naively hope for more. Not now that I knew he didn't want a wife.

He wanted a pawn.

When his fingers brushed my jaw, my eyes fluttered, and I looked up at him with too much hope for someone who'd already been made a fool by daring to rely on hope for survival. "Will I ever be free, Florian?"

His thick brows lowered.

As the riders and wagons began to fill the drive, I stepped closer and laid my hand over the black leather covering his chest. "Will you ever let me go?"

The wind whistled and threw my hair around my cheeks, Florian's expression and jaw granite and his touch falling away. "Never, butterfly."

I'd known what he would say. Perhaps that was why it didn't hurt to hear it leave his luscious, lying mouth.

I nodded once, resolve building brick by brick inside me.

There weren't many things I'd had the chance to excel at, but I was an expert at one thing.

Biding my time.

The king groaned a curse as I backed away to the steps, his nostrils flaring. Those depthless blue eyes lightened as they drifted down my body to settle upon my lower stomach. Loathing the way it quaked in response and how my thighs longed to squeeze together, I turned and strode up the steps.

"Tullia," Florian called.

It was the name that made me stop, but I didn't turn back as his alarmingly brittle order burrowed beneath my skin. "Do not leave the manor."

A tear threatened to spill from my eye.

I had no unearthly idea what was wrong with me. It wasn't as if I didn't already know I was a captive—*the enemy's spawn*—but his order to stay trapped indoors after I'd just reminded him of my life-long dream for freedom was another small cut to the chest.

Zayla followed me from the foyer as I kept my head down and hurried for the false safety of my rooms.

FIFTEEN

FLORIAN DID NOT RETURN TO HIS ROOMS THAT NIGHT.
The following morning, over a breakfast I couldn't stomach eating, Kreed informed me he was gone. He wouldn't tell me where, and I didn't ask. He did tell me that the manor staff and many of Hellebore's warriors were busy with preparations for the looming Frost Festival.

But I had no desire to make the most out of the quiet grounds.

As per the king's request, I stayed indoors and kept to my rooms. Not simply because he'd requested it, but because I was growing too uncomfortable to be anywhere else.

Night arrived with no return of the king. Days of increasing torture followed, and with them, no sign of Florian. After sleeping until midmorning on the third, I woke with a hunger I feared would be fleeting.

I tightened my robe to take Snow downstairs. Zayla had seemingly decided I was not in any state to attempt escape, for she was nowhere to be seen.

My bleary eyes snapped wide open when I caught his scent. It was fresh. We slowed on the steps as a voice I hadn't heard for days looped around my body and tugged.

"I do not want her there," Florian said from deep down below.

The door to his study must have been open.

Another voice followed. Fume, I noted, as we reached the landing before the last flight of stairs. "It's part of the plan, Flor."

Silence.

My hunger immediately abated.

Then Fume saying low, "Word spreads."

"Then let that be enough."

"But we both know it isn't. Let it be seen and wholly believed. Molkan will hear of it before dawn can touch the sky."

"The heat is upon her," Florian said after a long pause, as if he hadn't wanted to say it aloud. "Any creature can smell it should they get too close."

Fume cursed. A moment later, he suggested, "Just keep her at your side, as you should regardless." Carefully, he asked, "What are you to do about her evolvement, anyway?"

I assumed *evolvement* was a nicer term for what I was currently struggling to endure—the final stage of maturing into a faerie.

Typically, a full moon would prompt most young females of the age of twenty to evolve. A process that would grant us a heightened chance of finding a mate of the soul, and allow us to discover what our magical abilities might be, should we be blessed by the goddess with any.

And those of pure blood were almost always blessed with something.

I lowered to the bottom step above the landing, uncaring that either male could leave the study and scent where I sat—and know that I'd overheard them. Snow nudged at my hand with her damp nose, then laid her head upon my lap as she settled on the stone beside me.

When Florian finally responded, it was nearly too quiet for me to hear. "I wait until she asks for assistance."

My heart both bloomed and shrank, the feeling painful and aggravating the dull ache in every limb.

"You would see her through it?" Fume cursed again. "But you've never done it before, Florian."

Instant and intense relief shamed me at hearing that.

"That doesn't mean I'm not aware of what it will require from me."

My heart skipped and stalled in the stretched silence that followed. My bare toes curled over the dark whorls in the cream stone, my eternally flushed skin welcoming the touch of cold.

Fume's voice rose. "And what about what *you* require? How will you possibly be able to—"

"Shut your fucking mouth," Florian seethed. "You are not to talk of such matters, and you know it."

A screech of chair legs over stone. "I need to visit the barracks. I'll see you tonight."

Florian gave no response.

The warrior friend must have taken another exit, for his steps in the hall faded in the opposite direction to where I was still seated on the grand staircase with Snow.

The word *assistance* stalked me for the remainder of the morning and haunted my fever dreams of skin and teeth and pleasure and feeding.

I woke sprawled sideways across the bed, midafternoon casting my bedchamber in an orange glow, as the mattress dipped behind me. "You have not eaten today."

The first words the king had said to me in days.

I curled away from the tempting heat and energy emanating from him.

"Do you detest me and your circumstances so much that you would starve yourself?"

"I tried to eat," I croaked, my eyes closing. "And yes," I whispered. "I do detest you that much, but I would not give you the satisfaction of ending my life before it's even begun."

A touch of humor thickened his response. "You are not human, butterfly. Such a thing won't kill you." He paused as though thinking about that. "At least, not for many months."

Irritated by his hypnotic voice and struggling to find the will not to roll into him and ask for him to *assist* me through this torment, I snapped, "Was there something you needed, Majesty?"

Though I wasn't looking at him, I could sense he'd gone so very still.

I kept my eyes squeezed closed and curled tighter into myself.

My stomach cramping worsened with the emptiness I refused to ask him to fill.

"Roll over," Florian ordered, and when I ignored him, he leaned down and said to my ear, "Roll the fuck over, sweet creature."

I bit the inside of my cheek as the storm of heat and his harsh demand spread through my body in the form of a blistering caress.

I gave in and did as he said, but I wouldn't meet his eyes. I stared up at the canopy of netting coating my bed and nearly moaned from just the slight touch of his fingertips at my stomach. He opened my robe, and I knew it was over.

I was going to let him *assist* me, and skies, I couldn't even care to loathe myself for it.

His fingers brushed across my stomach. It contracted in response, expectation and exhilaration unfurling. The anticipation faded when he merely continued to stroke my skin.

"Do you ever eat, Majesty?"

"Florian," he corrected, but with none of his usual annoyance. "And did you not watch me eat when I took you to dinner?"

The memory of that night, of how confused and disappointed I'd been, returned. "I didn't watch you," is all I chose to say to that. "You never eat here."

"I do. Earlier than you in the mornings, and other meals when I get time."

"Where?"

The demand earned me a huffed noise that was almost a laugh. "Do you wish to poison me with something harsher than sea salt?"

"It would be fair play," I said, though the quiet words lacked conviction.

He chuckled, the deep sound brief but beautiful. From my lower stomach to my ribs, his cool fingers traveled and soothed.

"You've made your touch cold," I rasped and finally looked up at him.

His jaw was clenched, his gaze upon my exposed skin and breasts. "Too cold?"

"Perfect." My eyes closed at the sight of his throat dipping, the impulse to rise and lick his skin painful to fight. "When will this end, Florian?"

"When you decide it does."

I hadn't been solely referring to the torture my body endured in the name of full maturity. He was aware of that, but he said nothing else.

I then realized even if I pleaded for him to help me now, he couldn't. Not with the Frost Festival taking place at sundown. But I also knew he wouldn't refuse me, and the thought of ruining his grand plans to display me to his people made my desire to surrender and have him fix me nearly impossible to resist.

Yet the unbearable heat receded with every swipe of his fingertips over my skin. All too soon, exhaustion cloaked as if I hadn't slept in eons.

"You must think me extremely stupid," I whispered.

"For what reason?" Florian asked as though there were many.

My fingers curled, and I longed to reject his much-needed touch. I didn't. I couldn't. He was a poison I needed, his frost-tipped fingers a balm loosening every tense muscle.

Then he murmured, "I think you're young and desperate and without options."

I scoffed. "So, essentially, yes."

His next breathy huff washed my annoyance away. That is, until he said, "I also think you want me to feel guilty for taking advantage of that." He skimmed his fingers beneath the curves of my breasts. I shivered. "Even if I were capable of feeling remorse, butterfly, I would not."

The alarming admission was not malicious. He was being honest with me.

For once.

"Well, I'm no longer desperate," I said, the ire in my tone faint as sleep beckoned. "So kindly find someone else to tend to me throughout this heat."

His fingers stilled, his words a caustic rumble. "If I believed you wanted someone else..." His stroking resumed, moving to my lower back when I curled onto my side. "Then I would make you watch as I took my time ending their existence."

Chills erupted over my skin, the threat reaching the marrow of my bones.

"But you do not truly want me," I said, hating that I'd let such vulnerability be known. "You only want to use me to further humiliate my father."

Florian was silent for so long, I was falling into the warm depths of sleep when he whispered, "I can want both, butterfly." He traced the indent of my spine. "And I will have what I want."

Florian was gone when I woke to a knock on the door.

Zayla entered, eyeing me with amusement as I pushed hair from my face and sat up on the bed. "We leave on the hour."

It took a moment for sleep and the king's visit to leave and make room for remembering what lay ahead. "The festival."

Zayla nodded. "Delen will arrive any minute to prepare you."

With that, she closed the door, and I hurried into the bathing room to freshen up, feeling better than I had since I'd arrived in Folkyn.

It would seem the king's power and hands were good for more than wringing blood from his enemies. I still struggled to feel gratitude when I was about to be put on display as a show of his strength.

Delen was waiting outside when I emerged from the bathing room in my robe.

I was given only a nod when I greeted him. He entered silently with a moon-colored gown in hand that he draped over the chair in the corner of the room.

A pair of heeled slippers were carefully set by the door. He then stepped into the hall, and I assumed I would be readying myself, of which I would prefer, but he quickly returned with a small trunk.

His gray tunic was fringed in blue, matching the paint on his eyelids. I marveled at the glittering hue and the light rouge over his rock-hewn cheeks while he unlocked his trunk and opened several wooden compartments.

I moved closer to peek at the kaleidoscope of rouges and eye paints, but the look he shot me over his muscular shoulder made me retreat. "I'm only curious," I said. "I've never seen anything like this before."

His shoulders dropped, and he shifted to the side.

I smiled, knowing it was permission to inspect but to keep out of his way.

His skin was a light bronze, and his hair as white as my own. "You do not hail from Hellebore," I said after some silent minutes.

He didn't answer me.

He plucked the chair from the bureau and gestured for me to take a seat without saying a word. I watched as he placed a selection of colors upon the inside of his arm, and then as he picked two small brushes from a pocket in the lid of the trunk.

Delen was almost done applying the cool and sticky paint to my eyes when his lips parted, and I saw it. His silence was not because he too despised my presence here in this court, but because he couldn't speak.

Horror swept through me with steel wings that scored at my innards.

Gently, I clasped his smooth chin.

His shoulders and jaw stiffened. Narrowed gold-brown eyes met mine, his brows low with confusion.

"I just need to know one thing." My heart thundered at the thought. "Did Florian take your tongue?"

Delen blinked, staring at me as if unsure he should answer. After a moment, he shook his head. But the way his gaze hardened on mine caused my stomach to sink.

Rather than voice my suspicion, I released him and looked down at my fingers.

He was from Baneberry.

My gaze remained unseeing upon my hands as my fears and doubts and desires blended into an unsettling storm.

Delen gently threaded thick strands of my hair with dried flowers into a makeshift crown. My eyelids were painted a marble white that flicked at each corner. Kohl soaked my lashes, and a faint silver dust was brushed over my cheeks. My lips were a nude pink that matched the heeled slippers awaiting me by the door.

Delen inspected me, seemingly satisfied with his work. Then he bowed and left my rooms, allowing me privacy to don my lacy moon-washed gown.

It wasn't easy to wriggle into. I should have expected as much and perhaps asked Delen to wait and assist me. I did the best I could, tightening the silk ribbons at my back. The bodice sat loose, but it would need to do.

Florian was in the foyer, talking with two of his warriors. One of them was Fume, the other a male with silver hair cropped so close to his scalp, he appeared to have none until I descended the last few stairs and neared.

Florian dismissed them. Fume made his way to the doors, but the male I'd yet to see before gave me a once-over that tightened his ice-blue eyes.

"Something wrong with your feet, Shole?"

The male's full mouth curved as he took his time dragging his gaze from me. He gave his king a look that resulted in a glacial glare from Florian, then stalked to the doors.

Tension and something my senses failed to name emanated from the king. It worsened as he slowly turned to where I stood waiting before the stairs. The ice that kept his features perpetually as he wanted them—unmoving and unreadable—fractured with the parting of his mouth.

I chewed my lips, then winced. I rubbed them and inspected my finger, but there was thankfully no rouge. Whatever Delen's materials were made from was a magic that didn't exist in the middle lands of Crustle.

A glimmer of jewels caught my eye.

I soaked in the crown atop Florian's head, noting it was the first time I'd seen him wear it.

Stunned by the overt reminder of who he was, I lowered my gaze to his boots. The pair he'd chosen for tonight's festivities were knee-high and smooth black leather. His fitted pants coaxed my eyes to roam over those powerful legs to his torso.

A dress coat, black and edged in a dark blue with matching buttons, rose high at the collar and hung from his broad shoulders in intimidatingly sharp lines. He'd left it unbuttoned. A matching blue shirt beneath was tucked into his pants, molding to his broad chest and tapering temptingly at his waist.

By the time I reached his jaw, the bristle there not as heavy, he was standing before me.

My neck curled back, my smile one that conveyed I knew I'd been caught—and I didn't much care. "Majesty."

Florian's lips closed, curving slightly.

My smile fell beneath the changing hue of his eyes while he stared down at me. He didn't blink, though his long lashes dipped as his gaze danced with mine.

I might not have been exceptionally knowledgeable when it came to sex, but I was beginning to wonder if perhaps these staring games of his could not be defined as a hunter merely studying his prey.

For as much as I loathed to admit it, the longer he looked at me, the more I struggled to ignore it. The intimacy that aroused more than any words I'd read in books.

Discomfort stumbled with anticipation, and when the two combined, a wildness that begged to be unleashed was born.

"You look divine enough to eat," Florian murmured.

The heat he'd quelled just hours ago flared and forced my eyes from his. I hadn't eaten well in days, yet the only thing I hungered for was not what I should want.

"Turn around," he said gruffly.

I frowned, but he clasped my arm and gently turned me to face the stairs. My hair was gathered over one shoulder. His deft fingers liquefied my blood as he tied the ribbons of the silk bodice properly.

My breathing quickened. I told myself it was due to the tightened bodice.

I should have thanked him, this winter king who had tricked me into placing myself exactly where he wanted me upon his chess board. The urge to do so nearly got the better of me until his fingers met the exposed skin through the flower-shaped lace at my upper back.

The same lace spread down my arms, his touch tracing the material.

As light as a feather, his fingertips stroked, slowing at the skin the flowers exposed. The air became charged, hard to inhale, as his heat closed in at my back. His softened voice stirred my hair. "Your blood betrays you as much as your body, butterfly." His mouth brushed the arch of my ear. "It rushes to meet my touch."

Even if I could have trusted myself to speak, he gave me no time.

Cold washed in as Florian stepped back, and I turned as Olin neared with a shimmering cloak that matched my gown.

He bowed to his king, his shrewd lavender eyes appraising me for all of a second. I couldn't resist smiling brightly now that I knew the source of his eternally dour mood was Kreed.

Florian noticed.

He stepped close once more to drape the cloak over my shoulders. Rounding me, he fastened it at my neck, and I made myself stare at his squarely hewn chin with its slight dimple as my body and blood began to betray me yet again.

A curled finger tipped up my chin. The king's eyes narrowed. "Do not toy with Olin."

"I've done no such thing," I declared, all the while I fought back another smile.

Florian studied me. His own mouth twitched, then he stepped away with a rough exhale and held out his hand.

I looked at it, then at his eyes. "We're materializing?"

"Unless you think yourself too unwell. In which case, you are welcome to stay here and rest."

That I knew he would prefer that while I was victim to the heat had me stepping forward and folding my hand around his.

He eyed me curiously, as if sensing that I would endeavor to intentionally displease him, and took my other hand. He pulled me against his hard body. Another whisper was murmured to my hairline with tickling lips. "Hold on tight, troublesome creature."

SIXTEEN

THE ENERGY CURRENTS WERE NO KINDER TO ME THIS TIME. Screeching darkness stole my breath and every thought from my mind.

We were spat out with a force that would've sent me to my knees with nausea if it weren't for Florian's arm banding tight around my waist.

He held me to him as the world reshaped itself.

The call of owls and revelry nearby trickled in as the ringing in my head faded. My tight breaths soon slowed. My eyes opened to find the top button of Florian's shirt pressed against the tip of my nose.

I broke out of his hold and rubbed it. "Where are we?"

"Wattle Woods," he said, then remembered I had no idea what that meant. "We're at the base of Frostfall Mountains." He gestured to the trees climbing high over the dark hills behind us. "The manor and city are on the other side. Half a day's journey via horseback."

That would mean... "We're near the sea?"

Florian huffed. "A few hours on foot." A look at my shoes. "I must advise against fleeing for a ship in such impractical footwear, butterfly."

I snorted, inwardly admonishing myself for showing that he was humorous. Frosty kings with armies swarming and robbing another kingdom should not be considered anything but grotesquely immoral.

And immoral Florian most certainly was, but grotesque...

Unfortunately not.

Perhaps I would find it easier to cling to my hatred for his cruelty and duplicitous actions if he was.

That should have shamed me, and it did, though mostly because

I felt no shame for my own actions—and because I hadn't even considered escape until he'd mentioned it.

"Running anywhere in your state would not be wise," Florian said darkly, as if he could see my thoughts dancing all over my face. He likely could. I was not at all adept at hiding anything. "Though if you're truly desperate to try, I shall give you a head start."

A howl struck through the night. The eerie sound did not come from a beast, but from those in the clearing aglow with flickering firelight through the trees.

Florian grinned, the beautiful transformation of his goddess-blessed features anything but inviting. "I do enjoy a good hunt."

I glowered. "You wouldn't win anything if you caught me."

His brow arched. He closed the distance between us with a flaring of his nostrils and his brightening eyes drifting down my body. "If you say so."

His patience seemed endless—depthless.

Given all he'd planned and was now executing so meticulously, if this tension between us snapped in such a final way, I might as well be giving him the killing blade.

And I couldn't help but wonder if I hadn't discovered his true desires for me, if I'd have made my way to his rooms at the first signs of the heat's arrival, what we might have already done...

His wolfish grin waned, his brows lowering as though he would speak.

Then there was a violent shake of the ferns at my ankles, and I startled, turning and flattening my back to Florian's chest.

He grunted, his hands falling to my arms. Before his fingers could enclose around them, my heart stopped for a different reason.

I crossed to the ferns as a sniffing nose and beady eyes appeared.

I gathered my gown to crouch low and inspect it. The creature should have scuttled away, but to my surprise and delight, it waddled toward me on legs so tiny, its stout body was covered in dirt when I picked it up.

I brushed some from its smooth fur. Those beady eyes seemed unsure as they glanced at the king behind me.

I trailed a finger over its back. "Is it a peppin?"

"Close," Florian said. "A burshka." Carefully, he pointed at the wriggling ears, his fingers skimming mine. "See, the ears are more round, and they're twice the size of a peppin."

"Peppins must be tiny indeed." The creature's nose twitched as it shied away from the king's giant hand. "It's so soft." I pushed the critter toward him, forgetting how close we were. My arm brushed his stomach. "Touch it."

As though I were doing something ridiculous, his mouth quirked with his brow. "I've seen hundreds of them before, butterfly. Gnawing at carcasses or stealing food from camps and village barns."

He was as foolish as he was handsome if he thought that would deter me. "But have you ever held one?" The creature's little claws dug into my hand as I again offered it to the king.

He looked down at it with a slight shake of his head. He might have been itching to arrive at the festival, but he was far from annoyed.

He plucked the burshka from my hand as if it were nothing but the rodent it was. It squeaked like a miniature pig.

"Careful," I admonished, cupping my hand around his while stroking the milk-brown fur.

"Satisfied?" Florian asked, his eyes lifting to mine beneath his long lashes.

Sudden and severe dryness filled my mouth. I tried to say in jest, but whispered, "An unkind thing to say to me right now."

The heat he'd calmed that afternoon rose with a brutality that stole my breath as I briefly lost myself to imaginings of his mouth on mine, his hand fisting my hair, and his imposing form overpowering my weak and needy body...

Florian's eyes brightened with hunger, his jaw tight as he gritted, "Skies, Tullia." He dumped the creature into my hand, somehow knowing I would wish to pet it before I released it. "Reel it in, or we're going to leave before we've even arrived."

Embarrassed and unsure of what to say, I ran a finger down the burshka's back, then crouched to set the critter free. I watched it go, partly to try to do as the king said and calm myself, but also because I wondered what it felt like.

To have the ability to roam any place you wished.

Then I wondered why the thought of roaming Folkyn, or any realm, without knowing if I'd see Florian ever again unveiled a quiet terror within me.

Rising, I brushed my hands over my gown, wincing when I remembered it was easily soiled.

Florian tipped up my chin, his eyes searching mine.

"I'm fine."

"I'm not. You're fucking potent," he clipped, his jaw rotating and his thumb skimming the corner of my lips. He watched them part. "I miss this mouth."

He'd said it as if truly bothered—bothered that I hadn't kissed him and bothered that he wished for me to.

"Then perhaps you shouldn't have lied to me," I quipped and gathered my gown to pass him.

His fingers caught mine, twirling me back so fast I had to brace my hands over his chest to steady myself. "And you expect me to believe that if I had not, I would still be kissing you?" His snidely playful tone suggested otherwise. Clasping my chin, he lowered his mouth to mine. "You wouldn't have done what I needed if you'd known."

He was right. I wouldn't have signed that contract. He didn't need me to tell him that.

Though what else would I have done?

If Florian had admitted to wanting to squash the king who'd sired and hidden me, then would I have found another way to Folkyn? We both knew I would have failed and that, no matter what I tried to tell myself I would have done, there was no escaping Florian after that first meeting in the Lair of Lust.

My future belonged to him. My fate had been sealed the moment

I'd first laid eyes on him. Perhaps, warned a quiet voice, even long before then.

These endless walls I kept slamming into—the lack of control over my own life—made that building rage war alongside the sickeningly powerful desire of the heat.

I was almost afraid to discover which one might win as our mixing breath warmed the chilled air of the forest.

My voice was thick. "And now I can never believe a word you say." Ignoring the desire to kiss him until I drew blood and then slap him, I said with my mouth brushing his, "Nor can I believe for a moment that you suffer from lack of affection when you've indulged in others."

The images Queen Aura had painted of this king were hard to forget, yet also hard to match with the male standing before me. The only exception was the part pertaining to his pleasure seeking with as many willing partners as possible.

He was a king. Virile and tenacious and mouthwatering. He oozed pheromones and power as though they were a second shadow to lure his prey. And not only was I inexperienced in matters of pleasure, but I was also now unwilling to fall victim to all that he was.

I was about to turn away when Florian said roughly, "For feeding only."

The confession singed.

I stepped back.

Florian studied my features, his expression almost curious. "You're upset."

"I'm no such thing." I glared at the pine needles and rocks blanketing the snow-kissed ground, wishing they'd fly up to smack this deceitful king in his arrogant face. "I suppose I am shocked, but I shouldn't be." I began to walk toward the awaiting lights again.

Shocked and stupid.

For a stolen second there, I'd almost believed it might not be so terrible to surrender to the heat rather than the rage. I'd almost believed he'd spoken true when he'd claimed that he wished to have both

NECTAR OF THE WICKED | 203

me and his revenge, and therefore, maybe I could have used it to my advantage by slowly gaining his trust.

But he didn't want me badly enough. Otherwise, he wouldn't have fed from another.

An irrational way of thinking, certainly. The king needed to consume blood to nourish those magical abilities of his—to keep them as cold and deadly as his heart.

But I didn't want to be rational. For what upset me the most was that he hadn't asked me if I would be a willing source.

Though if he had, would I have surrendered that much at least?

Only the goddess would know now.

The forest clearing became visible through the trees. Bonfires rose toward the sky, ice garlands strung throughout the birch trees I neared. The twirling loops of crystal surrounded what looked to be a large valley, joining the fires to give light to the shadows of moving bodies.

Florian snatched my wrist, keeping me within the woods. "Stop walking away from me."

"Is that an order, Majesty?" Tearing my hand from his possessive hold, I fluttered my lashes.

"Florian."

My temper flared. "*You* stop *that* because it doesn't matter what I call you." I should have been concerned by this newfound ability to let loose such anger after so many years of swallowing every unpleasant feeling I had.

Apparently, I was not as afraid of this war-hungry king as I had been of Rolina.

Definitely stupid, I inwardly scolded.

Florian's own anger swelled. A blistering breeze that knocked my hair over my shoulders. But he only gritted, "It matters to me."

I knew he hadn't wanted to confess those words. And that he did made my ire and jealousy deflate.

He cursed, looking toward the sky as if Mythayla had cursed him even though he'd been the one to instigate all of this.

"Florian," I said softly, unsure why I was speaking to the monster at all. His eyes lowered, narrowing upon me as if he were on edge and braced for an attack. "You did upset me."

His features creased, the rare sight melting some of the resolve around my heart.

"I need to feed, Tullia," he said simply. "And soon, you might too." He scowled when I remained silent, as though he did not understand my unwillingness to understand him. "There's no one I wish to fuck but you."

My darkened lashes tickled my brows as my eyes widened. "How very sweet," I said dryly, even as my stomach bounced. "But..." I licked my lips, forgetting again they were painted and frowning at the berried taste. "It's just as intimate, isn't it? Drinking another's blood." The question was genuine and not mocking. I'd read and always assumed it was.

The detachment that once again made his features unreadable, as well as his silence, caused my chest and eyes to burn. I turned and headed for the tree line, and this time, he didn't stop me.

This heat was rendering me an unrecognizable and emotional mess.

The king caught up with me within two inflamed breaths, his stride unhurried and the warriors lining the woods parting to reveal our destination.

The hand at the small of my back felt more like a brand. A claim over a possession. Not a guiding touch toward the throne upon a wooden podium on the northern edge of the clearing. Beyond it, rippling in the breeze, was a large deep-blue tapestry of the royal insignia—a crimson hellebore flower backed by a gleaming white snowflake.

My skin itched as the revelry quieted to a low hum, and eyes fell upon us like needles poking at thread.

The final beating of a drum echoed through the deafening silence as he paraded me in an unmistakable display of power toward the throne.

A throne that was unlike anything I could have read in a book.

As dark as night, the ancient and curling wood glimmered with diamonds and sapphires reminiscent of icicles. The back of the giant chair arched in sharp spires and rose higher than Florian's head as he stood before his people.

An endless sea of glowing torches and fire-lit eyes.

The king looked upon them all with a taut chin and shoulders, then seated himself.

My hand was clasped in his. I couldn't remember when that had happened as I hadn't known until I was tugged gently onto his lap.

The annual celebration of this wintry kingdom continued with a violent pound of a drum.

Stunned by the sight of so many people looking at me—seeing where their king had placed me—I flinched at the sound, belatedly attempting to close the gap in the leg of my gown and failing.

Florian seized my waist. He turned me until my thighs draped over his and his erection pressed into my hip. "Cease fussing, pet."

"So I'm a pet again?" I asked, my eyes skirting the crowds of people adorned in blue and white and black. "Lovely."

Smoke rose from vendor carts at the opposite end of the clearing. The scent of meat and fish and even something sugary sweet traveled upon the air.

Stiffly, I sat and tried to ignore the male whose mere presence soaked up the undivided attention of all those closest to the podium. Painfully aware that they might overhear despite the noise, I whispered between tight lips, "If I am to be queen, then shouldn't I have my own throne?"

"Then how would I touch you?"

I both shivered and bristled.

His fingers circled idly over the bare skin through the lace flower at my hip. "You're still displeased with me."

"I'm not."

My ass was pinched. I jumped and scowled, glaring at him.

It seemed that was his plan—to gain my full attention. A pleased spark glinted in his dark-blue gaze when I met it with mine. His hand slowly rose from the small of my back. My hair tangled in his fingers, my skin igniting despite my efforts to act unbothered.

He leaned forward, whispering to my cheek, "I've not fed since your arrival in Folkyn, and butterfly?" A shaken exhale left me as he murmured roughly to the corner of my mouth, "I'm fucking famished."

I couldn't keep my eyes from widening.

His hand reached my nape, his fingers curling and squeezing gently. "So although I adore quarreling with you and the look of molten fury in your eyes, right now, my patience only extends so far."

Those edged words proved my earlier assumption wrong.

I didn't need to ask him to convey exactly what he'd meant. He was just as in need, perhaps even more than I was, and he would have to remedy that if I wasn't careful.

My thawing heart stuttered and drooped as what he'd said before failed to keep from nagging at me. I couldn't help it. Couldn't stop myself from saying, "You fed during the time we were meeting at the Lair of Lust."

His eyes darkened.

I turned away, my teeth catching my lip. I hadn't the room to care about the rouge. A red haze blurred my vision and swept through my body to tighten every organ. No matter how much I reminded myself that it didn't matter.

After what he'd done, it certainly shouldn't have mattered.

But for some reason, it did.

Florian's hand caught mine when I rose from his lap. "We need only stay an hour for appearance's sake. Then we can leave."

I painted a smile on my face and tugged my hand free. "Then I would like to spend it enjoying the festivities rather than tolerating them and your presence."

He scowled, a warning within his eyes, but he didn't stop me from taking the two steps down from the dais to the grass.

Maybe he knew my own patience was at an end, and if I remained, we would cause a scene by continuing to do as he'd warned we shouldn't—argue until one of us snapped in a way we could not take back.

The thought of humiliating him in front of so many onlookers both thrilled and nauseated me. That awakening part of me, likely tied to the heat, liked the idea of claiming that devious mouth in front of so many far too much.

Though the rest of me knew that to do so would only further suit his plans—and make me and my father's kingdom appear weak.

Two guards trailed me as I entered the thick throng of faeries. Scents crashed into me and caused my head to swim. Overwhelmed, I bumped into bodies when a female with hooves for feet nearly squashed my slipper-covered toes.

Her features might have been dusted in a light layer of fur, and her eyes that of a bovine, but I didn't miss the sharp sneer she gave me. Nor that from the cluster of goblins she'd been dancing with.

I could no longer see the warriors but knew they were watching from somewhere. My eyes caught on the twinkling throne I'd steadily moved away from, and I soon realized why the king had let me go.

A female with glowing crimson hair curling around slim shoulders now stood at the side of the podium.

Florian no longer sat on the throne.

I moved out from behind a line of dancing females, wine bouncing from their goblets, to see he'd descended the steps to speak with the red-haired female. She wrung her hands before her, but her smile was wide and bright. I could only see Florian's broad back and the crown atop the hair he'd tied to his nape, but I could tell from the glow of her face that they were not family.

The king of Hellebore had no living family.

For if he did, I would not be standing here, dazed in a field of faeries.

Needing air, and to keep from marching back to stop the king from standing so close to the creature of whom he was evidently very familiar with for him to leave his royal perch, I made my way to the tree line.

As predicted, the guards had followed.

A lightly muscled male with piercing brown eyes smirked when I neared him. "Looking a little unwell there, Princess."

The female beside him knocked his arm with her elbow. Her gaze remained steadfast upon the festivities, as if more of Molkan's spies might emerge and snatch me at any moment. "Don't, Fellan."

"Don't what?" he said, giving the female a feigned look of outrage. "I was only going to tell the princess not to worry, for dear Nalia is merely our king's only permanent lover."

He would only be merely screaming when I gave in to the temptation to snatch his dagger from his waist and bury it in his groin.

Shocked and a touch sickened by the flare of my violent temper, I closed my eyes and pleaded with the skies for this ghastly heat to hurry up and end. I couldn't keep feeling and acting this way.

I couldn't keep longing for something I couldn't allow myself to have—especially when all I truly needed was to find the father who'd sent me to the middle lands when I was born.

If nothing else, at least it was now clear that Molkan had been trying to protect me from Florian's wrath. A forgivable heartbreak, if only I was given the chance to give that forgiveness to him.

I didn't need Florian and the useless feelings and desires he conjured.

And right now, I just needed Fellan to shut his irksome mouth.

"Decades, I think it was. Wasn't it, Lorri?"

Lorri sighed. "I honestly don't care to remember."

"No, it was." Fellan went on. "She practically lived with him, Princess. Though I do believe in different rooms, so don't you worry."

My teeth met and gritted.

"Oh, the fun they had. Hardly monogamous from what I recall, but they were always together for every wild gathering." He laughed then. "I had a friend who walked in on one once. Females everywhere, he'd said. An endlessly magical sea of tits, cunts, and ass."

Lorri had apparently decided she did not wish to hear another goading word. I was tempted to follow her as she walked back toward her king.

Too curious and apparently masochistic for my own good, I stayed. It would help, I thought, to hate him just that little bit more.

"Wish I'd seen it myself, of course." Fellan tutted and stepped far too close. "If it weren't for his wildling of a sister and his heartbroken father dying, then I'd wager they'd still be at it."

I said nothing—wasn't given the opportunity.

Fellan feigned a forlorn sigh, his hand tightening around the hilt of the blade at his side. "Changed him well and truly, that did. But don't worry." He elbowed me hard, and I ignored the impulse to place a hand over my ribs as the sneaky brutality and his words knocked the wind from me. "Looks like they might be on the cusp of a sweet second chance."

His hoarse laughter stalked me when I finally drew away.

I was so enraged, so distracted by the knots that had replaced my innards, I all but threw myself back into the ever-growing crowds. Bodies crushed and shoved, and I ducked to avoid another blow from an elbow, this time to the head.

My hand was stolen.

Before I could react, a strange male with indigo eyes hauled me close. He grinned, fiendish, then twirled and spun me deeper into the suffocating swarm.

It took me a moment to realize he was dancing with me. That for the first time outside of my room inside of an apartment in the middle lands, I was actually dancing.

And not on my own.

But my awed smile slipped when another male grabbed my hand, and apprehension slowed my feet. His eyes flared a burning sky blue as he pulled me toward his chest and inhaled my hair. "The heat has her," he said, the words almost groaned.

The male who'd stolen me first pressed his chest to my back. "Are you looking for help with that, Princess?"

"No," I said, smiling tightly and attempting to push away from them. But they were too much muscle, too tall to see past, and too insistent on persuading me.

"We've done it before."

"Yet to have found a mate from it, either," the new one said over my hair at my ear. "So we're not breaking any rules."

"Who knows..." The other male's hands clasped my hips. "Perhaps our beloved Mythayla will decide you'll be our mate."

Before I could tell them I wasn't interested in them nor what the goddess might have in store, another male joined us. "Bold," he said, his dark eyes glinting as he tossed back a goblet of wine. "To be touching the king's plaything."

"He's occupied." The indigo-eyed male squeezed my waist possessively. "We checked."

The new arrival who'd been overtly ogling me looked over my head, and his grin spread. "History always repeats itself with those two."

Jealousy, that insidious poison, stole my breath and burned through my veins.

The males laughed at the expression on my face. The new one took the opportunity to steal my hand and spin me around. "You're better off with us anyway, Princess."

Hands seemed to be everywhere all at once, traveling over my hips, arms, palms, and even brushing my thighs and ass. Hard groins were pressed upon me as they held and then spun me between them.

My lungs tightened, dizziness paralyzing.

Firelight and fiddles and drums melded into a storm of song that jumbled my thoughts and unsteadied my feet. But the males didn't let me fall. They wouldn't, which was the only reason I refrained from screaming for help. Instead, I played along until a gap opened between them.

I darted through it, the world tilting so much that I almost fell.

A hand caught my upper arm right before my outstretched palms met the grass, then pulled until the disgruntled barking of the males I'd escaped faded.

My back was pushed to a rough surface, my hands reaching be-hind me and feeling the bark of a tree. Panic receded, even though I could barely see the ice garlands blurring with the darkness. I'd made it to the tree line, away from the crush of groping hands and warm bodies.

Then a cloaked male's scent infiltrated. A hurried whisper en-tered my ear.

The hands holding me up released me.

I stumbled, quickly leaning back against the tree to catch my breath—absorbing the words that had been pressed to my ear by the stranger I hadn't seen.

If you wish to go home, find a way to the city florist on Ashen Street.

I shook my head, my vision still blurry as I held the tree and rounded it. I searched for the group of cruel faeries I'd left, attempt-ing to guess which one had whispered to me while knowing whoever it was hadn't been with them.

My eyes found Florian's furious gaze instead.

Even with the distance between us, I could see the anger tight-ening his features—that stiffened his entire frame.

He stood below the podium. Alone.

Guards approached me, Fellan thankfully not among them.

I swallowed and looked back to the dancing bodies, but the males who'd been toying with me were nowhere to be seen.

I didn't wait to be caught like a nuisance pet who'd wandered too far. I met the guards halfway. Seeming shocked as I passed them, they then trailed me back to Florian.

As soon as I neared, the king captured my hands, and we mate-rialized to my rooms in the manor.

I wasn't given time to recover from the journey.

Florian released me and strode to the door.

Disorientated again from materializing, I gripped the bedpost to stay steady on my feet. "You're angry," I foolishly croaked, feeling as though I had to say something before he left.

He laughed, the sound cold and hostile. "Angry doesn't even begin to cover it, *Princess*."

"I didn't mean to—"

"I've never felt more murderous in my entire fucking existence."

Oh.

Shit.

Guilt and jealousy tangled, causing my mouth to open again when every instinct screamed in warning that it would be safer not to speak at all. "I saw you," I whispered. "With her."

He stilled, but only momentarily. He opened the door and entered the hall.

"Florian, wait." I followed. "Please, I want to talk to you."

He turned back, effectively backing me into my bed chamber as the fury roiling from him drenched me in a light sweat.

My very flesh trembled. There was nothing I knew within his gaze, within his features and his prowled steps.

Before me loomed a stranger—a male with hatred where his soul once lived. It bled through his eyes, the air growing so cold, I feared it would snow indoors.

He was no longer Florian.

He was now a ruthless king capable of reducing another kingdom to rubble, stone by stone at a time.

"Bad pets do not get what they want." My next breath sat in my throat when he wrapped his hand around it. My pulse punched at his fingers as he growled to my mouth, "Leave these rooms without my permission, and you'll earn yourself a lesson on what regret truly means."

His eyes bored into mine, swirling with a darkness that rendered them almost black. After a moment that brought tears to my eyes, I was released.

The door slammed, snow flurries melting upon the floor.

SEVENTEEN

S LEEP REFUSED TO TAKE ME AWAY FROM THE FEAR AND uncertainty that had me pacing my bedchamber into the early morning hours.

And when it finally did, Florian still hadn't returned to his rooms.

I woke with the first touch of dawn creeping into the ice-covered windows and a pounding ache within my skull and limbs. There would be no king willing to soothe it for me, so I crawled from where I'd fallen asleep at the end of the bed and drew a bath.

I donned my preferred robe, without a reason to dress even if I had the energy to, and wondered if breakfast would be delivered.

I combed my wet hair while Snow whined to be let out.

The door wasn't locked. I still hesitated to open it, worried I'd be met with Florian's wrath for merely letting the wolf cub find a way outside.

Snow scratched at the wood. I gave in and let her out, hoping someone would do the same when she reached an exit to the manor downstairs.

The aches had morphed into something reminiscent of a fever. I'd never had one. Fae did not fall victim to sickness as humans did. But I'd tended to Rolina when she'd been bedridden with them so often that I knew the signs.

I drank the remaining water in the carafe within the bathing room, my hands shaking as I leaned upon the stone wash basin. My eyes were murky, my cheeks too pronounced and tinged with a flush that would not recede when I touched them.

I stared at the ginormous bathing tub beside me, tempted to climb back into the water I'd yet to drain.

A knock sounded.

I left the bathing room as the door to my rooms opened.

Olin, grim-faced, said in a tone that made me clutch at my robe, "The king desires your presence in the downstairs drawing room." He scowled when I didn't move. "Immediately."

I swallowed and nodded.

Atop the stairs, I turned when Olin said quietly from behind me, "Do not test him. I've only seen him like this once before." His eyes seemed absent, and I knew he was remembering whatever had happened then. "This time is different. He's..." He shook his head and exhaled heavily. "Be very careful."

Although alarming, it was possibly the nicest the steward had ever been to me. I nodded again, grateful for the warning and for the indication that he did not wish to see me murdered.

Even as a bone-deep instinct reassured me that Florian wouldn't hurt me.

At least, not in the ways Rolina had.

That didn't stop my heart from rattling in my chest as I made my way down the stairs to the drawing room. It stopped beating when I entered the open doors to find three faeries tied by their wrists to a wooden beam in the ceiling.

Their swollen and bloody faces made them nearly unrecognizable. Though that wasn't what horrified me so completely.

Ice encased them all. From their toes to their mouths, it appeared to cocoon them.

Regardless, I still knew who they were.

The overwhelming scent of their fear matched that of the males who'd tormented and touched me profusely at the Frost Festival.

Dread heavied my slow-to-return heartbeat.

Florian sat in the armchair by the snow-piled window.

At first glance, he was the definition of composure.

But he was without a shirt, his knuckles bloodied and cut. The foot resting over his knee bounced. His elbow dug into the leather armrest. His thumb slid over his lower lip, blue eyes fixed on the prey he'd hunted.

The doors behind me creaked.

I glanced over my shoulder to Olin. He pulled the doors toward him, giving me a slight nod, then trapped me inside the room with the king whose rage seeped from him as a second scent.

The earthy caramel fragrance I'd come to obsess over had sharpened. It was headier but tinged with an acidic aroma that heightened the senses, his fury a blistering-cold energy akin to standing outside during the arrival of a snowstorm.

No pair of his many boots adorned his feet. They were bare and speckled with blood that I knew was not his. His hair was a tangled mess as if he'd continuously swept his hands through it.

It was then the full magnitude of this male I'd been recklessly toying with sank into my psyche with claws so sharp, I struggled to find my next breath. He was a storm given the form of a Fae king, his energy crackling with every heaved rise and fall of his chest.

My refined keeper and tormentor was gone. In his place was a beast freed from his gilded cage.

One of the males groaned.

A dagger made of ice flew from Florian's palm and plunged into his cheek.

He bucked, but only moaned some more.

Startled into taking a step closer, I saw that each male's mouth had been sealed. The ice encasing their bodies stopped beneath their nostrils, leaving their eyes the only way to communicate their terror.

"Who touched you?" Though the question was soft, it was edged in warning.

I kept staring at the males, but none dared to acknowledge me. Their eyes remained on the ceiling as if they were afraid they might fall upon me and they would be further punished.

"Tullia," Florian clipped.

The use of my real name jarred me. I looked at the king.

His eyes were on the males. I still knew he was aware of every burning breath I drew.

I shook my head, wanting to move closer to Florian to reassure him—to attempt to end whatever this was—but not daring when his energy flared in warning. "They all did, but they were only fooling around," I said, my words and tongue thick. "Just dancing."

"Just dancing," Florian said, his lips spreading into an unnerving and blinding smile as he rose from the chair.

I staggered back but croaked out, "Yes."

Florian slowly paced before the males, and two of them squeezed their eyes closed. The other continued to stare at the ceiling.

As heavy seconds passed, I wondered if Florian had calmed enough to be reasoned with. I stepped closer, then stilled when he stopped pacing and wrapped his hand around the frozen arm of the male in the middle.

Muffled screams were trapped behind the ice covering his mouth, blood vessels bursting in his eyes, as Florian pulled.

Blood sprayed red and unending over the stone floor.

I stared at the severed arm melting within a pool of warm blood. "Florian," I wheezed, my hand clapping over my mouth. "*Why?*"

I'd known he was not a good male. I'd known, yet I hadn't imagined him capable of something like this.

"They touched you," he said, and so simply, as he stared at the male who'd lost consciousness while he stood before the next one. "*Groped* you." He turned to me with eyes so dark and wild, I ceased breathing. He jabbed his finger at his chest. "My treasure. My creature." He turned and kicked the leg of the male behind him, roaring, "Fucking *mine.*"

More blood rained, and I fell to my knees.

I blinked at the severed leg, afraid I would vomit as the room twirled and twirled, and my stomach roiled.

Florian crouched before me and lifted my chin in a terrifyingly gentle hold. "Who took you into the trees?"

"No one," I rasped.

His eyes sparked at my audacity to lie, venom coating each clipped word. "Who took you into the fucking trees, Tullia?"

My eyes closed.

I had to say something—but I refused to give him everything when those whispered words of going home were all I had.

Find a way to the city florist on Ashen Street.

He growled, and I opened my eyes. "It wasn't any of these males, Florian, I swear. Someone helped me get away from them, and when I found my bearings, whoever it was had disappeared."

He searched my damp eyes, no trace of the male I'd come to know visible in his own. Every inch of him had surrendered to his baser instincts—to the predator that lurked beneath his skin.

I'd caused this. By walking away from the throne during the festival, by falling victim to feelings and desires I couldn't tame, I'd caused all of this.

And to make him stop, I would need to bring him back.

Guilt sliced sharp and deep, stealing my breath and then sending it from me in a heaved exhale.

Florian snarled, "I don't believe you."

My fingers shook as I unfolded them to grasp his wrist. He tensed, his upper lip curled, but the king did not recoil when I brought his hand to my mouth. I held his gaze as I pressed my lips to his bloodstained palm. "No one has ever touched me in the ways that you do."

His eyes, which had been fastened on my mouth at his hand, snapped to mine. His nostrils flared slightly as though he were sniffing for a lie.

There was no lie to be found.

"Florian, I need..." My words trailed into hoarse noise as my eyes flicked to the bloodshed surrounding us, and I ceased trying to ignore the desire within me.

Instead, I squeezed his hand, allowing the heat I could no longer battle alone to bloom.

His gaze slowly traveled over my robe, assessing and cold, yet I warmed further beneath his appraisal. "The heat." His head cocked. "So potent, I cannot sleep near you, knowing how much you need me." Unblinking eyes met mine. "You need me, don't you?"

I nodded, still clutching his hand at my cheek.

His thumb brushed the flushed skin there, his eyes narrowing when he discovered it wouldn't recede. "Tell me you fucking need me, Tullia."

I didn't hesitate. Not even the blood and horror marring this room could stop me from finally whispering, "I need you, Florian. Now."

Rather, such gruesome possessiveness had only made me all the more desperate.

The shame of my reaction to his actions faded, taking the guilt and sickness with it. For what he'd done, understanding why he'd done it...

I shivered, and the incessant ache in my core panged and swelled like never before.

Florian noticed, of course, and he cursed.

He plucked me from the floor. My arms and legs curled around his shoulders and waist as he carried me from the drawing room to the stairs. His unhurried steps and protective hold beneath my ass and the back of my neck were telling.

He would have me, and there was no stopping him. No turning back.

Fortunately, I didn't want to.

I wanted to end this torment once and for all, despite the numerous consequences that would follow—the reasoning I'd clung to for days. None of it seemed to exist now. Nothing existed but him and the press of his body burning through my robe, his scent singeing and melting my limbs as I inhaled deeply at his neck.

A rumbled noise climbed his throat.

I kissed it, laid my lips upon it, the molten heat inside me dancing with impatience. He held me tighter, and as soon as the doors closed to his rooms, warned to my ear, "There will be no running from me now."

"I don't want to."

A dark chuckle sent a shiver down my spine.

Strange cracking sounded.

My head rose as I was carried toward the bed to find ice crawling over the doors—sealing them. More crawled over the balcony doors.

"No one but me is allowed to hear your cries, pet."

Then I was set on my feet, my legs wobbling as Florian ripped open my robe. He groaned and pushed me backward onto the bed. I blinked up at the candles in the chandelier as he ordered, "Open your legs."

I surmised he was in no mood for teasing.

I did as I was told while he removed his pants, his stare plastered between my thighs. He rubbed his bristle-bordered mouth, cursing roughly. My own dried at the sight of all he was, my eyes unable to decide where to feast first.

I didn't get the chance to decide.

Muscle clenched everywhere, my legs gripped above the knee when the king climbed onto the bed.

His hold was bruising, but I forgot about the pain when he lifted my core to his mouth and rubbed me over his lips and nose. He groaned, then licked me, and that desperate entity inside me who'd been starving for what felt like eons ruptured at only the fifth languid swipe of his tongue.

I moaned as he hummed against me in approval.

Then he lowered my shaking legs but leaned forward and wrapped them behind him. His cock pressed to my entrance. He gave no other warning, no soft reassurances like those I'd read in books. He was incapable right now. Possibly always.

He eased inside my body in one slow yet determined thrust.

My back arched. My muscles seized.

My body bucked and screamed in refusal.

But Florian captured my hips and held me still, his cock deep inside me as waves of agony spread like fire. Breathless and trapped, I whimpered without sound.

My eyes opened to find the king's gaze crawling over me with unmistakable delight. "Sweet creature, am I hurting you?"

He knew he was. I still further pleased him by saying, "Yes."

"Good." His gaze fell to where we'd joined, pain locking my limbs. "You're broken now, butterfly," he said, still staring as he slowly withdrew from my body to the tip. His smile was feral satisfaction. "Your blood marks my cock."

He pushed back inside me, and a scream scraped my throat.

His neck rolled, muscle cording as a guttural groan trembled his giant frame. Then my hips were released and he was looming above me.

His elbow indented the bed beside my face. His wrist pressed to my cheek as his hand covered my mouth. The other caught my hands and held them above my head. He withdrew again, then entered me in a hard thrust, his hips grinding.

He groaned, loud over the sound of my smothered cries.

His head lowered aside mine, his every low and gritted word heating my ear. "My defiant, daring creature. Look at what you've done."

My thighs quaked as my feet dug into his smooth ass. My body curled up against his in search of both reprieve from the burn of his cock and more friction. He slid out, and though I tensed against the scalding ache, a different heat delivered relief when he sank back inside me.

"Are you proud?" He licked my pulse, teeth nipping. "Does it make you feel good to disrespect and torment me?" He kissed the skin he'd bitten, rumbling, "To rake your tiny claws over my chest and watch me lose my fucking mind?"

My heart clenched. I shook my head, attempting to talk—to tug my hands free—and failed.

"I think it does." His slow thrusts gained more speed, more

bruising power. "What am I to do with you now, Princess? It seems you were created solely to test me." Another groan. "And to take me." His teeth pierced my skin with his words. "But only me."

I bucked against him once more, but the pain receded when he sucked the wounds his canines had given.

Alarm prodded at my hazed mind.

He was feeding from me.

It left as quickly as it came as every ounce of pain began to fall away like water pushed over a cliff.

Warmth, so swift and drugging, flooded from my scalp to my toes. It was akin to standing in the sun after feeling cold for an eternity. I shivered and moaned. My legs tightened around his waist and my head tilted to give him better access to my throat.

"Good little pet," Florian crooned and lapped at my neck. "By the time we leave these rooms, you will hunger for me as much as I do you. And butterfly..." He circled his hips with a grunt. "We won't be leaving for days."

I gasped when he stole his warmth from me and rose.

I was pulled off his cock, his hooded eyes watching himself slowly leave my body. His chest heaved heavily, once, twice, while a glowing sky blue overtook his eyes. Then he lowered his head at the same time he lifted my legs from behind my knees, helping himself to my center.

"Florian..." I was about to warn him of the blood.

But of course, that would be redundant when it was blood he desired.

His tongue flattened and dipped, seeking every drop of my broken virginity. I orgasmed almost instantly and with violence, pain flaring and soothed by his tongue. He kissed my clit, then sucked it, and forced my thighs to stay open when I attempted to close them.

It was too much.

And not nearly enough.

He pushed his cock inside me as soon as my ass met the bedding again. "You're so fucking swollen, butterfly." My head was caged within the bulk of his arms, his bloodstained lips trailing over my jaw with his rasped, "Squeezing silk."

Remembering that my hands were free, I clutched his head while he moved in and out of me, wanting his teeth in my neck again. He sensed as much as I held him there, and chuckled, the sound primal and throaty.

The sharp puncture of his canines stilled my limbs, but when he suckled, I was once again given that unearthly bliss.

A bliss that matched the sparking pleasure from the movement of his hips.

"Come on my cock, Tullia," he ordered and licked at the blood I felt trickling toward the bedding. He groaned, tongue dipping into my clavicle, and began to fuck me harder.

My fingers clenched his hair, and my thighs shook.

He rose as I spasmed around him. "Fuck."

I moaned and met his thrusts.

He gripped my throat when my back arched and my eyes closed. To the corner of my mouth, he demanded gruffly, "Eyes on me."

His thrusts sharpened, learning where to strike to prolong the rapture racing through my veins and hitching every breath. His eyes were still aglow, his lips parted. His hand slid up my neck, his thumb rubbing my lower lip.

I caught it with my teeth and sucked.

His eyes flared. He stilled, then pounded into me three times before his head tipped back. His shoulders and throat corded with veins and muscle, his entire body shaking as he released with an animalistic sound inside me.

At that moment, I feared the consequences again, but for a different reason. As his thumb left my mouth and our gazes locked, I knew that even if I survived him, I would never recover from him.

Florian's chest heaved with another violent, exhaled curse.

Then he fell over me and pressed his mouth to mine, hard and fleeting. His nose skimmed my cheek, his lips dragging down my chin to my chest.

Reclaiming his hair, I stared at the ceiling and licked my own blood from my lips.

Panic and thickening desire broke through my skin in a light sweat as he sucked my nipple and rotated his hips, the shudders of his body gentling. "It feels worse," I thought aloud, fear entering my needy bones again.

His mouth left my breast with a wet pop, and the king I'd grown far too enamored with began to return.

He smirked down at me, but it was softer, his hooded eyes too, as he said, "I know." Then he rolled off me. "On your hands and knees, butterfly."

EIGHTEEN

PPARENTLY, I DIDN'T MOVE FAST ENOUGH.

He lifted and dropped me to the bed, and I yelped as he smacked my ass.

He gripped it, squeezing so tight I would surely bruise. I moaned through clenched teeth when his own nipped the flesh, then shook when his finger slid through the mess he'd made of me.

He rose behind me and knocked my knees open wider with one of his. A hand glided over my arching back, gooseflesh erupting and a purred sound leaving him. My hair was gathered and wrapped around his fist while he slowly circled my clit with his other hand. "Who put the bruise on your ribs?"

The need I needed him to quell faster flared so acutely, it almost hurt when he stopped touching me and waited for me to answer.

With the bodies likely still hanging in the drawing room two floors below, I couldn't find it within me to hand over the guard, regardless of whether Fellan loathed me. After seeing what Florian did to males who danced with me and dared to touch me too much, I couldn't imagine what he'd do to one who'd intentionally injured me.

I moaned with feigned frustration that was all too real. "I don't know. There were a lot of people at the festival."

He didn't like that answer. But it was the only one he would get.

My head was pulled back by my hair until my eyes met deep-sea blue. "Do not protect the undeserving."

"I need you to touch me," I pleaded truthfully.

He relented with a twitch to his eye, but his hold on my hair remained tight. "Where?" When I didn't respond, he tugged. "Your pretty little cunt?"

The word whimpered free. "Yes."

His chuckle was whiskey and ice. "Never have I enjoyed defiling a creature so much."

Jealousy pinched at my chest. I couldn't keep from remembering the female he shared so much history with. "Who was she?" I panted.

The king stilled, tugging until my gaze met his again as he loomed over my arched back. "Who?"

"The female you were speaking with."

His eyes narrowed, then gleamed. A rough chuckle caused that pinch to turn into a burn. "I see."

"That doesn't answer my question."

His finger slid to my opening, then inside me. My eyes fluttered, my toes curling with the digit as he stroked me with precision. "That I am here with you and satiating our needs should." An intentional pause before he clipped, "She is no one you need to worry about."

"I want to know who she was to you."

"And I want you to drench my hand before I stretch you with my cock again."

I shivered, fighting the encroaching orgasm.

Florian brushed my clit, and my thighs quaked. "She was then, and all I've been interested in for far too long is now." Those gritted words confused but warned me he would tell me nothing more.

He leaned over me to skim his mouth across my cheek. "Come." He dunked his finger in and out of me, the digit growing ice cold.

I startled, my flushed skin adoring the contrast, and gave in. All of me trembled as his magic-coated touch coaxed me to much-needed release.

His lips rubbed my cheek with his praise. "Perfect fucking creature."

His iced finger withdrew, but his hand stayed wrapped in my hair as he slammed into me from behind while I struggled to stay on my hands and knees. My skin hummed with pleasure, and my breaths left me hard and fast, as I clenched around his invading cock.

A groaned, "fuck," rumbled from him as he planted deep and allowed me a moment to adjust.

But only a moment. He reared back and eased back in. Once, twice, and on the third, he stopped. "You're still jealous," he said, smoothing a hand over my ass cheek. He slapped it when I didn't respond. "Answer me."

"Yes," I growled.

He laughed, a deadly song that ripened and chilled my blood. "And you were even more jealous when you wandered off and then saw me talking with Nalia last night."

Just hearing him say her name incensed. He didn't need me to answer that, and wanting to see how he'd punish me next, I didn't.

My silence earned me another smack and a squeeze of my breast. He tugged my head back again, then rocked his hips. I gasped as pleasure sparked. "You're intentionally trying to get into trouble, aren't you, pet?"

I sucked my lower lip, but I failed to hide my confirming smile.

He cursed and turned my head, his mouth claiming mine. His tongue swept in, then he stole my own with his teeth. He bit it, licked my upper lip, and broke away to stare at me intently. "You infuriate and arouse me like no other."

"The feeling is so very mutual," I rasped, then smiled as I added, "*Majesty*."

His eyes thinned, but his mouth quirked. I was relieved to see it—the return of his usual arrogance, though I couldn't deny that I wouldn't mind seeing the fury-charged beast who'd stolen my virginity again.

I also couldn't deny that I just wanted him.

All of him—every sharp and blisteringly cold and slow-to-warm facet. I wanted it all, and I couldn't find it within me to be fearful of that when he looked at me as he did.

As though he knew exactly what I thought, all I desired, and he was smug in his victory of taming me so thoroughly.

He licked my jaw, and I mewled like a fucking cat.

I had no shame, especially when he hummed his approval and released my hair to clasp my throat. Easing in and out of me, he rubbed my racing pulse and kept my eyes fastened on his, as he watched me rise toward the precipice of pleasure again.

As I came apart, he growled into my ear, "I'm going to fill you with so much seed, no male will even breathe too close to you when you eventually leave these rooms." Then he released my neck and leaned back to fuck me so hard, our skin slapped and sharp cries fled me.

A hoarse roar sent me over the edge once more as he gripped my hips and stilled.

"Fuck, butterfly." It pleased me to hear his breath ragged and feel his body jerk with violent aftershocks against mine. He heaved again, "*Fuck*."

He withdrew, leaving me unbearably empty, and I scowled as he fell to the bed and swept a hand through his hair.

"Tired, Majesty?" I taunted, shamelessly ogling the lean muscle of his thighs and lower abdomen. A light sheen of sweat glistened, and I leaned down to lick it from the dips in his abdominals.

His cock hardened. "I fear I'll never tire of you." His stomach and teeth clenched when I gripped his length. He groaned. "Sit on me. Put my cock inside you."

The ache within me that refused to relent demanded I do exactly that. I licked him first, from the base of his shaft to the swollen head, uncaring of the bodily fluids still dampening the rock-hard flesh.

He cursed viciously and tugged me over his chest. My legs settled astride him, my cheeks clasped in his hand while the other helped push his cock inside my body.

To my lips, he whispered throatily, "You're far filthier than I thought you'd be."

"Don't tell me you're disappointed."

"Sweet creature." He grinned, and his lips glided over mine with each word. "We've barely scraped the surface of all the many ways I wish to corrupt you forevermore."

Wings spread within my chest, fluttering. I swallowed all of him with my eyes fastened on his and a moan washing over his lips.

His lashes lowered and lifted when I splayed my hands over the tattoo covering his hair-dusted chest and leaned back. "Feel good?"

"Yes." He was so deep, it hurt. But I was so full, I'd never felt so good.

"Roll your hips." He watched my body move over his with his lip between his teeth. "Now tilt them back." He groaned as if being tortured, his eyes lightening to a bright blue once more. Then he rose and wrapped my legs around him. His fingers dug into my hair, his other arm banding tight around my waist to grip my hip.

I rocked over his length, my gaze fused to his, and said, "I want your mouth."

"Where?"

"Everywhere."

He smirked. "Would you like me to kiss you?"

"Yes," I breathed, the word a plea.

Softer than I'd expected, his lips meshed to mine.

He parted them. Unhurried, he devoured me with relish, and nipped my lips when I tried to do the same to him. His tongue skimmed under my upper lip, then dragged over my teeth.

"Where next?" he whispered, sucking my lower lip into his mouth and releasing it with a scrape of his teeth. I moaned, an orgasm unfurling, as he said, "Here, precious pet?" and pressed his mouth to my throat.

I mumbled something incoherent, my hips jerking.

His hold firmed, my breasts squashed against his chest, as waves of pleasure shook me. "You're going to be the end of me," he said, hoarse, then stole my mouth and lifted me from the bed.

Books fell to the floor as I was carried to the wall near the ice-sealed doors, still shaking from release.

He gripped my rear and thigh and chased his own release. I held tight to his broad back and shoulders while, over and over, he drove into me.

His teeth captured the delicate skin at my neck, but though I half hoped he would, he didn't break it. He sucked as his rhythm slowed. Pressing deep, he emptied inside me with a gravelly groan against my pulse.

I clutched the back of his head. My fingers rubbed and swam through the thick softness of his long hair. Needing more already, I tightened my hold, all the while wondering if this heat I'd dreaded would become something I might wish would stay.

For I could get far too accustomed to this—his bruising hands and soft mouth and the aggressive hunger that matched my own.

Sooner than I'd have liked, Florian set me upon the bed, and I smirked into the sheets as he collected the fallen books and placed them back. He entered the bathing room, and though I itched for him to return and douse the building need inside me again, my eyes closed.

They opened what might have been only minutes later, his scent and nearing heat heady to my ripened senses.

Florian picked me up as though I weighed nothing and carried me to the waiting bathing pool. Still holding me, he climbed in and set me upon a rock-hewn ledge within the water.

I blinked at him in surprise and confusion, unsure what he had planned for me now.

Reaching behind him into a basket, he plucked a caramel-scented soap and lathered it within his hands. "Come to me."

I dropped into the water and swam to him.

"Wet your hair."

The pool was as deep as I imagined, my knees only bending slightly as I did as requested. When I emerged and smoothed my hair back, his lips parted. I brushed water from my eyes and tucked myself between his knees.

He twirled his finger with a smirk, and I sat upon the rocky step between his legs and stared at the steamed window that spanned the length of the pool.

"Are you sore?" he asked, his talented hands running through my hair to spread the soap.

"A little, but not enough to care."

He was quiet for a minute, and I grew more aroused with every gentle rub of his fingers over my scalp. Ridiculous, I thought, yet I knew, even without the heat to blame, it would still be so.

"What does it feel like?" he asked.

"The heat?" Shocked not only by his curiosity but by the gentle hands cleansing my hair, it took me a moment to answer. "Hollow. Just so..." There was no better way to describe it other than, "Uncomfortably empty."

"Does it hurt?"

I shook my head. "It makes me feel sick when ignored for too long."

Florian hummed. "And how do you feel now?"

"Better," I said as his fingers massaged my scalp a touch harder. As if he were waiting on a more detailed answer. "But I still want more. I still..."

"Still what?" he asked, voice rougher.

"Ache to be filled."

His hands paused, and he hardened completely against my back. "I would pay good coin to hear you say that to me again and again."

I laughed and dunked my head underwater to rinse the soap.

When I emerged once more, Florian's hungry gaze warned me of his intentions. My stomach still lurched with anticipation as he pulled me over his lap.

"Put me inside you." After fumbling for only a moment, I did, and he whispered to my jaw, "Kiss me."

Delighted to finally be granted permission, I explored his mouth. I kissed each corner of his lips, licked the full shape of each, and bit him when he tried to kiss me back. He laughed, quiet and soft, and I ate as much of the delicious sound as I could.

My mouth traveled over his jaw, my tongue rubbing the sharp edge and the bristle. I ventured to his neck, found his pulse, and flattened my tongue to drag over it. He chuckled when I did the same to his Adam's apple, and I admitted a touch breathlessly, "I've been wanting to do that."

He stared, time dripping away and unaccounted for, as I luxuriated in the absence of his typically stoic features. He stared at me as if both in deep thought and lost to the way my breaths came faster through my kiss-swollen lips.

Then he kissed me, urgent and rough, before tilting my head back with his hand in my hair to torment my breasts.

I rolled my hips to make his cock press exactly where I needed it. It didn't matter that I'd already climaxed numerous times. The heat wasn't done. I was far from done with enjoying this king I should loathe and reject with every corner of my soul.

Though I knew with a certainty that should have shamed that even if I weren't drowning in the need to mate until this heat ended, my body still wouldn't care a thing for right and wrong and logic.

It would still refuse to obey me whenever he was near.

Release arrived swiftly, and on the cusp of welcoming it, Florian clasped my face. His mouth grazed mine. "Watching you come is a fucking addiction."

This unfeeling yet passionate king was an addiction. One I knew I would never crawl free from.

And as I was delivered in a sleepy haze back to his bed, I realized it wasn't the end of the heat that I feared.

I feared what it would cement between us long before it did.

I woke aching in strong arms.

Florian slept soundly, holding my thigh over his hip and my head at his throat. I didn't have the heart to wake him. I'd already done so twice since we'd left the bathing pool a mere few hours ago. So I tried to sleep some more.

Florian must have scented it, or perhaps he'd sensed I'd woken up.

He ordered thickly, "Roll over." His fingers squeezed my thigh. "You're to tell me when you need me, butterfly."

"You need to rest." Yet I was desperate enough that I rolled away from his chest to face the balcony doors, which were still sealed in frost.

He lifted my leg, his admission a throaty groan as he slowly pushed himself inside me. "My people believe it is an honor to see a female through the heat, and sweetest creature..." He licked the arch of my ear. "I've never felt so fucking honored in my entire life."

In an effort not to let those words burrow deep within my chest, I didn't respond. To let them in would be a mistake when this king hadn't a heart of his own.

NINETEEN

LORIAN SET A TRAY OF FOOD ON THE DRAWERS, THE DOORS clicking closed and resealing with ice.

I wasn't hungry. Not for food.

Two days had passed since he'd trapped me in his chambers. He seldom left them, and he certainly wouldn't let me leave. He'd forced me to hydrate, and he'd even withheld more orgasms until I'd eaten.

I studied his bare back, wishing he'd remove those pants and come back to bed. A bed that would need some serious tending to after this heat had left. I traced a smear of blood upon the bedding while he prepared dishes, his back still to me as he said, "Time to eat."

"You?"

He stilled, then eyed me over his shoulder. "Careful, butterfly."

But I'd meant it.

The hunger I now felt might have been foreign, but I was aware of what it was. The desire had grown with every hour spent together. I wanted to drink from him as he had me. It was a want so harrowing that my own blood pulsed in my ears with each step he took toward the bed.

He crooked his finger.

I crawled across the bedding to him without a shred of thought or shame, and gripped his pants.

He tutted. "Not yet." I glared up at him. He smirked, then ordered softly, "Open those lovely lips."

I did, and he bit into the strawberry before placing it between my teeth. With hooding eyes, he watched them sink into the fruit. "You make me want to kill anyone who's ever looked at you."

It hurt to swallow, both the small bite of fruit and his words.

234 | ELLA FIELDS

He swiped juice from my lower lip, then sucked it from his thumb before offering me another strawberry. I chewed as he returned to the tray of food, unsure how I was supposed to move forward after this. After all of the feeding and fucking and feeling.

I'd walked the finest of lines for weeks. Now, after the heat had forced my surrender, that line had disappeared.

The loathing, hurt, and fear twined in a protective barrier around my heart refused to stay. He'd unraveled it so thoroughly and expertly that there was not enough left to return to when this ended.

If it would ever truly end.

He'd bathed me, fed me, held me, taught and learned me. He'd tended to the overwhelming evolvement of my body with a stamina few males would possess.

I should hate him. A part of me still did, though it was now mostly due to the shame he made me feel for my growing obsession with him.

But most of all, I was just... grateful. Relieved that it was him seeing me through the heat, and that I hadn't needed to find a willing stranger or attempt to endure the impossible by waiting for it to pass.

"Thank you," I said, the word close to a whisper when he returned to feed me some bread and soup.

Florian's hand paused over the golden bowl, his eyes upon the creamy concoction within. Then he brought the bread to my mouth. "Do not thank me, butterfly." Lust brightened his gaze and dropped his dark lashes as he watched me eat. "I am far from selfless, especially when it comes to you."

I understood his meaning, and it didn't erase my gratitude in the slightest. "I'm sure many a male has desired another in the way you do me, but that does not mean they'd be so..." I gripped his wrist, taking the rest of the bread and smiling as I chewed and settled on, "Doting."

Florian huffed, again wiping at the food that'd escaped my lips and sucking it from his thumb. "Doting is not the right word," he said, and headed back to the tray.

Instead of asking what was, for I had a feeling he would not answer, I asked another burning question. "Who's watching Snow?"

He returned to me with more bread. "The twins."

I missed her. It hadn't been that long, yet I was beginning to miss the entire estate I'd thought to be my prison full of enemies. "Can I see her tomorrow?"

"Not unless I bring her to you." Noting my displeasure, he murmured with a gloss of his knuckles over my cheek. "You're still vulnerable."

I gently pushed his hand away when he offered me another bite of bread, forcing back a smile when he scowled. "I'm over the worst of it."

"I'm not," he said, gruff. "I want you where I know you're protected and can see you until it's over."

I sighed and bit into the bread, the pleased glint in his eyes tempting me to bite his fingers. He wouldn't mind, and so I didn't bother.

"What happens," I said, swallowing the dough, "after it's done?" I'd been so distracted with trying to survive it, then satiating it—obsessed with overindulging in this king with an appetite to rival any goddess-given heat—that I hadn't been able to give enough thought to what would come.

Florian glared down at the bowl, as if unsure how to answer that.

Cold slithered into my chest.

I attempted to ignore it by saying, "My abilities." I'd never expected to have any outside of materializing unless they were small and few, for I'd never expected to discover that I was a royal.

"Your ability to materialize will be easier, but as for the rest..." He dipped the bread and pushed it between my teeth. "We wait and see."

If I could materialize with more ease, and if Florian could teach me how to break into the energy folds for that to happen, then I could reach Baneberry.

I could reach King Molkan. My father.

Perhaps, I thought dangerously, I could even find more than the answers I desired about my family. Perhaps I could find more information about this hatred between Molkan and Florian.

And perhaps then I could help end all of this.

Unable to bite my tongue nor keep the gathering eagerness from my voice, I said far too quickly, "I want to test it. Materializing."

The king frowned as if knowing exactly why I would want to learn. "Not while the scent of your constant state of arousal still lingers so potently."

Of course, he would not teach me such a thing. He didn't trust me, and he was right not to.

I didn't take it personally. I would indeed run as soon as an opportunity arose, and Florian trusted very few. And though I knew he would tend to my every need inside these chambers, I did not trust him either.

If there was a way out of this game of war and revenge, I would not find it here. No matter how skilled the king was at tempting me to believe in this false sense of safety.

"It is a song," Florian explained in my silence. "A call to the wild that has found many their counterpart."

That piqued a new curiosity that was certainly better left alone. "A mate, you mean?"

He nodded once and turned back to the tray of food. "The heat repeats for a handful of years until a mate is found, or the female body simply learns to respect the soul's decision not to hurry the search for one."

I stared at the captivating expanse of his back, the question I didn't need to ask stuck like glue behind my teeth.

Florian braced his hands upon the drawers, seemingly lost in thought as he stared down at the food. Muscle bulged in his biceps when he clenched the wood, then swept a hand through his tousled hair.

It was best to talk of something else, so I decided to show him what I'd sensed after he'd left me alone in his chambers.

I stood and crossed to the drapes covering the balcony doors. "Look."

Florian turned, his brow furrowing and his lips forming a tight line.

"Baneberry royals have an affinity for nature, do they not?"

Birds filled the balcony. Every inch of the stone railing was covered, and some even perched upon the ground.

The king walked over to join me, and I expected the birds to fly away. They didn't.

Sunlight streaked across his cheek and torso, his taut skin close to gleaming in response and his eyes nearing a rare shade of purple. "Flora, usually." The belated words were absent. "That which grows from soil."

His quiet tone, and the hardening of his features, flattened my excitement yet again. "Perhaps they're drawn to fornicating royals, then," I tried to say in jest to lighten the unexpected arrival of tension, but my voice was weak.

Florian said nothing.

After another moment of studying the birds who still hadn't moved, he tore the drapes closed and returned to the tray of food. "Perhaps."

I stalked behind him and grabbed his waist, wanting to rid the heaviness that'd filled his voice and the room. "So perhaps you should stop feeding me food and give me something better instead."

Florian smirked when I slipped between him and the drawers, and he clasped the back of my head. His gaze danced with mine, his smirk falling with the growing hunger that brightened his eyes. Then he lowered his head to place his mouth over my thundering pulse.

He kissed it once before his lips moved lower, the only warning I had. His teeth sank into my neck at the same time he plunged two fingers into my body.

My legs quaked, euphoria rushing through my veins and pushing with cold heat against my skin.

The undulating mixture of bliss, coupled with his hooking fingers and the rumbled groan in his throat, rendered me instantly mindless. Stars danced before my wide-open eyes as I gripped Florian's head and his bicep.

"Delicious creature." He kissed the punctures in the curve of my neck. His arm lowered to hold me up while I convulsed over his hand. My chest heaved, my blood heating all over again when he slowly ceased pumping his fingers and carefully withdrew them from my body.

He brought them between us, his eyes aglow on mine as he sucked them clean. "Sweetest fucking thing I've ever had the pleasure of tasting."

Jealousy threatened to taint the warmth those words gave me.

I needed to cease wearing my thoughts on my face. That, or this male needed to cease being so damned perceptive. He smirked and undid his pants. "Your possessiveness is showing, Princess." Closing his lips over mine, he kissed me so softly, then murmured, "And it's making my cock throb."

"I do not wish to share you, Florian," I said without thinking.

Anger had taken hold, spurred by the sickness induced by the mere thought of him doing any of this with another. As well as remembering what that hostile guard had said—how he'd still indulged in others when he'd had Nalia as his lover.

Florian stepped out of his pants.

Embarrassed by what I'd said, though I'd meant it, I couldn't even bring myself to ogle all of him. I stared at the tray beside us with its leftover fruit and remaining mound of bread. Unsure what to say as the silence stretched but knowing I'd already said too much, I reached for the glass of water.

Florian allowed me two sips before setting it back on the tray. "What have I told you?"

"Not to make emotional requests, for they will be used against me."

Florian huffed. "And to fucking look at me."

Oh.

I gave him my attention, mortified even more.

Seeming amused and perhaps shocked that I remembered what he'd said in that room in the pleasure house, he loosened his jaw. "You think I would use such a desire against you?"

NECTAR OF THE WICKED | 239

"I am here to be used," I said carefully but firmly. "Am I not?"

He had nothing to say to that. He could not refute it. It was the cold truth.

Releasing a rough breath, he lifted me to the drawers and stepped between my legs. His nose trailed mine, his gaze holding mine captive. "You're here because it was always supposed to be this way."

Those words were meant to mollify me, I knew. They didn't.

His mouth crushed mine, his claiming kiss drawing blood and chasing away the darkness that had unfurled with his caged responses.

He left me panting to rub his cock through my center. His gaze stayed there, and I trembled with every nudge at my clit. "Feet up, sweet." I placed them on the edge of the wood, and he gripped me behind the knees. I was shifted forward and spread wide, his command strained. "Put me inside you."

We both watched as I did.

He released one leg to grasp behind my head, the wooden drawers groaning with every hard yet controlled thrust of his hips. I whimpered into his neck as a violent climax took me under, my teeth pinching his skin.

I didn't overthink it. I wanted all of him, needed to taste everything he was upon my lips and tongue.

And if he wouldn't give me what I needed, then I would take it with the same lack of remorse he'd shown me.

My canines pierced his skin.

"Tullia." His pace slowed, the hand in my hair tugging me back as the first heady drop of his blood met my lips. "Once you start surrendering to it, you will only last so long before needing it."

I swallowed, the copper and warm taste of him sliding down my throat. It wasn't enough. Not nearly enough. "I know." I licked my lips. "But it's natural."

"Some think differently." He looked at my mouth, his jaw and tone hardening. "Especially those from Baneberry." His eyes rose to my own. "Over time, it will weaken you. For it's one thing to drink blood, but to let that same creature take from you in kind can bind you."

He spoke as if I had not already bound myself to him in ways I would never escape.

"Well, I'm not in Baneberry, Majesty," I said, a touch too bitterly. "I'm here with you, and I want all of you." His nostrils flared, his pupils expanding. I frowned then, wondering if perhaps he had other reservations. "But if you do not wish for me to—"

His mouth slammed over mine, furiously bruising.

He moved inside me slowly while breathing me in. His hips halted when his mouth broke from mine with a rough exhale. "Go on, then, butterfly." He gripped my neck and cheek, then pushed my mouth to his throat. "Let me live inside you like you do me."

Though those words gave me pause, I greedily did as encouraged.

The taste of blood was not something I'd ever thought would appeal to me.

But feeding from Florian wasn't merely a consumption of the nectar that lived beneath his skin. It was a necessity I'd never known I needed. A nourishment I shouldn't crave but now knew I would indeed not last long without.

I needed no instruction for this. My legs twined tight around his waist. My teeth remained embedded in his flesh. My tongue lapped while I sucked. My heart soared as my body welcomed his essence with as much greed as my mouth.

I clasped his jaw to keep it tilted, unwilling to let him take this from me.

Not that he tried.

He cursed, a hard swallow sounding over my slight moans and bumping my nose. He was fire-coated ice, the warmth of him invading and spreading in a cold caress. The taste of him was pleasure and contentment unlike any other.

Intimate, indeed. I'd do atrocious things to make sure no one else could taste him in such a way—and to make sure I could do so again and again and again.

For if it were true that Mythayla provided an eternity of treasure to deserving souls in the last life, then this was it. Feeding from Florian would be it.

He groaned as I suckled and licked and swallowed, his hold at the back of my head gentling as he began to move inside me again. Within seconds, I came undone in an entirely new way. My release hit differently—a thunderous burn that tingled and cramped.

Tears filled my eyes.

The cries I'd smothered in Florian's neck were set free when he lifted my head, his thumb brushing over my cheek. "You're okay," he crooned. All the while, he didn't let up. He continued to fuck me with steady, unhurried thrusts. "Look at you." His eyes flared with his nostrils, then narrowed. "What have I done to you, sweet creature?"

I couldn't answer that, even if I'd been capable.

His smile was that of the true tyrant he was. He lifted me from the drawers and, still inside me, carried me to the bed. He laid me down and loomed over me. An exquisitely gentle kiss was pressed to my jaw with his gritted demand. "Answer me."

I croaked out, "You've ruined everything I've ever wanted." His head rose, tilting as he studied me with his gaze hardening. I smiled, reaching for the sharp crest of his cheek with fingers that still tingled. "You've ruined me."

His eyes flashed, his lips whispering over mine with his words. "You no longer seem so disappointed."

Because I wasn't, and he knew it.

I slid my hands into his hair and kissed him.

I might not have been disappointed, but I was unwilling to believe that the heat would change much of anything regarding Molkan and the kingdom of Baneberry's fate.

My kingdom's fate.

As night arrived and Florian returned from taking our dishes to the kitchen, I curled away from the drapes that blocked the birds still residing outside on the balcony. "When exactly do you intend on finalizing your plans of revenge, Majesty?"

That muscle feathered in his jaw. "Florian."

"*Florian*," I said, intentionally breathy.

He paused in kicking off his loose cotton pants. "Say that again."

I laughed, turning into the bedding. "Answer my question, and I'll consider it."

He smirked. "I'm afraid you'll need to be more specific."

"The wedding."

A tilt of his head as he neared the bed. "In a hurry to make sure I hold you captive forever, Princess?"

I scowled, but laughed again when he leaped onto the bed and tugged my leg until I was trapped beneath him. Above me, he was a darkness that blocked out all else, his eyes and teeth the only light. "I like it when you do that." He nipped my finger when I traced his mouth.

"Do what?" I whispered.

"Stare at me," he said gruffly. Lowering his head, he skimmed his nose over my cheek. "Smile at me."

My heart faltered, swelling when his lips grazed and gently tasted mine.

"Laugh because of me." He trailed a path of kisses down my chest to my center. "Time for dessert." That earned him another laugh that grew louder when he gripped my hips and nibbled playfully at my mound.

The following night, I woke starving but feeling more like myself than I had in weeks.

How that was possible when the changeling I'd been just weeks ago was now hard to see beneath all that had happened, I failed to comprehend while I searched the rooms for something to eat. There was nothing but a pitcher of water on the tray upon the drawers.

I drank half a glass, wondering about Florian's whereabouts.

I'd fallen asleep right after dinner, so it wasn't so late that Florian's absence was unusual. Mercifully, the heat had unlatched its claws. I wished I could have said the same about the desire for the male who'd seen me through it.

I opened the drapes to watch the birds that still resided on the balcony, and belatedly realized the ice encasing the doorframe was gone. Peering behind me to the doors giving entry to Florian's chambers, I found the same.

Even the door leading to my own chambers had been unsealed. I wasn't sure why that unsettled me.

Florian hadn't wanted anyone hearing us fuck night and day. But even as the heat had simmered to a milder burn overnight, we'd still spent all day doing just that.

He'd unsealed the doors tonight, then, I surmised, and walked toward them. That meant he was comfortable with me leaving, and although that fact troubled me, I still donned the robe Florian had hung in the bathing room and did so.

I crept down the stairs with fears of what tomorrow might bring now that I didn't need Hellebore's vengeance sworn king to feed, bathe, and soothe my every aching need. I should have felt relieved. I should have been thinking about the address whispered to me by the stranger I hadn't seen at the festival.

I should have been devising a way to get there to see if it would lead me to the only king who could answer the many questions still haunting me—my father.

The halls were silent save for the flower-shaped clock above the foyer entrance ticking toward midnight.

Which made the hushed conversation floating through the open doors to the manor all the more easier to hear.

"... finish this, Flor. Before she is taken and your precious advantage is lost."

"Do not give me orders, Fume."

I froze upon the landing before the last row of stairs, watching wisps of snow dance between the doors to melt upon the stone floor of the foyer.

"I'm not giving you orders. As your friend, I'm *pleading* with you to see reason," Fume urged. "I know the twist of fate makes it difficult, but you've come this far..." His voice dropped, but I still heard what sounded like, "To back down will only make you look even more distracted." A pause. "And therefore weak."

"Difficult," Florian said dryly.

Fume's voice became a whisper I could barely hear. "Just say the word."

Boots crunching over the pebbled drive sounded, shadows swaying over the stone of the entrance steps. My heart echoed in my ears as Florian barked something I missed beneath the screech of wind, and I strained to listen.

Then I heard him say, "No one touches her but me."

Their conversation then changed to fighting in the barracks and stolen weaponry near the border. It quickly became evident that Florian had a lot of catching up to do regarding the running of his armies and kingdom after spending so much time tending to me.

There was no guilt for keeping him from his duties. There was only confusion as I forgot all about heading to the kitchen and quietly walked back upstairs instead.

I couldn't make sense of what I'd overheard. Was Florian hesitant to marry me? To go forth with a celebration that would have all of Folkyn and beyond know it was official—he'd stolen and claimed his enemy's daughter.

Or was it something else?

Something that seemed so unfathomable, I couldn't even entertain the idea.

The only thing I knew with bone-deep certainty was that nothing was impossible where Florian's meticulous plans and wrath were concerned. So though it caused every ounce of me to protest, I knew I had no choice.

Further punctuating my thoughts, the clock downstairs gave one last echoing tick as I quietly closed the doors to Florian's chambers behind me.

It was time to make some plans of my own.

To sleep in my rooms would arouse suspicion when Florian assumed I was still asleep in his bed where he'd left me.

I failed to remember he'd catch my scent on the stairs and in the hall outside and know I was awake when he returned hours later.

The quiet sound of the doors clicking closed was akin to a drum pounding. "Where have you been, butterfly?"

I rolled to my back and stretched my arms over my head.

Florian stood by the chaise, unbuttoning his shirt. I chewed my lip and made a show of studying his broad chest. "Couldn't sleep. I was hungry."

Florian tossed the rippling black silk to the chaise, then unfastened his pants. "Need me?"

Incessantly, I thought but didn't dare say. I smiled. "For food."

He hummed, his gaze landing where the bedding had fallen from my breasts. "Not my cock, then?"

My smile grew, real this time, as he prowled toward me. He tore the blankets away to seize my ankle.

I squeaked, dragged to the side of the bed.

Just when I'd thought I'd gotten away with keeping my troubled thoughts to myself, he ran his hand down the inside of my leg. "Something upsets you." Panic bleated, and his eyes shot to mine as he heard it—the increased tempo of my heart. "Butterfly," he warned softly. "Tell me what has kept you awake."

"You," I whispered immediately, and honestly.

His hand stilled as he waited for more.

There was no point in not speaking of it, in hiding the truth when it might help me avoid admitting what I'd overheard earlier. "You're my mate, aren't you?"

He didn't answer, and he didn't need to.

He pushed his cock into my body and gathered my legs to his chest, causing him to sink so deep that pain flared. I moaned as he grasped my thighs and spread them, my feet at his hard shoulders, and slowly rocked his hips.

His head turned for his mouth to press to my ankle, and the action, coupled with his unrelenting gaze...

I closed my eyes, so confused and conflicted and cornered that tears threatened to arrive.

For once, the king didn't demand I keep them open.

He delivered my traitorous body to a release as gentle as the roughened fingertips trailing my legs, and then he followed with a snarled groan.

Afterward, he cleaned me, and I curled onto my side to face him when he returned from the bathing room. I searched those dark-blue eyes, and they searched mine.

And I wondered if we were both looking for something we were too afraid to find.

Fear had held me prisoner my entire life. More than Rolina. More than this male. And more than anyone else ever could.

I couldn't keep letting it control me. I had to stop letting it keep me where I didn't wish to be.

Here, that noose around my neck—the bond I'd found with this king—tightened. *I wish to be right here.*

But although I might have been a part of his plan, it couldn't be more clear, especially after hearing pieces of his conversation with Fume, that Florian was incapable of turning the tides of his own making.

And I'd been swimming toward nothing for too long.

Florian studied my every feature, his jaw firm. Yet he would not demand that I tell him what was ailing me again. Not when he did not wish to acknowledge things I'd rather not even acknowledge myself.

But I needed to.

I needed to use what I felt as a weapon, rather than let it use me.

I needed to use whatever he felt for me, however small, rather than let him play with me until he decided he was bored and his mission was complete.

So I said softly, "I still hate you, you know."

He tensed, something passing through his eyes.

Reaching out, I traced his cheekbone, whispering without enough air in my chest, "Most of all, I hate that I think I'm falling in love with you."

His lips parted slightly, but otherwise, he just continued to stare. He didn't blink. Florian did exactly what I expected and needed him to.

Nothing at all.

I rolled over to face the balcony doors and sleep, knowing he would leave me again and attempting not to let it wound. For although I hadn't thought I'd meant what I'd said, I supposed I had to some extent.

I was falling, and it was time to find a way out before his refusal to catch me killed me.

TWENTY

I'D ASSUMED CORRECTLY.

The following morning, Florian was gone.

It was what I wanted. What I needed. Yet alone in my own rooms, I bathed and angrily scrubbed useless tears from my cheeks.

A grizzly glance from Olin, when I ventured downstairs for breakfast and dared to ask of the king's whereabouts, conveyed the steward would rather swim naked in the iced-over lake than indulge any curiosity of mine.

He walked past me and up the stairs, nose in the air and a steaming cup of ginger-scented tea in hand.

Right. Still despised me, then. I sighed, even as I tried not to laugh.

One of the groundskeepers opened the manor doors to let Snow in.

The wolf bounded through the foyer toward me, bigger than I'd last seen and trailing mud behind her.

I crouched to nuzzle my face in her wet coat, then swiped dirt from her cheeks. "Did you miss me?" She licked my cheek, and I laughed. "I missed you more. Hungry?" I asked, rising and smiling as she raced ahead of me and down the hall to the kitchen stairs.

"Well, if it isn't the captive bride." Kreed wriggled his brows while I took a seat upon the stool at the island bench. "I'll need a minute to prepare you your usual." He pointedly cleared his throat. "After such a long absence."

Heat crept into my cheeks. I muttered scratchily, "It's only been a few days."

The cook grinned, blinding and mischievous. "*Four* days,

NECTAR OF THE WICKED | 249

Princess." He laughed, then whistled. "That's some prowess, even for a royal male."

I refused to tell him that I could have comfortably left the king's rooms yesterday, and that Florian had thought it best we be absolutely certain the heat was over beforehand. "Stop it," I hissed but smiled, then looked around. "Where are the twins? Though I'm glad they're not here to hear you tease me, I would like to thank them for watching Snow."

"Helping to clean up the melting mess outside." He dumped a cup of oats into a pot of water. "And no need. They tried to keep her, I'll have you know. I think you might have to share now."

I looked down at Snow, who was licking her bowl clean, relieved. Glad to know that should I find a way to Baneberry, then the wolf would be cared for. And if I never returned to this frosty kingdom, then she would be loved.

My chest clenched.

Forcing out a breath that shook, I feigned a yawn that made the cook laugh again as he finished preparing my breakfast.

I ate while lost in the gloom of my thoughts, and Kreed vigorously scrubbed the bottom of a large pot. Then what he'd said came back to me, and I stopped chewing to ask, "The snow melts?"

He shot me a smile over his shoulder. "The snow melts."

I frowned when he looked away, poking at my breakfast with the spoon. "You seem far too pleased by this." I would have thought the people of Hellebore knew exactly what living here entailed—terminal cold.

He laughed, the sound thick with dry disbelief. "Princess, it's been years of endless snow. Everyone is pleased."

I made a face. "The entire manor would be half buried if that were true."

Kreed snorted. "Believe me, it has been more times than I can count." He set the pot on the drying rack and grabbed the towel. "Florian hires some of Aura's people to help thaw things when it gets..."

He scratched at his jaw and made a strange noise, then finished with, "Particularly bad."

"So," I said, failing to understand his way of phrasing it. "Now autumn comes?" The only other season to grace this kingdom.

He gave me an odd look, then a pat on my shoulder as he headed for the stairs. "Only time will tell."

Before he could leave, I asked, "You wouldn't happen to know when Florian might return, would you?"

"As far as I'm aware, he's seeing to issues near the border. Could be days or mere hours."

Recalling that weaponry had been stolen, I asked, "The warrior camps?"

Kreed hesitated, gripping the doorframe. "Do not get my limbs severed, Princess." His flat expression said that Olin had already tattled on him to the king, and he'd since been warned not to appease my curiosities.

I winced. "Are the frozen males still hanging in the drawing room?"

He barked out a laugh. "Skies, no."

"Then..." I blanched, not wanting but needing to know.

Kreed gave me another look, then glanced up the stairs. Just when I'd thought he'd leave, he looked back at me and said quietly, "Guess most on the estate know, so..." He shrugged. "He killed them." Then he tapped the wood and left me to fester with all he'd said and wouldn't say.

Exhaustion and frustration and a gnawing sense of foreboding kept me from finishing my breakfast. I was so tired of this world of secrecy and deceit.

A world I'd desperately wanted to be a part of with such foolishly naive abandon.

I cleaned up my mess and left the kitchen, pondering a nap before I pondered plans of escape.

I withheld a groan when I found Zayla waiting in the hall.

My dismay evidently showed, for the guard smiled. "Try not to look too displeased, Princess. I'm merely in charge of making sure no harm befalls you." Eyeing me up and down, she pinched her lips. "Enjoy the heat?"

Her audacity punched a shocked laugh from me. I walked down the hall, and she quickly joined me. "I'd enjoy being able to go wherever I want more," I lied smoothly.

I highly doubted I'd enjoy myself so thoroughly ever again.

She paused before Florian's study. "You're not a prisoner, Tullia." The door behind her was cracked open. I could see the fireplace beyond the desk was empty, and there was not a trace of fresh smoke nor his scent.

He hadn't been in there at all today. Which confirmed he'd left for the warrior outposts while I'd slept.

I continued on. "That's exactly what I am, or you wouldn't still be following me everywhere."

"Would it help if I informed you that you are indeed permitted to go wherever you wish?" I turned to her, and the freckles upon her nose shifted as she smiled. "Providing you take a personal guard, of course."

Hope expanded so fast, I feared I'd wear it all over my face.

I cleared my throat and did my best to keep my features clean of anything other than a mild hint of expected excitement. I rolled my eyes. "Of course."

Zayla laughed.

I squinted at her with lingering disbelief. "Truly?"

She nodded, fixing the end of her long braid. "The king told me so himself right as he was leaving."

It had worked.

I didn't let that fool me into believing I now had Florian's trust in any form. But the confessing of my feelings, and acknowledging the reason for this unquenchable desire we couldn't shake for one another, that we were mates...

It had truly worked.

I stopped before the stairs, tempted to laugh. I calmed my features and tone. "Anywhere?"

Zayla bobbed her head. "Suppose it depends on how far any-where is."

"The city," I said, and probably far too quickly but beyond car-ing now.

It had worked, and it couldn't be taken back when Florian wasn't here. I could get to this florist on Ashen Street today.

A swooping took hold of my heartbeat while a sinking stone dropped to my stomach.

Zayla lifted her shoulders. "I cannot see why that would be an issue. I'll make arrangements with some of the other guards to escort you." She eyed me pointedly. "No plans of escape in my absence." A grim look at the drawing room beyond the stairs. "I do not wish to die so gruesomely."

I winced yet again, laughing humorlessly as I said, "Understood." Then I thanked her and watched her leave.

Once I knew she was gone, I let the hope and shaking nerves I'd tried to keep hidden propel me up the stairs in a rush to my cham-bers. Reaching the florist without the guards knowing would prove difficult, but if I could get close enough, perhaps I could outrun them.

That, or I would at least know exactly where to materialize to. Providing I could learn how when I'd only done so in dire situations thus far.

Dressing in a dark crimson gown with woolen lining and long flowing sleeves, I froze at the sight of the coat Florian had given me what seemed like so many moons ago.

Days. I'd been in Folkyn for mere weeks. Even more shocking was that I'd known Florian for less than a month.

In such a short time, not only had he changed my entire life—he'd also begun to change my beliefs and the beat of my heart. I couldn't imagine the damage he'd do if I stayed much longer, all the while knowing the chances of leaving Hellebore today were slim.

I would likely return to these rooms and to the male who'd given them to me. And I would again promise myself that I would find a way out when there was none to be found.

When perhaps I didn't truly want one.

I stopped at the door with the coat in hand. It would be too much with my gown, but after one last glimpse at the bed I hadn't slept in for four unforgettable nights, I donned it anyway and closed the door.

My growing affections for this kingdom's cold ruler were not enough to quiet the unrest inside me. An unrest he'd caused with his bloodthirsty plans, but that I could only fix myself. He would never change his mind, and he certainly wouldn't allow me to meet my father when he was the very reason I was here.

Florian could not love me, and trying to make him would not save me.

I would need to save myself. To seek all I needed before I fell into another trap I might have avoided if I'd only opened my eyes wide enough to see that something wasn't right.

And the befuddling conversation I'd overheard last night had been a stark reminder that none of this was right—no matter how differently the beating organ in my chest felt.

Downstairs, Zayla waited by the doors in the foyer. She sketched a playful bow. "Your wish has been granted, Princess."

"Thank you," I said, meaning it, as the portrait of Lilitha caught my eye.

Her mischievous eyes twinkled, and I could've sworn the young princess trapped within a painting attempted to convey something.

Shaking my head, I gathered my skirts to descend the damp steps to the drive.

I stopped at the sight of the guard leaning against the dark-blue carriage. He flicked ash from his tobacco stem and straightened with a grin. Smoke billowed from his mouth and clouded his face.

The ash floated across the royal insignia of the hellebore flower upon the carriage door, falling to the melting sludge upon the ground.

The driver, dressed in the regalia of a warrior, leaned down from his seat to smack the carriage. "Cease ogling and open the damned door, Fellan."

Zayla closed the doors to the manor.

Fellan shot the male a dark scowl and stomped on the stem with unnecessary vigor. "No one in their right mind would ogle Molkan's spawn." He glowered and spat at the ground.

I tensed and glanced at Zayla when she reached my side. "Apologies, Princess." A sharp warning look was given to Fellan. "He was one of few with a clear morning schedule."

"Wonder why," I muttered beneath my breath, and sighed as I walked toward the carriage.

Fellan opened the door, whispering far too close to my hair, "Heard that, *Princess*."

I ignored him and climbed inside, nearly tripping on my gown as Snow howled behind the doors to the manor.

Zayla sat beside me while Fellan sat opposite us with his legs spread. His jaw rotated as the carriage lurched forward, his gaze unwilling to leave me alone.

I did my best to act as though he wasn't there at all, all the while knowing it would be wise to never be caught alone with such a hostile creature. Perhaps I should have told Florian he'd bruised my ribs after all.

They were now healed, and the chance was gone.

Though smaller than the royal carriage I'd journeyed in before, it was no less grand. The seats had been upholstered in black leather, and matching drapes veiled the windows. With Fellan's unrelenting glower pressing like a burn upon my face, I pulled them open to view the woods.

"Close them," Fellan barked.

I finally looked at him, frowning. "I would rather not, thank you."

His dark eyes flashed, teeth meeting with a clack behind his thinned lips.

I never thought I'd meet anyone who loathed me more than Rolina had. But this male... Something told me he'd peel my skin from my flesh and use my bones to feast upon my organs if given the chance.

I withheld a shiver.

Zayla spoke before Fellan could, a look given to him that I

couldn't decipher. "We can better ensure your safety if people do not know you're in here."

I refrained from saying that not once had Florian told me to keep from looking out the window. Not during our long carriage ride through Hellebore, nor during our shorter trip into the city. Annoyance and a chilled feeling I couldn't name pricked at my skin.

But I let the drapes fall closed and caught a gesture from Fellan.

A gesture I'd assumed was vulgar, but it had been made with his fingers in his lap—so slight, I couldn't make out what it meant as I turned it over in my mind.

Then my peripheral snatched the movement of Zayla's quick nod. A flock of birds screeched overhead, and she shifted on the seat.

Fellan laughed, but it didn't reach his evil eyes. "Still got that fear of birds, Zay?"

She had no fear of birds, and the almost imperceptible confused purse of her lips before she played along said as much.

The screeching sounded again.

A warning I felt right down to the marrow of my bones.

Hair rose upon my nape and arms.

I didn't need another. I tugged the drapes aside just enough to glimpse the sharp turn up ahead. As I'd begun to suspect, we were not venturing to the city at all.

We were traveling across the mountain into deeper woodland.

I breathed, slow and quiet, through my nose in an effort to keep the guards from noticing the faster cadence of my heartbeat.

"Close the drapes, Princess," Zayla ordered, her tone gentle no longer.

I did, then forced an apologetic smile. "It's just beautiful, isn't it?" I said, wistful. "The foliage beneath all the melting frost." I needed to act as though I had no idea what these guards were up to until I could figure out a way to escape them and this carriage.

Fellan snorted. "If you say so."

I scowled at him, and he grinned. The grin of a warrior who was about to win a battle I couldn't see coming.

But I could.

Fear thundered through my heart now, wild and untamable. Although I tried, there was no calming it. For I didn't need to wonder what this male intended to do with me. It was written all over his smug face.

I looked back to the window and feigned a sigh.

I had to get out of this carriage before they scented my fear and decided to act while I was stuck like a caged animal. "I need to relieve myself."

Zayla tensed beside me. "We'll arrive in a few minutes, Princess."

"I'm afraid I cannot wait." I knocked on the carriage ceiling three times.

The horses complained as the driver tugged on the reins and the carriage lurched and slowed.

Fellan growled, "Sit down." Then he turned to the window behind him. He pulled the drapes and knocked on the glass, motioning for the driver to keep going.

But we'd slowed down enough that although it would still hurt, I could escape.

Now, instinct screamed.

I threw myself at the door.

It burst open, and the world spun in winter color as I hit the rocky road with a yelp and rolled down the embankment.

Shouts sounded from somewhere above, and I scrambled for purchase among the rocks and ferns. My nails split. My hands sliced on stone and stick. There was no stopping it, and knowing it was best to get as far away from the carriage as possible, I gritted my teeth and let go.

Pain careened through my arms, sides, and head.

The air knocked from me with the fall failed to return as I slammed into a tree and bounced faster downhill.

More branches and rocks scratched and gouged. My coat and gown ripped and tangled around my legs as I rolled over thorny plants and came to a stop by an unused road beneath the one I'd fled.

I moaned, splayed across overgrown weeds, and turned over with a hissed wince. Moss covered the dirt road beneath my palms as I pushed to my hands and knees, trying to catch my lost breath.

A quick inspection told me I wasn't seriously injured. Even if I was, it wouldn't matter. I had to keep moving. I climbed to my feet, dizziness swamping me, and made the fatal mistake of looking behind me down the mountainside road.

Fellan, atop one of the horses he'd untethered from the carriage, rode toward me. The sun, filtering through the treetops, made something glint in his hand.

A dagger.

Before I could turn to run, a hand clapped over my mouth from behind.

I screamed, the sound muffled. Zayla hushed me before saying in my ear, "I really do feel terrible about this, Tullia. Please don't take it personally."

"He'll kill you," I mumbled to her skin, and tugged and clawed desperately at her arm.

She laughed. "The king only cares about who plays with his toy, not who kills it. Want to know why?" she asked, and I kicked behind me to no avail, my dress hindering movement. "You were never supposed to live this long."

At that, my heart stopped.

All of me froze.

"Seduce, marry, fuck, mock, and kill," the driver said, climbing free from the embankment he'd slowly traversed. "The order might be a touch incorrect, but you get the gist."

Zayla had the ability to materialize.

Mercifully, Fellan did not. I was certain I'd already be dead if he could.

But he was closing in now. He dug his heels into the giant horse's flanks, the creature huffing and rearing when its dark eyes met mine.

Fellan cursed and growled at the majestic beast, "Easy, asshole."

I didn't want to believe it, but with Florian and Fume's

conversation still so fresh in my mind from the night before, it was irrefutable. Every word I'd ever heard them exchange now made perfect sense.

Florian had sought to humiliate me, to humiliate my father, and then he would take me from him the way my father had taken his sister.

There was no time for tears, but my heart didn't care.

My eyes filled as Fellan neared.

I closed them, knowing to surrender would haunt me in any last life to come but unable to do anything else. A tear escaped, and I opened my eyes as the cold steel of Fellan's blade skimmed my cheek.

He scooped the tear with the dagger, digging the blade into my skin.

I flinched, but though I'd lost the will to fight, I refused to beg.

I looked beyond his shoulder as he laughed and dragged the dagger down my other cheek. He reeked of sweat and tobacco and misdeeds. The lewd words and laughter he exchanged with his comrades became a buzzing I ignored when the forest gained volume.

Wet soil and pine and horse rode along the kiss of the autumn-touched breeze, drawing my eyes to the carriage horse.

He stood behind Fellan, restless and free.

I met the monstrous creature's eyes, and he settled with a huff.

As I stared, an unexpected peace, cool and soft and silken, unfurled from my chest. It erased the aches in my body and heart. If I was leaving this world when I'd only just begun to experience it, then I would do so without giving these guards the satisfaction of looking at them.

"Indeed, there is a chance we might be punished for taking this win from our king," Fellan was muttering now, the tip of the knife meeting the corner of my mouth. "But we'll be celebrated for taking another slice of Molkan Baneberry's soul." The blade rose, the steel catching sunlight a second before he placed it at my throat.

The horse I was still staring at reared.

My knees buckled as pain scalded from the slice of the blade.

Then it slid across my skin as Fellan shouted and turned to the advancing horse.

I tripped backward into Zayla as darkness invaded the edges of my vision, and my fingers tingled in a way they'd only done a handful of times before.

In a way that told me I was about to materialize elsewhere.

But this time, the magic that had only ever arrived when I was desperate might be too late, even as Fellan fell beneath the bucking legs of the black stallion.

Zayla screamed and left me to rescue him, but she too was knocked to the ground.

The driver looked at me and cursed, unmoving. His wide copper eyes jumped from me to Fellan, who was howling and growling beneath the hooves of the horse while Zayla scrambled back with her arm clutched to her chest.

I smiled as the soil ruptured and rose beneath my feet, and I slipped through the welcoming void of time.

The apartment was just how I'd left it.

I didn't stay. I stumbled into the hall and down the stairs, still winded and far too unbalanced.

I didn't dare seek help from Gane either. Florian would know where to find me, and it would not be long until he heard of my failed venture to the city.

A venture he likely wouldn't have allowed.

The pain in my chest flared, worse than the various bruising, cuts, and gashes. Worse than the deep slash at my throat. Clutching it as tears blurred my vision, I gritted my teeth against the desire to slide down the wall of the landing and scream at the flickering firelight of the stairwell.

Later. I could fall apart later.

Right now, I needed to make sure there would be a later. I needed a place to hide until I assessed my injuries and made a new plan.

I gave one last longing look at my very own secret entrance to the library, and then I continued downstairs.

The acrid scents of refuse and smoke overwhelmed as soon as I pushed open the rear door to the apartment building and stepped into the narrow alleyway beyond. Crustle had always been as gloomy and dank as people said, but now that I'd left and returned, I fought the urge to vomit.

It was likely shock or the repercussion of materializing. So I leaned back against the cold stone of the building, partly hidden beside a large rusted wagon.

A wagon filled with rotting food.

I gagged, misery squeezing my bones as I walked on.

Not a minute later, I stopped. A familiar male stood beneath the stairs to the Lair of Lust.

The male I'd met in the dressing room at the beginning of this journey I never should have taken paused. His tobacco stem fell from his fingers as he surveyed me slowly. "Mother of skies, pretty thing, what the fuck happened to you?"

"I need a place to stay," I said, breathless as each step made my ribs scream. "Just..." Startled by a clatter in the distance, I glanced around. Mercifully, it seemed to have come from the street. No one else lurked in the alley. "Just for the day."

His eyes widened upon the hand at my throat. "You need more than that," he said, his face creasing with an incredulous huff. "You're bleeding." He looked me over again, gold-dusted lashes flicking. "Everywhere." He sighed when I said nothing. "Let me get Morin. She'll skin me if I bring you in looking like *that* without checking first."

I attempted to nod, then flinched.

His head shook as he climbed the stairs and squinted down at me. "This place is no good for sweet creatures like you."

He was gone before he could glimpse what those words did to me.

What have I done to you, sweet creature?

A hitched breath spiked my pulse.

Disorientated anew, I leaned against the building beneath the stairs and closed my eyes over the wet that filled them. I silently recited my letters to the timing of each trembling breath, then I lifted my shaky hand from my neck.

Blood dribbled from the sliced flesh but didn't gush. Not too deep, then.

There was no relief. There was only pain. Tears left my eyes as I stared at the crimson covering my palm.

The air grew warm.

I tensed and clasped my neck again, sensing I was no longer alone.

My heartbeat drummed in my ears.

Boots, large and bulky like some of Florian's, entered my blurry line of sight.

I couldn't recall seeing a chestnut pair in his collection. Nor had I seen him wear a brown cloak. Slowly, my eyes rose over a thick pair of olive-green britches and a fitted brown tunic to meet the male's gaze.

Gold eyes.

"Finally." Thin lips spread into a wide and bright grin. "Been spending far too much time in this cesspit, waiting for the moment you came to your senses." His tone turned mocking as he bowed deeply. "My *princess*."

I forced a smile, all the while inwardly whining like a babe. I just needed a skies-damned minute. "I wouldn't recommend staying out late," I rasped, gesturing to my neck and hoping he'd assume I didn't remember him.

A dark brow rose, humor sparking in those unforgettable golden eyes.

He was with the hunt, yet he'd been waiting for me? I couldn't make sense of it—lacked the ability and time to make sense of anything right now.

My mind was cotton. My beaten body remained upright from adrenaline and survival instinct alone.

All I knew was that I needed to get away from power-hungry males, and that he was but another one. Whatever he wanted was guaranteed to be no good for me. So I shrugged and straightened to walk back to the apartment building.

But my unbalanced feet faltered as he lifted a gloved hand. He opened that hand to reveal a small pile of dirt-colored dust. He smirked.

Then he blew.

I turned away and blocked my face. But it was too late. The faerie dust, acidic and laced, was inhaled into my lungs.

The alley dripped away in an instant, and I fell into his arms as day turned into starless night.

TWENTY-ONE

I WOKE ON A BED IN A CIRCULAR STONE ROOM, CONFUSED AND wondering if the dreamless sleep had now become vivid.

Then it all came rushing back in patches of pain and fear and blood and horse hooves.

I rolled over and expected to feel it still—the aches and stings of my wounds—but found there was only one.

And it radiated from my chest with the memory of dark-blue eyes and a feral smirk.

Wherever I was, Florian wasn't here; here was nowhere I'd been before.

He would be furious indeed, I thought as the pain of betrayal flared. Furious that his captive had escaped before he was done with me.

Hairs rose upon my skin, and I finally sensed I wasn't alone.

Tears cleared at the sight of a male seated in a woven cane chair against the wall.

It creaked when he leaned forward and clasped his hands between his spread knees. He wore his features similar to the male I'd escaped—with cool indifference. His were not as easily seen, hidden beneath a dark beard that reached his broad chest.

I didn't need to ask who he was.

I knew before he said, "You look like Corina." His voice was rough, sand over concrete, and his scent a similar mixture of pine and eucalyptus to the male who'd blown dust into my face. "Your mother."

I'd always wondered if that were true, and I'd always dreamed of one day hearing someone say those words to me. Though I'd never imagined them being said in a tone as empty and matter of fact as his, and certainly not from the male I assumed was my father.

The Fae were not known to be warm and welcoming creatures, but they were fiercely protective of those they did care for, especially their family.

A kernel of disappointment joined forces with the hurt already fracturing every heartbeat. Still, I rasped, "You're Molkan."

The male nodded once, slowly. The chair creaked again as he leaned back, a large hand rubbing over his mouth. The sound of coarse facial hair scratching his palm echoed too loudly in the small and otherwise silent chamber.

"So you escaped him," he said, the first sign of something within his voice—disbelief. "The meticulously ruthless Florian."

Merely hearing his name was a knife grazing wounded flesh.

Though the answer was obvious, I said, "Yes," and to hide my emotions, I pushed up on the bed and inspected my arms. I was still wearing my ruined gown, but my coat was gone. I tugged up the sleeves but found only blood-marked skin. "Someone healed me?"

"Of course," Molkan said. My *father* said.

Mother melt me, this could not be real.

My gaze flitted over the wooden trunk beneath the circle-shaped, glassless window. There was a chest of drawers beside the bed, though, with the exception of the chair the Baneberry king sat in, nothing else.

"Thank you," I said belatedly.

I could feel his eyes on me. My stomach tumbled as I forced myself to tuck the bedding over my waist and look at him. A hard male, certainly, his skin sun warmed and faintly lined—his body big and burly but mostly muscular.

His clothing was similar to the golden-eyed male's from the alley, a brown tunic and pants. Molkan's were not britches but loose, and his giant feet were shockingly bare of shoes.

"I had hoped to reach you before he snatched you," he said, still rubbing slowly at his mouth as though deep in thought. "Alas, by the time we confirmed it was indeed you who Avrin encountered during the Wild Hunt's visit to Crustle, it was far too late. You were as good as gone."

"Avrin?" I questioned.

A slight smirk lit Molkan's charcoal eyes. Eyes so very similar to my own. "The male who brought you here."

Gold eyes.

Remembering that night in the alleyway right before I'd left the middle lands with Florian, an onslaught of regret twined through my bones. If I'd have known the male with gold eyes had been working with my father, then so much would have been different. So much could have been avoided.

Such as finding a goddess-given mate of the soul in a king who intended to murder rather than claim me.

I now understood why Florian hadn't said a word when I'd asked if he was my mate. He had intended to kill me, and that would prove difficult if he acknowledged what I was—*his*.

Florian had no heart. It had been torn from his chest long ago, rendering him merciless and calculated enough to make sure it would never dare to beat again.

For he would let nothing stand in the way of everything he'd spent years working to achieve.

I fought back a new wave of incoming tears, my lungs tight as I stared down at the ivory cotton linen of the bed. Beyond being an enjoyable pet in his games of revenge, I didn't matter to Florian. Not nearly enough to change anything. To change him.

I pushed thoughts of him and what he might be doing in my absence aside as the silence in the room swelled once again. "I thought the hunt was composed of those who choose not to belong to any faerie court?"

Molkan lifted his hand from his cheek, saying casually, "They are exactly that." Noting why I was confused, he smiled slightly, and the sight gave me a modicum of comfort. "Avrin's brother is a member, and so he is permitted to travel with them from time to time when scouting for things we need." His expression hardened. "Things that have been stolen from us."

He hadn't meant me, yet I was too hesitant to ask what he did mean.

"Artifacts, books, coin, seedlings," Molkan explained. "Even magic-infused items used to help ward our palace walls."

"How do you ward a place with items?"

Molkan flashed his teeth in a quick grin. "They contain my blood, you see, but once they're removed from my land, they become nothing more than collectibles for the curious."

I frowned. "Florian takes such things from you?"

His brow arched. "You say his name with significant ease."

My cheeks threatened to flush and give away all of the mistakes I'd made within enclosed rooms and carriages—skies, even atop a horse.

But I maintained eye contact, relieved when Molkan said, "He and his beastly blood-drinking ilk take all that and more, yes."

Now would be a good time to ask why, but I already knew.

He seemed to assume as much, nodding once with a rough exhale. "You have less questions than I thought you would."

"I was almost killed," I said, ignoring the urge to touch my throat. "And my lifelong desire for answers is the reason for that, so..." I smiled as best I could, and nervously combed my fingers through my blood-streaked hair. "I think I just need a moment to remember them all." My fingers snagged on a small twig. I pulled it free, inspecting another reminder of what had happened on those mountain roads in my lap.

"So he finally decided to do it," Molkan said with a huff. "I was beginning to think it might not happen."

"You knew he intended to kill me?" I asked, unable to keep my voice from rising in shock.

"Oh, with certainty." He laughed at my expression. "I'm not the one to harbor anger toward. You were placed in the middle lands for this exact reason, young one."

I looked down at the twig. "To keep me from Florian."

Silence arrived, and I almost thought he'd leave until he linked his hands over his stomach and seemed to come to a decision. "When Lilitha died, he vowed to take everything I loved," Molkan said, voice low and more rough. "We do not love in the way humans do, but when we care for something, it is almost the same thing."

"And if you do love something?" I asked.

Molkan smirked. "Then the fiery pits of Nowhere will extinguish before anyone gets away with taking it from us."

I swallowed. "And Florian loved his sister."

"As though he were her father," he said, almost wistful, almost regretful, and as if recalling the male Florian once was. "Mother Mythayla knows Hammond Hellebore ceased wishing to breathe after Lilitha's birth resulted in the death of his beloved queen and mate."

He knew them—had known them well. I couldn't resist asking, "Why did you kill her?"

I thought his amused hum would be all the answer I'd receive. But he sighed and said, "We were all close, as they say in the mortal realm"—he waved his hand—"once upon a time." Then, for what might have been the first time since I woke, Molkan averted his eyes from me.

He looked down at the patch of woven carpet covering the stone floor at his bare feet. "I think we'll let you get acquainted with this home I've kept you from." He rose from the chair, his height staggering. "Before I give you information that might just make you wish to leave it."

A humorless laugh escaped me. "After everything..." I shook my head. "Nothing much can surprise me now."

The door creaked open, revealing more light stone.

Molkan stood in the doorway for a prolonged moment, then said, "I do advise against tempting our dear goddess to prove you wrong. I'll have one of the servants along to show you where to bathe shortly."

The door closed with an echoing click.

I stared at it while his warning chilled the sun-warmed room, unsure what to do now that I'd received everything I thought I'd never get.

A male with shorn white hair arrived within the hour.

He said nothing as we walked down the arched sandstone hall toward windows in the same shape. They lined the expansive length of the hall we entered, giving view to rows of gardens and fruit trees beneath.

Beyond them, woods backed and curled around a glimmering lake to meet with small stone buildings. It was odd to see water that wasn't frozen, and even more startling to glimpse all of the fresh vegetation, green and ripe and swelling with life.

It shouldn't have come as such a shock, for I'd already known the seasons of Baneberry rotated between autumn and spring. Yet the lack of ice upon the mild breeze crawling through the arched windows caused something within me to flinch.

Something that recoiled at the mere thought of never feeling the cool touch of Hellebore again.

Of course, that was ridiculous when the source of such weather was a king who'd pulled me from my old skin with such expertise, I'd have never known he was nothing but a hunter savoring the chase of his next kill.

My steps slowed at the sight of the rumored sandstone wall.

It encircled Baneberry Palace, stretching beyond into the tree line feathering the large lake. Guards in brown and green uniforms walked along the wall and stood within three towers. I assumed at least three more stood upon the other side of the palace. Silver armor glinted from chests, heads, and shoulders.

The male I trailed stopped at a darkened doorway to the springs I could hear beneath the steps behind him, and bowed.

"What is your name?" I asked as he began to walk away.

He paused and made a face, then motioned with his hands. Not understanding what he meant, I shook my head.

His mouth pinched, and he looked over his slim shoulder. Looking back at me, he opened his mouth.

To show me he had no tongue.

He closed it and gave me a grim smile, then walked back down the hall to the one containing the room I'd woken in.

I took the winding stone steps down to the gurgling springs, light flaring from sconces on the damp walls, and thought of Delen. Thought of why I'd now met two males from Baneberry who were without the means to talk.

There were two springs to choose from. One was long, the length of a small dam, and the other as small as a garden pond. Heat rose in tempting curls from the latter. Needing something not so sweltering upon my skin, I decided against it.

I stripped out of my ruined clothing and carefully climbed the mossy steps into the wide-open warmth. Rocks lined each end of the large spring and rimmed the smaller one. Moisture dripped down the stone of the underground chamber in fascinating rivulets.

Home.

I dunked my head underwater with a smile.

As I emerged, I pushed hair from my face and ran my hands down my neck. My fingers faltered over raised and tender skin. Indeed, someone had healed me, but Fellan's attempt to slit my throat might leave a scar.

And if he'd been successful, the daring trio would have needed to remove my head or stab me in the heart for certainty.

I shivered, leaning against the stone as I attempted to calm an onslaught of racing thoughts and breaths I couldn't seem to control.

"You've been a busy little changeling."

Water crashed as I instantly covered my breasts. Though it was dark and murky enough that he'd hopefully only see the outline of my body at most.

"Relax, I'm not interested in Florian's toys." Avrin straightened from the bottom of the stairwell, a crooked grin sparking those gold eyes as he strolled closer. "Or shall we call you his failure?"

I will have what I want.

Fresh fear chilled my nape. Florian and the word failure would never coexist.

I shrank deeper into the water until it tickled my chin. "I'm trying to bathe."

"Oh?" Avrin's smile stretched. He tore off his tunic and unfastened his tight pants. "Unfortunately, Princess, these springs are communal." He pushed his pants down. "You must share."

I snapped my slack mouth closed and scowled, averting my gaze from his toned and tan abdomen.

"How's the neck?" the rude creature asked, descending the steps into the pool entirely naked and far too slow.

"Fine."

He swam to the other side of the spring, then slipped underwater. I was more annoyed than impressed by his dramatic exit from the water.

He swept his fingers through his short black hair. Droplets slid over sculpted cheeks and clung to his long lashes. "I'm curious, Princess."

I nearly told him not to call me that, but it could no longer be ignored. It was who I was, no matter how ill-fitting.

"Curiosity indeed kills," I drawled instead and stared at the formation of sharp rocks behind his head. "Or at least it tries."

"Yet here you are." I could hear the grin shaping his words. "How *did* you escape him?"

I met his gaze then, absorbing the unwavering way he watched me. Almost laughing, I suddenly understood why he'd rudely joined me in the springs. "You think he sent me to you?"

Avrin said nothing, just continued to stare.

"I wish," I admitted, though it lacked the sarcasm I intended, my fingers climbing to my neck again.

His eyes followed and narrowed upon the healing skin. "He did that to you?"

"No," I said. "Some of his loyal guards with a hatred for this kingdom did."

Avrin's head tilted, his lips pursed in thought. "Florian is not the type to have others do such a deed for him. Not with someone as important as you. He'd make a show of it." At my failure to respond to that, he concluded with a touch more tact, "He didn't know." A pause. "You were ambushed."

He was good, whoever this Avrin was to my long-lost father.

I could only nod while pushing my hands back and forth through the water in an effort to keep the burn within my chest from reaching my eyes.

"You will be asked more questions regarding him, Princess. The winter king is skies-bent on plucking your father's flesh from his bones until he bleats in surrender, and you've spent a great deal of time with him."

"That's fine," I lied, as it was to be expected, and I reluctantly understood.

"But is it?" Avrin pressed.

I made the mistake of glaring at him, and he barked a laugh.

His teeth caught his lip, his study of me completed with furrowed brows and a slight shake of his head. "He burrowed beneath your skin, didn't he?" There was no use in lying, but that didn't mean I would put voice to the truth. "As was his plan, I suppose," Avrin murmured with a smirk.

I looked away, my chest cinched tight. "What will be asked of me?"

He continued to watch me, and it was confirmed that he hadn't merely decided to take a bath. The interrogating had already begun.

I would need to grow used to it, though all I wanted was to return to my small chamber and sleep until I could find the excitement I should be feeling over finally being exactly where I'd always longed to be.

"Well, you will be asked how you managed to get away from those guards for a start."

"I materialized."

His arched brow said he knew there was more, or I would have materialized long before a blade caught my throat.

"I jumped from a carriage when I realized it wasn't heading into the city." I saw no harm in telling him, even as I found it hard to explain. "The horse. One of the guards untethered a horse and chased me, and when he dismounted, and I was trapped, I wished only to keep from looking at him if I was going to die."

The peace that had encompassed me so entirely at that moment still baffled me. If there was ever a time to feel anything but utter contentment within my being, it was when a hate-riddled male with a dagger was trying to end my existence. "I stared at the horse, and the creature reared when the blade..."

"It helped you," Avrin finished.

I nodded. I'd been too hesitant to admit even to myself that it had happened. But it had. It had, and I didn't know how I'd done it. "I remember meeting his eyes, the horse," I said. "And as I did, everything just washed away. The forest around us seemed to mute all else. I was no longer afraid."

"Your mother had such a gift," Avrin said.

My lashes lifted, my lips parting.

Avrin informed, "The bond with animals. Most in this kingdom with noble blood do, but for some, it runs deeper. A form of communication where no words are required—only feeling."

Some of the ice encasing my heart thawed. That I'd been blessed in such a way...

Avrin squashed my awe, his tone mocking. "A useless gift, really, but in this case, it served you well." A crooked smile curled his mouth, and I wanted to punch it. "Do not despair. Have you any affinity with the land?"

I glowered. "What do you mean?"

"The soil," he said with a tug of his brows, as if I should know. "And what grows from it."

"No," I said, wondering if I should be ashamed when I didn't care.

Perhaps I should have been. Avrin wiped his hand over his mouth, evidently hiding another stupid grin, and shrugged. "I suggest finding out if you do. Vines and quaking earth make for far more impressive escapes, Princess." He dunked into the water, emerging some feet away near the mossy steps. "I'll give you that privacy you were seeking now."

I didn't dare look at his naked form. I listened to the slap of his wet feet over the stone and the unfolding of a sun-dried towel pulled from a carving of shelves in the rock. "Avrin," I said. "Do all the servants have no tongues?"

I sensed that he'd stilled, the rubbing of the towel over his body ceasing.

Carefully and quietly, he said, "Would you keep help in your household who might one day be captured and forced to tell the enemy every secret they've heard within your walls?"

My empty stomach roiled. I turned to rest my arms on the ledge of the spring. Water dripped down my hairline.

Avrin watched its descent to my chin. "Didn't think so," he said softly.

I didn't tell him that one of their servants, who I now understood had been captured by Florian, was employed by him and likely various other nobility within Hellebore.

My eyes shifted to the ripples in the water as Avrin padded to the stairs and left me with, "Most are illiterate, too."

TWENTY-TWO

MY EYES OPENED WITH THE INCOMING DAWN. SLEEP HAD been elusive, and the patches of dreams that visited haunting.

Blue eyes. Soft hair. Cold and bruising hands.

I might have crossed the border into a different realm, but I knew I would never escape him.

The same silent male who'd taken me to the communal springs beneath the palace delivered breakfast to my room. It was a small affair of citrus fruits, lemon and honey tea, water, and buttered bread. I ate it all despite hunger being a distant thought shrouded by too many others.

The male returned not an hour later to take the tray.

The palace was awake, yet there was no sound save for that drifting in through the lone glassless window. I sat on the edge of the bed, admiring the never-ending grid of stone and wood beyond the formidable palace wall.

"Thank you," I said to the servant, still staring at Baneberry's royal city of Bellebon.

I sensed the male pause. Then his steps, as light as a feather over the stone, neared.

He stood next to the circular window, his lime-green gaze meeting mine as he cocked his head. Bold, I knew, without even knowing wholly as to why, that he would linger and dare try to communicate with me.

He gestured to me, then to the window. To the north, I realized after a moment of frowning at his slender hands. "Hellebore?" I whispered.

He nodded. Unsure how to ask me what he clearly seemed desperate to know, his features creased. He scrubbed his hands over his cheeks and hair.

I smiled with uncertainty, saying low, "I don't know what you're trying to tell me. I'm sorry."

He stepped forward as if he'd touch me.

I froze, and so did he. Lips pinched between his teeth, he then motioned toward my face. He was asking permission to touch me.

That he'd asked earned him a nod of acceptance.

My hands clasped tight in my lap as he set loose a relieved smile and stood before me. Softly, he made a motion of brushing over my cheek, his fingers nearing my eyes. They closed, and as his fingertips traced my eyelids...

Gasping, I took his wrist. "Delen."

The servant's eyes flared, his hand falling. He glanced warily to the closed door and stepped back. He didn't seem to breathe, inflating with tension as he nodded.

"He was a beautician here, too," I surmised, as he must have years of experience with such skill and pride in his craft.

The white-haired male nodded again, slowly, as his eyes filled. I studied them, and the rigidness to his jaw, the height of his refined cheekbones. "Your brother?"

Another nod.

I stood, took his hand and squeezed. "He is well, if that's what you're asking." For I knew Delen was, no matter what atrocities Florian continued to commit.

Relief loosened his shoulders, and he squeezed my hand in return as he placed his other hand over his heart.

I wanted to tell him more—that Delen worked in Hellebore and that he glowed with good health despite it. Something held me back. As if the servant knew, indecision flickered in his wet gaze and made him swallow.

He shook his head, indicating I should indeed say no more.

Then he shocked me by bowing deeply and placing a light kiss to my knuckles.

I watched his thin and towering form head to the door with my breakfast tray, wondering if perhaps I'd been the only stupid creature on this entire continent who hadn't feared the king of the north.

Not until it was too late.

Molkan arrived moments after I'd donned a weightless lemon dress. Intentionally loose around my torso, the luxurious cotton flared into pleats at my hips. The material whispered against my knees, my bare toes curling over the cool stone as I finished with the three large buttons at my chest.

The king of Baneberry knocked once before entering, then paused in the doorway as I fussed with the oddly unfitted bodice that felt more like a tunic. When I'd returned from the springs, the dress, a wooden comb, and a small brush for my teeth had been left upon the trunk by the window.

I'd only had the chance to use the latter before deciding I could no longer stand feeling the crimson gown I'd worn in Hellebore upon my skin.

Molkan cleared his throat and ripped his studious gaze from me. "Take a walk with me, Tullia."

It was not a request, and I doubted I would have spared a thought to denying him anyway.

We walked in stiff silence, even as the king who'd sired me kept his hands clasped behind his back in a relaxed manner. I felt out of place in my soiled slippers. He wore no shoes, his linen pants similar to what Florian would wear to bed and his tunic a cream rayon.

The halls were shaded between windows, all of them arched and cracked by time. We meandered through three before the sun brightened a wide set of stairs. Potted ferns sat astride the top of each balustrade, and roses choked the thick sandstone rails, thorns awaiting to prick the skin.

Beneath the stairs was an enclosed terrace patterned with dark and bright sandstone in the shape of diamonds. The palace gates loomed large straight ahead with guard towers on either side. We veered right, leaving the terrace and heading toward hedges that bordered blossoming gardens.

The silence grew warmer than the spring sun as we walked the perimeter of the palace grounds.

Before I could find the courage to break it, Molkan did. "You've undoubtedly experienced harrowing horrors at Florian's hands due to his hatred of me. But if you're willing, then I would like to tell you my side of the story."

Horrors was not the word I would have chosen to describe my time with Florian.

I did not say that, but I did feel the need to inform him, "I wasn't captured." Slimy and sharp, shame crawled through me. Unable to be masked, it stained my words, making them low. "I went to Hellebore with him willingly, not knowing his true plans."

Molkan's steps slowed, as did mine, his eyes traveling the expansive surroundings of his royal home. A home that should have been mine. A home that could perhaps still be mine. "And how long before you realized you'd ventured into a viper's nest?" he asked.

My cheeks flushed, and not due to the sun.

Molkan deduced enough from my silence. A touch of pity that only made me feel worse lined his voice. "You are young, and though you were born here, you are not at all familiar with the deception and trickery of your own ilk."

I refrained from saying I was more than familiar now.

We reached the shade of a large apple tree. Molkan plucked one from it, inspecting the glossy red fruit before he passed it to me.

I thanked him, my fingers rubbing over the smooth skin of the apple as he nodded once and we walked on.

"Your mother was my first love," he said, hands again tucked behind his back and his eyes fastened on the workers who tended a vegetable garden along the wall in the distance. "But she was not my only."

I paused in bringing the apple to my lips and lowered it.

"Corina's father was a filthy rich merchant and a dear friend to my own father. Years before they were both lost to the sea during one of their annual adventures across the Amethyst, they'd made plans for Corina and me to marry."

A smile carried his words. "We dragged our feet, of course. We'd been friends our whole lives, and though we loved one another far more than any friend should, we did not encounter any sign of the Mother-blessed bond. Which worried us, and for a good reason."

My mind skipped forward, guessing where this tragedy was headed.

"But when our fathers died, well..." Molkan lifted his shoulders, his eyes still glued to the gardens while I tried not to trip while gazing at his bearded profile. "We decided it was time. Corina's father's fortune was hers, but not until she married could she rightfully claim his vast estate along the coastline of the Elixir Sea." A smirk sparked his eyes. "Her father always got what he desired, and it seemed not even death would stop him."

"So she couldn't inherit until you were wed?"

"Barbaric, isn't it?" Molkan said. "Not two weeks after their ship went down, the nymphs hired to search for our fathers' remains finally found enough evidence to suggest that sea beasts had helped themselves to everyone on board, and so we were wed."

Just imagining the brutality of dying in that way...

The teeth and scales and mountainous muscle of the sea monsters I'd glimpsed within books turned my stomach.

Molkan huffed, as if he'd glanced my way to see the color drain from my face. Then he continued, "Your mother grieved her father terribly for many years, but I was glad to be rid of my own. He was prone to violent outbursts. So much so, my mother was laid to rest in these gardens after perishing from one of his tempers. We were to never speak of it. As far as anyone knew, when my father was alive that is, she died from complications of a miscarriage."

Sadly believable. Miscarriage and birth were feared killers of faerie females.

"My father never wanted to be king," Molkan said quietly. "He loved the sea a great deal more than he could have ever loved my mother and me. He felt trapped, and though I hated him, I eventually empathized when I first saw Lilitha."

Something cold coiled around my heart, my fingers tightening upon the large apple.

"Some decades ago, we had an annual tradition that is now no longer. Each kingdom would meet right here in Bellebon upon the spring equinox. For three days, we'd celebrate. The palace was open to every noble and creature of importance from across Folkyn, and the city outside overflowed with citizens and visitors from our neighboring kingdoms."

There was no mistaking the nostalgia in his voice, nor the slight thickening that hinted toward regret.

"Lilitha had been confined to her kingdom until she reached seventeen years, and I do believe Florian would have kept her there until she'd fully matured—had he been able to." He released a gruff bout of laughter. "She escaped, of course, after convincing her father that she had an urgent message that must be delivered to her brother immediately."

Recalling those mischief-glazed eyes in her portrait, I couldn't help but smile.

"Hammond was beyond caring what his daughter got up to, and he certainly hadn't enough soul left within him to keep her from danger. So dressed in his night robes, he materialized his daughter to these very gardens, merely nodded when he'd found me gaping at his unexpected entrance, and then vanished. Lilitha, who'd been slow to shake off the dizziness of her arrival, first looked at me, blinking such huge blue eyes."

We slowed as we neared bowing workers along the far wall.

Molkan's voice dropped even lower. "I knew instantly, and I suppose she did, too. For although I resumed mollifying a courtier who'd finally gained my attention, Hellebore's princess walked straight to me." He chuckled. "She just waited there in a shimmering silver gown, her long dark curls over her bare shoulders, until the courtier grew tired of failing to keep my stolen attention."

We wended back across the plush grass toward the palace.

"I'd like to say I avoided her. She was so young." His sigh was more of a groan. "As I said, she hadn't even reached the age of full maturity, but I am certainly no saint, and she was incessant. First a dance, then too much wine, then she dragged me beyond the lake and deep into the trees to seal our fates."

"But she knew you were married," I said, then remembered she had been all of seventeen years, and evidently lost to the over-whelming intensity that came with finding such an attraction. That came with finding a mate.

"We both forgot that fact entirely too quickly," he admitted so-berly. "Florian was the one to find us. To this day, I still don't know how. I assume someone informed him, for last I'd known, he'd been in the springs with a horde of females and higher than the moon on toadstool dust."

Even as my very bones protested at the thought of him with others, I almost snorted.

Almost.

It was hard to imagine the rigid and refined Florian in such a way.

Which must have shown on my face, for Molkan said, "I do hear he does not partake in such revelry any longer. In fact, I've heard he's become quite the cold bore. Like his father but at least with ambition." A darkly humorous hum. "Suppose that's my doing, of course." He exhaled heavily. "So Lilitha was immediately mate-rialized back to Hellebore, and Florian was sitting in my chambers the following morning, watching my wife and me sleep."

My eyes widened, although the image was much better matched with the arrogant king I knew.

"He hadn't needed to say it," Molkan said. "The way he'd stared at Corina was warning enough."

"He was going to kill her?"

Molkan chuckled. "Skies, no. He was not so cold-blooded back then, but he was certainly cruel when he wanted to be, and his entire frame pulsed with his desire to be as menacing as I'd made him feel by daring to touch his young sister."

"He would tell your wife." I swallowed, finding it odd to say, "My mother."

Molkan nodded. "And despite quietly vowing to never touch Lilitha again, he still did. He smirked at my pleading and waited for Corina to stir, then he rose from the chair to crouch by her ear and whisper my transgressions, his eyes on me while I tried to keep from leaping over our bed to knock the audacity from his pretty face. He vanished before I could, and your mother..."

A warning. Florian had issued a warning to this father of mine to keep far away from the sister he'd raised when his father, Hammond, could not.

Quiet reigned for some minutes as we passed the apple tree and more silent yet bowing workers, and I absorbed all he'd divulged.

When we reached the shade of the terrace, I had to ask, "Did she forgive you?"

Molkan gazed up the stairs, appearing lost in thought. "Never, but as time passed, she did come to understand. I'd found a mate, and rejecting a force that has been ordained by the mother of fate is near impossible. I still tried. For some years after that life-altering night, I tried and tried." He sighed. "And tried."

He needn't have bothered saying more. He'd tried, and he'd clearly failed. Molkan hadn't stayed away from Lilitha, and now, here we all were.

He said nothing more as he climbed the stairs, with the exception of parting words. "We will resume tomorrow."

I'd been dismissed, but after all he'd said, I didn't mind.

I stared at the apple in my hand, then looked back to the sunlit gardens that had seen so much history.

For the remainder of the day, I walked the halls and viewed the scenery beyond the windows and palace walls, lost to the beauty of this land I longed to explore more of and the chaos of my thoughts.

I bathed alone and quickly, not wanting to find myself in another awkward position, then ate a light dinner of pork and a large leafy green salad delivered by a different male servant. There were few items in my room to amuse myself with—only a handful of dusty books and the view from the window.

So I sat upon the bed with a novel containing historic uses of poisonous flowers, and mostly gazed through the window to the city aglow with soft touches of night.

The next morning, I was awake and ready when Molkan arrived, better rested than the day prior but still haunted by blue eyes and careful and cruel lies.

"How are you finding the food?" the king asked once we'd reached the bottom of the sandstone steps.

This time, we didn't veer right toward the gardens we'd traversed yesterday. Molkan strolled toward the western side of the palace. He waited when I paused at the sight before me. "I suggest leaving your shoes behind."

I smiled and kicked off my slippers.

A pond, almost a dam, rich with algae and water lilies, stretched along the base of the western wall. Beside it was another terrace that met with the emerald grass, vines crawling up the pillars of the stone shelter.

Remembering he'd asked me a question, I stammered out, "The food is delicious, thank you."

Molkan hummed, fingers curling at his back once more, and licked his teeth as if pondering his next words before he set them free. "We would have more in the way of meats, but our livestock has diminished, and now our poultry, too."

Florian.

Though I didn't need to ask who was responsible, I did say, "What has he been doing exactly?"

The wagons—of which I knew were likely just some of many that had been taken elsewhere—and the conversation I'd had with Kreed swam within my mind. My toes scrunched over the soft grass, but my blood chilled when Molkan spoke again.

"He has his warriors steal our livestock. They're resold for a hefty sum in the middle lands, where meats are not as rich and bountiful. And if they cannot be stolen from us and used for his own gain, then they're destroyed or poisoned."

I wasn't surprised. I'd known he'd been tormenting Baneberry.

Yet I found myself struggling to understand all of this in its entirety. "All because you loved his sister?"

"Love," Molkan said, squinting toward the harsh glare of the sun. "A strong word, though sometimes not quite strong enough." He lowered his gaze and scratched at his beard, then re-hooked his fingers at his back. "Lilitha was an obsession, an addiction I could not quit."

"What happened next?" I couldn't resist asking. "You said you tried to stay away but you knew she was your mate."

"Well, I didn't see her again for years. Of course," he huffed, "when I did, she made sure it was when she was maturing—the heat upon her like an iron noose around my throat."

I failed to suppress the rising memories of my own experience with the heat. Memories of molten lips, possessive hands, and the insatiable hunger within glowing eyes that stalked my dreams and imprinted upon my soul.

Those endless days and nights were a crushing weight within my limbs. A poison I'd forever carry in my heart. No matter how much I wanted to rip them from my memory and wake wishing they'd only ever been a dream.

Molkan, as if lost to memories himself, cleared his throat. "I couldn't refuse Lilitha. She'd learned to materialize and appeared in my study, desperate and sick, and I just..." He blew out a rough breath. "We stayed in the cabin of one of my father's prized and forgotten boats along the river, and it would be some days until we left. Then I made the mistake of materializing her home, thinking that would be it. That I could walk away for good."

A lizard, blue and mottled violet in the sun, scuttled across the terrace to the rocky bank of the large pond. The spikes upon his tail changed from cream to gold when he reached the water and turned to flick his forked tongue our way.

"I told your mother I was away with unexpected business, and though she didn't believe me and ignored me for weeks on end, she never did question me. But a month later, she finally ceased her silence with a stern request for a babe. A test," he said. "One I was determined not to fail, for I'd already failed her too much."

"A test?" I questioned.

"She wanted to know just how lost I was to this connection with Lilitha, and though I was lost beyond being found, I still adored Corina. I still wanted our lives to remain as they were. We were blessed, and I'd foolishly thought bringing another blessing into the world might keep me where I needed to be. Might keep me from continuously falling prey to temptation for what I could not have."

There was a heavy pause.

"As you might already be aware, for those of us with royal blood, there is no such thing as termination of marriage. It risks upsetting the bloodlines, you see."

It was impossible to keep my shock from showing, so I lowered my gaze to the grass. My cheeks heated with yet more shame and fury.

Another lie Florian had hand-fed me like food for the pet I had been. That should both parties agree, a marriage could be terminated. He'd known royals were forbidden to leave a marriage, no matter what, and he'd known I was too desperate to know any better.

A relief, then—that he'd dragged his feet on the matter.

We hadn't married, and as Molkan walked in silence while nodding to some passing groundskeepers who kept their gazes from me, I had to wonder if Florian had ever truly planned to make me his wife.

My relief burst beneath more flames of hurt.

Once we were alone, not another soul to be seen or heard as we traveled the length of the towering palace, the king went on. "Corina was due for another contraceptive potion, so in answer, I told her not to take it."

Alarm spiked sharp and sudden.

Not because I recalled Florian offering me a contraceptive potion he'd brought with one of many trays of food to his chambers during the heat.

But because that merciless creature had *given* me the choice.

Too early in the heat to care about why he'd presented it in such a way, I'd swallowed the brew without thought, desperate for Florian to tend to me again.

Molkan knocked me from my stomach-snatching confoundment.

"Six months later, you were swelling her stomach and feet. We felt the pregnancy had taken well enough, so we eagerly spread the news." He gestured wide with one hand and nostalgic words. "Celebrations took place throughout the city in the days to follow, your mother and I watching it from the balcony of our rooms." His hand returned behind his back. "But the bliss and hope and the feeling of finally making things right was short-lived."

"Lilitha found out," I guessed.

"She was always wild, untamable, Hellebore's beloved yet reckless princess," he mused quietly. "But never more than when she discovered Corina carried you. In the middle of the night, not three days after we'd set the news free, I woke to find her standing at the side of our bed, tears in her eyes as she gazed at my sleeping wife." There was a slight croak to his voice. "At Corina's growing stomach."

Skies, I couldn't imagine. Waking to find someone watching you sleep was concerning alone, but witnessing the evidence of betrayal from a mate you thought had been yours despite everything he had or hadn't promised?

I willed the empathy morphing into a scaled beast unleashed by unbearable hurt to fade.

It didn't.

It writhed within my chest as Molkan said, "I should have been the one to tell her, I know. I see that now, but back then..." He made a sound of flat humor. "I was only concerned about my pride and the marriage I had to keep. So I forced Lilitha from the room before Corina woke, thankful that the pregnancy kept her sleeping like the dead, and we fought for hours in these gardens while she paced and cried and failed to understand why I would betray her by impregnating my wife."

We'd reached a large cropping of rocks at the rear of the palace, damp from the water I could hear trickling between the gaps from deep below. The springs, I surmised.

Walking on, we crossed the grass to the shade of swaying leaves from a thick line of maple trees.

"Lilitha left, but she came back. Time and again, she returned and waited right there." He gestured past the row of stone houses, likely for the palace staff, to a lone wooden corpse of a tool shed. "Despite telling her not to, she came at least once a week for two moons until Florian caught wind of what she was doing."

He laughed low. "I should have been grateful for his intervening, but it was too late. I'd given in so many times by that point that I was almost as resentful of your impending arrival as Lilitha was."

Before the sting of his words could settle deep, he sighed. "The following week, I received a sparrow instead of a visit from my mate, Lilitha's tears smudging the parchment and ink. She'd been caught and forbidden to see me again. But when Lilitha disobeyed Florian not two weeks later, he arrived minutes after his sister, and he knew."

"That you were mates."

"Yes," he said. "We were friends, allies, but of course, I ruined that when he first caught me with Lilitha when she was but seventeen years. Though finding out why I'd been with her, and that we were mates, did not redeem me in any way. He knew Corina was pregnant, and he knew we were forever bound by marriage."

"What did he do?" For he'd certainly done something.

"Florian took her home and returned that night to warn me that if I broke his sister's heart any more than I already had, then he would marry her off to one of his most trusted warrior friends—someone who would not take kindly to another sampling what wasn't his to claim."

I couldn't help but wonder if that particular warrior friend had been Fume.

"I'd never been so angry in my entire life, but he left without another word or warning. Florian knew how much I cared for Lilitha, despite my failed attempts not to. And he knew to shackle his sister to anyone she hadn't chosen herself would slowly kill her."

"So you let her go."

"We had what I'd thought would be a final meeting, and I told Lilitha it was finished. That it had to be. I told her of Florian's threat. She called me a liar, claiming her brother would never dare do such a thing to her. It was one of the hardest decisions I've ever made," he said roughly. "Like plunging a knife into your own chest and watching your blood stray from you, but it had to be done, for her sake and mine."

Birdsong filled the following silence.

Just as I began to assume we would turn back, Molkan lowered to the grass beneath the maple trees. He patted it, and I sat a few feet beside him and pulled my skirts over my bent knees.

"I was planning a small trip," he continued, so soft, I almost missed it beneath the volume of birds above. "Your mother wanted to sail down the Heartline River one last time before your arrival, and I was willing to do just about anything to see her happy, for doing so made some of the longing and misery within me lessen enough to remember what was right."

Molkan folded his legs beneath him. His eyes remained cast upon the lake and the stone houses surrounding it.

"Lilitha had sent an urgent request to meet, and so we did by the docks during my inspection of the boat." He shook his head with a grimace. "I had to know she was okay, and it would seem she wasn't. An arrangement was being made. She would marry one of Florian's friends after all." Contempt filled and lowered his words. "The mere thought made me sick. I couldn't have her, but she was still mine."

I ceased stroking the velvet blades of grass.

"I told her so, and she told me it was my fault. That I was a coward for not killing my own wife." His laughter lacked humor. "For not choosing her. She pointed her dagger at my chin, saying I was a stain on her soul. A mistake made by the goddess, and that she would see to Corina's end herself regardless of the babe in her womb."

"My fear and fury were such that dirt crumbled beneath her, and my mate stumbled to her knees. I snatched the blade she'd dropped and gazed down at the wild creature who'd made it her mission to ruin my life so thoroughly."

I knew how this ended. He'd killed her.

My heart still raced. My eyes stuck to Molkan's profile, of which was half hidden by sunshine and shade.

"I knew it would destroy me, but it had to stop." He pressed his lips together momentarily, then parted them with a harsh breath. "At that moment, I knew within my soul that it would *never* fucking stop. That I would want Lilitha forever, but I could never truly have her."

So he'd made sure no one would.

Despite knowing what had happened, horror still gripped my chest.

"Yet I didn't mean to. It's all a strange fog. One second I was staring at her with so much anger, it burned as hot as the sun, and the next..." He groaned. "She was limp in my arms, the dagger in her chest. The pain," he rasped, his hands unfolding from his lap for one to splay over his chest. "It was so acute that I burned alive for years, wishing I had turned that blade on myself instead." He thumped his chest. "I still feel it even now, though there is nothing in here but scorched earth."

I didn't try to fill the somber quiet.

I sat with the destruction Molkan had depicted and rose only when he did. We walked in silence along the line of maple trees toward the eastern grounds.

When he finally spoke again, his voice broke. "Lilitha just..." He coughed a little. "Perhaps she didn't think I had it in me, for to lose a mate is unthinkable, but to kill your own..."

Fume and Florian's conversation returned to me then.

Difficult, Florian had said, as though the word barely scraped the surface of accuracy. Perhaps that was why Florian had stalled in his vengeance against Molkan, and I still breathed.

Perhaps I was still foolish enough to want to believe that.

"She threatened my wife—and consequently you. I did what I had to, though it killed half of my soul, and she didn't fight me," Molkan said, as if angered that Lilitha hadn't. "She just let me sink that blade into her beautiful heart. And if she had known I was capable, then maybe she'd *wanted* me to end it. The suffering we continuously endured at the hands of a fate meant to be a blessing." A short and clipped laugh. "Not a fucking curse."

We traversed a slim pebbled path between hedges, the sun beginning to drop.

"I couldn't hide it. I didn't want to. I had her taken home, and then I began to fortify my own to forever trap me with my regret. He came before I'd succeeded, of course. Mere days later, word of Lilitha's and King Hammond's passing reached every corner of Folkyn."

We'd almost circled the entire palace, and though I wished for more shade and water, I wanted to know. I needed to know. So I said nothing and waited for Molkan to give voice to what had transpired next.

"Florian came with his threats and his heartbreak, and he terrified my wife. I didn't wholly believe him, this pompous prince who only wished to fuck and drink himself stupid, but Corina did. She believed he'd seek vengeance until the day she left me. So much so, she tried to flee—to leave out of concern for your safety. I found her, of course. I vowed to take her fear seriously, and I did. I warded our walls, and I sent you away."

Molkan's rough and milder tone returned as he went on. "His sister's death was my fault, and that of his father too, who'd taken his own life just hours after learning his daughter's fate—as he'd had even less to live for." He swore under his breath. "He blamed me, yet Hammond had wanted to leave this world for *years*. Florian knew that, but they'd once been as close as any father and son could be, so I suppose he could not bear it. Hammond would take Florian everywhere with him. Trained him. Taught him. Made him. Skies, some say he even read to him when Florian was old enough to read on his own."

That fissure in my heart panged. "Before his mother died?"

"Right. Crystal's death began the slow erosion of the Hellebore family. A unit that was once the source of envy across the land for the seemingly perfect life Hammond and Crystal had made for themselves." He hesitated before saying, "Many talk of Lilitha with fascination. We faeries love nothing more than a bloody tragedy. But more quietly, for fear of Florian's icy wrath, Lilitha is spoken of as the creature who cursed her family—sent by the beast of Nowhere himself."

I frowned down at the grass, wiping my sweaty palms over my teal-green skirts. Then I carefully asked, "And what do you think?"

As though shocked I'd asked, his thick brows rose and he gave me a small smile. "I think none of us were ready for Lilitha, but should I ever meet her again"—determination gritted his voice as he looked toward the sky—"I will be."

The terrace neared, and I thought our conversation might be done for the day.

Then the king said, "Florian vowed to take everything from me. When you were born, your mother's dying wish was for you to have no part in his revenge. After she was gone, I was lost to grief, to the realization I'd lost not only my mate but also my wife, so I told my most trusted to decide what to do with you. Admittedly, I hadn't cared. I spent days, months—years, really—wondering if that was how Hammond had felt, but I refused to leave my people. I refused to give in to the longing to end it all, for I was the one who'd caused it. I would endure my penance."

I wasn't sure what I'd expected when he finally gave voice to dumping me in the middle lands, but such cruel honesty wasn't it.

"It would be years before I even cared about Florian's threats, and by the time I did, he'd already started toying with me. It started small. Most of it insignificant enough to arouse mere annoyance. Prized mares were found missing from the stables, our boats overturned along our rivers." A flick of his hand. "That type of thing. But I should have known..." He shook his head. "He was simply flexing his muscles."

"Now, he has taken our people, killed and kept them chained to him in surrender. He has burned and butchered factories and greenhouses and fields of staples. Coin, finery, livelihoods—he takes it all. Our ability to trade with the other kingdoms. Even our jewel troves hidden within tunnels beneath our city walls were stolen a decade ago."

One part puzzled me. "I thought the other kingdoms were not involved."

"Oleander might claim they want nothing to do with this feud, but all that means is they want nothing to do with me. And Aconite," he explained, referring to the realm in the far northwest of Folkyn, "even if King Ruben would trade with me, I am not so desperate that I would sell my soul to a Nowhere-bound hellion such as he."

Evidently, only so much could be gleaned from books and murmurings. I was almost tempted to ask more about King Ruben, but Molkan wasn't done.

"Florian humiliates me to no end, wearing me so thin that when he finally decides to take this very soil from beneath my feet, I will have no choice but to surrender." He paused, and I did too, shocked as he turned to level me with a dark look. "I might have robbed him of what little heart he once had, but this has gone on long enough." A careful lowering of his eyes over my features was followed by a slight smile shaping his full mouth. "With you now in my possession, I have hope we can turn this tide."

"How?" I asked, a little breathless from all he'd told me.

I couldn't yet decide how to feel about it, nor understand *why* I couldn't. It should have been obvious, especially after all I'd endured, that Florian was a monster who needed to be stopped.

But just as Gane had warned countless times, nothing was ever as it seemed within these lands.

Molkan only winked, then resumed walking. I followed, my steps lighter from just that one wink, as he said, "The heat. Have you already succumbed to it?"

The way he'd ignored my question had left me wondering about his plans, so I was about to blurt the truth until something stopped me. "No," I said, my cheeks warming. I let them, as it was to be expected. "Not yet."

Molkan slid his gaze to me, but he just said, "Do make sure you let me know when you start to feel the effects." Then his pace quickened toward the stairs.

I stayed behind, afraid to ask what he would have done if the heat hadn't already swept through me like a raging storm. Would he have had one of his servants tend to me? Or perhaps his golden-eyed adviser?

Relief gnawed like a parasite.

Florian had intended to kill me, yet I still couldn't envision it—giving myself to anyone as wildly and completely as I had him.

TWENTY-THREE

I WAS SHOWN TO A DINING ROOM FOR DINNER THAT NIGHT, THE king's tragic tale still stopping my every attempt at new thought.

A round table big enough for twelve stood in the center. Candles in varying sizes and citrus scents sat upon the rattan cupboards and slim shelves lining the room. The arched fireplace was empty and dark behind the grand chair likely reserved for the king.

There were two place settings, but the king would not be dining with me.

Avrin entered long after the meals had been delivered.

I'd grown tired of waiting. I'd thought I would be dining with Molkan, who was my father, and so I'd assumed he wouldn't mind. If I'd known he would not be joining me, I would have served myself the lemon-crusted fish and fruit salad far sooner.

I lowered my cutlery, shock pausing my chewing as the golden-eyed male took a seat before the other place setting. He immediately helped himself to the food while saying dryly, "Thank you for waiting, Princess."

I scowled and finished chewing, then sipped some water. "I've grown accustomed to dining alone."

"There are two place settings."

"I do have eyes," I stupidly said.

He snorted. "Doesn't seem like they work very well."

"What's that supposed to mean?"

"It means..." Done with dumping fruit onto his plate and licking cream from his fingers, Avrin smirked at me. "That you're maddeningly blind."

I knew he was referring to Florian. I refrained from taking the bait. Instead, I merely said with a false calm that made me proud, "What's done is done."

"If you say so," he murmured, and reached for the wine. After taking a slurping sip and setting his goblet down, he noted I hadn't poured any. "So ashamed of your bad decisions you would keep from one of life's finest delights?"

I half rolled my eyes. "If you consider wine to be a source of happiness, then I don't know what to tell you."

"Oh but I have many *sources*," Avrin emphasized with a flash of his teeth, "of happiness."

I carved up more fish. "Am I supposed to blush?"

"Rumor has it you were eternally red for a certain frosty king."

My attempt at remaining unbothered was officially ruined. I choked, coughing as I snatched my water.

Pleased, Avrin went on, his tone riddled with knowing. "Of course, rumors are often disappointingly inaccurate, but in this case..."

I'd had quite enough of arrogant males.

The goblet of water hit the table with a thud. I made to stand to take my meal to my room until his chuckle and waving arm halted me.

"I'll stop," he said, and though I didn't believe him, I sat back down. Mirth and unmistakable judgment sparked in his gaze, in the smile that didn't quite reach those bright eyes. "It seems I've touched a very tender spot."

I cursed, but before I could stand, his hand stole mine.

Shocked, I looked down at it—at the way it covered mine on the table. "Stay," he ordered, then added gently, "I apologize. I loathe him, and that you've spent any amount of time with him just..." He released a harsh breath. "Well, it blows my fucking mind in the worst of ways."

I stared at his hand, then looked at his seemingly earnest features.

I made my tense shoulders slump, and I slipped my hand free to resume eating. Making new enemies was incredibly unwise, especially within a court I would need to start thinking of as my home. "I loathe him, too," I finally said.

Sensing that I'd meant every word, Avrin blinked. "Is it too soon to ask what he did to you?"

I nodded once.

Quiet settled as we ate, the dark growing and the candles surrounding us glowing and swaying.

"So, Molkan." Avrin amended, "Your father, told me he had the talk with you."

Having eaten enough, I set my cutlery down. "He has indeed."

Avrin watched me as he chewed, but I kept my gaze fixed on the finger I trailed around my goblet of water.

"And?" he pressed. "How do you feel about it all?"

"I don't know," I confessed, frowning slightly. "He told me so much, yet I still have so many questions."

Avrin waited, then spread his hands. "Such as?"

The glinting silver of his cutlery made my fingers curl with the desire to touch the almost healed slash at my throat.

I studied Avrin and wondered why he would humor me. He was adviser to the king, or so it seemed. I had the growing suspicion he was far more than that. Spy, confidant, perhaps even something like a son.

My question wasn't at all what I thought I'd ask first if given the chance. "Where is Rolina's daughter?"

His features did not change, save for a small crease between his brows. "Who?"

"Rolina. My guardian. The woman you killed and turned to nothing during the hunt's trade visit to Crustle."

"Right, the woman who kept you sequestered within a cage of loathing for twenty years," he said, then reached for his wine when I didn't respond. He took a hearty sip. His lips smacked together as he finally confirmed, "Her daughter is dead, of course."

That shouldn't have bothered me. Perhaps guilt over being the reason she was killed was the reason it did—though I'd had no say in any of it. I'd likely been only days old. "Why?"

Avrin ate another mouthful before cutting me an amused and confused glance. "What do you mean why? It's just how it is. If a faerie babe is dumped outside of Folkyn's borders, then the babe they swap it with is of no use to us."

Maybe I'd spent too much time amid humans and creatures who wanted and no longer had anything to do with Folkyn, as I failed to stomach such horrific cruelty. I took another sip of water, that tiny part of me who empathized with Rolina's actions thankful she'd died before knowing of the fate that had befallen her babe.

"Many thought you dead too, you know, and Molkan didn't care to correct anyone." Avrin shrugged. "But I wasn't here then, Princess."

Surprised he'd decided to stay on the topic, I set the water down and gave him my attention.

"I was plucked from the streets maybe four or five years after you were born, so I don't know for certain what happened to this guardian's babe, but I do know she is probably dead as that is the way of our ilk."

No humans were permitted in Faerie. There were rumors of exceptions, such as witches and half-breeds, and humans kept by nobility and the wealthy to feed their fetishes and give them something different to feast upon.

But I knew, and I think Rolina had also known, that the Fae were not inclined to care for much outside of themselves. Certainly not a human babe.

To be polite, I waited until Avrin finished his meal to leave, but he excused himself first with a mocking grin. "Sweetest dreams, Princess."

Annoyance pricked at my nape.

I reached over and snatched the wine to pour a small amount into my goblet.

There was no stroll through the grounds the following morning. After waiting in my room until midday, I finally took to the halls to do a little exploring.

At the bottom of the sandstone steps I'd taken with my father for the past two days, I paused and looked across the terrace to the grass-lined drive.

Imposing and taller than the wall they arched between, the iron palace gates stood dark as night in the shine of the sun.

Upon the drive before them, three guards stood in conversation, dressed in uniform with swords and daggers at their backs and sides. Above them, two watch towers climbed toward the sky. Another guard descended the ladder rungs while laughing at something his comrade said from high above in the enclosed wooden lookout.

These people were victims, but they were ready and anticipating an attack.

Florian's manor was heavily fortified, yet there was no wall. No warriors in towers watched every move the civilians made beyond Hellebore's royal home.

The winter king might have had his reasons, but after hearing Molkan explain everything, I failed to understand how such hatred from Florian could withstand so much time. Twenty years, and it hadn't lessened. From what Molkan had said, Florian was patiently increasing the tension—tightening and tightening until it snapped.

Until Molkan snapped.

I intend to go to war, Florian had said what felt like a different lifetime ago. He'd deceived me in many ways, but as my mind fell within the dangerous disorder of memories, I couldn't resist wondering if he had also been speaking the truth.

After all, there was no one more skilled in the art of veiling lies within truth than the Fae.

The thought of Florian and his warriors flooding this city, breaking down those gates, the once laughing guards dead upon the ground...

I turned back and walked up the stairs, my hand trembling as I curled my loose braid over my shoulder.

Avrin was already eating when I entered the dining room for dinner.

I hid my surprise and curiosity over his presence by muttering, "Thank you for waiting," just as he'd said to me the previous night.

He huffed but said nothing.

I lowered into my chair, lacking the desire to fill the silence that followed. I remained quiet and contemplative as I pushed my food around my plate.

Although the adviser ate without saying a word, his eyes tracked every move I made.

Irked by it, and by the thoughts that clouded my mind until the only option I could settle on all day was inaction, I spoke first. "Why are you here?"

Avrin showed no sign of shock at my rude tone and question. Amusement filled his voice, and I looked up as he reached for his goblet of wine. He swirled it, then took a sip. "Here in this palace, or here dining with such a sullen princess?"

I almost bristled. Then decided I didn't much care about his opinion of me after all. "Both."

"Well," he said, wiping his mouth with a lace-edged napkin. The cream cloth came away smeared with tomato soup. "If you must know, I usually dine here."

"Alone?" I lifted a spoonful of soup to my mouth, swallowing as he watched with narrowed eyes.

"Your father hasn't dined in this room since I arrived here, and I'll wager he didn't for years prior." He glanced around, his attention falling to the empty yet beautiful fireplace with gold and ruby inlaid in the stone hearth. "A room like this deserves to be utilized."

I silently agreed, peering around as I tore my bread in half and stifled the rising memory of the last time I'd eaten soup.

Open those lovely lips.

I dunked my piece of bread violently, uncaring as soup splashed over the lace table linen. Then decided to distract myself by any means necessary. "You said you were plucked from the streets?"

I could imagine a room such as this—and that this entire palace—was something he would marvel at standing within for many decades to come, then.

He nodded, lifting his bowl to his lips and slurping.

Irritation prickled, but the playful gleam in his eyes made me suppress a smile as he set the bowl down. "I was starving and desperate enough to try pickpocketing an off-duty soldier." He licked his lips, and I half hoped the intrigue the shape of them aroused would create more—would kindle an interest for a male who did not carefully plot my demise. "I was too young to be executed and too wild to leave unpunished."

"The soldier brought you here?"

"He brought me to his commander." Avrin drank more wine. "The king just happened to be visiting the guard barracks, conversing with the commander and two others."

I surmised that the largest building among the clusters of stone houses deep within the palace grounds must belong not to servants, but to members of Molkan's royal military.

"I really should have been executed, and he knew it." As if lost to the memory, Avrin's gaze fell upon his almost finished meal, absent. "But he gave me the groundskeeper's storage shed, said if I worked well for Helain for a year, he would see about letting me go."

I chewed slowly, then paused. "But you never left."

"Why would I want to?" he said, then laughed. "I had no parents, only an older brother who was relieved to no longer need to look out for me while he fended for himself. Here"—he gestured to the window—"well, you've seen it. I was barely eleven years, but even then I knew a good thing when it was shoved right before my face. So when the year was up, I said nothing and neither did Helain, and the king never noticed me again until I was pushing sixteen years and outgrowing half of his matured soldiers."

"He made you enlist."

He nodded. "As part of the royal guard. A few years later, Florian's second-in-command killed his adviser and personal guard during an attempt to negotiate peace terms, and the king trusts no one, so..."

Fume, I guessed again but didn't say.

"But he trusts you," I said instead.

"He trusts me more than most, but let me be clear"—his voice lowered, and he tossed a glance over his broad shoulder—"he trusts *no one.*"

Similar words had been said to me about a different king.

I pondered that for longer than I should have, imagining what it must feel like—being so guarded. My hand curled around the bread, crumbs crumbling, as it occurred to me. As I acknowledged that I was dangerously close to knowing exactly what that felt like.

I had no choice but to trust those around me, at least to a certain degree, to get what I needed and to remain breathing. And I was beginning to hate it. That I might never know true safety and the life of comfort that came with it.

I wished I could roam freely throughout this land and any other without fear. I wished I could further get to know the male who was my father and have him smile and wink at me again without feeling like I needed those tiny displays of affection. Hints that he cared for me.

This kingdom was supposedly my own, yet I couldn't shake the sense that one wrong move might cause all of it to disintegrate and cave in around me.

I wanted to be accepted here. In a way I hadn't been accepted in Crustle or in Florian's court. In a way that finally made me feel like I'd found it.

Home.

Avrin dropped his spoon with a clatter, then leaned back in his chair.

Sufficiently shaken from the anxiety that refused to let me feel at ease, I was grateful. "And your brother?" I asked, recalling that he was a member of the Wild Hunt.

"He wanted no part of this kingdom or any other. He left with the hunt the moment he matured and proved his worth to them."

Curious, I asked, "What did he have to do?"

Avrin grinned, then rose from his chair and said with a seriousness that shocked, "Trust me when I say you're better off not knowing everything, Princess."

The following afternoon, I ventured down those sandstone steps to the terrace once more.

Determination kept my stride steady and my shoulders back as I neared the gates that would open to a world I'd yet to experience.

And I was tired of waiting.

Tired of sitting within a pretty palace, awaiting my father's attention when I was beginning to fear he saw me as nothing more than a creature to be kept in order to keep me from his enemy. I should have been grateful for such protection. But the safety I'd found was nothing like I'd envisioned.

This time alone had made it clear that all I'd found since beginning my hunt for something so elusive was more uncertainty, violence, and questions.

I wanted no part of this war. I wanted to live without being used by scheming males. I wanted to breathe without feeling the burn of betrayal and missing someone I never should have wanted.

I wanted to escape everything I'd foolishly hoped to find and have the freedom to find something else.

Maybe I would find a place of my own. A place where no one would bother me. And if I had to find such a place in the middle lands until these kingdoms forgot that I existed, then so be it.

I couldn't return to the apartment. It would be the first place Florian and Molkan looked. I'd have to work my way farther south toward the wood-laden borders of the human realm, and gain employment along the way to help me achieve that.

The guards ceased talking and separated when they became aware of my approach. Both moved to the center of the gates, chins high and their hands drifting to the weapons at their sides.

I stopped a few feet away, frowning. "I wish to leave."

Neither of them responded. They didn't need to.

My heart sank, my new plans dissolving upon the warm breeze. I was evidently not permitted to leave the palace grounds.

Footsteps crunched down the drive behind me before I could set my panic-induced anger free by demanding to be released.

I whirled on Avrin, seething quietly, "Why won't they let me through?"

"It's not safe for you out there. You know that better than anyone after almost having your throat carved wide open."

The reminder made me instantly tense. "I can fend for myself, Avrin."

"Of course." His lips twitched. "With the help of some creatures, if they just so happen to be around?"

I glowered at him. "Let me go. Whatever happens to me is of no consequence to you and Molkan." I swallowed thickly, suddenly desperate to run through those gates when his brows rose and his arms crossed. "I have no intention of being captured by Florian, if that's what you're so worried about."

Avrin gave the guards behind me a slight nod, an unreadable command in his gold eyes. Then he looked down at me and whispered through lips that barely moved, "We cannot talk here."

Confused, I let him escort me back to the terrace and up the steps.

As we neared my room, my impatience and anger returned. I hissed, "I didn't realize I was a fucking prisoner."

His brows jumped at my crassness.

But I wasn't sorry. In fact, something loosened in my chest at having been so careless with my actions.

It was then everything I'd held inside for days while hoping to be proven wrong—while hoping that I'd merely grown jaded from all I'd been through—exploded. "He barely even looks at me, Avrin. Not *once* has he asked me about myself, about the things I love and the life I've had..." My chest heaved, my eyes blurring with unexpected tears. "I want to leave. Please," I croaked. "Just let me leave."

Avrin licked his lips, casting his gaze to the end of the empty hall.

When he looked back at me, he murmured, "You're not a prisoner, Tullia. But until we've formally announced your arrival at the introduction ball tomorrow evening, we would like you to remain in the palace."

My breath stalled with my thudding heart.

I shook my head, not wanting to believe I'd overreacted with my outburst. But perhaps I had. "A ball?"

Avrin's jaw clenched. He nodded and lingered after he stepped back, as if he wished to say something else. Then he walked away.

I blinked at his tense form, so stunned, I almost flinched when he cursed and turned back.

"No," he said with a humorless laugh. "You want to know what I think?"

He didn't give me a chance to answer. My eyes widened as he advanced on me.

"I think even if you *were* a prisoner, you should be nothing but grateful. You live better than most while trapped within these walls among this huge estate. You've spent time with the enemy that seeks to eradicate this kingdom from the map of Folkyn, yet we still treat you with respect although you're reluctant to talk about anything you've experienced during your time at Hellebore Manor."

"I..." I stepped back against my closed door, at a loss for all the words I'd thought I still wanted to voice.

"I should hate you." Avrin's smirk was cruel, his scent a rising spiced mint as he loomed over me and set his hands on either side of my head upon the door. "I *want* to hate you. You're ignorant and insufferably trusting and naive, and it drives me mad, but that is also why I can't. This..." He gestured around us. "This prison you're referring to?"

His hand slapped back against the wood by my head as he leaned so close, I could see the flecks of brown within his gold eyes. "It's supposed to be mine, and now, I can't help but be glad that I might have to share it, and it fucking enrages me."

Shock stole my voice, my thoughts, then my breath as his mouth fell over mine.

Without a second of hesitation, he kissed me.

Rough at first touch, then immediately slowing to a rubbing

caress. A stunned breath left me, and he rumbled a groan in response, his tongue seeking entry to my mouth. I gave it to him, but only for a moment.

His taste, a softened sweet wine, startled.

Something within me recoiled. My head turned, forcing his lips from mine.

Staring at the stone arch while Avrin seemed to inhale my scent at my neck, I withheld the urge to push him away—and the urge that pleaded for the return of his kiss to help erase the stain of another's. I whispered thickly, "Thought you weren't interested in Florian's toys."

He stepped back, his hands slowly sliding down the door. "I lied."

When I finally dared to look at him, he was gone.

I didn't sleep.

I tossed and turned in the spring warmth, uncomfortable in my own skin and mulling over Avrin's words. He thought I would take all he expected to inherit—and I would. I should. Yet just imagining such a thing, that I would one day rule this place...

I couldn't imagine it at all.

Avrin had been wrong in so many ways to say what he had. But he'd also been right. I didn't deserve this, and I clearly didn't want this. Not in the way he did. Though there was one thing he'd said I couldn't understand, and it chased me from bed and into the quiet hall.

He wasn't awake. No one would be. It was long after midnight.

It didn't matter. I walked to the end of the hall to the row of arched windows that gave view to the star shine over the lake in the distance.

A harsh laugh echoed from down the hall. From the springs, I realized. About to head back to my room, I stopped at hearing my father's voice.

"... marry you. I will not have her used as a weapon to bring me to my knees."

A pause. "And if she refuses?"

"She cannot."

Silence.

I crept closer but didn't dare get too close to the stairs that twirled down beneath the ground to the springs.

Several failed heartbeats later, Avrin murmured, "You cannot mean..." Another pause. "She is your daughter."

Molkan growled, "I went without one for twenty years, only to be handed a creature sullied by my enemy." His voice dropped. "I care not for her fate. I cannot afford to when more important things are at stake."

More silence followed. A silence so loud, I feared my chaotic heartbeat might be heard. I gripped the window ledge, knowing I should walk away before I heard anything else that might leave another scar.

Then Avrin spoke in a hard tone. "Tullia is not an object to claim or discard, Sire."

A gruff, humorless laugh bounced up the stairs and echoed down the hall. "Yet that is exactly what she has become, and if you truly desire to one day take my place, then you must learn from my mistakes." Molkan barked, "Cease thinking with your fucking cock."

TWENTY-FOUR

THE WHITE-HAIRED SERVANT DELIVERED A SHEER GOLDEN gown that would leave minimal to the imagination.

Although I was far from pleased with the finery, I still smiled and gestured for him to lay it on the bed.

He lingered a moment, his features tightening as he looked from my uneaten breakfast to me. I hadn't the energy to reassure him. And I hadn't the energy to ask if there would be anything else to accompany the revealing material that resembled more of a seductive nightgown.

I gave my eyes back to the window, my stomach in endless knots and fear my only companion as the door quietly closed.

The first sign that something was wrong was the dress. The second was that no one came to decorate my face nor do my hair.

And as the sun dipped low and the stars began to sprinkle across the darkening sky, apprehension stilted my movements when I finally donned the gown.

A knock sounded.

Avrin entered my room a moment after, dressed in the regalia fitting for his high rank. The brown jacket was fringed in a dark forest green that matched the crest of a baneberry flower over his chest and the three stripes at his broad shoulders.

He eyed me up and down, his hands clasped behind his back. The posture and stance resembled my father far too much.

A father I hadn't seen in days.

I pondered whether we'd get to talk before this ball. But as Avrin's gaze dipped down my body, I became keenly aware of every shape and curve I was forced to put on display. "I believe I'm missing a slip, perhaps." I laughed, but it was lacking in humor. "Or, at the very least, a cloak."

Avrin didn't speak as he crossed the room to where I stood.

My stomach squeezed at his silence and nearness, a nervous breath rattling free. "I need a minute. I still need to do something with my hair."

His giant boots stopped, the toes almost kissing my bare ones. My eyes stayed there as Avrin leaned close to kiss my cheek, whispering, "I'm sorry, Princess."

Thinking he was referring to the harsh words he'd thrown at me before he'd kissed me, I maneuvered a smile into place as I lifted my eyes.

It fell when he leaned back with tightening features reminiscent of the male I'd met the night Rolina had died.

A burning cold enveloped my wrist.

My gaze dropped as he seized the other, and I flinched from both the burn of the iron and to get away.

It was too late. Iron manacles encircled my wrists.

I glared up at him, horror filling my chest and my eyes. "What is the meaning of this?"

He reached into a pouch at his waist, and I knew before he pulled it free. I knew what would be blown into my face, and I stumbled back.

It made no difference. Even as I turned and covered my nose and mouth, the glittering dark flecks still reached me.

Avrin, at my back, gently tugged my hands down, the chains clanking. I screamed, but it fell into a whimper as I inhaled and blackness entered my vision.

Laughter and merriment cloaked like a faraway song.

My eyelids were heavy, gritty as I tried to keep them open.

I soon discovered I would have been better off keeping them shut. The room appeared in patches. A glowing chandelier dotted with orbs of fireflies twirled slightly from the stone ceiling.

Turning my head to the side, I startled.

Three males stood there, goblets in hand, gesturing to me while muttering, "beautiful" and "goddess-damned shame."

The gown I'd donned, the gown I'd felt insecure about wearing for how much it revealed of my body, was now gone. And I'd have given anything to have it back.

I was naked.

Naked in a shining bronze cage barely wide enough for two males.

Red welts marred my wrists. The chains were gone, and they were unnecessary. The only method of escape appeared to be via the top, but the cage was so tall that I'd surely fail and only injure myself trying.

The door was latched closed with a golden padlock.

I shook it, my teeth clacking with the force of my desperation to wake from this insanity.

Just a nightmare.

Just a nightmare, I kept repeating, and if I made enough disturbance, then I could wake up and find myself—

A hand clasped my rear and squeezed.

I flinched, my knee banging into the metal cage, and pushed up to sit against the bars. Pointless. Males, and even some females, still ogled me while smirking and laughing. Their jeers and leering became a cacophony that buzzed like a swarm of bees in my ears.

The room swirled as my vision blurred with tears and excruciating fear. Not just any room, but a throne room. At the opposite end was a dais with two males atop it.

My father sat upon his throne. A crown of wreathed golden leaves glinted on his head.

Behind him, standing tall and proud and observant of all the guests flooding the room, was Avrin.

He'd chained me and stripped me of my gown, then caged me like an animal.

Why?

The question slammed into each corner of my mind. Trapped

breath burned within my lungs, leaving me panting and dizzy. Bile crawled up my throat, and I pushed it down while closing my eyes.

A rasped male voice crooned to my ear, "Hello, pretty whore."

I screamed and moved back, only to fall into the hands of another male on the other side of the cage. One of my breasts were clasped, pain screeching as I pulled free and the fingers refused to relinquish my nipple.

It was endless. Endless and barbaric and it couldn't be real.

It just... it couldn't be.

This ball of which was supposed to welcome me into my kingdom was nothing but a nightmare. It had to be—

"My fine and loyal friends." Molkan's voice boomed above the laughter and crass names hurled at me, and the room slowly descended into silence. "Our feature for this evening is finally awake."

Had anyone touched me while I'd been asleep? How many people had seen me unclothed, helpless, and had... *oh, goddess.*

I curled into myself and vomited.

A male hissed his displeasure as it splashed through the bars and onto his shoes. He reached through them and slapped me.

My head crashed into the bronzed metal, and I slumped to the cage floor.

The king needn't have yelled anymore.

He had the entire room's attention as he said, "Some of you might think you know who this creature is, but let me make one thing abundantly clear." There was an intentional pause before he declared, "She is no daughter of mine. She is a traitor."

Murmurs and soft laughter arose.

I flicked damp strands of hair from my face. Rising, I looked across the room to the male who'd sired me.

"She is enemy-bound." Molkan's eyes met mine, empty and dark. "The secret wife of Florian Hellebore."

Everyone gasped and shouted their outrage.

I flinched as wine was thrown at me. Spit followed, as well as fruit and goblets that clanged against the bars and punched into my skin.

I cried out, but quickly muffled it behind clenched teeth when I realized reacting only encouraged more of them to torture me.

None of the pinching fingers, insults, and bruising blows hurt nearly as much as Molkan's next booming declaration.

"This traitor was sent to our beloved kingdom to spy for her husband under the guise of wanting to escape him and to know her people, wanting to know *me*"—he laughed—"and under the guise of wedding one of our own loyal warriors, but we caught her."

None of that was true. Not a single fucking word.

"No," I croaked—would have screamed if only someone would have believed me. No one would, I knew, when they did not wish to.

"Quiet, traitorous filth," a female spat from beside the lust-gazed male she clung to.

I ignored her and looked at Avrin, only to find him finally staring at me.

His jaw was fixed. Gold eyes unreadable.

This was insane. Avrin had come for me. He and many others had been sent to retrieve me, and we all knew I wasn't yet married...

My stomach curdled, my hand clapping over my mouth. I closed my eyes as the realization threatened to make me sick again.

The contract.

Florian's inability to tell me when we would be wed.

"The winter king has requested the return of his wife," Molkan went on. "This spawn of mine that he stole with the intention of humiliating me."

I glared through wet lashes.

Florian was not the type to make requests.

"So tell me..." Molkan's voice echoed, utter silence trembling within the cavernous room. His eyes met mine again, a gleam within, before he said with smug amusement, "Who's humiliated now?"

Laughter crashed against the walls of the room in unending waves.

My heart splintered, cracked wide open and filled with the sound and the stares and the vulgar gestures and my own endless stupidity.

The king of Baneberry said nothing more. He stepped back with stone features and lowered onto his golden throne.

Avrin stood beside him, clean-shaven chin high and staring beyond me.

Behind my enclosure, a small group of violinists stood in gold and brown formal wear. The whine of their instruments returned, and conversation rose with it. Now that the explanation for my presence had been delivered, no matter how false, many had seemingly lost interest in me, dancing and drifting throughout the room.

But some only moved closer.

Groping hands snatched my arms and even attempted to slip beneath me to pinch my rear. I gave up on trying to move when there was nowhere to go. I kept my arms over my breasts, my legs tucked and crossed. The bars of the cage slowly closed in. My ears rang with the howl of my heartbeat.

I closed my eyes tight and folded over with my head upon my knees.

How could this have happened?

All this time, I'd been married while assuming I was not. All this time, I'd thought I'd known who the enemy was, and I was wrong.

There wasn't just one. I was trapped between two evils.

I could scream like the hawk that soared low past the row of arched windows flanking the side of the throne room. I could plead with the goddess and those around me to stop, and to believe me as I explained that I hadn't known.

None of it would matter.

Florian had wanted me thoroughly ruined and humiliated before he killed me.

And this father I'd stupidly thought would shelter me from him...

His conversation with Avrin in the springs spun through my violent thoughts. If Molkan couldn't wed me to his precious adviser because I was already married, then I was of no use to him. I was only as he'd claimed—just a weapon for Florian to use against him.

Both kingdoms were intent on being my doom.

And I had no one to blame but myself for ever daring to believe that a home might be found for someone like me within these treacherous lands of Faerie. Gane had warned me. Even Hal, with his stolen jewels and missing digits, had warned me.

Yet I knew the entire population of Crustle could have warned me, and still, I would have ignored them all.

I still would have wanted to know.

Now I knew, and regret spiked like thorns around my pulsing heart. Each shallow breath grew tighter, and my knees soaked in tears, as the touching ceased but the insults and probing gazes assaulted in never-ending torrents.

I recited my letters faster than ever before, the volume rising to a scream trapped within my mind each time I finished and started again. But I could only get away with pretending to ignore what was happening for so long.

My hair was pulled, and I lurched to the side. A hand wrapped around my throat.

I snarled, attempting to tug it free.

The male with orange-flecked brown eyes laughed, a tobacco stem hanging from wine-red lips. His laughter ended with unexpected swiftness as his fingers uncoiled and he backhanded me across the face.

I met the bars again, the room twirling as I contemplated giving in entirely. As I fought the temptation to just lay there and let them all do as they wished.

I saw her then.

A row of portraits hung at the back of the room, half covered in shadow, but I was only interested in one.

A portrait of a queen with a tiny silver crown and large hazel eyes. Her cheeks were rounded and high just like my own. Though cropped to her shoulders in voluminous curls, her near-white hair was just like mine, too. Her nude-lipped smile was guarded grace.

My mother.

An onslaught of flapping wings and birdsong dragged my wet eyes to the ceiling.

Avrin,” I said as the guard stepped aside, but my voice broke.
I was taken down a hall and then another, then down a spiral-

"Avrin, wait." I knew if I was placed in a cell, I would likely not leave until it was time to meet my end.

He ignored me and led me past the twin rows of empty cells.

"This is all a mistake. I'm not a spy, and I'm not Florian's wife. Whoever told you that is lying."

He stopped at the last cell, then opened the iron bars and released me into the dank space that housed nothing but a rotting cot.

Avrin didn't speak until the grate was closed, and I was trapped behind it. "You heard what the king said."

"But none of it was true." I reached for the bars and hissed when they singed the tips of my fingers.

"Florian has requested your return," Avrin said, toneless. His golden gaze roamed over me, and I clutched the cloak tighter.

His cloak, I noted, judging by the scent. That he'd given me that much meant he might be the only one I could reason with.

He spoke before I got the chance to think of a convincing argument. "If I were you, I'd give your father anything he desires so that you're not sent back to your soulless beast of a husband in pieces."

The word husband was another slap to the face.

I shook my head. "What is the point, Avrin? Molkan will kill me." I knew it within my bones. There was now no leverage to be gained with my existence—only with my death.

Avrin said nothing, apparently waiting to see what else I might divulge.

"I didn't know." I swallowed as a spell of dizziness arrived, and leaned against the cold stone beside me to keep upright. "I didn't know we were married."

"You expect us to believe that?" Avrin glowered and stepped closer, growling low, "What is your plan, Tullia? Tell me what Florian has sent you here to do, and I swear I will do what I can to get you out of this alive."

"I have no plan because *I did not know*," I gritted, tears leaking from my eyes. My voice softened with dismay. "I didn't. I had no fucking idea, Avrin. He had me blood-sworn before he brought me to

Hellebore, and I assumed the contract was merely an agreement to marry, not the actual..."

"Marriage contract," he finished for me, brows crinkled.

I nodded, my throat tight. "I didn't even know who Molkan was—that he was my father. Florian never told me. I found out when one of your spies was captured and brought to the estate to be tortured, and I snuck into the dungeon."

Avrin's frown deepened. "Frensroth."

"Yes," I said.

"His head was delivered to Molkan amid a wagon of fresh produce riddled with his bones. Straight to the palace gates."

My eyes widened. I hadn't thought I'd still have the ability to be horrified. Nevertheless, my blood churned, and my stomach quaked. Exhaustion, heavy and unexpected, followed.

I stumbled back to the corner of the cell, tripping over the cot.

Avrin watched, his brows remaining low. "Are you injured badly?"

"Would it matter?" I slumped to the bloodstained blanket on the cot, dizziness deepening the dark of the small cell. "What will happen to me now?" It was all I could think to ask, all I could manage to ask, as my bones seemed to melt and adrenaline faded into dust.

Avrin didn't answer. I supposed he didn't need to.

He gave me one last assessing look as his jaw tightened further, then he left.

TWENTY-FIVE

I HADN'T INTENDED TO SLEEP.

My body apparently hadn't cared. I woke with a scream when a warm hand gripped my arm and tore me from the cot. I didn't know how long the brief respite had been until we left the dungeon and I closed my eyes against the harsh glare of the rising sun.

Sleep hadn't helped. The heavy weight of weakness had only seemed to worsen, and when I recalled all that'd happened the night prior...

My empty stomach quivered with my knees.

Glimpses of halls were fleeting. I was led up another flight of stairs that seemed to never end to a room tucked away behind a locked door. Shelves filled with various vials and baskets lined the walls. Two windows displayed the bright-blue hue of a new day.

I feared it would be my last as I was tugged into the room.

The guard's grip firmed when I stumbled over the edge of a coarse carpet, an impatient grunt leaving his gnashed teeth. Not carpet. A large strip of hessian fabric. Atop it stood a metal type of table.

"Lie face down on the bench," the guard ordered.

I turned to him as he released me, his dark red hair aglow in the early morning light and his scarred lip curling with disgust. There would be no asking him questions.

I looked back at the bench as steps sounded.

"Get on, or I'll force you," the guard snapped.

"I'll take it from here."

Avrin.

I was shoved forward by the guard.

Avrin growled, "I said I'll take it from here, Jellinson."

Thoroughly warned and dismissed, he left. I looked from the awaiting bench to Avrin, unsure what to do as the door closed with an intentional slam behind the guard.

"Climb on," Avrin said.

"What will happen when I do?"

A dark brow arched. "You don't really have a choice, Princess. Climb on and just make sure you answer what is asked of you."

I gnawed at my lip, fear stampeding through every tight muscle. My heart stopped when the door opened again.

Molkan entered, throwing the wood closed behind him. "Get her on the bench."

Avrin seized me.

I shrugged him off. Still only wearing the cloak, I climbed atop the cool metal.

Metal rings glinted on either side of the carpet. I stared at the fibers, tense as Molkan clipped brisk instructions to Avrin behind me. The cloak was tugged from my body, and I tried to sit up to reach for it, but a heavy hand pushed me down.

Molkan's hand.

My neck protested as my head swung harshly over the edge. "Restrain her now," Molkan ordered. "Then hand me the stencil."

I didn't bother fighting the inevitable, and that should've shamed me. I'd grown too numb, too accepting of this nightmare I couldn't seem to wake from, to feel anything, as Avrin chained my wrists to the metal loops within the stone floor.

He did the same to my ankles, the iron forcing my teeth to grit. A large piece of soft material, then the brush of something wet and sticky, met my back.

From my shoulder blades to my lower torso, my skin was carefully decorated with swirling patterns.

My teeth unclenched, though I didn't relax. Then they met again with a clack when a sharp blade sank into the painted skin. My back arched as the knife dragged.

I cried out for them to stop, writhing but unable to move as Molkan finally did stop and said, "Another set here."

More chains were wrapped around my upper thighs, bound tight beneath the metal bench.

Gathering enough of my bearings, I sobbed, "What are you doing?" But the question broke into a scream that scraped claws over my lungs as another slow drag of the blade curved through the skin of my back.

"For every refusal, you will earn a mark." Molkan's tone was that of the king who'd spoken in the throne room while he'd allowed his loyal subjects to torment me. "Easily understood, so let us begin."

My eyes were closed tight against the overwhelming burn radiating up my back, but I sensed movement. Avrin now stood in front of me when he said, "What did Florian ask you to do before he sent you here?"

"He didn't send me here. You even found me in Crustle your—" I screamed, my eyes bulging wide and blackness entering the edges of my vision, as Molkan carved into my back once more.

"Where does he intend to strike next?" Avrin asked before the blade had even left my skin.

I could scarcely breathe, let alone talk.

My silence was taken as a response.

Molkan sliced again. This time with a circular shape between my shoulder blades that seemed to never end. The entire room swam with red and black before my eyes closed. My limbs pulled taut, attempting but unable to move.

Avrin's gritted voice forced me to remain in this wretched reality. "How many units of warriors await his orders in the Frostfall Mountains?"

I couldn't have answered if I'd wanted to, and as the blade returned to make another circle over my shoulder blade, anger kept me conscious. And I knew, even if I did know anything, I would give them nothing.

They deserved nothing.

None of these assholes who'd taken advantage of me and my foolish heart would get a scrap of what they desired before my last breath left my lungs.

Sweat gathered at my nape as soon as the knife left my skin. Molkan tutted. "A shame. Truly such pretty skin."

As if it mattered when I would be dead before I could worry about what horrors might forever scar my back.

My breath shook, and my legs twitched uncontrollably.

"How weak you are. You fed from him, didn't you?" Molkan asked, and when I didn't respond, he sighed and resumed his torment.

I must have lost consciousness.

I was slapped awake by his hand over my battered flesh, a whimper fleeing my clenched teeth. "Feeding from humans is one thing, but to feed from your own kind when the consequences can be so fatal..."

My ears rang, barely hearing his words. Deep grooves in my palms from my nails leaked blood when I uncurled them and drew in a breath that choked.

"Lilitha went mad, you know. First from abstaining from her mate and then from drinking from another when she'd bound herself to me. Blood is a poison that ruined her, and she had no one to blame but herself."

Confusion warred with blistering agony as I tried to match what he'd told me during our walks throughout the palace grounds with what he'd just said.

So gently, it hurt, the male who'd sired me swept his fingers over the wet mess of my back.

Over the blood.

"This is but yet another result of her rash and bold decisions." A chuckle, both dry and light, preceded his next words. "My, how she would enjoy the unending mayhem she caused."

Avrin cleared his throat.

Molkan ignored him. "That is why the court of Hellebore is cursed—damned by Mythayla herself for their immoral acts. Nothing but death and doom blooms in the winter realm, and giving yourself to another in such a way will only damn you, too."

Avrin shifted.

Another laugh from Molkan. "But I suppose it already has. Just look at you." The tip of his knife dug into my skin, then he pulled. "Weak and filthy creature."

Mercifully, I lost consciousness.

When I came to, it was to the sound of a foreign and urgent voice. "...been poisoned. Blood froths from every orifice."

Molkan cursed. "Nulbon's gone?"

"Yes, Sire. But they timed the concoction well, for he was sent back to deliver a message before he ceased breathing."

"And?" Avrin clipped. "What is the message?"

"He comes." A harsh swallow. "And a sparrow arrived just minutes ago from Chip, who says the outposts along the border are nearly empty. The frost moves southeast."

I didn't open my eyes. I hadn't the energy, and to do so would bring forth more punishment. I had no desire to even remain awake as every inch of my torso throbbed in fiery waves.

"Ready the encampments," Molkan said after a long moment.

"Sire?" the messenger questioned, a touch of alarm in his voice.

"We won't need them. She will be long gone before the frost can even cross the marshes."

The door closed, and the sound of shifting opened my eyes. Boots, drops of blood speckling the rounded leather toes, laced around tight brown britches.

Avrin still stood before me. "She's awake," he said.

"Let us resume," Molkan said, as though he hadn't just been given word that armies were potentially heading toward his kingdom's most populated territory.

I didn't delude myself into thinking Florian's decision to march upon Baneberry had anything to do with me. Rather, I was willing to wager I was positioned perfectly for the next stage in his meticulous planning.

I was the excuse he needed.

Providing the news delivered to the king was even true. Judging by what Molkan had said, this was not the first time the royal city of Bellebon anticipated an attack from the winter king.

"Where does he intend to strike first, Tullia?" Avrin asked. Then, "The city or the surrounding towns and villages?"

I said nothing, and though I'd braced for it, the return of the knife to my skin was worse than ever before as it carved through torn flesh and marred the rest in a vicious circle.

Molkan's patience had come to an end. "Wake her up."

"She is awake."

I finally drew a breath, a cry leaving with it.

Avrin asked with a hint of his own impatience, "Where are Florian's spies hiding, Tullia?"

I blacked out again right as the blade left my skin after another circle was made upon my other shoulder blade.

A light tap on my arm brought me back—brought everything screaming back without mercy. My entire body shook, my teeth clacking with each trembling breath.

Crouching before me, Avrin lifted the curtain of my hair. The gentle action was a painful contrast to the agony he'd helped inflict. "Answer," he said, almost pleaded. "This is not a brand you want to wear, Tullia. Answer, and it will cease."

"I cannot answer," I rasped through my teeth and groaned as my back spasmed, "when I do not have the information you fucking seek."

I could have sworn Avrin winced as the king attacked my back yet again. Could have sworn my response made the king dig the blade far deeper than necessary.

Endless, the questions came, and the knife followed.

My body was reduced to nothing more than a half-numb burn. So much so that when it stopped, I nearly failed to notice.

Avrin had moved what might have been hours ago to stand against the wall and ask me questions he knew would remain unanswered. All the while Molkan's fury seemed to cloud the room with the copper essence of my blood and the smell of something acidic that had been delivered and set somewhere behind me.

Then the stool he'd been using tumbled from the makeshift carpet absorbing my blood to the stone floor, as Molkan rose with a flare of temper he tried to keep from showing within his rough tone. "Last chance," he warned. "Once iron is poured over the wounds, you'll forever walk the realms with the mark of a traitor."

"Not just any traitor," Avrin said—seemed to urge. "But that of a betrayer to their own kin."

It was a snake.

I knew without asking. Without much room for any thought at all. The lines and shapes made by the blade had already told me as much.

So again, I remained quiet, save for that of my labored breathing.

But my silence and the agony I'd grown familiar with were erased when Molkan made good on his warning. Not that I'd thought he wouldn't.

Painstakingly slow, hot iron was poured all over my back.

The last thing I heard was my unending scream and Avrin's brittle curse before I tumbled into the safety of bleak nothing again.

This time, blue eyes were waiting and aglow in the dark.

It seemed the goddess I'd unknowingly pissed off was not content for me to escape anything, for those eyes remained a constant light during the abyss of unconsciousness.

I was eventually dragged away from them when the chains keeping me trapped against the metal bench were unwrapped from my body.

Avrin crouched before me again, whispering, "Time to get up, Princess."

I couldn't imagine doing any such thing.

The pain was so absolute, so endlessly depthless, I closed my eyes against it and silently pleaded for unconsciousness to take me again.

Avrin released a tormented-sounding groan, and I felt him move to my side.

A scream scraped my raw throat as he carefully hauled me into a sitting position. He may as well have forced me up by my hair. I wouldn't have felt anything but the torrential ripple of flames engulfing my torso.

I hunched over, bile rising. Nothing left my mouth. There was nothing left within me to evict. Still, I heaved and whimpered and swayed.

Avrin took my wrists. Something heavy and scalding was fastened around them. Then he said, his voice a little hoarse, "We need to go."

"Fuck you," I mumbled absently, staring at the dried patches of crimson upon the mesh-like fabric beneath my hanging feet. Blood dribbled down my legs, catching between my toes.

A soft huff, and then he pulled on my bound wrists. "If I help you stand, it will only hurt you more. Better to do it yourself."

"More," I said, laughing then groaning when I lifted my head. Tears fell as I pushed off the metal to my feet. They were numb. My legs wobbled, and I gripped the bench. A cry parted my lips but created no sound.

I made it into the hall filled with guards before my knees buckled.

One of them laughed, but he fell quiet when Avrin bent low to maneuver me over his shoulder like a sack of rain-ruined grain.

My eyes closed, each step Avrin took sending flares of fresh pain throughout my entire body. If they were going to kill me, then I silently prayed to Mythayla that they would hurry up and do it. I wouldn't survive another round of their torture.

I had a feeling I wouldn't want to.

Minutes that felt like decades later, cool air hit my cheeks and stirred my hair. My head turned at Avrin's upper back. A procession of guards trailed us—spread themselves along the drive as we left the stone terrace.

"I've done all I can," Avrin said, barely a whisper. "This is it."

I was set down on my bare feet.

Not wanting to but unable to help it, I clung to Avrin's tunic as my legs failed me. He let me until the king made his presence known by barking, "Open the gates."

Then Avrin gripped my upper arm, and I was delivered through the gates to the awaiting road and bridge beyond. Across it, the royal city of Bellebon shone beneath the late afternoon sky. Civilians and buildings dotted the river like stones against sand.

The breeze grazed my butchered skin. It was then I finally had enough awareness, and the ability to feel more than pain, to realize I was still naked.

There was little point in trying to shield myself against the eyes behind me and what awaited in the city outskirts ahead. So much of me had already been seen by too many, and it was the least of my concerns.

Avrin gently pushed me toward the bridge.

Agony raged through my limbs from the battlefield made of my back.

A guard stood waiting before the curving mixture of wood and sandstone granting passage over the river. He came forward to meet me as I concentrated only on placing one foot in front of the other.

If I thought of anything else—if I stopped—then I would crumple like wet parchment.

"Let it be known that not even blood can save a traitor, and Florian's supposed wife means nothing to us," Molkan boomed from atop a guard tower, his shadow cast across the sandy ground absorbing my trail of blood. "His capture and corruption and defiling of this creature were in vain."

I didn't turn to take one last look at the home I'd always longed for—nor the parent I'd been so eager to meet.

I walked on as the gates closed behind me with a blood-chilling creak.

TWENTY-SIX

LEFT WITH NO CHOICE, I FOLLOWED THE GUARD ACROSS THE slow arching bridge.

On the other side, more people in the streets ceased their afternoon activity.

They began to flock to the river's edge as I stumbled down the crest of the bridge and into the city encircling the palace in the shape of a sun-bright horseshoe.

I expected to be paraded through the streets naked and bearing the sign of a traitor before I was beaten by my own people and left for dead. I hadn't expected the guard to spit at my feet before turning on his heel to cross back to the palace.

There was no relief. I would still need to walk through the city naked and bloody and marked. A mark I would forever wear due to the wounds being iron-infused.

The brand of a traitor. A traitor to the people surrounding me.

Vultures to a carcass, they glared and murmured. Some turned their younglings' curious gazes away. Others studied me with a mixture of disgust, awe, and horror.

The world became too bright. Too loud.

There would be no horses to save me from a humiliation that somehow felt worse than any encounter with death.

Eyes were akin to needles upon my exposed skin—hundreds of prodding iron pokers.

Iron.

As the voices of the gathering crowds grew louder, my thoughts quietened. I looked at my bound hands but didn't dare look back to the palace gates. Beyond them was my father's loyal adviser who'd chained my wrists in iron.

The golden-eyed male who'd told me this was all he could do.

For although my hands were shackled, the heavy manacles were not locked.

Perhaps Avrin had saved me. If that were true, then I shouldn't have felt as if I'd indeed been damned instead. As if flames fell from my scorched back to lick at my feet, and I would feel their burn for all eternity.

The warmth of the sun was too hot. Sweat misted my raw skin. I stopped when my feet met cobblestone, then closed my eyes over a fresh wave of tears when someone shouted, "She bears the mark!"

Behind my closed eyelids, midnight-blue eyes found me again.

Distance and energy are no match for desperation.

Something hard, perhaps a stone, slammed into my shoulder. It forced my eyes open as I stumbled back a step. Tears were now free to stream down my face.

Murmurings of "Florian's whore" and "winter king's wife" reached my ears.

Birds screeched overhead. Gasps mingled with laughter and insults. Horses whinnied and hounds barked while I just stood there, surrounded by hatred and frozen with fear and unending pain and unable to make it stop. Unable to do anything.

Someone lobbed another object at me. It splattered over my chest, the scent of a tomato following.

I barely felt it.

I barely felt anything as the crowds grew into something monstrous, and I began surrendering to the helplessness I'd been forced to face. Deep within me, that dark pit of despair and heartbreak opened.

Distance and energy are no match for desperation.

I pushed the darkness wider. Shook and shoved the iron cuffs from my wrists.

They clanked to the cobblestone as I welcomed the rapid fleeing of my breath. As I begged the rifts, the mother—whoever was responsible for such an ability's existence—to take me the fuck away from this nightmare-ridden land I never should have stepped foot in.

Butterflies circled and tickled my cheeks. The breeze stirred granules of dirt around my feet and ankles.

"She's materializing," someone yelled.

"Return to your wretched husband," another hollered and laughed. "Not even he will have you now."

Laughter echoed and then faded.

A blue butterfly followed me into the rifts that stole me from the encroaching civilians with a soft violence I'd never felt from materializing before. That all-consuming and swirling darkness encompassed, an iced and gentle caress.

And it set me upon the dusty floor of an uninhabited apartment.

The wood floor blurred.

In the sudden quiet, my heart was a drum beating in my ears. Survival a song now screaming through my veins.

Move.

Everything ached as though it were as fresh as the moment I'd been branded, but I had to move. I couldn't stay in this apartment. Not when every faerie who wished me ill would begin the search for me here.

A brief glance around showed no sign of breaking and entering. No sign of new residents or that Madam Morin had been here at all. Everything was still just as I'd left it. Just as Rolina had wanted it.

I had no time to be puzzled over that.

I opened the door and hurried to the stairs. Too fast—I stumbled and winced, slapping a bloodstained hand to the wall. Drawing a breath through my nose as pain spiraled up my back, I slowed my pace.

But there was no slowing the beat of my heart when I saw the familiar door in the wall. I shoved it hard. So hard I fell through in a bloodied, tangled pile that made Gane shriek like a crow.

"Mother of murderous skies, Flea."

I blinked up at the mildew-dotted rafters in the ceiling, so relieved to see them again that more tears left my eyes.

Then I rolled to my side as Gane scuttled from his desk and came close to shouting, "You're naked. Why are you..." His voice trailed into an odd-sounding gasp. "The mark."

I couldn't seem to say a word.

Now that I was here, safe—even if only for a short period until I figured out where to go next—every drop of adrenaline fled. The mess Molkan had made of my back flared with blistering heat.

I groaned, curling my legs into my stomach.

Gane was muttering. Whether it was to himself or me, I didn't know. Something soft was soon draped over my lower body. Color leaked from the library, not even its comforting scent capable of keeping my eyes open.

I forced them wide and flinched when my hands were touched. I pulled them toward me.

After setting down a bundle of bandages and a knife, Gane raised his hairy hands. "I just want to check your injuries." His eyes were damp. I'd never seen his eyes damp. "That's all."

The sight shocked me enough that he could turn my wrists carefully. "Iron burns," he said softly, and then he pushed my blood-streaked hair from my face. I recoiled slightly, and a tear fell from his dark eye to his bushy cheek. "You should've listened to me, Flea."

I just blinked, unable to argue when he was right and I was hurting too much to care.

His voice was hoarse. "I need to get better supplies, okay? I'll be right back."

I thought I might have nodded. I heard him walk away, and I stared at the kitchen knife he'd left lying next to the useless bandages in an effort to stay awake.

The temperature dropped.

A warmth of awareness brushed at my nape.

Gane hadn't returned from his private quarters, yet I sensed I wasn't alone in the library. I scrambled to pull the blanket around my body and sit up, my hand slipping. I looked down at the wooden floor. Blood.

More blood.

A snow flurry floated toward it like a moth to a flame.

The haze filming my mind cleared as the invading presence slid along my skin like the threat of a new blade.

Booted steps neared. Measured and unhurried. I'd recognize the sound of them anywhere. I'd know the touch of his energy—that cold heat—lifetimes from now.

The aching agony ceased to throb with the paused beat of my heart as I looked down the aisle of books.

Snow flurries drifted in his wake, a dagger in one hand and a large sack in the other.

Though his features had been honed into indifference, menace rolled from him to flood the library in an acidic cloud that glossed at my skin in warning.

Adrenaline finally returned.

I slid over the blood, seizing the knife Gane had left.

Books tumbled to the floor as I used the shelves before me to rise on weak legs while clutching the weapon and blanket tight at my chest.

His hair was unbound and finger-swept. The near-black strands swayed over his shoulders with the winter breeze he'd brought with him.

The dagger glinted in the late afternoon sun when he twirled it in his hand and slowly came to a stop mere inches from me. "Do you wish to stab me, butterfly?" Florian's iced features cracked with a cruel smirk. "Make it quick."

I trembled, failing to draw breath as the tip of his blade whispered across my jawline and his gaze brightened.

Cold violence soaked his rasped words. "I've a wife to punish."

Don't miss the heart-wrenching conclusion to the
Deadly Divine Duology...

WRATH OF THE DAMNED

MORE FANTASY ROMANCE BY ELLA

Kingdom of Villains
A King So Cold
The Stray Prince
The Savage and the Swan
The Wolf and the Wildflower

STAY IN TOUCH!

Follow on Instagram
www.instagram.com/ellafieldsauthor

Website
www.ellafields.net